THE DOCENT

Also by Tom Kenny

The Morning Line

The Docent is a work of fiction produced for the entertainment of its readers. It is not intended to portray any actual person or persons. Any suggestion of a connection to, or resemblance of, any actual person, living or deceased, business entity or historical event, is entirely coincidental.

Book and cover design by E. K. King

For the lawyers and judges who always walk the right path, often providing well beyond what is asked or required, often at personal cost, often anonymously.

GREATER BOSTON

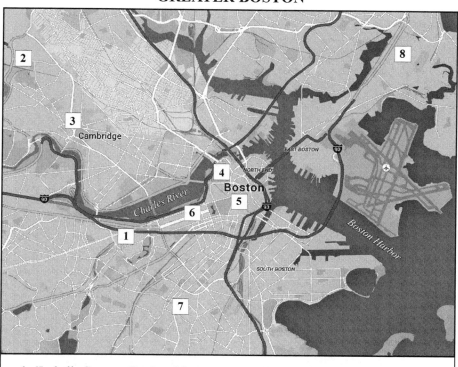

1	Isabella Stewart Gardner Museum	**5**	Downtown Boston
2	North Cambridge	**6**	Ritz Carlton Hotel
3	Harvard University	**7**	Dorchester
4	Beacon Hill	**8**	East Boston racetrack

Tom Kenny

PROLOGUE

BOSTON - WINTER, 1990

"Hey, Mr. Nice Guy, you come into the Goose just to see little ol' Julie again?"

The B-girl, slim, early twenties, wore a sleeveless purple minidress. She slid onto a barstool next to the bespectacled customer in the navy blue bomber jacket and put her hand on his forearm. Julie Santos' ready smile revealed perfect, snow-white teeth. She was happy to see the weekly regular. A normally slow winter afternoon was even slower because of the weather. Slush and freezing rain was keeping foot traffic sparse on lower Washington Street. Julie had been working the bar at the Frisky Goose Lounge for about a year and a half and wondered how long it could keep its doors open. Boston's "Combat Zone" was gradually losing its strip bars and porn shops. Suburban competition fired with first amendment oxygen, and constant pressure on the zoning board from civic leaders of next door Chinatown, were exacting their toll.

The plump bar patron, his ample backside tucked into a pair of gray chinos, provided a brief respite from Julie's gloom. A couple of splits of phony champagne bought for her by this loner would mean a sawbuck. She was glad to provide the guy company, even though she'd never scored a premium from him for booth action in the lounge's adjacent, barely lit "restaurant" section (which had not hosted a plate of food in the last decade). She figured him for about forty, maybe a little more, maybe a little less. He reminded her of a snowman with a small circle for a head, set on top of a pair of large circles. And he always seemed nice, like the snowman would be if he were real.

"Okay if I sit, Hon?" Julie asked, after the fact.

Mr. Nice Guy shifted his attention from an unenthused, G-string clad dancer straddling a shiny pole on the stage behind the bar and turned to Julie. He liked the way she looked. It seemed she didn't need make-up, just a little lipstick. And her brown eyes were always shining and happy. He smiled back at her.

"Sure. How are you, Julie? Having a good week?"

"Yeah, I guess. How's it going for you?"

"I'm doing okay." He bent toward the floor with a soft grunt and came back up holding a ***Filene's Basement*** shopping bag by its string handles. He displayed it to Julie. "I had some luck down in the Basement."

"That's nice. You go shopping in the Basement a lot?"

"Yeah. I like to go there on my day off, and it gives me a reason to come in here."

"I'm not reason enough?" was accompanied by an impish grin as Julie tucked a few strands of short brown hair behind an ear.

"Sure you are."

The customer leaned over and stood the shopping bag back on the floor beside his barstool. When he straightened up, Richie, short and bald, was placing a glass of Coke on a napkin in front of him, next to his red and blue baseball cap. The bartender glanced in Julie's direction, then back at his customer. "A drink for the lady?"

"Yeah, sure."

"Thanks, Hon," Julie said. "If it's your day off, it means you have a job. You know, I've been seeing you for a long time now, and I never asked you what your name is, or what you do for work."

"Well, my name's Eddie and I'm a...," Eddie hesitated, thinking Julie would probably not recognize the word, then, hoping she'd lose interest and avoid a possible awkward moment, mumbled in a quiet voice, "docent."

"I'm sure you do a good job, Hon. What is it you're decent at?"

"No, Julie, not decent, docent. It's like a tour guide, but not outside. I'm inside, in a museum. I answer questions for people and tell them things about the paintings, sculptures and other things in the museum."

"No kidding? I could tell you were a smart guy. You know..." Julie was quiet while the bartender placed a small, opaque green bottle and a glass in front of her, then walked to an end of the bar. She resumed talking as she poured the ersatz wine. "... I go to a museum every week."

"You do?" Eddie asked, pushing his thinning brown hair back with his hand. "Here, in Boston?"

"For sure."

"Which museum?"

"That fancy castle place over in the Fenway area. Isabella something or other."

"Stewart Gardner," Eddie said, quickly filling in the name. He straightened up on the barstool.

"Yeah, that's it, Hon, the Gardner Museum. But, the truth is, we don't go over to look at paintings. It's not even open when we go."

"What do you mean, not open? And who do you go with?"

"Just between us, Hon, okay? You know the long drink of water with the red hair that goes by Maggie?"

Eddie pictured the tall, skinny woman he had watched perform every now and then at the Goose. "Sure. She goes to the museum with you? When it's closed?"

"Well, we're working girls, Hon, you know?" Julie said, keeping her voice low, even though she and Eddie were alone at the center of the long bar. "And that museum's got a couple of real horny guards that watch the treasures during the night. They get two of their own treasures early every Sunday morning. When the Goose closes at one o'clock, me and Maggs grab a cab right off and head on over." Julie smiled at Eddie. "Nothing like a regular trick. Can count on that money to help with the rent."

Eddie had lost all interest in the dancer, now at a pole at the end of the bar, her body contorted in a dip in front of a few young men in Harvard sweatshirts. "How can you even get in the building?" he asked. "The museum's locked up tight as a drum when it's closed."

"Those security guys throwing the party sure as hell aren't gonna lock out the entertainment. They just leave the alley delivery door unlocked and shut off the alarm. We waltz right in and head upstairs to the room with no windows and all those fancy rugs on the wall."

"Wow."

"Why 'wow'? You guys have your brains down here." Julie gave the docent's crotch a gentle pat. "When guys are thinking booty, nothing else matters. Those guards are really into it, too. A little kinky. You know, ropes, handcuffs."

As Julie sipped her drink, Eddie asked, "Do you lock the door after you go in?"

Julie shrugged, and said, "Nah. We just slam it shut. Nobody's around in the middle of the night."

"Yeah, I guess not. How long does the party last?"

"At least an hour or so, usually more. They close the big doors to the room, turn on the boom box, break out the booze and have at it. An atomic bomb could go off in the place and they'd never even know it. A good time's all they got on their minds, nothing else. I'd never hire them to keep an eye on my treasures, if I had any, that is."

"Believe it or not," Eddie said, "I work at the Gardner Museum. That's where I'm a docent."

Julie's mouth opened, and her eyes rolled upwards. "Oh, shit!"

"Oh, you don't have to worry, Julie. I'll keep your party night a secret."

"You will, Eddie? Promise?"

"Yeah. I promise." Eddie paused a moment and smiled at Julie. "I wouldn't want to ruin anyone's fun. Really."

"Thanks, Eddie. That makes me feel lots better."

Julie rubbed goose bumps on her bare arms and turned in the direction of the open Washington Street door. A half dozen college kids were digging out their ID's for the doorman's cursory glance. Cold air rushed around them and down the length of the bar.

"Close the damn door," Julie shouted, then turned back to Eddie. "I wonder if these college boys ever go to class."

Left over from a weekend of St. Patrick's Day revelry, green and white streamers hung from the ceiling and cardboard cutouts of shamrocks and leprechauns decorated the Goose's walls. It was about ten-thirty on Monday morning. Julie Santos sat alone at the bar, the front page of the *Boston Globe* spread out in front of her. She sipped from her Dunkin Donuts coffee cup as she stared, wide-eyed, at the daily broadsheet. "Oh my God," she whispered to herself. "Oh my God."

A voice from behind startled Julie from her trance-like state. "What's so amazing, Jules? The world about to end, or what?"

The question came from Julie's co-employee, and business partner of sorts, Maggie, who had just come into the Goose. Recognizing the voice, Julie did not turn, but simply pointed at the *Globe* headline:

$200m Gardner Museum art theft –
2 men posing as police tie up night guards.

Maggie's mouth fell open. "The Gardner Museum? Oh my God, that's our museum, Jules! When did this happen, last night?"

"You're not gonna believe this, Maggs. It says it happened yesterday morning, early, at about one-thirty. That's just after we got there for our St.Patty's Day party with the guards and their buddy."

Still staring at the headline, Maggie, a large red pocketbook slung over her shoulder, moved to the barstool next to Julie. She sat, staring at the *Globe* headline, and placed a steaming cardboard cup of coffee on the bar. "The robbers tied up the guards? Tied up our johns?"

"That's what it says, Maggs. The guards say they were tricked into opening the door by fake cops, got tied up and the place was robbed."

"The other john, the guards' buddy, he get tied up, too?"

"The story says just two guards were tied up and handcuffed to a pole. Doesn't say anything about a third guy. Maybe he had something to do with the break-in, you think?"

A shiver ran through Maggie. With a shaky hand, she pulled a pack of Newports from her pocketbook, and then asked, "What should we do, Jules? This shit's big time."

Julie glanced toward the Washington Street door as it opened, letting in a shaft of sunlight, along with two uniformed Boston policemen. As the two cops walked over to the bar, one, who Julie thought looked familiar, caught her eye, smiled and doffed his hat. In seconds, Richie placed two empty shot glasses and two bottles of Bud in front of the cops. Watching the men, Julie thought, again, back to her conversation with the Gardner Museum docent, Eddie, two or three weeks earlier. She didn't know what, if any, connection there might be with the break-in. She quickly realized she didn't want to know. As the bartender poured shots of Canadian Club for Boston's finest, Julie turned to Maggie, who had lit her menthol cigarette and was taking in a long drag.

"I don't think we should do anything, Maggs. Let's stay under the radar on this one. Not a word to anyone, okay?"

"Absolutely, Jules. Nothin' to nobody," was followed by a stream of smoke.

5

PART ONE

THEOPOULIS V. THEOPOULIS
SUFFOLK SUPERIOR COURT

1

SPRING, 2002

Senior Auditor Martin Hanley of the Massachusetts Department of Revenue planned to leave his office at one o'clock. He had scheduled a visit with a small packaging firm on the South Shore - questionable retained earnings - for tomorrow morning, but his appointment calendar would show his on-site audit began this afternoon. Hanley knew no one would be checking to see exactly when he showed up at Bubble-Pac. Yesterday, he'd played the back nine at the Hatherly Country Club in just two over par. The middle-aged civil servant was anxious to get back on the course this afternoon, before he forgot exactly how he'd stroked the ball. As he pushed a pile of documents into his briefcase and stood from his desk, he heard a muted buzz. Hanley paused a moment, staring at his phone, groaned, then sat back down and reached for the receiver.

"Hey, Marty, got a minute?" the caller asked. "I've got questions on the Finish Line corporate return, and the Theopoulis Trust return."

Hanley recognized his first assistant's voice, and the names of two very substantial state taxpayers. "They can wait, Herb. I'll be back in the office tomorrow afternoon. Bring the returns up then."

"Don't know about waiting, Marty. The Finish Line lawyers are already raising hell because they're looking for a big number refund. But there's something screwy about the returns, especially the trust return. It's your ass that's on the line. Remember, Finish Line's the largest privately held company in the state, and there are some real heavy hitters in that trust."

Phone in hand, Hanley pushed up and out of his chair and walked a few feet to the window. He looked at the pedestrians fifteen stories below. Many were in shirtsleeves, enjoying the gentle heat of spring. Perfect golf weather. He accepted his fate. "Okay, Herb, bring the damn files up."

An hour later Marty and Herb, sleeves rolled up and ties loosened, sat across from each other at a document strewn conference table. They agreed that there was no logical explanation for the failure of the trust return to report what appeared to be a substantial capital gain. Thousands of shares of stock in Finish Line Corporation, owned by the Theopoulis Trust, had been sold by the trustee. The trust's sole beneficiaries were Harold Theopoulis and his sister, Helen. The trustee who sold the stock was Cosmos Theopoulis, Harold and Helen's uncle. The buyer of the shares was a limited liability corporation which identified the same Cosmos Theopoulis as its sole manager. But there was no entry showing the stock sale on the trust returns, and no capital gains tax had been paid to the Commonwealth.

"This is either a huge oversight, or someone thinks the DOR is dumber than dirt," Marty said while he rubbed his bald spot. "What do you think?"

"Could they have just screwed up the return?" Herb asked.

"You're a hell of a lot kinder than I am. The cynic in me says they assumed we still operate this department like we did in the old days, when they probably would have gotten away with it. But you caught it, Herb, so I'll leave it up to you. You can call the lawyers and ask them about this little mistake, or figure the past due tax, glom on the interest and penalty, and make a formal demand. That'll get a response."

"Let's give them a chance to explain it," Herb said. "I'll call the trust's lawyer. It should be an interesting conversation."

"Okay, but before you make the call, go back and check the last few years of returns. Let's see if we have a pattern." Marty glanced out a window, then at a wall clock. "Two-thirty. I can still get out of here before the whole afternoon is wasted."

As he began collecting the papers from the table, Herb asked, "Where you playing, Marty?"

The next afternoon Herb strode into Hanley's office and pulled a chair up to the front of his boss's desk. A wide smile lit his face beneath his gray buzz cut. "You're going to love this, Marty."

"Anything to take my mind off an eight on the ninth hole yesterday. Screwed up what started as one hell of a round."

"This'll get your mind off golf."

"Do tell," Hanley said. He popped a spearmint Lifesaver in his mouth. "Can hardly wait."

"I checked the Theopoulis trust returns over the last five years, like you suggested. The sale of Finish Line stock has been going on for the last four years, but a capital gains tax has always been paid, except for this year."

"That's hardly interesting. What am I going to love?"

"Well," Herb leaned in toward the desk, "I don't know who entered the phone number on the Theopoulis file to call with questions, but it wasn't for a lawyer or an accountant. It was for one of the beneficiaries, Harold Theopoulis. When I explained why I was calling, he wouldn't believe anything I told him about the stock sale."

"Why?" Hanley asked. "Tax preparers make mistakes all the time. This was a big one, but because the tax on the gain was paid the previous years, this would appear to be an oversight. There'll be some interest to pay, but there won't be any penalty."

Herb shook his head, the smile returning. "No, no. Listen, Marty. The guy didn't know anything about the sale of Finish Line stock, this year or in past years. The trust returns, all the tax stuff, is taken care of by his uncle Cosmos. He said he and his sister just sign whatever the uncle sticks under their noses. Cosmos has taken care of everything to do with the family business since his brother, the kids' father, died ten years ago."

"So, over the last four years, uncle Cosmos sold all this stock in Finish Line, and his dead brother's kids had no idea it was happening?"

"That's what the kid says. And, Harold also said that out of respect to their father, there's no way he and his sister would ever sell the company stock. It's a family loyalty thing. Says he's going to talk to his lawyer."

"Your right, Herb, it is kind of interesting. But there are usually two sides to these things."

"I checked with the corporations division at the Secretary of State's Office. Uncle Cosmos' LLC now controls one hundred per cent of Finish Line stock. It's not traded. The tax returns show what the Theopoulis Trust was paid for its Finish Line stock, but I wonder what it's really worth."

2

"My father told me about this restaurant. He says it has the best seafood on the Cape. He always gets their Lobster Savannah."

Roger Metcalf looked into the green eyes of the woman in the skimpy black dress sitting across from him. Paris Par La Mer was the priciest restaurant he had ever set foot in, but whatever Angela Theopoulis wanted, he was anxious to provide. She had it all as far as Roger was concerned. The raven-haired 30-year-old was, without question, movie-star gorgeous, and unreal in the sack, a four-post version of which was waiting for them at the nearby Chatham Bars Inn. The fact that Angie was a member of one of the wealthiest families in Massachusetts added to her allure.

"Does your dad come to Cape Cod often?"

"Hell, he seems to go everywhere often. Cosmos Theopoulis never stops moving. It can be work or play. Whether it's his Porsche, his Lear, or on foot, he's a perpetual motion machine. A hyperactive geriatric. I don't have half his energy."

"What makes Cosmos run?"

"Originally, I think he just wanted success for its own sake. You know, son of immigrants, make it big, make his parents proud. He spent all his time working along with his brother. Once their business was a big success, he kept working, but began to fill in his life. My dad had waited to marry and have a family. He's a good father, always interested in the kids, there are four of us, but work always comes first, making money. He likes the power it brings."

"He can relax now, enjoy his so-called golden years. Why doesn't he?"

Angela drained her martini glass and answered as she chewed on the olive. "My dad's sure he'd die if he stopped working. Could be right. I love him to pieces, but he'd drive anybody crazy. He's an incredibly demanding person, has no room for anyone else's opinions and, if you're supposed to do something, you sure as hell better do it right. Makes no difference if you're a janitor or a US senator, and he's told both what to do and where to go. Daddy has no interest in excuses. Believe me, I learned that early in life."

"He's connected politically?" Roger asked, as the sommelier arrived at table-side.

"Very. He contributes lots of money to all kinds of politicians. He's like that old TV ad. When he talks, they listen."

"Sounds like an interesting guy. Maybe I'll get to meet him someday."

As Roger glanced at the wine list, sudden activity at the entrance to the dining room drew Angela's attention. A short, slight and wiry man in a dark suit, gray chest hair pouring out of an open-neck white shirt, stood next to the maître d'. He was running a hand through unkempt, salt and pepper hair. Standing next to him, taller by a head, was a young woman in a short red dress.

"That day has arrived," Angela said, staring beyond Roger at the couple standing at the arched entryway.

"Huh?"

"I said that day has arrived. I mean, to meet my father. That's him." Angela gestured in the direction of the couple.

"Really?" Roger turned and looked. "Is that your mother with him?"

"Come on, Roger. My mother has to be older than I am." Angela half stood from the chair and waved to her father.

Cosmos Theopoulis's face lit up when he saw his daughter. His smile displayed a top row of teeth that were too perfect and too white for the lined face. He spoke a few words to the maître d' and started across the floor, swiveling to barely avoid a collision with a table of four. In a few seconds, Cosmos was at his daughter's table.

"Angie, Honey, I didn't know you were on the Cape."

In short order, furniture was being rearranged. Under the curious gaze of the roomful of diners, a pair of busboys moved a table for two from a far corner, married it to Roger and Angela's, and quickly set it with silverware, napkins and glassware. There were quiet apologies for disruption to nearby diners. Snapped fingers and circular hand motions from the maître d' to a nearby waiter would bring peace offerings of drinks and hors d'oeuvres.

Without introducing his stranded companion, who had tentatively made her way across the room, Cosmos sat. The young woman in red offered a weak smile and took the remaining chair. Angela introduced Roger. As the blonde introduced herself simply as Suzanne, Cosmos reached across the table and took a slice of cranberry bread from a wire basket.

"What keeps you busy?" Cosmos said, gesturing at Roger. "Besides my Angie," he added with a smile.

At six foot two, trim and handsome, Roger generally experienced a feeling of confidence, if not superiority, when dealing with other men. That feeling was absent.

"The law, Mr. Theopoulis. I'm a lawyer."

"Yeah? What kind of lawyer, and whereabouts?"

"I'm a partner in a Boston firm, Keene and Metcalf. We're involved in most civil areas of the law. I specialize in litigation."

"I hire and fire lawyers all the time. You any good?"

"I like to think so. My clients seem satisfied, at least for the most part."

"Maybe I'll give you a call about something that's just come up." He looked at his daughter. "Be sure to get his phone number to me, Sweetie."

"Roger's interested in being a judge, Daddy," Angela said. "He used to be a federal DA, or something, in Washington."

"Prosecutor, in the US Attorney's Office," Roger said.

"Any political connections? That's what you've got to have, you know, to get a judgeship. State or federal bench, makes no difference. I can pick up a phone and be connected to the governor or a senator in a minute." Cosmos took a bite of the cranberry bread and spoke while chewing. "How old are you?"

The question made the 38-year-old Roger feel inadequately young. "Moving in on forty."

"Ah," Cosmos waved his hand as if shooing a fly, "you've got plenty of time. Hell, if you ever get your ass on the federal bench, they'll have to dynamite you out of the chair. No mandatory retirement. Bastards stay 'till they croak. Remember that son of a bitch, Douglas? Horny old prick just refused to die. Kept marrying young broads. Kept him young, I think. Take your time. When you're really ready, let me know. Maybe I'll make a few calls." He looked at his daughter, smiled and added. "If Angie says to, of course. Let's eat. Where the hell's the fruity waiter? They're all fruits in these fancy places."

3

Roger Metcalf hurried into a private dining room at the Parker House Hotel as dessert was being served at half a dozen round tables. A middle-aged woman dressed in a business suit stood from the head table at the top of the room and shook his extended hand. After a brief conversation, Roger was at the center of the table, raising a microphone to accommodate his height. As the group of thirty or so lawyers assembled in front of him began to work on servings of Boston Cream Pie, Roger, the featured speaker at the Boston Bar Association's Bi-annual Ethics Meeting, smoothed the front of his navy blue, pin-striped suit and looked out at the men and women. He knew well enough not to take up too much time of those who had drawn the short straw at their firms. He tapped the microphone, quieting the group who had gathered for the luncheon.

"I'm sorry my schedule kept me from enjoying lunch with you, but, trust me," he smiled, "I won't be keeping you for long. Just a few words of wisdom, and warning, about some recent disciplinary decisions from our Supreme Judicial Court, and you'll be on your way back to billing your well-served clients. Now, let me suggest what we should be doing, and what we shouldn't be doing."

An attractive, short-haired brunette seated at a table toward the back of the room smiled, thinking back to a weekend bar seminar on Martha's Vineyard. "That's the same line he used on me last year," she whispered to the female lawyer sitting beside her.

"I thought he was married," her colleague responded. "Is he divorced?"

"Should be," the brunette said.

Across the table, a man in a rumpled suit shook his head. "This is the last guy to be telling anyone what to do. I had a client come in last year who wanted to sue Metcalf and file a complaint against him with the Board of Bar Overseers. Claimed Metcalf over-billed him big time. I talked my client out of it. Told him how tough it is to prove those cases. My guy could easily afford the bill anyhow. Also, I know what a pain in the ass those complaints can be for lawyers. I told Metcalf about the favor I did for him, kind of a heads-up to watch his billing. He thanked me a few months later by telling me where to stick it when I needed an extension to file an answer to a complaint. Long story short, my guy got defaulted by a judge who wouldn't give me a break. If I don't get it tipped in the Appeals Court, my client's going to sue me. So much for doing this shit a favor. Metcalf's one rotten son of a bitch."

Within thirty minutes, Roger had completed his comments to the group. Once again, he shook the hand of the committee chairperson, then left the hotel and started to walk to Locke-Ober Restaurant, located in an alley off nearby Winter Street. He had arranged lunch with Frederick Poole, a colleague on the Judicial Oversight Committee, and a senior partner of one of Boston's prestigious law firms, Wiggins, Lewis and Poole. As he strode along the crowded Tremont Street sidewalk, Roger rehearsed what he would be saying to Frederick. It had to go down just right.

Seated amongst the city's power brokers in the stately, polished wood Locke-Ober dining room, Attorneys Metcalf and Poole finished up servings of New England clam chowder and lobster stew, mixed with the small talk of Boston's legal community. Once the dishes were cleared from their table, Poole, early seventies and bordering on rotund with a whisper-like fringe of white hair, listened with interest as Roger got into the background of the reason for the meeting.

"Theopoulis v. Theopoulis was filed in Suffolk Superior Court two weeks ago. The family corporation, Finish Line, is also a named defendant. The plaintiffs are seeking an accounting and damages for deceit and violation of fiduciary duty, that's basically a count in fraud. They're looking for triple damages under Chapter ninety-three A. They're also looking for a declaratory judgment saying they have a controlling interest in the corporation. Simply put, Frederick, it's a classic family feud. The son and daughter of a company co-founder claim they're being screwed out of their dead father's share of the business by his surviving business partner, Cosmos Theopoulis, their uncle."

Roger's monologue was followed with the sound of the last of his beer pouring from his Heineken's bottle into a Pilsner glass. He sipped the beer, then leaned back in his chair and pushed some hair from his forehead. He had never felt so much the pitchman, even when addressing juries with closing arguments.

Noticing a lull in the conversation, the stealth-like waiter appeared at table-side. Crumbs disappeared under a silver brush and simultaneously, or so it seemed, the server poured two cups of coffee, placed the silver urn on the table and padded off. Reaching for a packet of Sweet 'n Low, the sleeve of Poole's cord suit coat moved up, displaying a white starched cuff pinned by a gold link.

"I know it's the first inning, but any idea of how strong a defense you'll have, Roger?"

"It seems solid, even from the little we know from Mr. Theopoulis at this point. Basically, he says the kids' claim is bull, and that he's been doing his dead brother a favor out of family loyalty. For ten years, he's acted as the sole trustee of a trust that benefits his niece and nephew. He was named to that position under his brother's will. He has very wide discretion to decide on investments under the terms of the trust. Until they filed this lawsuit, the kids never complained. He's never lost a dime of trust assets, and he's always told his niece and nephew what was going on. He says that's documented. The kids were never in the dark. They were just too lazy to bother to pay any attention.

"The demand for multiple damages, claiming fraud, really seems off the wall. The statute just doesn't apply to this kind of case, Frederick. It's as if they're trying to make new law. This just may be a frivolous suit."

"If it is frivolous, why does your client think his niece and nephew sued him?"

"Because they're a couple of losers. They hit the sperm lottery, and they want more. Simple greed. They're both in their late twenties and never worked a day in their lives."

"Family hate is deeper than any other," Frederick said. "What amount did you say is potentially involved?"

"Worst case? If you consider the possibility of a judge awarding multiple damages under the statute, my client's exposure could be as much as a billion dollars."

"Yes, yes. I can believe that. Theopoulis is one of the wealthiest families in the state. That's an incredible amount of money at risk." Frederick paused, tapping his fingers on the tablecloth. "There will be untold billable hours in this case."

"Millions in legal fees, Frederick. Millions."

"Yes, yes. And the likelihood of a compromise short-circuiting lengthy, expensive litigation, Roger?"

"When I asked my client about settlement, his response was he'd be gelded by the track vet before he gives those kids a penny. To him, they're just a couple of ingrates."

Poole smiled and sipped his coffee. He enjoyed hearing about the characters prone to involvement in rancorous feuds, often leading to litigation. Frederick seldom saw this side of the law. His contribution to the business of law was the same as the Pooles who had preceded him - rainmaking: luring lucrative accounts to the white-shoe firm. He was a lawyer who did not lawyer, but rather produced the clients who required legal services for themselves and their businesses. An Ivy League background and family contacts had worked splendidly for Frederick, as it had for his paternal forebears.

To his relief and satisfaction, being a part of the more conservative branch of Boston's gay community, which he neither promoted nor hid, had not seemed to harm his business prowess. In his opinion, it may have helped. His grapevine had identified more than a few old and new clients of the firm as being shadow members of that same community. Frederick had not only maintained most of the viable clients lured to the firm by his ancestors, but had also substantially added to that number.

"Tell me, Roger, how did your office get involved in a matter of this magnitude?" Poole paused, just an instant. "Of course, I don't mean to imply for an instant any lack of capability. No question, yours is one of the finest young firms in the city. Your reputation as a litigator is outstanding. It's just when the stakes are as high as you say, well, I would think that a larger firm, a White and Doar, or a Ropes and Gray, would have likely gotten the call."

Roger smiled. "Or a Wiggins, Lewis and Poole?"

Poole smiled in acknowledgment of Roger's observation. "Well, we certainly have the resources."

"You sure do. Fifty or so lawyers to our half dozen. And, realistically, I know our office would be stretched. We'd just about have to put the rest of our business out to pasture. That could be suicide in the long run. That's why I suggested this meeting, Frederick, to invite, actually request, your firm to come in as co-counsel. And, to answer your question, I met the client through his daughter, Angie. We've been seeing each other for a few months."

"Be faithful to her."

"That's no problem with Angie," Roger said with a slight shake of his head. "I know in your world it can be like musical chairs, but for me ..." Roger immediately regretted his comment. He watched the color begin to grow in Frederick's face and neck above his starched white collar. "I'm sorry, Frederick. I, I..."

Frederick waved a hand dismissively. "Not to worry. Here I am in my seventies and still reacting to such comments. Shame on me. But they don't bother me as they once did. It's okay, Roger. Really, it is."

"Thank you, for being the gentleman that I'm not."

"You're welcome."

"Angie and I were at a quiet little restaurant with a fancy French menu down on the Cape when, all of a sudden, there was a hullabaloo at the door. In just seconds, the maître d' has a table dragged over next to us and seats Angie's father. He's with a real attractive young woman who was not his wife, Angie's mother. This, apparently, is acceptable family sport because there wasn't the slightest embarrassment, just introductions all around."

"Interesting."

"Angie mentioned to her father that I was a lawyer. We talked a little about what I had for experience. He seemed impressed with my years at the US. Attorney's Office in DC. I also mentioned a couple of my recent courtroom successes. He said that he anticipated need of a blood and guts lawyer for a family problem that was beginning to spout like Vesuvius."

"Did he retain you before the entrée? Could make the dinner deductible."

Roger chuckled at the small joke, and then said, "Actually, it was just a week ago that he hired me, my firm. He appeared at the office with his corporate vice-president, and without an appointment. He met with me and my partner, Bill Keene, for about fifteen minutes. Then he announced he was hiring us to defend the lawsuit filed against him by his dear brother's rotten children, his words.

"I explained that if we agreed to accept the case, we may want to bring in co-counsel because of the anticipated scope of the litigation. He said fine, whatever I think, whatever I wanted or needed. He then asked if I was taking the case. I told him we'd have to discuss it with others in the firm."

"And?" asked Frederick.

"He said that was nonsense. If I had to ask anyone about taking his case, everybody in the firm needed a fucking shrink, his words again. If I didn't have an immediate answer, he was getting on the elevator to go upstairs to a real law firm. I had no intention of letting this tuna off the hook. We took the case. Without asking me what I needed for a retainer, Mr. Theopoulis nodded to his vice-president, who never opened his mouth while he was there. He wrote out a retainer check for a half a million dollars."

Poole took a Gran Habano cigar from his coat pocket, undid the cellophane wrapper, and stuck the expensive smoke into his mouth, rolling it around his tongue. After a few moments he took the cigar out and spoke. "It sounds like your Mr. Theopoulis is a unique fellow."

"From what I've seen and been told, he's an opinionated, bossy little bastard. He's obviously used to getting his way, and willing to pay to get it."

"These clients don't come along every day, Roger. And the fee is paid, of course, win or lose."

"Damned right. But I'm not even thinking about losing, Frederick. With the combined abilities and assets of our firms, and the Theopoulis money, we can mount one hell of a defense, plus I anticipate we can come up with a few counterclaims. I'm thirty-eight years old, and I don't expect I'll ever have an opportunity like this again. This case can make my reputation, establish my office. For me, this is huge."

"When did you say the complaint was filed?"

"Two weeks ago. The suit names Theopoulis personally, and in his capacity as trustee. His limited liability corporation is also a named defendant. The plaintiffs are his niece and nephew, Helen and Harold, both Theopoulis, and the Theopoulis Trust."

Frederick rolled the cigar on his tongue again and permitted himself a small smile. "There will be counterclaims as you suggest, Roger, huge amounts of discovery, mountains of pre-trial maneuvering. A case as complex as we could make this one will drive a cadre of motion clerks to early retirements." Poole patted his lips with his napkin, then placed the triangle of sky-blue linen next to his coffee cup, and stood. He was a rainmaker for his firm, and prided himself on doing his job well. "Yes, Wiggins, Lewis and Poole is in. And, Roger, thank you for an excellent start to the summer."

Roger quickly stood and reached to shake Frederick's extended hand.

"Now, if you'll excuse me," Frederick said, "I'm headed to the bar to take a few puffs of this cigar. Of course, you're free to join me and a few of my tobacco loving brethren."

"No thanks. I want to get back to the office and let my partner know of our collaboration."

"Enjoy the rest of the day."

4

Roger decided to take advantage of the perfect, early summer weather. Leaving Locke-Ober for the walk to his office in the city's financial district, he chose the longer route, one that skirted Boston's tawdry "Combat Zone." His spirits had been lifted by Frederick's agreeing to involve his firm as co-counsel. Wiggins, Lewis and Poole could be of enormous assistance in insuring a defendant's verdict. Frederick's firm had a corps of aggressive litigators, some of whom had earned Roger's respect in personal courtroom battles. More importantly, the firm had manpower – highly paid junior associates fresh from great law schools, eager to outdo one another, to bury themselves in the library to prepare for paper discovery, depositions, critical pre-trial motions, and a lengthy trial. Roger knew preparation was where success was spawned in the business of adversarial law. Perry Mason moments were few and far between.

Involving co-counsel would mean sharing the fee, but considering the mammoth amount that would be generated, that was not a concern. Establishing a stellar reputation was more important to Roger. He knew a clear victory in this civil action which, considering who was involved, would be one of the city's most notorious cases in decades, could lead to that result. Suffolk County juries had been good to him. Roger liked to think he knew why - he was just tough enough, but no real jagged edges; nice enough, polite, but no one would ever think of calling him a patsy; and, he talked their language - no airs for Roger Metcalf. Simple, they liked him. A few winks over the years from some of the jurors, mostly female, reinforced his self-image. The jury in the Theopoulis case would be in his corner. He anticipated a defendant's verdict, on all counts, nothing less. Roger glanced at his reflection in the plate glass front of a Chinese grocery store as he walked along Stuart Street. He smiled at his image. No wonder jurors ate him up.

Ten minutes later, Roger entered the lobby of the Bay State Business Towers, a smile and nod directed at the young woman behind the information desk. Keene & Metcalf's half-dozen lawyers occupied the north side of the building's fifteenth floor. The firm's decision to lease in the high-rent area wasn't an easy one. Until Cosmos Theopoulis opened his wallet, Roger wasn't sure how the rent was going to be paid in the foreseeable future. He was thinking the firm's costly location might end up spelling the end to the fledgling group of legal eagles. Now, with the sizable retainer in the escrow account, and a billing rate starting at four hundred dollars an hour, that problem had been nudged off stage. Roger walked from the elevator, through the office reception area and down a corridor. As one of two founding partners, he had the advantage of a private secretary. Martha, a gray-haired perfectionist, sat at her desk tucked into a partitioned area at the door to Roger's office. As he approached, he heard her side of a phone conversation.

"Oh, hold on, sir. He's just coming in now." The call put on hold, Martha looked up. "It's Mr. Theopoulis. He's quite excited. I figured you'd want the call."

"Right. I'll pick up." Roger stepped into his office, snatching his desk phone as he sat. "Mr. Theopoulis, Roger Metcalf here."

"For starters, tell me if I have to let my nephew onto the grounds here at the track right after he sues me and tells all the world that I've cheated him out of his inheritance, or can I throw him out on his little royal ass?"

"Okay, Mr. Theopoulis, okay. Try and calm down just a bit. I haven't had time to familiarize myself with your company yet. I've got a few questions."

"Ask."

"Rather than the phone, Mr. Theopoulis, can you make yourself available to meet with me as soon as possible? I can come over to your office. If I'm going to be looking for a restraining order to keep Harold off the grounds, I have a lot of learning to do."

"Come to the track at four o'clock and go to the top floor in the clubhouse. That's where the company offices are."

Roger placed his phone back on the cradle and looked up. His secretary stood at his desk with a sheaf of papers in her hand. "The interrogatories on the Williams case."

"Never mind that, Martha. I'm off to the racetrack. Tell Bill Keene and Mickey Kratz I'll see them in the conference room at six o'clock today. We've got one crazy Greek bastard on our hands. I think we better get used to him. Cancel everything on my schedule for this afternoon, and tomorrow. Get anyone who's available to cover if you need a body."

Martha shook her head about the rescheduling as she walked out of the office.

"And Martha," Roger called after her through the open door, "phone over to Wiggins, Lewis and Poole. Get a message to Frederick Poole. Tell him that I've gone to the track and I'll call him in the morning to bring him up to speed."

At quarter of four, Roger paid the driver and stepped out of a Yellow cab at the entrance to the Patriot Downs clubhouse in East Boston. As he looked up at the white, three-story building, the public address system was barking the start of the fifth race, a claimer at six furlongs. A little over a minute later, as the track announcer was calling the order of finish, a uniformed usher pointed Roger to an elevator tucked into an alcove on the ground floor. Riding to the top floor, Roger pictured the slight, wiry man with the head of unruly hair he had met on the Cape ten days earlier. He thought Cosmos Theopoulis looked like his personality - abrasive, demanding, and full of piss and vinegar. The doors slid open directly into the office of Finish Line, Inc. Roger introduced himself to the receptionist and asked for Mr. Theopoulis.

"Let me see if I can spot him," the tall, gum-chewing blonde said. She stood from her desk and turned to a picture window overlooking the race track. She looked to her left, towards the homestretch. "He's at the eighth pole. Should be up in just a few minutes, unless one of the railbirds gets his ear."

"May I?" Roger, standing in front of the receptionist's desk, asked as he pointed toward the window.

"Sure, come take a gander."

Roger walked to the oversized window and stood next to the receptionist. He was overlooking the oval dirt track, which encircled a grass track. On the far side of the dirt track's inner railing, he watched a small man in black shorts and a gray T-shirt jogging on the vibrant green grass, or turf, track. The runner was barefoot and headed in the direction of the finish line. He waved at the fans and received a few cheers and shouts in response as he reached the grandstand area.

"Mr. T takes a run around the grass track every day, rain or shine. A solid mile. Pretty good for a seventy-eight-year-old."

"No kidding," Roger said as he recognized the mint aroma from the receptionist's gum.

"Ready for another one of his habits?"

"I guess so."

"A sauna and locker room are at the end of the hall." With a thumb the gum chewer gestured to the right. "The lockers are unlocked and there are towels on the bench. Mr. T will meet you in the sauna."

"Really? You're serious?"

"Yep. He conducts his business meetings in the sauna. He says naked people are more likely to tell the truth. Thinks people hide behind their clothes."

Roger scratched the back of his head. "Does he ever discuss business with women?"

"The ladies get robes to cover up," the receptionist said. "But Mr. T says I'd be shocked at how many don't bother to wear them."

"Do you find this custom a little unusual?"

"I've worked here at Finish Line for thirteen years. Nothing's unusual when it comes to that little devil."

A stream of water poured from an oversized wooden ladle splattered onto the bed of hot lava rocks, creating a sizzle and hiss along with a cloud of steam. A naked Cosmos Theopoulis dropped the ladle into a water bucket and climbed to the higher of two wooden benches against the sauna's back wall. Short legs hanging, he looked through the steam at Roger Metcalf, who, except for a white towel draped around his neck, was also naked, and sweating profusely.

"Hot enough? I'm getting ready for hell, Metcalf. But before I die I plan to see my dear brother's kids learn that you need to have respect in this life. Without respect, you get shit."

Roger, sitting against a side wall on a lower bench, wiped his brow with his towel. He'd been in steam rooms and saunas before, but nothing this hot. He looked up at Mr. Theopoulis, noticing the grass-stained soles of his dangling feet.

"Respect is very important in life, I agree. But, when I go into court and ask for a restraining order to keep Harold and Helen off the company property, the judge is going to be interested in facts, not manners. Tell me, Mr. Theopoulis, since your brother died, have Harold or Helen been at the office on a regular basis, or any other basis?"

"Helen? Never. Harold shows up every now and then, usually when the horses are running. He's supposed to be connected to the PR office, but just sits around and reads the paper, harasses the office gals, then goes down to the clubhouse for lunch on the house and watches the races. The little prick never does anything worthwhile. I'd never let him near anything important anyhow. By the way, call me Mr. T. Saves a lot of time."

"Is Harold an employee of Finish Line? Is he paid anything? Does he have his own office in the building, any keys?"

"Used to be on the books with Finish Line. A grand a week for doing shit. That ended the second the sheriff walked up to me and slapped those papers across my chest. By the way, I want to sue *that* son of a bitch for assault."

"Let's keep our eye on the ball. When did Harold get notice that he no longer had a job with Finish Line?"

"Today, when I told him to get the hell out of here. You know what he said to me, his uncle, who has protected him and his sister since the day of my dear brother's death?"

Roger looked up at his client. "I could probably guess."

"He said that he has as much right to be here as I do, and that he and his sister would be kicking my ass out the door before this was over. That's what he said! You're my lawyer! I hired you to handle this kind of crap. I don't care what it takes. I don't care how you do it. I want that little bastard to know he cannot disrespect his uncle." Cosmos wiped the palm of his hand and his fingers across his sweating forehead, flicked his wrist and flung perspiration at the floor. "He's not entitled to drink my sweat. What can I do to the little bastard?"

"First of all, we ask a judge for a temporary restraining order. Until we get that, I suggest you keep paying Harold's salary. I don't want to give them anything to bitch about."

"What judge?"

"Judge King, at the Suffolk Superior Court. That's the court where the lawsuit is pending."

"Who's this Judge King? I don't think I know him."

"Not to worry, Mr. Theopoulis. Sorry, I mean Mr. T. He's a solid guy. He'll do the right thing."

"When?"

"This Friday morning, first thing. I can put together a request for a TRO, that's a temporary restraining order, between now and then. I'll tell the judge why we need to have your nephew and niece kept away from the business property. I'm sure he'll grant a restraining order on the papers alone. No testimony necessary. Just your signature on an affidavit that says what you just told me, that the kids, the plaintiffs, never really did any work around here. I'll add something about your being worried about security and get that over to you tomorrow for your signature."

Cosmos pointed at the wooden water bucket and made a pouring gesture with his hand. "More steam. Hotter."

Roger scooped a ladle of water and poured it onto the lava rocks. Listening to the sizzle, he wondered if, indeed, he could be representing the devil.

5

Jennifer Metcalf met her husband when he took the seat next to her in their sophomore Modern World History class at the University of Connecticut. Coincidentally, both were from the gritty industrial neighborhoods of Springfield, Massachusetts, about thirty-five miles north of the UConn campus. That same night, Roger became Jennifer's first and, to this day, only lover. They married a month after graduation. For the next three years, Jen waited tables at an Italian restaurant in Hartford while Roger attended UConn Law. Jen was willing to sacrifice. Hell, life had been no bed of roses so far, and everyone told her lawyers made fortunes once they got established. Following law school, a professor who had taken an interest in Roger used his connections to ease his student's way into the US Attorney's Office in Washington D.C. After five years of prosecuting white-collar criminals and defending civil claims against the government, Roger decided it was time to leave the Justice Department and test the private sector. He accepted an offer from a small Boston firm. He and a pregnant Jennifer packed a U-haul trailer and moved to a rented house in the suburb of Weymouth.

That was eight years and two kids ago. During that time, they had bought the house from their landlord with the hope and expectation that it was just a "starter," to be followed by bigger and better. Nine months ago, Roger, his reputation as a top-shelf civil trial lawyer firmly in place, established his own law firm in partnership with Bob Keene, a high school football teammate. He told Jen it was a necessary risk if he was ever going to really make it in the Boston legal community, and generate some serious fees. But, lately, life sucked in Jen's view. Never enough money, and she was sure Roger was screwing around on her.

Jen stared into her postage stamp-sized backyard. It was a little after six in the early summer evening. Wearing a tank top and shorts, she was sitting at a round metal table on the tiny deck off the kitchen, sipping from a plastic tumbler of lemonade. She hated the rusting deck furniture, but long ago decided that her "house" money could be better spent elsewhere, like the Macy's jewelry counter at the South Shore Mall.

About a half hour commute from downtown Boston, the small Cape style house always seemed cramped. Soon Emily and Rob, 6 and 7-years-old, would need separate rooms, and there would go the den/playroom/office, further crowding the house. Whoever the hell kept saying that all lawyers were making fortunes never met Roger Metcalf, Jen was thinking. Leaving a decent firm to strike out on his own might prove worth it in the long run, but it sure as hell was no picnic in the beginning. The anticipated riches of a big city lawyer always seemed at least another client away.

Feeling less guilty because the kids had overnights with friends, Jen lit a cigarette. Smoking was an addiction she had enjoyed since freshman year in high school, and she knew the kids would insist she stop once they really had standing to complain about it. She was trying to cut back, and rarely smoked if the kids were home, convinced that to do so would send an "it's okay" message that would give her guilt feelings forever. Anyhow, this evening she needed the calming influence of her Virginia Slims.

Her intuition told her that Roger's dalliances had morphed from the occasional bar pick-up while trying a case out of town, to an on-going affair, and she was about to confront him. Jennifer heard a car door slam and steeled herself. Just moments later, her husband walked directly into the backyard from the adjacent, cracked concrete driveway.

"Hey, Jen," Roger greeted his wife as he stepped onto the deck and draped his suit coat over a chair back, "enjoying the great outdoors?" He stooped over and planted a kiss on her forehead. Then he set his briefcase on the deck, scraped a chair over to the table and sat. "Back on the cigs, I see. That means something's bothering you. Want to share?"

"Funny, Roger, that's exactly what's bothering me, sharing."

Jennifer was surprised at the ease with which she dived into the subject.

"I've had a long day, Jen. No riddles, please."

Jennifer stared back into the yard and continued speaking in a normal, calm voice. "Roger, I may not be the best and the brightest, but I'm not stupid, and I'm a wife. I know you're having an affair and, quite frankly, I'm wondering just what to do about it."

Roger reached over and placed a hand on his wife's arm. "Jen..."

She shook her arm free. "No, Roger. Don't say anything until you admit that I'm right, because I know I am." She looked away and took a deep drag on her cigarette.

Roger had worked to avoid even thinking about the likelihood of Jen discovering his affair, yet he felt it was inevitable. Angela Theopoulis was becoming more of a presence in his life. He would hear from her by phone every day, and, lately, she had begun to appear at his office without warning. During a visit late last week, she had nearly seduced him, the sexual interlude being embarrassingly halted as it was beginning by the unannounced appearance of his secretary, Roger's mind being elsewhere when the phone intercom was buzzing. Ironically, it was Angela's father, whose calls were to be put through without exception, who had given Martha a reason to enter Roger's office uninvited.

He didn't know if it was his wife's intuition, or a "friend" doing Jen a favor by ratting out her cheating husband, but he saw no sense in trying to deny it.

"I won't lie about it, Jen. Yes, for a short time I've been involved with someone else, but believe me, I feel awful about it, and it's about to end."

"Feel awful? About to end?" Jennifer swiped at her lemonade. The tumbler flew off the table and the sweet drink splashed onto the deck. "What the hell are you saying, Roger? My God, cheating on your wife isn't something you schedule ending, you just end it!"

"No, no, of course not. That's not what I mean, Jen." Roger reached again for his wife's arm, this time grasping her wrist in his hand. "Look, Jen. Please listen to me for a minute, and I'll tell you what's going on here. Why this is different. I know you'll understand."

Walking through the city's financial district as he chewed on a bagel the next morning, Roger was invigorated, actually pleased, with the results of the confrontation with Jen. He had guessed she knew, and he had to explain his behavior in a specific way. Of course, the affair had to end, but now Jen understood the delicate situation with the dream client. The tacit agreement was accepted by her suggested label for his continuing philandering: "Don't ask? Don't tell?" The discussion ended inside the house, on the couch. The lovemaking made Roger wonder, for just a moment, why he'd strayed in the first place. Then he pictured Angela.

6

The uniformed Suffolk County court officer sat in the front row of the jury box. He put down the *Boston Herald* on the chair beside him as Roger Metcalf walked into an otherwise empty seventh floor courtroom at 8:30.

"Morning, Rog. What's cooking so early in the day?"

"Need a TRO. The clerk just took the papers into Judge King's chambers."

"You mean Judge Valdes's chambers, like in Senorita Zelia Valdes."

"Get your bearings, Gerry, this is Judge King's session."

"Wrong, counselor. At least for today, this is the foxy lady's courtroom."

Roger was suddenly concerned. Judge Elliot King was the father of a college football teammate. Roger knew his motion for a temporary restraining order was sure to be allowed if decided by King. He probably wouldn't even look at the pleadings, let alone study them. It would be a five or ten minute visit to discuss UConn's upcoming gridiron season. Roger had called in a favor at the clerk's office to be sure to get the motion scheduled in King's session. Now it seemed to be blowing up in his face. He realized the motion itself was mostly for show, a tactical move, and to keep Mr. T happy. What really concerned him was the court procedural rule that kept a case with the judge who made initial rulings, such as on a motion for a temporary restraining order or an injunction. Roger wanted Judge King sitting on this case.

"Valdes? Where the hell is King?"

"His brother, or sister, or someone out on the left coast, died a day or two ago. He's in La-La land 'till next week. Got Valdes sitting in. I'd think this would be good news for a lady killer like you."

"Shit, this is not good news." Roger set his briefcase on a table. "Valdes used to be a public defender. Doesn't she usually sit in criminal sessions?"

"Actually, I don't remember her sitting in any civil sessions. Cheer up, Rog. I'm sure you'll charm her."

The barrel-chested, curly-haired court officer picked up his *Herald*. Roger took a seat at a desk in the front of the courtroom and pulled a file from his briefcase.

It had been just after midnight when the three lawyers and two paralegals from Wiggins, Lewis and Poole completed the final draft of the motion for a temporary restraining order and request for a preliminary injunction, along with a supporting memorandum. The documents were then delivered by taxi across town to the office of Keene & Metcalf, where Roger Metcalf slept on a sofa. It wasn't that Roger couldn't have been sleeping at home with his wife and kids, but, if ever questioned about billing hours up to 2:00 a.m., he wanted to be able to answer that he was at his office, which could be confirmed by the security officer who called up from the lobby when the cabbie dropped off the package.

Roger glanced at his watch, found a copy of the memorandum in the file, and began to read, rapidly. He hadn't figured on being quizzed on its content, and now he needed to take a look. He was hardly into the twelve page document when an assistant court clerk poked her head around the corner of a short hallway and into the courtroom. "Judge Valdes will see you now, Mr. Metcalf."

Roger walked into the judge's chambers, a long narrow room, as the clerk was taking a seat on a worn leather couch set against a wall. For a moment, he stared at the woman standing behind the desk, her right hand extended. She was of medium height and slim. Shining brown hair fell to her shoulders. Every aspect of her physical appearance seemed perfectly proportioned. Roger recalled thinking how strikingly attractive Zelia Valdes was when he watched the television newscast of her being sworn into the bench. Even though the memory was a few years old, it was clear. This morning, wearing a tan skirt, a simple white blouse and a string of pearls, she offered a welcoming smile. "Good morning, Mr. ...?"

"Metcalf." Roger filled in his name.

"Yes, of course, Mr. Metcalf. You'll have to excuse my lack of familiarity. I'm pretty new to the civil session. Have our paths ever crossed in the criminal sessions?"

"No, Your Honor, I don't practice in the criminal court very often. Occasionally, but only over in the federal court."

"Please have a seat," the judge said as she sat. "I've looked at your motion. In all honesty, I only scanned the documents, but I'm sure I've got the gist of it. Your first prayer is for a temporary restraining order, but it seems to me that a short order of notice on the preliminary injunction, returnable as soon as, let's see...," the judge leafed through her court calendar, "... a week from today, Friday, the twenty-eighth, will work. That will give the plaintiffs time to digest your argument and prepare a response. I'd like to hear from them before interfering with the status quo."

Roger, now sitting in a hard chair in front of the judge's desk, resisted the urge to stand. He moved to the edge of his chair. "Judge Valdes, this is exactly the type of situation that justifies an ex parte TRO from the court. I realize that you're new to ..."

"Mr. Metcalf," the judge raised the palm of her hand, stopping the lawyer in mid-sentence, "no one is more aware of just how green I am on civil matters than I am. But I'm sure you'll agree that irreparable harm is required to support a TRO without notice to the other side. So, tell me, exactly what is the irreparable harm to your client if his niece and nephew are not barred from the company premises? There is nothing in the pleadings, including your client's affidavit, that spells out the concerns. Are they likely to trash the place? Go postal? Just what do you anticipate between now and a hearing on an injunction a week from now?"

Roger wasn't concerned with anyone going postal, unless it was Cosmos Theopoulis. As they sweated in the sauna earlier in the week, Roger had assured his client of a court order by this morning that would keep his brother's children locked out. Irreparable harm? There had to be something.

"The computers," Roger flustered. "It's the computers that my client is concerned about, Judge. Proprietary information about the corporation and its businesses is locked away in the company computers. And there's always the possibility of important company secrets being stolen. That's the irreparable harm, Judge. That's why we don't want them on the premises at all. We need the TRO. We're afraid of closing the barn door after the horse is stolen, Your Honor."

The judge cast a wary eye across the desk. "Staying on the farm, Mr. Metcalf, aren't you putting the cart before the horse?"

"How so?"

"Why would the plaintiffs want to harm the company, particularly at this time? Among other things, their complaint is seeking control of the business...," the judge glanced at a document and continued, "...that would be Finish Line Incorporated. They claim they've been cheated out of their rightful share by your client, who happens to be their uncle. Nasty family stuff, yes, but it would make no sense at all for the plaintiffs to do anything to harm a business which they are seeking to control. It's not logical that they'd be sabotaging it, certainly not at this juncture."

"But, Judge, this is critical."

"I'm sure it's critical to all the parties, Mr. Metcalf. Both sides deserve a chance to say their piece." Judge Valdes looked at her desk calendar. "I see my new law clerk is starting next Friday. Let's give him a good family fight for breakfast." She then turned toward the clerk who held her pen in hand, an open notebook on her lap. "Barbara, a short order of notice on the preliminary injunction, returnable Friday, the twenty-eighth, at eight-thirty."

Two hours later, a packet of court pleadings in the case of Theopoulis v. Theopoulis was delivered by courier to the Dunn Law Office, located in a suburban office park on Route 128. Enclosed in the parcel was a court notice stating that on Friday, June 28th, at 8:30 a.m. Judge Zelia Valdes would consider a request for a preliminary injunction barring Harold Theopoulis and Helen Theopoulis from entering onto the business premises of Finish Line, Inc. At noon, Joe Dunn arrived back at his office, fresh from a game of handball at a nearby athletic club.

Dunn's paralegal, a casually dressed young man, greeted him as soon as he entered the office. "There's a hand-delivered motion for a preliminary injunction and a memorandum on the Theopoulis case on your desk, sir. Suffolk Superior, next Friday at eight-thirty. Also, there's a copy of a motion for an ex-parte TRO. I called the clerk's office and was told that the case has been assigned to Judge Zelia Valdes, and that she denied that motion this morning."

Dunn wasn't surprised that the motion was filed. When he'd arrived in the office earlier in the week, Harold Theopoulis was waiting for him. He was still steaming while he sputtered the story of his ejection from the Finish Line offices at Patriot Downs. Dunn knew some legal maneuvering would soon be in the cards.

"They're looking to draw first blood. Who's representing the old man?" Dunn asked the paralegal.

"Roger Metcalf from Keene and Metcalf and Frederick Poole from Wiggins, Lewis and Poole are the attorneys of record."

"Call Harold and his sister. See if they can come in about two o'clock."

"Why is it so damn important to keep us off the premises, Joe? I've only been there maybe three times since our dad died ten years ago." Helen Theopoulis was pacing about the office as she asked the question.

"The simple answer is that it's not important. They're pulling your chains. Interested in flexing some muscle." Dunn turned to Helen's brother. "Harold, how often do you show up at the office?"

"Since Dad died, probably once or twice a week. Usually, I'm going to the track anyhow, so I stop up in the office to say hello to a few of the old-timers who still remember my father, check any mail and make a couple of phone calls. Don't need the damn office, but, what the hell, it was my father's office. It's our family's space. I usually didn't even see Uncle Cosmos. I don't give a damn about access to the place except out of principle. Where the hell does he get off, a goddamn thief, telling us we can't visit our own damn business."

"They went in for a temporary restraining order," Dunn said. "That means they claimed some sort of emergency existed and they had to keep you guys off the grounds immediately."

"Emergency? What is this crap?" Helen asked.

"Easy, Helen," Dunn responded. "The judge, her name's Valdes, denied the request and said they could come back and argue for an injunction once we had notice. That gives us the opportunity to argue against it. Next Friday we can tell the judge why you and Harold have as much of a right to be on the company property as your uncle. Between now and then, I'd suggest you guys stay away from the office. Let's at least try to keep a lid on this."

"What kind of an emergency could they have claimed? They must have said something," Harold said.

"My understanding is that they argued something about computer security being jeopardized if you were permitted into the offices."

"You gotta be shitting me," Harold said. "I don't even know how to turn the damn things on."

7

Upon learning on Friday that the defendants' motion for a temporary restraining order had been denied, Frederick Poole scheduled a working lunch with Roger on the following Monday at the Harvard Club in Boston's Back Bay. The discussion would center on why the TRO request had been denied, and the handling of the request for a preliminary injunction, scheduled for a hearing on the coming Friday.

Roger's cab dropped him at the stately brownstone at twelve-thirty. As he walked into the club's Boston Room, he spied Frederick at a table by a pair of windows overlooking Commonwealth Avenue. To his surprise, Frederick was not alone. Also at the table and sipping from a martini glass sat a large, fit-looking man without a hair on his mahogany-hued head. Roger hesitated just a moment, then responded to a wave from Poole and walked to the table. As he approached, Frederick and his companion stood.

"Roger Metcalf, say hello to Martin Robinson," Frederick said and stepped back to permit a handshake. "Actually, my partner is more casually known as Otto."

"A pleasure," Otto said, and both he and Roger smiled and sat along with Frederick.

"Can't say that I know too many Ottos," Roger said.

"The name is from his magnificent off-Broadway performance years ago as Othello," Frederick responded. "I asked Otto to come over to the club for a celebratory drink. He's just heard that he's been named an associate drama coach at Emerson College."

"Congratulations," Roger said as a waiter placed a bottle of Heineken, previously ordered by Frederick, and a Pilsner glass in front of him.

"Thank you. I was fortunate," Otto said. "An old friend from my New York theater days recommended me for the position. Not much of a stipend, but I love drama, and teaching. I'm really quite excited about going back into that part of my world." Otto finished the last of his martini and stood. "I'll leave you gentlemen to delve into boring legal things. Thank you, Frederick, for the drink, and I'll see you at home. A pleasure, Roger."

Roger glanced at the menu, wondering if Frederick had invited his partner as an "in your face" gesture in response to his comment during the Locke-Ober lunch. He silently accepted the supposed retaliatory gesture, admitting to himself that he was impressed with Frederick's mate.

As soon as the waiter took lunch orders, small talk quickly gave way to the Theopoulis case. Frederick, himself not a litigator, had been prepped by the firm's team that had been assigned to the case. He expressed concern about the jockeying going on in preliminary matters, that early rulings could establish an initial momentum that could carry throughout the litigation. The conversation then turned to the judge.

"Tell me, Roger, how is it that this young lady judge with virtually no experience on the civil side of the court decides that she knows more about temporary restraining orders than you, one of our city's top trial lawyers?"

"Thanks for the compliment, or was that a velvet fist that just slugged me?"

"Oh, a compliment, by all means. But I wonder about this inexperienced Judge Valdes getting involved at all with a case of this magnitude. I imagine you did a little judge-shopping for your TRO request. What made you think she was likely to do the right thing? And, under our new court rules, is she the right judge for the case as it continues?"

"Yes, we did do some judge shopping. I filed for the restraining order in the seventh session because Elliot King is sitting there this month. That is, was sitting. He took time off because of a death in the family. I discovered that only after the file had been put under Judge Valdes's nose. An early warning from the scheduling clerk would have been nice, but he told me later he had no idea King was on bereavement leave. No way to withdraw the damned thing. I was called into Valdes's chambers to make my pitch for the TRO five minutes after I found out there was a change in judges. You'd figure that a relatively new judge would be anxious to make a few of us more distinguished members of the bar happy with an ex parte order. Remember, Frederick, your firm's name is also on our pleadings. But, I guess she isn't easily impressed."

The conversation lulled while shrimp cocktail was served.

"I'll see if we can develop a little background on Judge Valdes. It may be helpful when you argue for the injunction on Friday. Perhaps we can have some information by mid-week. Regarding your argument, Roger, is there any real problem with the plaintiffs having access to the company premises?"

"For our client? Sure," Roger said. "He hates his brother's kids."

"I'm told this injunction is very important. I understand it's critical to set the tone in this case."

"We have a first class brief filed. Your research team came up with excellent precedents, and on short notice. I am preparing some additional comments for the hearing to emphasize the difficulty in having the parties to this lawsuit in close proximity. It will be at the judge's discretion, but I think we'll be okay."

When the last shrimp had been devoured, Frederick dabbed the cocktail sauce from his lips with a crimson-colored linen napkin, then said, "Occasionally, we used to have horse meat on our menu. A few slabs were sent over from the Faculty Club every now and then. Very tender and sweet. Lean, loaded with protein. A healthy red meat."

"No longer available?"

"Nope. Back in the eighties it disappeared. Caved into the PETA gang, I guess. I can live without it. It's the principle, Roger. No one should tell us how to live our lives, including what we choose to eat."

Early Wednesday morning, a mahogany-paneled elevator sped Roger Metcalf to the fourteenth floor of the financial district office tower that housed the firm of Wiggins, Lewis and Poole. His raincoat deposited with the receptionist, Roger now stood by a leather couch in Frederick Poole's spacious office. As he thanked Frederick for arranging the early meeting, there was a soft knock on the door.

"Come right in, Anik," Frederick said as he opened the door. He introduced the junior associate to Roger and led her to an armchair turned from the front of his desk and positioned opposite the couch. "Tell us what you've discovered about Judge Valdes."

Although Anik was 26-years-old, more often than not she was carded on Friday nights at the Faneuil Hall area bars frequented by the city's young professionals. As she sat she pushed strands of hair from her brow and faced the two men, now sunk into the soft leather couch. Being somewhat elevated over her audience took a little of the nervous edge away. Anik carefully crossed her legs, thankful she had chosen a mid-length skirt, and opened a binder. She looked at Mr. Poole who smiled and nodded. The young associate began her well-rehearsed presentation in a strong, even voice.

"Judge Zelia Valdes is thirty-nine-years-old. She was born and raised in the Cuban section of Miami, Florida known as Little Havana. She has no siblings, but she lived with an extended family of aunts, uncles and cousins, which is not unusual in that community. Her mother, Gloria Morales, fled Cuba by boat for Florida in 1962. When she left Cuba she was pregnant with her only child, Zelia, now Judge Valdes. It is assumed that Zelia's father stayed in Cuba. Of course it's possible that he never knew he had a child."

"Zelia Morales excelled at Miami Coral Park High School. She was a member of the National and Spanish Honor Societies. She graduated in 1979 at age sixteen and went on to Wellesley College where she majored in fine arts."

"That's a hell of a leap, particularly at sixteen," Roger interrupted. "How did she end up at Wellesley?"

Anik, pleased with the thoroughness of her research, developed a small smile. "Zelia Morales was the recipient of the Lazlo Gutierrez Scholarship. Gutierrez was a wealthy Miami car dealer. The scholarship paid college and graduate school tuition, living expenses and a cash stipend to the two Cuban-Americans chosen each year. Judge Valdes won her scholarship in an essay contest. The title of her essay was 'Family Allegiance.'" Anik sensed an opportunity to editorialize. "She probably was able to draw on her own history, an advantage..."

"Indeed, my dear," Frederick interrupted, and then immediately grimaced and said, "Apologies. Please accept my apologies, Anik. I should not have addressed you in that manner. I most certainly should have used your name."

Anik, surprised and embarrassed, cleared her throat and said, "It's okay, Mr. Poole. Really, it is."

"Thank you, *Anik*. Please continue."

"Zelia Morales graduated cum laude from Wellesley College in 1983."

"Any extra-curricular involvement?" Frederick asked.

"Yes, sir. Three years as a writer for the Wellesley News, that's the student weekly newspaper, three years on the swim team, and two years in the art club.

"The month following graduation, June of eighty-three, she married a Wellesley College assistant art history professor, David Valdes, a Spanish immigrant from Barcelona. The following September she started at Boston College Law School. The summer after her first year of law school, she gave birth to a son, David, Jr. However, she managed to complete her degree, magna cum laude, on schedule in 1986."

"Politics?" Roger asked. "A lot of Cuban immigrants are known to be pretty conservative."

"Judge Valdes is not enrolled in either party, Democrat or Republican. In the year 2000, she contributed five hundred dollars to a fund set up to send Elian Gonzalez back to his father in Cuba." Anik decided to withhold an explanation of who Elian Gonzalez was.

Roger pushed up from the couch and walked to a rain-spattered window which provided a distant view of Boston Harbor. "That's kind of interesting. I thought the Cubans in Miami wanted that kid to stay in the US."

"How do we know the information on her contribution to the Gonzalez fund?" Frederick asked.

"The agency we use, sir, produced copies of tax returns and credit card statements." Anik pulled some documents from her binder and held them toward Poole.

"No, no." Frederick raised both hands at Anik. "I'm sorry I asked. Please go on."

Anik waited a few moments, and then resumed speaking. "Judge Valdes passed the Massachusetts bar examination and was sworn into the bar the fall after graduation. She was then employed by a medium size suburban law firm, Walker Associates, located in Natick, for two years.

"In 1988, she was appointed an assistant district attorney in Suffolk County. She was with that office for six years, and was highly regarded. She was trying capital cases by the time she left the DA's office in 1994."

Roger walked from the window and half sat on the edge of Frederick's desk. "Was that the year of the accident?"

Frederick looked up from the couch. "Accident?"

"Yes, sir," Anik answered. "In June of 1994, David Valdes and their son, David, Jr., were on their way to a Little League game in Needham, where the family resided. It was late afternoon and their car was struck at an intersection by a drunk driver who was being pursued at high speed by the State Police. Mr. Valdes and his son were both killed."

"My God," Frederick said in a whisper. After a few moments of silence, he asked Anik to continue.

"The accident resulted in a lawsuit against the drunk driver, the bar at Logan Airport where he had been last served, the rental company where he leased the car, and the Commonwealth."

"The claims were settled for a total of nine million dollars," Roger said. "One of the largest tort settlements in Massachusetts history."

"Six months after the accident," Anik continued, "Judge Valdes joined the Massachusetts Public Defender's Office. She became one of that agency's chief defenders."

Roger walked back to the couch. "You'd think she'd have gone back to the DA's office to prosecute with a vengeance."

"It's impossible to know what motivates people sometimes," Frederick said. "How does someone, a wife and mother, get over a tragedy like that, and then lead a productive life, one that contributes to our society?"

Without hesitation, Anik responded to Frederick's rhetorical reflection. "She does it in their memory, sir. She does it for them. In a way, and surely in her mind, it keeps them alive."

Frederick cast a smile at the young associate. "Yes, Anik, of course. And what a fine way to express your thought."

"Isn't Judge Bettinger in charge of the Public Defender's Office?" Roger asked.

"He was, sir," Anik answered, turning in Roger's direction. "I think he may have retired a short time ago." She looked down at her notes and continued her report. "In fact, after Judge Valdes spent four years with the Public Defender's Office, Judge Bettinger spoke on her behalf at her judicial confirmation hearing in front of the Governor's Council. That was a little over three years ago. Obviously, she was approved by the Council, and has been on the superior court bench since May of 1999."

Frederick turned to Roger. "Bill Bettinger is one of the finest men I've had the good fortune of meeting in this profession. He must have been a terrific mentor for this young lady judge." He nodded at Anik and then said, "Anything further?"

"Judge Valdes moved to a condominium on Beacon Hill soon after the accident. She usually sits in the criminal sessions in Suffolk County superior court. She has not remarried." Anik breathed deeply and closed her leather binder.

With some difficulty, Frederick pushed himself up from the soft leather cushions.

"Thank you, Anik," he said to the young lawyer who stood from her chair. Frederick walked her to the office door. "That was an admirable report, and very well delivered. Please see that copies are in the hands of our Theopoulis team members, and leave a copy with reception for Mr. Metcalf." Frederick closed the door and turned back into the office. "Anything useful there, Roger?"

"Possibly. The judge sure has an interesting background. Not that it's necessarily relevant, but I wonder what she has for a private life. She's one very attractive lady, let me tell you, and she's been a widow for a good amount of time. What's she doing living alone? No stone goes unturned in this case, Frederick, not a single one."

8

Across the city, in the Newmarket Square Industrial District, a middle-aged beef carcass trimmer threaded his way through a crowd of men and women, most carrying lunch pails. The Quality Meats graveyard-shift was headed for the plant's exit gate. "Hey, Matlock, wait up," shouted the trimmer. Catching up with his colleague, nick-named for the TV trial lawyer, the cold room worker handed a white envelope to the tallish, dark-haired twenty-five-year-old. "The boys and Marie took up a little collection. It's not much, just a few hundred. We know you missed your pay check while you're getting ready for your final law exams."

"Oh, come on, Georgie. I can't take this," Tony Cipriano said, looking at the bulging envelope. "It's great of you guys, but maybe give it to the Jimmy Fund, or something like that."

"Bullshit. It's for you, Tony. You worked your ass off for the last four years. And even though we had to listen to your corny jokes every night, you had to put up with us, too. You earned everything that comes your way. Marie told me to give you a big kiss, too, but I'll skip that." As Tony stuffed the envelope into a front pocket, Georgie patted his back. "Good luck, Kid. When's graduation day?"

"Tomorrow, and then I start work on Friday. No rest for the weary."

"Don't turn into a big shot. Come back and say hello now and then."

"Will do, Georgie. By the way, you know what they call a phony noodle?"

The meat worker shook his head. "I'm afraid to ask."

"Impasta."

Just before noon on Thursday, Anna and Frank Cipriano emerged from the underground **T** station into a wet and windy Copley Square. Short and stout, 71-year-old Anna led her husband across the Square toward the Old John Hancock Building on Berkeley Street. She walked quickly, with a tight and confident stride. Two days earlier, she had made a practice run from her home in the Dorchester section of the city. Her trip on the **T** into and under downtown Boston had been without a hitch, just like today, except for the rain. She was glad she and Frankie left early.

Frank, eight years Anna's senior and hunched over from decades on the assembly line at Continental Cardboard, huffed behind his wife. Relieved at last to enter the dry building, he was eager to find the men's room. Minutes later he rejoined Anna in the marble lobby fronting John Hancock Hall. The white-haired immigrants from the Campania region of Southern Italy waited, Anna's foot tapping away, for the sets of large doors to the sloping hall to open.

Anna and Frank were the first guests to arrive for the Bay State Law School graduation ceremony. The parents of Caesar Anthony Cipriano claimed their seats in the center of the row immediately behind those roped off and reserved for the law school faculty. Forty-five minutes after their arrival, the remaining thousand seats under the curved ceiling were full, and Frank was wishing Anna had planned more carefully. He nudged his wife of fifty-one years, interrupting her one-way conversation with the woman to her left. In a loud whisper, he voiced his urgent complaint.

"I should not be in the middle here, with people on both sides. I have to go."

Anna, staring ahead at the stage, responded in her own, louder whisper. "You always have to go. Why didn't you pee before the seats got all filled up? No, don't go."

"Even at the box factory, they'd let us use the bathroom."

Anna glanced at her watch and shook her head. "Frankie, you can't go now. It's almost one o'clock. Just hold it, you'll be okay. If you leave now you might miss out." She turned to look at her husband. "What if you miss Tony?"

Frank, already uncomfortable from wearing a suit borrowed from his wife's cousin, jiggled in his seat, used to accepting his wife's decrees.

To the chagrin of the woman to her immediate left, Anna resumed extolling the virtues of her only child, Caesar Anthony. She told her captured audience of one about the unbelievable schedule her Tony had managed for the last four years. A full time job at a meat packing plant, starting at midnight and finishing in the morning- you know, the grave something. And then, after just a few hours sleep, back to studying before the night-time law school classes. Not only was Tony handsome and polite, but also really smart.

"After all, you do not become the second best student of the Baystate Law School without a good brain." Then, in a whisper, Anna went on. "You know, I was right at the end of my chance to have him, when God answered my prayers and blessed me, just like that lady in the bible. Maybe it was because Tony started, you know," Anna dropped her voice another level, "when me and Frankie did it, in May. That's Mary's month."

The listener was thinking that God probably gave in, wanting to shut the woman up, when recorded music mercifully announced the arrival of the graduates as they began to file into the auditorium.

Anna and Frank hurried from the auditorium as soon as the commencement exercise concluded. They were seated at the street-side window in nearby Charlie's Bistro before most of those attending the ceremony had met up with their graduates. Frank, after a visit to the men's room, followed Anna's orders and stationed himself at the door of the restaurant. He greeted Tony as he made his way through the bottleneck and led him to the table by the window. Tony sat in the chair across the table from his parents.

"Tony, you look so handsome in your nice blue suit and red tie, doesn't he, Frankie?" Anna beamed at her son. The waiter arrived with an eleven-dollar bottle of wine. "A nice glass of wine to celebrate." Anna said.

"Thanks, Ma, that's great." Tony then looked at his father, an unusual sight in a suit and tie. "You look terrific, Dad."

The waiter poured a finger of wine into Frank's glass and stood by silently. Frank cast a curious glance in his direction. Tony came to the rescue.

"You're supposed to taste it, Dad, then tell the waiter whether or not you like it."

Frank smiled at his son and reached into his pants pocket. He peeled a pair of one-dollar bills from a role and held them out in the direction of the waiter.

Catching Tony's eye, the waiter sent him a discreet wink, and then took the offered gratuity. "Thank-you, sir," he said with enthusiasm and a bow, and then continued pouring the wine.

Anna grasped her wine glass and nodded at her husband, her instruction to Frank to do the same. "A toast to our Caesar Anthony. The second best student in the Baystate Law School, and he will be the best judge's law clerk, ever."

When the glasses were set back on the table, Tony looked into the eyes of both of his parents. "I owe everything to the two of you. All the things you did for me. The extra jobs, Dad, to get me through college. All the things you did for me, Ma. You guys did everything."

"You, Tony, are our lives," Anna said softly.

"I'll never be able to pay you back."

"You pay us back every day, Tony," the usually stoical Frank said. "It was my honor to do things for you. You are a good son, and you are a good man. I am very proud of you."

Tears welled in the eyes of both parents, and Tony. Frank stood and held his arms out to his son. Tony stood, then leaned over the table and into his father's arms. The men hugged.

"And me?" Anna stood and reached for her only child. "I'm as proud as your father is proud, you know."

After the tears of all three had been wiped away and the waiter had taken the orders, the conversation turned to Tony's immediate future.

"Tell us, Tony, about your new job," Anna instructed her son.

"I was real lucky. A lot of new law school graduates want to stay around Boston and would love to get one of these law clerk jobs. It'll be great training for me and will open a lot of doors for other jobs after a year working at the court. I'm all set to start tomorrow."

The waiter arrived with a basket of bread. Tony tore the end off a hard roll and chewed.

"You were almost the best student, Tony. Why not a bigger, more important job? Doesn't a clerk just push papers around? I don't understand why it's such a good job to start with," Anna said.

"That's a different kind of clerk, Ma. What I'll be doing is working directly for a superior court judge. Sitting in on cases while the trials are going on, reading the papers the lawyers file, doing research in the law books and writing drafts, you know, Ma, like practice decisions for the judge. That kind of stuff."

"Wow, Frankie," Anna placed her hand on her husband's arm. "Our Tony, only twenty-five-years-old and already deciding who wins and loses, and he just graduated."

"No, Ma, no. The judge will tell me what she thinks and ask me to write a paper to say what she's decided. I'll write something that's like a practice decision. Then she'll read it to see if it makes legal sense. She'll actually decide the cases."

"She?"

"That's right, Ma, a woman. I told you about her after my interview a few months ago. Remember? She's kind of young, very nice and very smart. There are a lot of women judges now. Starting Friday morning, I'm going to be working with Judge Zelia Valdes."

"Zelia? That's a funny name for a judge, Tony. You better be sure you have her name right."

A Formica-topped table took up most of the kitchen in the Cipriano's Dorchester apartment. The top floor of the three-decker home was the only address Anna and Frank had lived at since Tony was born. Anna had permitted herself to think that now, with Tony becoming an important lawyer, maybe a little house out of the city was possible. She had cousins who lived in nearby Braintree and owned a small restaurant. Maybe she could help out with some pastries and other cooking. There was a **T** stop there, so they could get back to visit the neighborhood without too much trouble. She placed a steaming platter of sausages in red gravy on the table.

"Tony, get the napkins, and tell us what you will do tomorrow, on your first day of being a lawyer?"

Tony placed a stack of paper napkins on the table, sat and reached for the bowl of pasta. "I'm not sure, exactly. I'll show up at the courthouse at eight-thirty and..."

"Be there at eight. Do you think you should maybe take a taxicab to be sure to be on time?"

"Ma, I've been taking the subway downtown most every day for years. It's more reliable that a cab in traffic."

"Okay, but eight o'clock."

"Yeah, Ma, sure, eight o'clock." Tony ladled red gravy and sausages onto a mound of ziti. "Anyway, then I'll find out exactly what I'll be doing. I asked someone who's had the same kind of job what I should expect. At first it's mostly learning the ropes. Then doing what the judge needs. Probably looking up some legal things for her. You know, research and that kind of thing. Whatever she asks."

"When do you start deciding who wins and loses?"

"Ma, like I told you at the restaurant, I don't do that. After a while, the judge might ask me what I think, but that's all. The judge decides, and sometimes might ask me to write it out. That's all."

"That's all." Anna exaggerated a shake of her head. "Imagine, Frankie, Tony writes out who wins and loses, and he says, 'that's all.'"

"Can I have the Parmesan, Dad?"

Before Frank had an opportunity to respond, Anna reached over and pushed the bowl of grated cheese to her son. "You be sure to take your medicine with breakfast tomorrow. If you forget, you could be in a bad mood. That would be a bad way to begin a new job."

"I'm out of pills, Ma. Remember? The school health insurance ended."

"You have to get more pills."

"I'll get new insurance at work. It kicks in after a couple of weeks. Then I can get a new prescription."

"Don't forget. And I ironed your good white shirt and the trousers to your suit. Wear the red and blue tie. Red, white and blue. The lady judge will think you love your country without even really knowing why. I read about that kind of thing. Sub something. Anyway, Tony, it's important. Everything is hanging in your closet. And don't forget your raincoat. They said on the TV it will rain again tomorrow."

"Thanks, Ma."

"You shine your shoes tonight."

Tony's glance at his dad earned a smile.

9

Tony arrived at Judge Valdes's chambers on the seventh floor of the Suffolk County Superior Courthouse at precisely eight o'clock on Friday morning. As he was led into the small office by a court officer, the judge stood from her desk and greeted him with a smile.

"Good morning, Mr. Cipriano. Welcome to the courthouse, and congratulations on your graduation." The judge gestured toward an empty armchair. "Have a seat."

"Thank you, Your Honor," Tony responded as he sat. "I'm really very pleased to be here."

"The feeling is mutual. You'll have a little while to learn the ropes around here, then, as I recall, you said at your interview that you were planning to take the bar exam the last week of August."

"That's right, Your Honor."

"That will work out just fine. I'm going to be on vacation the last two weeks of August. You can use that time to prepare for the exam. If you need to take personal leave for a bar review before that, I'm sure it can be arranged."

"That's great. Thank you."

The judge glanced at a wall clock. "Okay, let's get to work."

Tony's early arrival gave the judge an opportunity to give him a brief explanation of the motion for a preliminary injunction scheduled for eight-thirty. At about eight-twenty the judge suggested that Tony familiarize himself with the courtroom.

The new law clerk walked into the large courtroom with high-ceilings and tall windows. A half dozen portraits of retired, mostly deceased, judges hung on off-white walls. Tony immediately noticed the only other person in the courtroom. He was a short, slight man with salt and pepper hair.

Cosmos Theopoulis sat in the front row of the public area in a black, pin-striped suit and open neck white shirt. He held a cell phone to his ear. Listening to the man argue over the price and availability of various cuts of beef and pork, Tony smiled, thinking back to the shouting matches he overheard during his days at the meat packing plant. He poked around a few moments, and then took a seat in the back row of the empty jury box. A minute later, the court officer with short curly hair who had led him to the judge's chambers came into the courtroom carrying a Styrofoam cup of coffee. He walked over to a chair next to the jury box and introduced himself to Tony as Gerry. The hefty officer immediately began his third degree reserved for new faces. He was delighted to have another set of ears for his courthouse scuttlebutt.

By 8:25, four more men had come into the courtroom and walked beyond the wooden rail, or bar, that separated the public area from the space reserved for lawyers trying cases. All were wearing dark suits and white shirts. Three of them stood at one of a pair of tables in front of the judge's elevated bench, the fourth sat alone, hands folded, at the remaining table. The standing lawyers were arranging small piles of documents. At eight-thirty, to the accompaniment of "All rise!" from the court officer, Zelia Valdes climbed the pair of steps to her bench and stood behind a high-back leather chair. The sole seated lawyer stood. The other lawyers abandoned their busy work and straightened up, more or less at attention. The court officer made the formal call for anyone with anything to say to the Suffolk superior court to come forward and be heard. Judge Valdes then sat, followed by all others in the courtroom, except Cosmos Theopoulis, who had not bothered to stand.

"I've read the briefs, gentlemen. The moving party has the burden of persuasion." The judge glanced down at the assembled lawyers. "Mr. Metcalf, what do you, or your designated co-counsel, have to say?"

Tony listened with rapt attention for the next fifteen minutes as Roger Metcalf argued that Harold and Helen Theopoulis should be enjoined from entering onto the Finish Line business premises. Tony found Attorney Metcalf's impassioned plea non-persuasive. But it was his first day on the job and he had no intention of trusting his own opinion. Especially after the court officer had told him that Metcalf was one of the top lawyers in the city.

Attorney Joe Dunn stood and began to argue the other side of the issue. With no small amount of satisfaction, Tony listened as Dunn poked some of the same holes in Metcalf's argument that had occurred to him. Judge Valdes then asked a few questions of both lawyers. At nine o'clock she stood and announced that she was taking the matter under advisement and would have a decision on the motion early in the following week.

Back in chambers, Judge Valdes draped her black robe over a peg on a wooden coat tree, sat at her desk and motioned to Tony to take a seat. "Welcome to Suffolk Superior, Mr. Cipriano. I'm sorry I didn't have the chance to speak with you more before the hearing. We'll be working together for the next year or so. What do your friends usually call you?"

"Tony, from Anthony, my middle name," Tony said as he sat in a straight-back wooden chair.

"Okay, Tony it is. As I told you, I like to start the day early. I'm usually here by eight o'clock. If there are motion hearings on the docket, they start at eight-thirty, and you should be here by then. What did you think of the arguments you just heard for and against the injunction?"

Tony was surprised, not expecting the judge to care what he thought about anything. "Well, both sides seemed to make some good points."

The judge half-stood, reached over to a window and, with effort, raised the sash a few inches. She then sat and reached over for a pack of cigarettes and a lighter from her nearby handbag, also hanging on the coat rack. "Do you mind?" Tony shook his head. "Good." After taking a small silver foil ashtray from the desk drawer, the judge lit up.

"I feel like I'm a teenager again, sneaking a smoke in the girl's room at high school. Okay, let me tell you a little more about the allegations in this case, Tony." The judge pointed to a thick stack of papers on her desktop, "It's all set out for the world to see in the twenty-four page complaint that's on top of that pile of papers."

"In 1947, the Theopoulis brothers, Cosmos and Charles, Greek immigrants, both in their early twenties, started a pushcart food business in downtown Boston. After a while they started selling their food -

sausages, gyro sandwiches, that kind of thing - at various city events, outside the Boston Garden, Fenway Park, the old Braves Field, and at some neighborhood festivals and the like. In a few years, they got a decent stake together and convinced the owners of the local race track, Patriot Downs, to let them operate the food concession. Before long, the brothers also operated the food concessions inside the two major league ballparks in town - Boston had the Red Sox and the Braves back then - and at the Boston Garden.

"The plaintiffs' complaint goes on to say that, in the early seventies, their father and uncle mortgaged their food concession business, which by then had spread throughout the Northeast, took the money and bought Patriot Downs and a few more race tracks. Today the family corporation, Finish Line, owns a half dozen race tracks and is the biggest food concession business in the country. They estimate the value of the corporation at over a billion dollars.

"In 1993 the younger brother, Charles, died. Cosmos was left in control of the company. It was, and still is, a closely held family business. No publicly traded stock. No sunlight on the financial niceties, accounting procedures, etcetera. Cosmos allegedly assured Charles, a widower, on his death bed, that he'd take care of his children, Harold and Helen, and that their half share of the business would be protected."

"I'm guessing maybe the kids think that didn't happen," Tony said.

"As you'll read in the complaint, the kids allege uncle Cosmos has been fleecing them for at least the past four years. They claim that he, without their knowledge, sold their stock in Finish Line to another corporation that he, uncle Cosmos, owns outright. They claim further that the sale of the stock was at a bargain price. The niece and nephew discovered this because of a problem with a Massachusetts Department of Revenue audit. Boiled down, the pleadings paint Cosmos as an out-and-out thief."

"I was watching him during the arguments," Tony said. "He looked pretty miserable."

The judge took a final drag on her cigarette and stubbed it out in the ashtray. She blew a stream of smoke toward the window sash, then continued.

"I saw the same thing, Tony, but a lot of people look miserable when they're in a courtroom. Of course, I'm not prejudging anything.

I'm only aware of allegations at this point. The facts will show up later. These plaintiffs could be way off base. That'll be up to the evidence."

"Is there any chance of a case like this being settled?"

"I've only sat on a few civil cases, and never practiced outside of the criminal courts, but having asked colleagues about the reputations of the lawyers on both sides of this case, and having read the pleadings, I think this one is likely to run the full course. Possibly a trial date next March or April."

"Do you have any thoughts yet about the injunction?" Tony asked.

"Yes. After reading the memoranda and hearing today's arguments, I do. The defendants started with a huge hill to climb, and they haven't done that. They want this court to order the plaintiffs to stay away from the corporate offices that they've had access to for years, but they haven't substantiated any real likelihood that their having access would be a problem. If there is going to be a problem, it seems as likely to originate from the defendants as well as the plaintiffs. In any event, they can come back and ask again if they have new evidence." The judge pushed the thick stack of documents across her desk. "I will deny the defendants' motion to keep the nephew and niece off the company premises. However, when they are at the Finish Line offices, they will be under the reasonable direction of their uncle Cosmos, who is, after all, the CEO.

"I will also issue an order, sua sponte, to prohibit the transfer of any company assets outside of usual and ordinary business transactions for both Finish Line Incorporated and the LLC managed by Cosmos Theopoulis. I'll need a four or five page draft decision by Tuesday, Tony. Use language from a half dozen cases. Both memorandums are amply cited, so a lot of your work has been done for you. Be thorough. The parties in this case have unlimited funds, and very aggressive lawyers. Any decision I make in the course of this litigation could end up being appealed. We have to be ready for that. You don't want to start your career, Tony, with your judge being reversed upstairs."

"Okay, Your Honor."

"'Judge' will be just fine. By the way, unless I decide to change the protocol, if you disagree with my rulings, say so, and tell me why. Go get yourself some coffee."

Tony's departure left Zelia alone in chambers. She sat back in her chair and closed her eyes. As often happened without her willing it, she thought of her husband and son, her Davids. She immediately tried to focus on the family's visits to relatives or other happy memories, all stored within easy reach. She used those memories to construct a wall around the day of destruction, to blind her mind's eye. As it usually did, the defense crumbled. Zelia traveled back in time, just about eight years.

It was mid-week, a warm, early summer day. The windows were open in the third floor courtroom in downtown Boston. She was reaching the zenith of her blistering cross-examination of a defense witness in an armed robbery case. The jury was dialed in. Her glance at a wall clock told her it was four-thirty. Even though late in the trial day, she knew the judge would let her finish with the man in the witness chair. This judge never interfered with prosecutors when a witness was about to crumble. Suddenly, a court officer came through the front door of the courtroom and strode quickly to the judge's bench. Everything stopped as he whispered in an urgent manner.

The judge stood, grim-faced, and, without explanation told the jury they were dismissed for the day, and to return at nine o'clock the following morning. When the last juror disappeared into the lobby, the judge ordered the courtroom cleared of all others, except the prosecutor, Assistant District Attorney Valdes. Lawyers, witnesses and onlookers left, as directed by the court officer, through the rear door, many glancing with curiosity toward Zelia. She stayed, puzzled, concerned - Why me?

A moment later, a Massachusetts State Trooper came into the courtroom through its front door. Cowboy-style hat in his hands, the trooper glanced up at the judge who nodded in Zelia's direction. Moments later, Zelia was shaking her head at what the State Trooper was telling her. Once again, she re-lived her scream. As always, it jolted her back to the present. Her stomach was in knots. She stood from her desk. A shiver ran through her.

"Just what the hell does 'under advisement' mean?" Cosmos Theopoulis demanded as he and Roger Metcalf walked to the elevators.

"Most judges don't like to give their decisions on motions while the lawyers are still in the courtroom," Roger responded. "The guy who loses is likely to start arguing all over again." He pushed the elevator call button.

"I'm not sure I liked her questions. And why didn't she let me testify when you asked?"

"In motion sessions, there often isn't any testimony from witnesses."

"How old is she, this judge?"

"Late thirties. Young for a judge," Roger said. "Must have been something the governor liked about her."

"You can see that unless you're Mister Magoo, or queer, which I know isn't your problem. By the way, Angie said to say hello. She's still on Mykonos. Doesn't know when she'll be back."

The ride down to the main lobby in the elevator was silent. The silver doors slid open and Roger, Cosmos and the few other riders emerged. The lawyer and his client walked across a wet marble floor, stopping at the main doors. Outside, a wind-blown rain swept across the wide plaza that fronted the courthouse.

"I don't like this judge," Cosmos said. "And I don't think she likes me, or you. I just got this feeling that she's going to let that little piss-pot keep his office at the track. I know that doesn't really mean squat. He's hardly ever there anyhow. But I don't like to lose anything, and this will be a bad sign if we lose at the beginning, before the trial even starts."

"I'm not so sure you're right about who the judge does and doesn't like, but in every war the winner will lose a few battles. It's the big picture that counts."

The front door was pulled open in front of a gust of air that blew in with a half dozen lawyers. A few recognized Roger and commiserated in silence as his client shouted at him.

"Don't go giving me shit about losing battles! Big pictures! You're a big shot lawyer. Get that judge the fuck off this case."

10

AUTUMN, 2002

As always, it was a busy Friday evening at the Elms Restaurant. Zelia Valdes handed her coat to the maître d', who also functioned as the coat checker. The judge was meeting Jack Ralston, her former colleague at the Public Defender's Office, at seven o'clock for dinner at the popular Beacon Hill bistro. Coat check ticket in hand, Zelia stepped directly into the wood-paneled bar from the foyer. She glanced around the crowded room, bustling with loud chatter. Not spotting Jack, she made her way across the room to a stand-up bar. Looking for the bartender, Zelia inadvertently nudged a portly man, prompting a greeting from a familiar, but unexpected, voice.

"Evening, Judge Valdes," Eddie Smelton said.

"Oh, hello, ... Eddie?" a somewhat startled Zelia responded to the greeting. Used to seeing her former client from the Public Defender's Office at his Gardner Museum docent post, Zelia was surprised to bump into him elsewhere, particularly in a the highbrow district of Beacon Hill.

Over a wrinkled dress shirt and knit tie, Eddie wore a suit coat that did not match his corduroy slacks. A sheepish grin lit his face.

"I know you wouldn't expect to see me at a fancy place like this, Judge. I'm not in this area of Boston very often, but I come here for dinner on October fourth every year," the docent explained. "I always order the same thing - sautéed sweetbreads. The food is very good."

"Well, it is nice to see you, Eddie. You're quite the gourmet," a less rattled Zelia said. "Is October fourth special for some reason?"

"In a way. It's Jean Francois Millet's birthday. He's my Mom's favorite, so I celebrate for her every year. Actually, it's her idea."

Zelia caught the attention of the bartender. "I'd like a mojito please, and my friend will have a, what, Eddie?"

"Oh, that's okay, Judge, really. I can get one for myself."

"One what, Eddie? It's my treat."

"Well, I was going to order a White Russian."

"That's surprise number two. I don't suppose your meeting, say, Meryl Streep for dinner, now, are you?"

"No, Judge. No. That won't happen. Just me."

Zelia looked at the waiting bartender and ordered Eddie's drink, then turned back and said, "Things seem to have slowed down at the Gardner."

"A little bit. The crowds are smaller with the summer over. Now, the education department has some time to catch up on the histories of the exhibits."

"Well, I'm glad you get a little breather," Zelia said.

"The Gardner is a wonderful place to work."

"How's your mom doing?" Zelia asked.

"She's doing okay. This is one of the few nights that I leave her."

"You're a dedicated son. She's very fortunate."

"Mom looks forward to the crossword magazine every month. That was really a nice thing you did, getting her the subscription."

"As I recall, Eddie, the cost of the subscription is about a dollar a month. The cost of her medicines runs you what, six hundred dollars a month?"

"Almost eight hundred, now. The cost goes up every year. But that's okay. What else would I spend my money on, and," Eddie smiled, "those payments reduced my bank account and made me eligible to be represented by the Public Defender's Office." He paused and glanced toward his shoes. "I got the opportunity to meet you."

"Indeed, Eddie," Zelia said, "and I got the opportunity to meet you, and your mom, as well."

The bartender placed the drinks on the bar. Zelia reached over and picked up her rum-based highball. Eddie took the crystal glass holding the sweet concoction of coffee liqueur, vodka and cream from the zinc surface. Zelia raised her glass in the direction of the museum docent.

"To the memory of Jean Francois Millet."

They both sipped, then Eddie used the tip of his tongue to wipe a narrow line of creamy residue from his lips.

Zelia glanced in the direction of the busy foyer and spotted her dinner date. He held a hand up and pointed a finger into the adjacent dining area. She turned back to Eddie. "I see my dinner companion has arrived and he's motioning that our table is ready. I hope you don't have a long wait for your table and that you enjoy your annual feast, Eddie."

"I don't mind waiting a while, Judge. Maybe I'll see you at the museum soon."

After enjoying dinner, Jack and Zelia left the Elms and walked along Charles Street, his arm around her shoulder, hers around his waist. The early fall night was cool, and the aroma of wood-burning fireplaces was carried on a light breeze.

"What's with the guy you were talking to when I arrived?" Jack asked. "I didn't get a close look, but, from a distance, he seemed a little, well, rumpled."

"I was surprised to see him there. He's an interesting story, that's for sure. You wouldn't have had any reason to meet him before, even though he was a client of the PD's four or five years ago. I was appointed to represent him when I was covering arraignments for the office at the Boston Municipal Court."

"What was he charged with?"

"Shoplifting neckties at Filene's Basement."

The couple turned the corner and trailed a loose collection of leaves being blown along the sidewalk.

"Did you plead him?" Jack asked.

"Hey," Zelia removed her arm from Jack's waist and poked an elbow at his midsection, "my defense never rested."

"Oops, sorry. I should have known that. Not guilty?"

"Yes, Jack, not guilty. He, like a lot of folks back then, browsed in Filene's Basement on a regular basis. Store security thought they recognized him pocketing a few ties on their grainy surveillance tape. The next time he came in they detained him and called the BPD. My client claimed he was at home at the date and time stamped on the tape."

"Home alone, I suppose. Defendants are always elsewhere, and alone, at the time of the crime."

"Not this time. His mother was his alibi witness. The poor woman had severe arthritis, and a touch of dementia. She testified from her wheelchair. Fortunately, she was firing on all cylinders on trial day. She said her son was indeed at home when he was supposedly lifting the neckties. She was very convincing. Also, the trial was just before Christmas. Maybe the jury was feeling the holiday spirit. After they left the courtroom," Zelia smiled, "Judge Meagher complimented my guy on his Gerry Garcia necktie."

"Meagher is sort of a comedian," Jack said.

"I got to know Eddie, I mean the defendant, pretty well once I started representing him. He's a very bright fellow in some ways. He's kind of savant-like when it comes to paintings, at least old masterpieces. He uses that knowledge, working as a docent at a museum."

"How did Eddie become eligible for a public defender if he had a regular job?" Jack asked. "We're only supposed to represent those in need, the indigent, remember?"

"Or marginally indigent, which he was, actually still is. His mother doesn't have any health insurance and refuses to accept government aid. A large part of his salary is spent on prescription drugs for her, and he's her sole caregiver. I don't think there's anything in his life except his mom and his job. No siblings, he's a bachelor and his father died years ago."

"I guess that's why he's at the Elms by himself."

"Most likely. His mom sits by her window in their home during the day and waves at the cars when the drivers beep the horn. It seems very sad, but she appears to be a very content person. I'd never want to be so restricted of course, but I kind of envy the simplicity of her life."

Jack took Zelia's arm and the couple walked in silence for a few moments, reached an intersection and stopped at the curb. The pedestrian light was blinking **WALK**. Zelia pulled Jack into the crosswalk.

11

WINTER, 2003

The beginnings of an early February blizzard were frosting Boston. Anticipating afternoon commuting problems, trials had been curtailed for the day and Suffolk County courthouse personnel had shrunk to a skeleton crew by one o'clock. Preliminary matters in the case of Theopoulis versus Theopoulis were being heard in courtroom 702. Judge Zelia Valdes poured water from a carafe into a plastic cup, sipped and looked down from her bench at Roger Metcalf. The defendant's lead trial counsel was in hushed conversation with four other lawyers from the defense team. Attorney Joe Dunn sat at the plaintiffs' counsel table alone and tapped his pen on a yellow legal pad. Looking up at the judge, Dunn's bored expression suggested things were dragging. She agreed.

"Mr. Metcalf, do you think we might move this along to a conclusion? I can see out the window that the snow is beginning to get heavy. We don't want to get stranded in the courthouse. You have had my undivided attention for these motions for two full hours today, after all of yesterday morning."

Roger turned back to the judge from the group of lawyers. "Of course, Judge. And we appreciate your patience. We are close to the end."

"You have ten minutes to sum up, starting right now."

"I'll only need five, Your Honor."

"These shrimp are huge," Jennifer Metcalf observed as she dipped one into the crystal bowl of cocktail sauce. "Mmmm." She closed her eyes and chewed away.

It was Friday, and the roads from the South Shore into the city had been cleared of the mid-week blizzard remains. The Metcalfs were dining at the Bay Tower Room of Boston's 60 State Street office tower. Their table was covered with white linen and subtly lit with a small hurricane lamp. The immediate view through the 33rd floor window wall was of the historic Custom House Tower. In the distance city lights reflected off the waters of Boston Harbor. Jennifer's husband smiled at her unintended oxymoron.

"What's tickling you, Roger? Something I said?" Jennifer asked.

"Oh, ah, no, Jen," Roger said, not wanting to offend his wife who, he had concluded soon after they met at UConn, was super thin-skinned when it came to any perceived shortcoming. Sixteen years of marriage hadn't changed that perception. "I was just thinking of the difference between my lunch and this dinner. Lunch was at a downtown greasy spoon, and now," Roger gestured at the table, then at the harbor beyond, "nothing but the best."

"You can say that again. It's nice to have turned the corner financially. At least it seems that way since you opened your own office." Jennifer smiled and reached over for her husband's hand. "I like this life, Roger. I understand what had to be done. And I appreciate your honesty about it, even though I don't like to think about it."

"You should be thanking Cosmos Theopoulis. He's been paying just about all the bills for a while now."

"He's paying the bills, Roger Metcalf, because you're the best lawyer he can get in Boston, that's why. And you'll win that case. You'll see."

"By the way," Roger said, "our pre-trial motions and other stuff wrapped up Tuesday. The trial starts in two weeks. Once that gets going, you won't be seeing too much of me. My guess is it will go on for at least a couple of months."

It was a week after arguments on the pre-trial motions had concluded. Mid-morning sun poured through east-facing windows of the main conference room at Wiggins, Lewis & Poole. Five men and two women sat in leather armchairs at a large rectangular table. For a group of advocates who earned their livings with words, there was an eerie silence, broken occasionally by the ruffling of papers or a nervous cough. The meeting had been hastily arranged. A set of French doors opened and Frederick Poole walked into the room, Roger Metcalf on his heels. Both wore dour expressions. As they sat in chairs at the center of the table, Metcalf dropped a sheaf of documents onto the shiny surface. He pushed back in his chair as he glanced around the table.

"The Honorable Zelia Valdes has denied every preliminary motion we filed and allowed every motion filed by the plaintiffs. Importantly, our motions in limine have all been denied. Every damn one of them. This means the evidence the plaintiffs will offer will not be limited. We will have to rely on our objections being sustained at trial. Based upon the attitude that Judge Valdes has displayed to date, that would appear to be damned unlikely. Furthermore, if we constantly object, the jury is going to think we're simply obstructionist bastards, and that's never helpful. I am open to suggestions from this highly paid brain trust, even though our strategy to now has, simply put, sucked."

Frederick Poole tugged at his starched shirt cuffs and spoke. "I would like to make it clear to the team members from Wiggins that I share Roger's deep concern and disappointment with the direction this case has taken. Although we feel that a persuasive effort on behalf of our client has been made, we seem to dig our hole deeper and deeper. We have run into a judge who, for reasons unknown, is favoring the plaintiffs in this matter. Having no evidence to believe that anything underhanded is involved, we will assume that she is simply inexperienced in civil matters, and not qualified to sit on a case of this type and magnitude.

"But, ladies and gentlemen, that comes with the territory. We must play the cards we are dealt. We get paid handsomely for overcoming these roadblocks. We must, *and will*, re-double our efforts."

From his chair near the end of the table, a young attorney borrowed from the firm's corporate division broke the spell of silence following Frederick's remarks. He fiddled with thick, black-framed glasses as he spoke.

"Assuming Judge Valdes continues to be plaintiff-oriented, shouldn't we be placing more emphasis on limiting damages, rather than putting all our eggs in the win-at-any-cost basket? If the jury finds for the plaintiffs, they will decide the amount of any actual damages suffered. In addition, a major problem could develop in the fraud counts. The judge has reserved the right to rule on those counts. Under the statute, if she enters a fraud judgment, she can double or triple whatever amount of damages the jury has awarded."

Frederick turned to Roger and asked, "Tell the team what we're looking at, Roger. Worst case scenario."

"Worst case? A possible three hundred to three hundred and fifty million dollar jury verdict. If there's also a finding of fraud by Valdes, as much as one billion dollars."

There was at least one audible gasp. The team of attorneys seemed to sit up straighter.

"This case is in the limelight," Roger continued. "If you can believe it, the last motion session was covered by the *Globe* - a goddamn motion session. And both Frederick and I have had calls from the *Wall Street Journal*. I expect a reporter from the *Journal* will cover the trial."

"Our professional reputations, ladies and gentlemen, our firms' reputations, are in the cross-hairs," Frederick said. "And let's not forget our client. We are charging Cosmos Theopoulis an absolute fortune. Let's earn it. This trial begins a week from Monday. We are going to win." He stood. "Losing is not an option!"

12

The trial of the civil action of Theopoulis versus Theopoulis began at 10:30 on the third Monday of February when Judge Zelia Valdes directed the plaintiffs' attorney, Joseph Dunn, to call his first witness. On the first Monday of April, Attorney Dunn called his final witness, the defendant, Cosmos Theopoulis. For the past hour the trial lawyers had been sparring with each other and the judge. As a result, they had managed to fit in only a couple of questions for the short slight man with the bushy eyebrows and beady eyes who sat in the witness chair.

"Overruled," Judge Valdes said as she reached for the water carafe. "The witness shall answer the question."

Cosmos Theopoulis snapped around and shot a venomous glance at the judge from the witness stand.

Roger Metcalf leapt to his feet, his straight-backed chair nearly tumbling behind him. "You have to be kidding!"

"Come on, for God's sake! You're in a damn courtroom!" Attorney Joe Dunn shouted at Metcalf.

"Okay. That does it. Mr. Metcalf, Mr. Dunn - chambers!" Scowling, Judge Valdes stood from her high-backed chair. She turned to the fourteen rapt faces staring at her from the jury box. "Members of the jury, as you can see, lawyers in the heat of battle are not always polite. In fact, some of them act like spoiled brats every now and then. You have the court's apology for this behavior. They're not just wasting their time, but yours as well. We will be in recess for fifteen minutes.

Perhaps their manners will improve while they cool off. If not, they'll have problems they never dreamed of."

A knot of supporting lawyers milled around the front of the courtroom as Metcalf and Dunn followed the judge down the short hallway and into chambers. Closely behind was the rotund, perpetually red-faced court stenographer, his machine writer hanging from a canvas necklace.

"Harvey gets the chair," the judge said.

The stenographer sat in the straight-back chair. Metcalf and Dunn continued to stand as the judge hung her robe on a coat tree. She then reached into a drawer as she sat at her desk. Moments later a stream of cigarette smoke darted beneath the window sash, already open an inch or two.

"Excuse me for smoking. I don't like being a scofflaw, but I'm addicted, particularly when I feel stressed, and, believe me, I feel stressed."

"With due respect, Judge, you don't have a monopoly on stress in that courtroom," Metcalf said.

The judge looked at the court stenographer whose hands were poised over his writer. "Let's go on the record, Harvey," she said and looked up at the two lawyers. "You're two outstanding civil trial attorneys. That's what my colleagues on the bench have told me and that's what your colleagues at the bar have told me. Now, you tell me why you're acting like a couple of alley cats in my courtroom."

Dunn spoke up. "Judge Valdes, I have clients who ask only for their day in court. Quite frankly, that's not what they appear to be getting when, without basis, my brother objects to virtually every question I ask. Mr. Metcalf simply..."

"Hold on, for Christ's sake," Roger said. "I have every right to be damn sure that the questions asked are permissible, that this trial is fair, that..."

"I thought insuring a fair trial was my function, Mr. Metcalf," Judge Valdes interrupted, leaning across her desk, lit cigarette in hand, pointed toward the standing lawyer. "Your client has been getting a fair trial for the last month and a half, even though his lawyers, that's you and your team, seem to be working overtime to confuse the hell out of this jury and render the facts in this case indecipherable.

"One more outburst like the one that just occurred in that courtroom, Mr. Metcalf, and you will be held in contempt. And don't think you'll goad me into a mistrial by my kicking you out of my courtroom. You have half a dozen competent associates, any of whom can step right in as lead attorney for Mr. Theopoulis."

The judge's barely smoked cigarette sizzled as it connected with old coffee remains in a cardboard cup. She looked to the couch where the plaintiffs' lawyer had taken a seat.

"Mr. Dunn, the caveat goes to you as well. I'm the one who rules on objections, regardless of how baseless they may be. Okay, lecture over. Look, we're all beat. Let's get this case tried and finished and get on with our lives. Okay?"

13

At four o'clock on the fourth day of deliberations, the Theopoulis case jury foreman asked a court officer to deliver a note to Judge Valdes. It read that some of the jurors wished to be released for the day because it was Holy Thursday, and they had evening church commitments. The jurors were led back into the courtroom and the judge asked if they were close to a verdict. The foreman reported they required just another hour or two to complete their work. Hoping to keep the trial from continuing into the following week, when no objections were raised to returning to the courtroom on Good Friday morning, the judge ordered the twelve jurors and pair of alternates to return at 8:30 a.m.

The wall clock read ten-fifteen on Friday morning when the court officer announced to those crowding the seventh floor lobby that the jury was coming in with its verdict. Within three minutes, except for the chairs in the jury box, every seat in courtroom 702 was filled. Five minutes later the jury filed back into the jury box for the final time.

Frederick Poole fidgeted in his chair. He had been inside a courtroom hardly a dozen times during his decades at the bar. Rainmakers had little to gain by spending their time at the litigation battleground. He and other lawyers sat just inside the wooden rail separating the public gallery from the area reserved for trial participants. He watched as the court officer took the verdict slip from the jury foreman and walked to Judge Valdes's bench to hand it to her. Frederick could not understand how Roger, who sat alone at the defendants' counsel table a few feet in front of him, was able to appear so calm.

Roger Metcalf made it a habit not to speculate about a trial's outcome during the jury's deliberations. He had learned early in his career as a trial attorney that there was no victory until the appeal period has run, let alone before a jury honors you with a verdict. However, unable to block out his gut feelings, Roger had a foreboding about this jury. During the course of the trial it had been clear to him that most, if not all, of the fourteen jurors were enamored of Judge Valdes. If it wasn't for what he discerned as her bias against his client, this jury's appreciation of the judge would not have concerned him. It was easy to understand - she was not only the most attractive and polite person in the courtroom by a wide margin, she also seemed genuinely concerned about the jurors, aware that their lengthy public service was having a real impact on their lives. Judge Zelia Valdes had them eating out of her hand.

All eyes in the hushed courtroom were on Judge Valdes as she unfolded and, with no visible reaction, examined the verdict slip. The judge finished her review and looked up at the public area of the courtroom. "Let me remind all of you that we are in a court of law. There is to be no verbal reaction to this jury's decision in this courtroom." She handed the verdict slip to the court clerk and instructed her, "Please publish the jury's verdict."

Waiting those few seconds for the jury's verdict to be announced, Roger had that familiar feeling of being nowhere. The only words the clerk read that both Roger Metcalf and Frederick Poole would recall were: "*we find for the plaintiffs*" and "*three hundred and thirty-three million dollars.*"

The following day, Saturday, Frederick and Roger sat at a window table in Locke-Ober Restaurant, both nursing hangovers, neither showing much interest in the creamed fin and haddie on their plates. Frederick took a swallow of his ale, set the long-stemmed glass back on the table and took a roll from a wire basket.

"Thank-you for joining me for lunch, Roger. I suspect you'd rather being doing most anything else, something not connected to the trial. Truth is, I expected you had forgotten about our date."

"Gotta eat."

"For what it's worth, I thought your closing was brilliant. Cosmos

Theopoulis has to have been the most unsympathetic litigant in the history of Suffolk County. Clarence Darrow couldn't have salvaged this case. To have fashioned a cogent argument, beautifully woven with the law, was pure art. And, your delivery was perfect."

"Actually, Frederick, it was a third of a billion dollars imperfect. Months of trial, and that bitch murdered us with thirty minutes of jury instructions. The real killer was her tone. Everyone on that jury knew exactly where she stood, what decision she wanted." Roger pushed lumps of yellowish fish around his plate, cutting trails through a puddle of cream sauce. "Three hundred and thirty-three million dollars. And I can guarantee you Zelia Valdes will rocket those damages into the stratosphere when she rules on multiple damages in the fraud counts. And she'll do it even though she has no basis for it, not one bit."

"I'm afraid you're right, Roger. The disaster keeps spreading. But, that's why we have appellate courts. By the way, I apologize for leaving the courtroom in such a hurry. I did not feel well. I mean, I actually was ill after the verdict was read. I'm sure I don't want to know, but what did our client have to say, post disaster?"

"It was short and to the point - 'Do something, and quick, or you'll be hearing from real lawyers.' Then he added, 'at the least.' What he meant by 'do something' I don't know. I don't want to think about his last comment."

"I'd like to think he may cool off, but I doubt it," Frederick said. "At least our billing is up to date, and paid."

"In spite of the fact that Cosmos may have screwed his snotty nephew and niece out of a few hundred million dollars, we should have won this case. The evidence and the law did not support this jury's decision. That judge's rulings throughout the trial killed us."

"What's your best guess, Roger, on when the judge will make her rulings on the fraud and deceit counts?"

"She probably had her clerk drafting them during the final week of the trial, but I think she'll wait, make it appear that she's given it substantial thought. I expect she'll keep us hanging for at least a month, maybe two."

"In the meantime, it behooves us to prepare for the worst. Any suggestions?"

"It's hard for me to do any real thinking today, but of course we have to do whatever is necessary to stay the enforcement of the judgment until the Appeals Court rules. I'm meeting with the team on Monday at your place to start on post-verdict motions, including the motion for a stay."

Frederick brushed imaginary crumbs from his purple sweater and stood. "Perhaps a walk around our beautiful Public Garden will help bring me back to life. Lunch is on my account, Roger. Happy Easter."

Tom Kenny

PART TWO

THE AFTERMATH

14

SPRING, 2003

Forty-one-years old, an even six feet, slim, but being challenged by the beginnings of a pot belly, Jack Ralston Jr. sat alone in the second row of the public gallery in the First Suffolk Criminal Session. Courtroom 510 was sparsely populated in the early afternoon in mid-May as Judge Zelia Valdes finished up her lengthy instructions to a jury. The men and women had sat through seven days of gruesome testimony involving the Chinatown murder of an alleged drug dealer. Jack, supervising attorney for the Massachusetts Public Defender's Office, was a spectator for today's final arguments. One of the reasons he was in the courtroom was to see first hand if his assignment of defense counsel for the accused was a solid one. After listening to the closing argument by the young woman from his office, he'd decided it sure was. He also figured there was a possibility of a not guilty, a rarity of late in Suffolk County. As the judge started into her rote advice and admonitions to the jury concerning the proper ways of deliberation, Jack stuffed his lined notebook into his well-worn briefcase. He sat back, closed his eyes, and waited for the judge's concluding remarks and the departure of the jurors to commence deciding guilt or innocence.

Jack guessed he may have been the only graduate of his class at the Yale Law School to become a public defender, and he knew exactly why he chose public defense - his father despised the concept of legal entitlement, and Jack despised his father. From the cradle, through the day he left the suburban Lake Forest, Illinois mansion for freshman orientation at Stanford, Jack saw little of his father. Senior spent virtually all of his time in the city of Chicago. He could ordinarily be found either at the helm of the law firm of Kensington and Ralston, where he fully expected Junior to follow in his footsteps, or at the firm's convenient, and not-too-discreet, urban townhouse.

When Jack reached the age where he realized that human plumbing was also capable of a very pleasurable function, and human nature bent towards variety, it also occurred to him why his father probably spent the greater percentage of his time away from Lake Forest. But his absence was a blessing. It meant less opportunity for Senior to berate, and, Jack was convinced, physically abuse, Jack's timid, God-fearing mother.

Within a week of graduating from Yale Law, Jack was involved with a storefront legal clinic for under-privileged citizens of New Haven. Two years later he found his way up Interstate 95 to Boston and the Massachusetts Public Defender's Office. He had quickly developed a heart-felt concern for those standing in the dock, realizing that many of them were victimized by poverty, lack of a decent education and discrimination. Jack agreed that those who were simply bad apples were also due decent representation under our system. He was a champion of the common man, and those beneath, and liked the feeling, the satisfaction it gave him. Jack, now in his fourteenth year of providing yeoman service to the criminal law firm for the indigent, was head of the PD's office, and was proud of his service.

Since the end of a serious romantic relationship eight years ago, the office accounted for most of his time, and also for most of what he gave two hoots about. When a surf-green 1957 Chevy Bel Air convertible, seasons tickets to the Bruins, a bi-weekly Spanish class and the swimming pool at the Y were added, Jack was kept occupied. And then there was Thurgood, a black and white mutt rescued from the animal shelter. Jack had named the Border collie-Lab mix after realizing how damn smart he was, and that the Borador had real guts. Nothing intimidated Jack's canine pal, like nothing had intimidated Thurgood's namesake, the justice from Baltimore.

Jack was a patient man. His life as a lawyer was good, but he knew something, actually, it was someone - someone he absolutely loved - was missing. That someone had just finished her closing remarks to the jury. Then, her instruction to the court officer - *Please swear the jury.* - sounded in Jack's head and roused him.

As the court officer led the jury out of the courtroom, Jack caught the eye and smile of Judge Valdes as she turned to leave the bench for chambers. She discreetly pointed to the door off the courtroom leading to her chambers. Jack nodded as he held up an "in just a minute" finger. He waited in the courtroom for the defense attorney as she exchanged polite, post-trial "good-jobs" with the assistant district attorney. Jack was thinking the veteran prosecutor probably had just had his ass handed to him. A minute later, the young staff lawyer joined him and took a few deep breaths, her first murder trial securely under her belt. She smiled in obvious relief. Jack smiled back and gave her a hearty handshake and glowing words for her summation. With a promise to discuss the trial in detail after the jury's verdict was in, Jack patted the lawyer's shoulder, then turned and followed the route taken by Judge Valdes to her chambers.

"Boy, it's nice to be back in the criminal session, Jack. A few months of a civil case loaded with family venom makes you, or at least me, hungry for a good murder trial. Can you open the window a couple of inches?"

"Sure," Jack said and reached part way over the judge's desk and grunted, finally succeeding in raising the heavy, paint-peeling window sash a couple of inches. Sitting, he said, "I've got just enough time for a cigarette. Someone's waiting for me at the office."

Zelia dug into her desk drawer for a pack. "By the way, I see a bright future for that young lady from your office. She's got a terrific courtroom presence. I wouldn't be surprised to see this jury come back with an NG. She had them all the way through the trial."

"She kind of reminds me of a young woman who came into the PD's office eight or nine years ago. I think she had some Cuban ancestry."

Zelia smiled as she offered her pack of Marlboros to Jack who shook one free for each of them. He accepted a light from the judge, who then lit her own and asked, "Still swimming?"

"A few days a week. Trying to balance my pasta and Regina's addictions. Living in the North End can be hazardous to your waistline."

"I should get back in the pool. I miss it."

Jack and Zelia produced a combined chuckle after they said, in unison, "Haven't seen you since the *February Sucks* office party."

"I'd really like to change that, Zelia." Jack said. "Is that possible?"

"I'm sure you know how I feel about you, Jack. Often, I almost get to where I need to be so I can walk through that door, but never quite get over the threshold. In all honesty, I don't know if I ever will. I won't ask you to just wait around. I can't ask you to put your life on hold for me. If you find someone, or just have had it with me, that's your choice, and I'll understand," Zelia hesitated, her eyes began to fill with tears, "and I'll have to accept that."

If Jack was able to pat himself on his back for anything, it would be for his wealth of common sense. It told him long ago he had no choice. His heart had been renovated by Zelia Valdes, and only she could fit the space.

"No tears, remember? We agreed to that in February." Jack stubbed his barely smoked cigarette out in the throw-away foil ashtray and stood. "My faithful dog will have to provide me company for the time being. Don't worry, Zelia, if you come around, no, make that *when* you come around, I'll still be here."

"Oh, God, Jack, I hope so. I really do." Zelia stood and stepped around the desk toward Jack, her arms extended.

15

If not in the courtroom or the judge's chambers, Tony Cipriano could most likely be found in the courthouse library. With the Theopoulis trial finally concluded, and Judge Valdes's Chapter 93 fraud rulings in final draft, he was now able to devote more time to employment prospects beyond his court appointment, which was scheduled to come to a screeching halt in just about a month and a half. He tapped a few keys on a computer and sat back in his chair, hands locked behind his head. A printer on a shelf behind him began to hum. As it printed out the latest version of his resume, a mop of rust-colored hair poked around the partition.

"Hot chocolate? Coke? Muffin? Tijuana Gold? I'm headed to the cafe."

"Yeah, Marilyn, grab me a Sprite and a glazed donut, okay?" Tony stood and pulled a five dollar bill from his pocket. As he passed his colleague the bill, she glanced at the computer screen.

"Still working on the resume, Tony?"

"Yeah, but I'm not having a lot of luck out there in the private sector. I only have one interview scheduled. Not really sure I've got what anyone wants."

"You don't like it here at the court?"

"Sure I do. It's great experience, learning a lot, and it looks good on the resume. But it's just a one-year appointment and that's up pretty soon. Anyway, it's time to make some money in this business. Problem is, nobody seems too interested."

"Don't worry. I got reappointed to a second year. If nothing comes along, you can go that route, as long as your judge likes you. In the meantime, you get to hang around with me, and tell your stupid jokes."

At noontime a few days later, Tony was sitting up straight at an oval conference table. His mind was racing. *Am I too rigid, been smiling enough, body language right? Am I reacting okay to the questions? Do I seem loose enough? But I have to remember the serious nature of the legal profession, and that I'm fortunate to have the opportunity to meet with the committee.* He looked directly at the questioner, a bald middle-aged man who constantly swung gold-rimmed glasses from his fingers, and responded. "About ten months, Mr. Purcell. I've been working exclusively with Judge Valdes, except when she's on vacation."

"And?" inquired the woman sitting next to Mr. Purcell.

"And, what... ma'am?" Tony silently cursed, having forgotten the name of the woman with the man's haircut in the charcoal suit. She had been the clean-up hitter, asking the follow-up questions, making sure that nothing was avoided, either deliberately or accidentally. She looked directly at Tony, no smile. Her tone was stern.

"*And* what were your responsibilities when Judge Valdes was on vacation?"

"Oh, ah, I get it. I was mostly filling in for other law clerks who were on vacation or out sick. In motion sessions usually. A couple of times I was asked to prepare drafts of decisions in minor, jury-waived cases." Tony continued looking at the thin, needle-nosed woman, expecting a follow-up. He got one.

"I didn't realize there were minor cases. I expect the parties involved didn't view them as such."

"I don't mean unimportant, ma'am. I was referring to the dollar value. Of course, all cases are important."

The third member of the three-person committee, a young man who Tony figured for early thirties, pointed to a copy of Tony's resume and asked, "What kind of people go to night law school? I mean, are they mostly older than the ordinary law student, or married, looking to start out on second careers, maybe?"

Tony was taken aback by the "kind of people" reference. Throughout the interview, Tony sensed an attitude from Attorney Robert Bean, an attitude that seemed to say *why are you wasting our valuable time?* He gave his answer to what would be the final question of the interview.

"Not sure, Mister ..." Tony deliberately hesitated. He recalled this inquisitor's name, but chose to suggest it wasn't worth recalling. "Ah, there must be some reason. In my case it was because I had to work during the day. I can't speak for anyone else. The people in my classes seemed like pretty nice, pretty normal," Tony paused a beat, "people."

Attorney Bean stared at Tony, then smiled and said, "I think that about does it. Thank you so much Mr. Capriatti for giving us the opportunity to get to know you. By the way, are you related to that terrific tennis player, Joan, or Jane or something Capriatti? Great flat forehand." Then Bean grimaced and said, "Oops, sorry. I think I'm getting names mixed up."

Tony, necktie stuffed into his suit coat pocket, sat at the Starbuck's window counter on the street level of the International Place Building. He was twenty-two stories below the conference room where his first, and he was certain, his final interview with White and Doar had just taken place. With some disbelief, he reviewed his interview. *God! Am I crazy? Answering that last question like a wise ass? Maybe that shithead was just testing me, seeing how I'd react in an adverse situation. Hell, your life as a lawyer in a high-powered firm has you in tough spots that require cool thinking. That's got to be what he was doing, just testing me. Shit, I really blew it! I just hope to hell these big firms don't compare notes. If so, I can kiss a career in a decent downtown firm good-bye.*

Tony sipped from a bottle of cranberry juice, gazing through the plate glass wall at the overcast day. Scraps of paper tumbled across the open space fronting the high-rise building. A young woman in a bright red jacket, head bowed into the wind, drew his attention as she made her way towards Atlantic Avenue. With a start, he recognized her face, one he hadn't seen in months.

Tony met Kate Rosenfield when a group of Harvard Law students spent a morning in Judge Valdes's courtroom last fall. After a few movie dates, what Tony had seen as a potential romance seemed to cool all of a sudden. When he asked why, Kate confessed that a former boyfriend had resurfaced. Tony made a couple of stabs at keeping the relationship alive, but to no avail. The Theopoulis case had finally pushed Kate from his thoughts. Now she was back in his head. Instinctively, his arm shot up, seeking to grab her attention through the plate glass window. Kate glanced in his direction. A half minute later she was shedding her shoulder bag, redoing her brown ponytail, and sitting on the stool next to him.

"What brings you down to this end of town?" Kate asked.

"I took some personal leave. Had an interview upstairs," Tony thrust his thumb straight up. "What about you? Booted out of the People's Republic of Cambridge?"

Kate pointed in the direction of the nearby Federal Reserve Building. "My Dad's in town on business. He invited me in for lunch. Says he needs a break from the 'yes' men. Who'd you interview with?"

"White and Doar."

"Really? Wow, that's impressive, Tony. They don't talk to just anyone. Nice going."

"My guess is the letter of recommendation from Judge Valdes got me through the door. I've discovered the big firms like to keep the judges happy. Also, I think I was their token night-school interview."

"How'd it go? What kind of questions did they ask?"

"The usual stuff to start with. Why did you choose the law? Did you find school challenging? Who are your heroes? What are you most proud of, ashamed of? Then a few questions about my clerking for Judge Valdes."

"What'd you tell them about that?"

"That I did a lot of note-taking in court and in chambers, a lot of research, writing up some draft decisions on motions and, once, a draft decision on a jury-waived case. I threw in a few comments about how the judge would ask my opinion about the parties, or witnesses, every now and then. Now that I think of it, I probably made myself sound a little more important than I really am."

"People being interviewed exaggerate more than just a little. Everybody expects some puffing from job applicants, whether it's at a big law firm or McDonald's. It's part of the game, Tony. You have to toot your own horn."

"Yeah, but I think I struck out. One of the guys asking questions made a snide remark about night law school students. It was also pretty clear he wasn't crazy over surnames ending in vowels."

"World's full of jerks, Tony. Got to get used to it."

"I know, Kate, but it still got me pissed. I tried to shut him up with a wise-ass answer. I probably cooked my goose. That's when the interview ended."

Kate picked up Tony's cranberry juice and took a sip. "Good for you, putting these effete snobs in their place. Don't worry about White and Doar. You'll do just fine."

"I'll believe that when I see it." Tony hesitated, wondering if he should pry, then decided to plunge. "Still seeing that guy from Michigan Law?"

"Nope, that's over. Definitely over."

Tony's attitude went up a few notches. "Really? When?"

"A month ago." Kate stood. "I have all morning classes this semester. If you're available, I can meet you in Harvard Square, or take the subway in town for lunch. Give me a call if you want. I've got a new phone number." Kate pulled a pen from her bag and scribbled her number on a napkin. "Okay?"

"Ah, yeah, sure. The pressure's off at the court, at least for the time being. We just wrapped up a major case."

"Great." Kate moved off her chair, slipped her bag over her shoulder, and planted a quick kiss on Tony's lips. She headed for the door. "Can't keep my father waiting."

Tony watched Kate hurry across the plaza. He was suddenly happy. Very happy. The compliment, the promise of lunch, her apparent interest in his existence. And the kiss. She had kissed him. And it seemed so natural. The hell with White and Doar.

That evening, at the Murphy Ice Rink in South Boston, five minutes remained in a Colonial League game between Paddy's Pigs and the IBEW Shockers. Tony Cipriano, a Pigs' defenseman, wasn't paying attention, just gliding, picturing Kate, and remembering the kiss which had dominated his thoughts for the last seven hours. Suddenly, he was slammed into the boards by a vicious check. As he pushed himself up from the ice, he watched the kid who played for BU last year flick a wrist shot into the upper right corner of the net.

"Earth to Tony, you're fuckin' dreamin' out there!" shouted the goaltender as he fished the puck out of the back of the goal.

Ten minutes later Tony sat in the cluttered locker room imbued with the reek of years of sweat-drenched hockey gear. Paddy's Pigs, made up mostly of BPD and state cops from Southie, were on the losing end of the 6-2 contest. Tony unlaced his skates while a teammate sitting next to him on the scarred green bench offered his opinion.

"Maybe it didn't cost us the game, but what the hell you doing in never-never land during a fucking hockey game, Cipriano? We're not exactly the Bruins, but we do have some pride, and you could end up in the fucking bone yard."

"Yeah, Billy, sorry. Thinking about other stuff. No excuses." Tony rubbed his left hip. "That son of a bitch really whacked me."

"He was playing the damn puck that was going through your legs."

"Yeah." Tony grunted as he pulled off a skate. "Maybe I'm getting too old for this game."

"Tony, I'm thirty-seven. Believe me, you're not too old to play a little hockey now and then, if you pay attention to what you're doing." Billy stood and dropped his green hockey pants to the floor. "By the way, you still living with your ma and pa?"

"Yeah, why do you ask?"

"Don't be so defensive. I was asking because one of the guys in our house is leaving at the end of the summer. We're going to be looking for a replacement. If you're interested, it's the top two floors in a triplex, four guys, four bedrooms, two bathrooms, great location right here in Southie."

The image of his home life flashed in Tony's mind's eye. The family of three pushing a bowl of pasta around the table. His mother telling him what, when and how to do everything. Dad sitting mute, a resigned look on his face.

Then he thought of Kate. Maybe nothing would develop, but it seemed more likely something could if he wasn't living with his parents in a third floor walk-up in Dorchester. Billy pulled a sweat-soaked T-shirt over his head. "Well, you interested or not?"

"Maybe. Yeah, Billy, maybe. It sounds perfect. I'll let you know. Can you hold off filling the slot for a little while?"

Finally stripped, Tony's teammate grabbed a towel from his locker, turned and started to the showers. "Sure, we can hold it. Won't have any problem filling it if you don't want it."

As he walked to the steamy shower room, Tony examined his left hip, wondering when the bruise would surface. Then he smiled, thinking again of Kate, and the noontime kiss.

The weekend started out bright and warm, mirroring Tony's attitude. He'd arranged to meet Kate at noon at the Harvard Square kiosk, a stop on the T Red Line. Tony didn't have a car and the Cambridge landmark couldn't be much more convenient. A five minute walk brought them to the Casablanca Restaurant. By twelve-thirty a waiter was delivering a hamburger to Tony and a Nicoise salad to Kate.

"Ever see the movie?" Tony asked, studying a mural which depicted Humphrey Bogart and Ingrid Bergman, with Rick's Cafe Américain in the background.

"Sure. Half a dozen times. A lot of people around here know all the lines. They recite them, word for word, when the movie's playing at the Brattle Theatre."

"That's kind of cool, I guess," Tony said and reached for the ketchup. "Do you have anything lined up for work after graduation?"

"Slye and Connolly in Washington is kind of my safe harbor. I'm waiting to hear on some federal clerkships." Kate sipped her coke through a straw. "I'll take the Massachusetts bar in August. If I pass it, I won't have to take the exam for DC because I can be admitted by motion. When does your court appointment end, Tony?"

"Supposed to be for a year and that's coming up soon, but Judge Valdes has told me I can stay on while I'm job hunting for at least a couple of months. Working with her has been great experience. I've been able to see what goes on in the courtroom, the right way to do things, and the wrong way. I think she's really bright, and loaded with common sense. She actually seems to be interested in what I think about the cases she hears. Anyhow, yesterday I was able to line up two more interviews. Maybe they'll go a little better than the last one."

"Anything interesting going on in court now?"

"We just finished a first degree murder case. Drug gangs involved."

"Guilty?"

"Nope. Not guilty." Criminal cases are Judge Valdes's area of expertise. She was a Suffolk ADA for a few years, and then with the Public Defender's Office for three or four years before she got her judgeship. The murder case was a real change of pace from the notorious civil case that took up a good chunk of the winter. I may have mentioned it when I saw you in town."

In response to Kate's raised eyebrows, Tony said, "Maybe you read about it, the Theopoulis case? Cosmos Theopoulis?"

"Sorry, but when I'm in school I just go into a cocoon. What was it about?"

"Theopoulis was accused by his niece and nephew of defrauding them out of millions, actually hundreds of millions. It was pretty complicated, but it got to be pretty clear that the kids were right. The trial lasted a couple of months. The jury awarded the niece and nephew three hundred and thirty-three million dollars, and Judge Valdes could treble the amount, to a cool billion, under the fraud statutes."

"Wow, that's real money. Actually, more than real money. The case is over?"

"The trial is over, but the appeals are just beginning. The defense lawyers are claiming all kinds of error, judicial prejudice and whatever else they can think of."

"Who are the lawyers?"

"Joseph Dunn is representing the niece and nephew. Theopoulis is represented by two firms that are acting as co-counsel. The lead trial lawyer is a youngish guy, Roger Metcalf. Co-counsel is Frederick Poole of ..."

"Oh, I know who Poole is, Kate interrupted. A real big shot in the city. On lots of charitable boards and stuff."

"How do you know about him?"

"A few months ago my mother had me co-host a cocktail party because her boyfriend was out of town. Poole was one of the guests. Do you know anything about him?"

"Other than he's a big shot in the Bar Association, and probably loaded with money, nope."

"That's all true," Kate said, then added, "and he's openly gay. That may not be such a big deal now, but before, when gays always stayed in the closet, Poole never denied it. He lives with his partner, a guy named Otto." Kate speared a few green beans and a chunk of tuna from her salad.

"How do you know all this stuff?" Tony asked.

"My mother knows everything about everybody on the social register. And I met this Otto at the party. He's a big bald black guy. Really quite striking. Dresses and speaks beautifully."

16

Federal District Court Judge Fred Milton was a big man, six and a half feet tall and just a few pounds under three hundred and twenty. His career as an offensive lineman with the New England Patriots ended on a snowy Sunday afternoon in western New York about twenty-five years ago. An equally large man who played left tackle for the Buffalo Bills was blocked by one of Fred's teammates, fell over another of Fred's teammates, and landed on Fred's left leg. There was serious, career-ending damage. During his brief football career, Fred had heeded the advice of his aunt, a professor at Suffolk University in Boston, and enrolled in that school's evening law school. Fred graduated from Suffolk and passed the Massachusetts bar exam the summer before his leg got crunched.

His career as a general practitioner came to a conclusion thanks to a governor who happened to be a Patriot's season ticket holder. Fred was appointed to the Massachusetts bench. After seven years in the state court system, a combination of his legal talent, political connections, and reputation for plain speaking resulted in a seat on the federal bench at Boston

It was mid-morning of a late spring day, which happened to be the tenth anniversary of Judge Milton's appointment to the federal bench. Fred was in his chambers at the Moakley Federal Courthouse in South Boston. His imposing bulk sat across his desk from Attorneys Roger Metcalf and Robert Bean. The three men were half an hour into an off-the-record settlement conference. Fred Milton was used to cases on his docket settling when he thought they should, like this one. It was time for the hammer.

"Boys, this is supposed to be a settlement conference. You know, both sides give a little, get a little. But I think you guys seem to be more interested in churning the holy shit out of your bills." Judge Milton pointed a gold letter opener at Attorney Bean. "Mr. Bean, I know your firm has perfected the art of hourly billing, but let me tell you something. If this case goes to trial, as you know, it will be a bench trial, no happy faces in the jury box on civic duty vacation, and I will be presiding. I will make it clear to your client that the case, and his wallet, could have been closed months before, on better terms than he is likely to get in my verdict, but you, his attorney, refused to exercise common sense."

The judge moved the letter opener, now pointing it at Attorney Metcalf. "Mr. Metcalf, you should have settled the case for the Greek guy with the long name over in Suffolk Superior a few weeks back. You let your ego and bank account get in the way, and the jury scorched your poor client for a goddamn fortune. Do the right thing this time. Settling this case will save money and agony for your client, and help clean up my docket." The judge then raised his ham hock of a right arm and pointed at the door. "Boys, go talk a little bit more, and get rid of this fucker."

Within an hour, their case reported settled to the clerk's office, Metcalf and Bean left the courthouse and walked together over the Northern Avenue Bridge toward downtown Boston.

"Sorry about that big loss you took last month, Roger," Bean said. "Interesting factoid for you. Your trial judge's law clerk interviewed at our firm a couple of weeks ago. Blew his horn about being involved in the Theopoulis case. Seems to think he was pretty important. I didn't like him. He thinks the world owes him a living because he went to law school at night. Shit, that jockstrap we just left went to night law school."

"What exactly did the law clerk have to say, Bobby?"

The setting sun illuminated the Hyatt Regency Cambridge Hotel overlooking the Charles River. Bathed in orange light, the pyramid-shaped hostelry glowed along with the nearby buildings on the M.I.T. campus. From the flagstone terrace of Frederick Poole's Back Bay penthouse on the Boston side of the river, there was a sweeping view of the silver ribbon as it snaked toward Boston Harbor from the western suburbs.

Wearing creased khaki slacks and a white polo shirt, Poole stood at a waist-high brick wall. He was sipping from his second glass of Long Island iced tea and beginning to feel the effect of the whiskey-laden drink. The glass door from the adjacent study slid open and Roger Metcalf stepped onto the terrace.

"Hello, Frederick. Otto let me in. Why the urgent call?" Roger looked at Poole's face. He suddenly felt light-headed. He stated matter-of-factly, "You have Valdes's decision on the fraud counts, don't you."

"Yes, I do, Roger. A contact in the clerk's office had a copy hand-delivered to the office." Frederick glanced at a stack of papers clipped together on a glass-topped table. "You can take that copy with you if you'd like, but I can abstract it for you. We lose, in every way imaginable."

Roger plopped into a wrought iron chair next to the table.

"Everything? We lost everything? She tripled the damages? Transferred controlling interest in the company?"

Frederick nodded, turned back to the patio wall and set his glass on its slate cap. He pushed his hands into his pockets and, staring at the river, said, "I had a friend at college who wanted desperately to get into medical school, any medical school. Couldn't get accepted anywhere. He claimed to have received rejections from schools he'd never even applied to. I didn't believe that. I thought he was paranoid, until I just received a critique of the decision from one of the firm's appellate aces. Judge Valdes made findings the plaintiffs could never have dreamed of receiving, and she supported them with arguments they never made."

"Well, I guess that leaves everything up to the Appeals Court," Roger said.

"I'm also told that Valdes did one hell of a job in crafting her decision. Very tight. Written with an eye toward holding up on appeal."

Roger stood and walked across the patio. He leaned against the half wall, next to Frederick, looking at the river. "There's got to be something we can do. This is taking weird twists. This morning a federal judge shit all over me for screwing up this case. Suggested I didn't know what the fuck I was doing. That's the kind of thing that's happening to my, to our reputations. For months this goddamn Zelia Valdes treated us like dog shit, and then she led that jury by the hand into an outrageous damage award. Now she's put the cherry on top with this treble damage fraud decision. We have to do something. Maybe there's something outside the record we can use. We should get an investigator on her, like I've been suggesting, Frederick."

"What could possibly be outside the record? You're not thinking bribes and such, are you?"

"I have no idea what we might be able to dig up, Frederick. But we have to look. What the hell, we've lost a billion dollars, why not spend something on an investigator?"

"I have my boundaries, Roger. I'm not about to agree to setting the hounds on a sitting superior court judge. In any event, my guess is that she was simply inexperienced, in over her head."

Roger walked back to the table, grabbed the stack of papers and strode toward the sliding door. "Think about it, Frederick. We sure as shit have to do something."

17

Wearing jeans and a green V-neck sweater over a button-down shirt, Roger walked across the lobby of the Boston Harbor Hotel, headed for the Sea Grille restaurant. As he approached the hotel's main dining room, he saw Frederick and his partner, Otto Robinson, both attired in tan linen sport coats, chatting with the maître d' just inside the eatery's entrance. Roger was struck by the reflected light from a chandelier shining on the bald pates of the men he was meeting. The thought of Frederick and Otto buffing each other's heads, as they might do to the tips of their cordovan shoes, came to mind. Seeing Roger approach, Frederick gave a concluding compliment for the pan-roasted halibut to the restaurant host and he and Otto walked into the lobby.

"Eight o'clock on the dot. Good timing, Roger," Frederick said. "We're very interested to know about the idea you have. We can't imagine how Otto can help out in the Theopoulis case. Shall we talk here in the lobby, or would you rather have a drink at the bar?"

"The lobby will be fine," Roger said as he eyed an empty sitting area tucked into a corner behind a marble staircase. Moments later, he pulled an armchair up to the coffee table in front of the couch occupied by Frederick and Otto.

Frederick looked across the glass table and said, "Okay, Roger, you sounded very excited when you called. What's your idea?"

"After reviewing Judge Valdes's decision last week with the appellate lawyers, it has become clear to me that we have to be proactive in our effort to get this disaster reversed. If we do nothing, and just rely on the record on appeal, I'm afraid that a year from now this matter, as decided, could be final, with all appeals exhausted. My idea begins an aggressive course of action on behalf of our client.

"I have solid information that Judge Valdes's law clerk, Caesar A. Cipriano, he's called Tony, by the way, is looking for employment in the Boston legal community when his appointment to the court ends. That is supposed to happen sometime this summer. As part of that job search, I also know that Cipriano has bragged around the city that he plays a very large part in Valdes's decision making. Of great interest to us, Cipriano has made specific reference to his influence with the judge regarding the Theopoulis case. If what he is bragging about is accurate in any way, it is possible, no, make that probable, that Judge Valdes has violated her judicial oath by irresponsible, and illegal, delegation of her judicial responsibilities to her law clerk, who has only recently graduated from law school."

"Just where are you going with this, Roger?" Frederick asked.

"I am hoping that it's the first step of a journey to get this decision reversed. We need to create enough smoke to permit the Appeals Court to reasonably infer fire when it considers this matter. If we can get the case sent back for a new trial, we have to insure that it is assigned to a different judge, not the judge who has crucified us."

Frederick moved back in the couch, his head shaking. "Roger, I share your disdain for how Judge Valdes has treated the Theopoulis case, but what exactly are you suggesting?"

"Hear me out. I have a proposition."

Fifteen minutes later, the three men stood from the couch and armchair. "Perhaps it's not harebrained, Roger, but it's certainly close. Nonetheless, at this point we're grasping at straws. And, as you have just suggested, we may even have some sort of ethical obligation to the bar to look further. With that as my primary motivation, most reluctantly, I'll go along with your plan. While you and Otto figure out the nuts and bolts, I'll head home if that's okay. I'd rather not know the details."

Roger and Otto left the hotel lobby by the harborside door, heading to the illuminated foot path running alongside Boston Harbor. The cool weather was more suited to fall than mid-June. Coatless, Roger dug his hands deeper into his jean's pockets. He hunched his shoulders against the night air being pushed off the harbor by a steady breeze. Otto pulled the collar of his sport coat tight against his neck.

"How well do you know this law clerk, Mr. Cipriano, Roger?"

"Not too well. He was in the courtroom often during the trial, observing, taking notes. I spoke with him every now and then. Seemed like a nice enough kid. Polite, respectful, stayed out of the way."

"How do you know he's looking for a new job?"

"Recently I had a settlement conference over at the federal courthouse. The lawyer on the other side of the case is on the recruiting committee at a big firm in the city. We were shooting the breeze after the conference and Judge Valdes came up in the conversation. He told me about a job interview Cipriano had with his hiring committee a couple of weeks ago. Cipriano did a lot of boasting about how important he's been to Judge Valdes. How he discusses cases with her, and he claimed she was very interested in his opinions, including what he thought about the credibility of witnesses. He actually bragged that he wrote her findings of fact in the Theopoulis case."

"Is that what law clerks usually do? Are these some of their functions?"

"Yes and no. It's a question of degree. I'm thinking that this kid might have been given some of the duties, been doing some of the fact-finding that Judge Valdes should have been handling herself. You know, given too much authority. Judge's aren't supposed to delegate their responsibilities to their law clerks."

"I've been on interview panels, Roger. Applicants for all sorts of positions are prone to a little exaggeration. Could that be what happened at your colleague's firm when they interviewed Mr. Cipriano?"

"Maybe some of that, Otto, but I'm thinking there's some truth to his bragging about his responsibilities."

"So, you want to show that the judge relied too much on her clerk."

"That's the bottom line. We have to be able to show that Valdes based her decision on the fraud counts regarding our client's alleged deceit, at least in part, on something, or someone, or some influence, other than what was introduced as evidence at the trial. We have some of the top appellate lawyers in the city on this case. They keep looking for something to bolster our argument. They're not finding much of anything. The burden of reversing a decision on appeal is straight uphill.

"That's why, Otto, putting it bluntly, we have to have Cipriano set up. I need to record him saying things that will help us get this case reversed and sent back for a new trial, in front of a different judge." Roger paused, and then continued. "I don't like dragging the kid into this. I guess he's collateral damage, and maybe the only way to get this goddamn decision set aside by the Appeals Court."

Otto pulled his coat tighter. "Go over your plan again, please, Roger."

"I want to get Cipriano to agree to a job interview, but it will be a charade. It has to be in Canada, so I can legally record him without him knowing it. Secret recording of a private conversation is a crime in Massachusetts, and probably many other states, and the audio tapes would not be admissible in any legal proceeding. But it's okay to make the recordings in Canada. Cipriano has to be convinced that a company is interested in offering him a very lucrative job. Then, even if we have to lead him a little at the interview, I want him saying things that strongly suggest, reasonably infer, that he influenced Judge Valdes in the Theopoulis case. We need his actual voice, his words, on tape. That's what we need. Nothing less."

"When does this have to happen?"

"Yesterday, Otto, yesterday."

Otto paused and watched the lights of a plane rising from Logan Airport across the harbor. "I've seen how this case has affected Frederick. I've never seen him so low, and he's drinking more. He's diabetic, you know. He can't handle alcohol. This problem, this case, is taking a real toll on his health."

"Probably on mine, too," Roger said.

"All right, Roger. Let's see if Mr. Cipriano bites. I have a friend who can do most anything with her computer. I'll have her create a letterhead and set up a web page for a bogus head-hunter agency in case Mr. Cipriano looks on-line. Then we'll send out our letter offering him the interview." Otto paused a moment, then continued, "Just thinking, Roger, it may be helpful to refer to the young man's law school transcript in the letter. Can you get your hands on his law school record?"

"I'm sure I can do that somehow. As soon as I have it, I'll get it over to you, along with suggestions for what to put in the letter," Roger said. "Then get it printed and in the mail as soon as possible. That's the first step. If he agrees to an interview in Montreal, Otto, you can handle that as well?"

Otto showed a contented smile. "I'm still in regular contact with a theater troupe in New York. They'll be happy to take their talents on the road. If the law clerk is interested, there won't be a problem arranging the interview. Then we'll have to come up with a name and web page for the prospective employer as well. That won't be a problem either."

"If it's a go, Otto, I'll get together with you to arrange the logistics and go over an outline of what we need to get him to say at his interview."

The men arrived back at the hotel and stopped at the waterside patio, emptied of guests by the cool weather. Otto turned and motioned in the direction of the hotel, its windows glowing warm amber against the darkening night. He tucked his hands under the arms of his sport coat.

"Let's go inside, Roger. I'll buy you a hot toddy and you can assure me that we're not breaking any laws."

18

The supper dishes wiped dry, Anna Cipriano hung a striped kitchen towel on a wall hook and groaned softly.

"What's the matter, Ma?" Tony asked, looking up from the *Boston Globe* which was spread out on the kitchen table between a glass of milk and a plateful of brownies.

"Oh, it's all those steps every day. Up and down for Mass in the morning, then to run errands during the day, then to get the mail. My bones are getting too old for all the steps."

"Where did Dad go?"

"To church, for the men's club meeting."

"What do they do at those meetings, anyhow?"

"They sit around, drink coffee and talk about all the rumors they hear on the radio about big-shots in Boston. Ha, men's club. They should call it the old ladies' club instead. I think your father just likes to get out of the house."

Anna picked up a letter mixed in with a variety of junk mail on the counter and handed it to her son. "Here, Tony, something for you that came in today's mail."

Tony glanced at the envelope. Not recognizing the printed return address of Hynes & Associates in New York City, he casually dropped it on the table. "Just someone trying to sell me some law books or something. New lawyers get a lot of that stuff."

"That's all? Okay. I'm going to start over to church to meet your father. I'll walk home with him, then, up the stairs again." She shook her head as she walked to the door.

Tony drained his glass of milk, then remembered, and opened the letter from New York.

Dear Mr. Cipriano:

Hynes & Associates is a human resource firm headquartered in New York City with offices in major cities around the globe. Our mission is to fill the upper echelon personnel needs of major corporations and professional associations.

Hynes is presently researching potential matches for a position of first assistant legal counsel at an international, London based, banking group. Although this position may require occasional travel to London, the person chosen will work out of Boston or New York City, whichever is most convenient for him or her.

Our research has concluded that your background provides an interesting possibility in reference to this position. Data (all retrieved within the bounds of United States privacy laws) was recently forwarded to the client and a favorable, indeed enthusiastic, response has been received. We at Hynes have been asked to follow up.

Although we have no reason to believe you are discontent with your present position, we would ask you to consider being interviewed for this opportunity. The responsibilities of the position are interesting and the opening remuneration is at a level on par with a new hire associate's salary at major New York City law firms. Please call our New York office at the above number within the next week to advise us of your availability. You will not be billed for any services of Hynes & Associates. We are compensated by the employers.

Thank you and we look forward to your phone call.

Sincerely,

Hynes & Associates, by,

Bradford Johnson

Tony read and re-read the letter. After a few minutes reflecting on its contents, he stood and walked to the kitchen phone, anxious to call Kate and tell her about the letter. He started to poke her number on the keypad when he heard his mother on the stairwell, carping about forgetting her purse. Kate would have to wait to learn about the London bank. He hung up the phone.

Commuting home from the courthouse the next day, Tony stood in the hot crowded train as it sped under South Boston and into Dorchester. During a mid-morning court recess, he had called Hynes & Associates. What he was told by the head-hunter firm seemed too good to be true. Although surprised by the location, he had quickly agreed to travel to Montreal to be interviewed for the available position. He anticipated his mother's reaction. He was right.

"Montreal? Frankie, did you hear that? Montreal! In another country!"

"Yes, I heard. I'm sitting right here at the table with him."

Anna walked from the kitchen counter and sat at the table. She shook her head in disbelief, then used a paper napkin to wipe up some drips of red sauce.

"Tony, tell me again. You say that someone might give you a new job, but you have to go way up to Canada to talk to them? This sounds fishy. Why Canada, Tony? Did they tell you why? It's fishy to me." She turned to her husband. "It sounds fishy, Frankie."

"The man I have to speak with is from England, Ma, and he's going to be in Montreal for business. It's just more convenient for him, that's all." Tony turned a piece of bread in his hands "It's no big deal, Ma, really, and the company pays all my travel expenses."

"They know how you did so good in school. Isn't that enough to give you the job if you want it?"

Tony used the bread to sop up the remaining red sauce from his plate. "Law school grades aren't the only thing that counts with companies like this one. They have to see if you can answer questions, how you do in a face-to-face interview, that kind of thing."

"I don't know about this. I like the job you have with the lady judge. It's right here in Boston, and you can take the subway to work." Anna stood and picked up her dish. She walked to the sink. "Why change now?"

"Money, Ma. It's as simple as that," Tony said, chewing the bread. "You understand, don't you, Dad?"

Frankie looked across the table at his son, smiled and nodded.

"If you stay with the job you have, maybe you could become the judge," Tony's mother spoke over the sound of water rushing into the sink. "Bring your plate over if you're finished."

"That's not how it works, Ma. And it's time for me to move on anyhow. I told you that clerkships with the court are only supposed to last a year. That's over now. The judge is letting me stay on while I hunt for a job. She could change her mind anytime, and then I'd be out of work."

"The judge change her mind? Ha!"

"Whatever, Ma. But I can't pass up any possibility of a decent job. Tony stood from the table and carried his dish and glass to the sink. "It's time to make some money. I'd really like to help get you guys down from the third floor."

19

Ten days after meeting with Otto and Frederick at the Boston Harbor Hotel, Roger received a padded FedEx envelope at his office. The return address was in New York City. The packet contained only a micro-cassette of the prior day's phone call between the law clerk and Otto's actor friend. Roger loaded the cassette into his recorder. After hearing a nervous Tony Cipriano introduce himself, he heard the second voice.

"Good morning, Mr. Cipriano. Thank you for calling so promptly. Our client is very, very interested in you. Their human resources chief, who is a senior vice-president, called personally to emphasize his firm's willingness to be competitive. I am authorized to tell you that the client is London Group Equibank."

"That's really flattering. Do you know why they're so interested?"

"I can't definitely say, but I know you have an impressive background. I can tell you that they have the benefit of your law school transcripts. The company officer I spoke with was impressed with your grades, particularly in the international law and banking law courses. He also told me he was familiar with the reputation of a couple of your professors. There's really no rule of thumb when we get involved with filling positions at this level. Something just hits the client the right way. Makes them want to take a closer look."

"Well, I can tell you that I am interested. What should I do next, after this call?"

"A personal interview is the next step."

"When, and where, Mr. Johnson?"

"Bank officials will be in Montreal for business meetings this coming week. They would like to interview you while they are there. Could you be available on Saturday, the twenty-eighth of this month? In Montreal? Of course, all costs are paid by Hynes."

"Ah, Montreal? On a Saturday? June twenty-eighth? Yeah. Sure. I can do that."

"Excellent. Your plane tickets, flying out of Boston's Logan Airport, and information on hotel accommodations will be delivered with your itinerary by the end of the week."

"Hotel?"

"Yes. For convenience, you'll fly in the evening before, on the twenty-seventh. The interview will be at your hotel the following morning at nine o'clock."

"No kidding? I mean, okay, and thanks. Thanks a lot."

Roger turned off the tape player, leaned back in his chair and cradled his head. *So far, so good.*

20

"The flight was okay?"

"Yeah, no problems at all."

"I suppose they had a limo waiting at the airport."

Tony, phone to his ear, pushed back on the pillows stacked against the bed's headboard. "Of course, Kate. What would you expect for this hotshot from Boston?"

"Really? They really had a limo?"

"Yup. So far, it's been great. London Group EquiBank is top shelf all the way. First class on Air Canada, a Lincoln limo waiting at the airport, and a great room here at the Ritz-Carlton. I think I could adjust to the private sector."

"What's next?"

"The interview. Nine o'clock tomorrow morning, in a conference room in the hotel. Then I'm scheduled on a three o'clock flight back to Boston."

"Are you nervous?"

"Yeah, maybe a little."

"I wish I could give you some advice, but I don't know what you should expect. Just be yourself and you'll do great."

"Thanks, Kate. I'll call you when I get back to Boston, okay?"

"Know what, Tony? I can pick you up at Logan tomorrow. I have a morning class, then I'm free for the day. What time does your flight home arrive?"

"Four-thirty. Air Canada again."

"I'll be waiting outside the terminal in my mother's car, a red Jag."

After filling glasses and cups with juice and coffee, the retreating waiter closed the double doors to the Ritz's Salon Vert executive meeting room. To Tony, it seemed as if there should have been a clang, like a jail cell door being pulled shut. He breathed deeply, once again hoping he looked less anxious than he felt. That hope was dashed when his host, a slim man with a full head of white hair combed straight back, who introduced himself as Philip Mortimer, spoke.

"Just relax, Mr. Cipriano. We promise no root canals today, just some friendly questions. While we're asking them, please enjoy breakfast." Mortimer smiled, and then spread his hands in front of the tabletop which hosted platters of scrambled eggs, breakfast meats, various breads and sliced tomatoes. "Please, help yourself."

Tony heard what he imagined as the perfect British accent. The words suggested all was well in the speaker's world, and, if Tony measured up, he could share the contentment. Tony pegged Mortimer for about sixty years old. He wore a closely-fitted gray suit over a white shirt with a maroon tie. But something seemed askew to Tony - *was that a wig? Probably not. Just a fancy English haircut.*

Tony had arrived at the small meeting room on the hotel's second floor at eight fifty-five. Having no hint that breakfast would be served, and not wanting to head into the interview on an empty stomach, thirty minutes earlier he had discovered a Tim Horton's Donut shop around the corner from the hotel, and downed a couple of chocolate crullers. Nonetheless, he followed the lead of Mortimer's colleague, an attractive woman seemingly about half Mortimer's age, and introduced as Beatrice Longheart from 'legal', who was helping herself to the food. Tony scooped up a serving of eggs, and then, with silver tongs, pinched a pair of plump sausages.

Fifteen minutes of eating and small talk took the edge off the meeting for Tony. He was pleased that he was able to put the food away with no trouble, actually enjoying his second breakfast. The waiter reappeared and took away the remains, leaving a fresh pot of coffee. Tony felt his confidence building. As the doors behind him closed again, he recalled an interview tip he had read: *Interview them - they have to know that you think it's a two-way street.*

"Mr. Mortimer, if I perform to the standards you require, where can I expect to be in the organizational structure of The London Group in five years?"

"A very good question." Mortimer paused long enough for his colleague to fill her coffee cup. "I'll pass that on to Bea."

The svelte Beatrice was blessed with a pretty face rimmed with long blonde hair. Tony noticed how the color of her hair was set off perfectly by the room's green walls. She looked at him with a soft smile.

"The answer is not a simple one because of the dynamics of the international banking industry," Beatrice said, "however, it is reasonable to assume that you would be one of our top three persons in legal, and responsible for our North American operations."

Tony was delighted with his question, and not really concerned with the answer which, at this point, meant absolutely nothing to him. After forty-five minutes of general questions about law school courses and his law-clerking responsibilities, Mortimer mentioned the Theopoulis case.

"Hasn't there been a rather famous, or perhaps infamous, case decided by Judge Valdes in your courtroom recently? I believe I saw mention of it in the *Wall Street Journal*, the Theopoulis case?"

Tony liked the reference to "your courtroom" and responded with a hint of braggadocio. "I suppose you could say that. Actually, it was a very interesting case for us. The decision made one side pretty happy and the other pretty miserable."

"I'm sure that's the truth," Beatrice chimed in. "You've mentioned how you work with Judge Valdes on an everyday basis, Mr. Cipriano. Maybe we can get into a little detail, give us a clearer picture of your responsibilities at the court. Let's use that Theopoulis case, for example."

"Exactly what would you like to know?" As soon as he heard himself ask the question, Tony recalled the admonition from Judge Valdes on his first day as a superior court law clerk: *Nothing, Tony, absolutely nothing said or heard in chambers about any court matter is ever repeated to anyone, anywhere, anytime.* "Of course," Tony quickly added, "I can't repeat anything that was learned in confidence."

"Of course, Mr. Cipriano, we would not ask you to violate the confidential nature of your position." Beatrice said. "What we are interested in is details of your duties as a law clerk to a superior court judge, but only as you are permitted to relate them." She looked at Mortimer, who immediately affirmed her explanation with a stern-faced nod and follow-up comment.

"Certainly, certainly. Our organization is built on integrity, Mr.

Cipriano. Without integrity in the business of banking, there is no business. Your appreciation of the confidential nature of your present employment is heartening, indeed." Mortimer moved his cup of coffee aside and then asked, "I'm sure this is public knowledge, Tony. Just how long did that litigation take? I think the *Journal* said about ten weeks. Is that about right?"

The questions continued for another forty-five minutes. Once the interviewers had rung as much information out of Tony as they thought was available, and deemed that information sufficient to meet their marching orders from Otto, the meeting was directed to a conclusion by Mortimer.

"Anything else you'd like to offer, Tony?"

Tony hesitated, thinking he may have painted a harsher picture of Judge Valdes than justified. "I'd just like to make it clear, Mr. Mortimer, that my experience with Judge Valdes has really been great and she's taught me a lot. And I don't want you to think she's just some kind of narrow-minded legal scholar. She's interested in a number of things outside of the law. For instance, there would often be days she'd take an extra couple of hours for lunch, if the afternoon calendar was clear, to visit museums and other places around the city."

"You don't say. Did you ever accompany the judge?"

"No. I always had work to catch up on. But I know she made up the time in the evening. I'd come in the next morning and find more work that she'd left for me."

Just before five o'clock, Tony, carrying a garment bag over his shoulder, spotted the red Jaguar waiting at the main doors of Logan Airport's international terminal. Kate popped the trunk, stepped out of the sedan and greeted him with a bright smile. "I'm dying to know. How'd it go?"

Tony, not sure of what Kate's reaction might be, resisted the temptation to approach her for a hug, maybe even a kiss. He placed his bag into the trunk, slammed it shut, and stepped to the passenger door. He answered Kate, talking across the top of the car. "Seemed to go pretty well. I think they liked me. They said they'd like a follow-up interview."

"Great. I want to hear all about it. I'm hungry. How about you?"

Tony agreed and ducked into the car as a state trooper approached, motioning Kate to move the Jag.

Fifteen minutes later, seated at a window booth at a nearby diner, Kate jabbed at a plate of salad greens. "Did they zero in on anything in particular?"

Tony took a bite from his pastrami sandwich, washed it down with a long gulp of Coke and answered. "Yeah, I was thinking about that on the plane. There were two of them. The guy in charge, a Mr. Mortimer, sixty or so, and his legal assistant, a much younger woman named Beatrice. They said up front that they weren't interested in specifics, but they did kind of get into detail about the Theopoulis case."

"Well, from what you told me, they'd know about that case from the newspapers, if they read the Boston or New York press, anyhow."

"Mortimer said they followed the case in the *Wall Street Journal*. I remember a reporter from that paper being at the trial who wanted to interview me."

"Really?"

"Yeah, but Judge Valdes nixed it."

Kate picked up a French fry from Tony's plate and chewed on it as she asked, "How come you can talk about that case now?"

"It's over. I think I told you, the plaintiffs were awarded a fortune."

"Yeah, but you also said it's on appeal. It is, isn't it?"

"Yes, but..."

Kate peered across the table at Tony. "What did you say about it?"

Tony's interest in his sandwich suddenly waned. "I probably should have kept my mouth shut about it."

"Don't worry. I was just wondering what they wanted to know, and, I guess, why. But I'm sure you didn't do anything wrong."

"Actually, we didn't really get that specific about the facts of the case," Tony paused a moment, "although, they seemed pretty interested in what Judge Valdes thought of the people involved - the parties and the lawyers. They asked if she made any comments about them."

"Why so nosy about the judge, I wonder?"

"You know, Kate, it never really hit me until now. I was so caught up in the interview, I kind of lost track of the things they were asking. They were really pretty smooth with their questions. Mixed things up, kind of slid questions in here and there about the case, and how Judge Valdes handled it."

"What did you tell them?"

"Nothing, really. Just that she didn't talk about anyone in detail, might make a comment every now and then like anyone would, but that it didn't seem personal. That she was much classier than that. I was probably trying to impress them with how well I knew the judge, like, I mentioned that she was really into art."

"Yeah?"

"Yeah. I told them that sometimes, on slow days at the courthouse, she leaves early and heads for museums in the city. She says it's a great stress reliever. The judge studied art history at Wellesley." Tony sipped from his Coke, paused a moment, then asked, "Remember you told me once that everyone does some puffing in job interviews, kind of blows his own horn?" Chewing away, Kate nodded, "Well," Tony continued, "I'm guilty."

"Oh, come on, Tony."

"No, really. I was thinking about it on the plane. I realized that this Mortimer guy kept going back to the Theopoulis case. Really wanted to know how much I had to do with the decision, how much of it I wrote out, the judge's attitude about giving me responsibility, that kind of thing."

"Well, you were involved, and that case took up a huge amount of the court's time."

"Kate, from what I told him, if he wanted to, he could probably conclude that I decided the case. I said things like, well, for instance, that the judge asked me my thoughts about some of the witnesses, what statutes applied, case precedent, just about everything that goes into making the decision."

"Well, did the judge ask you about those things?"

"Kind of, but she'd pick apart my answers, and really critique the memos I gave her. I think she was just teaching me. I sure as hell wasn't telling her what was going on. I'm beginning to think I might have overblown my responsibilities, even for someone interviewing for a job."

"Oh, don't worry about it, Tony. These people are big shots in the international business world. They expected you to exaggerate, and that anyone would do that. You have a tendency to be too tough on yourself."

As their waitress slapped a check on the table, Tony leaned back on the padded bench. "Maybe, but when I think of it, it seems like they were really suggesting I had a slew of influence with the judge. I guess I liked hearing it, and didn't really disagree with the conclusions they were making about how important I was."

Kate smiled and said, "I bet they thought you were terrific."

Tony brightened with the compliment. "Maybe. I hope you're right. They're talking some really decent money, and thinking of opening an office in Boston. I'd travel a lot, but the home base could be right here, in the heart of Red Sox nation."

"Sounds perfect. When will they call you?"

"Mortimer wasn't sure. He said they had a few more candidates to interview, but they'd like a follow-up meeting, probably within a couple of weeks. I still find it hard to believe they're interested in Caesar Anthony Cipriano from Dorchester."

Kate stood from the vinyl-covered bench and reached for the check. "This one's on me, Dorchester boy."

Roger Metcalf gulped the last of his Heinekens from the bottle as he pulled his trilling cell phone from a pocket with his free hand. The cell screen told him the call was from Frederick Poole's home phone. Roger stood and answered the call as he walked back a few feet to get away from the noisy bar at Jacob Wirth Restaurant on Stuart Street, one of his primary watering holes.

"Hello, Roger," the voice on the other end said. "This is Otto. I have a message from Montreal which I think is good news."

"Great. What do you know?" A roar from the bar crowd watching the Red Sox game sent Roger toward the restaurant's door. "Hold on a minute. Let me get somewhere I can hear you." He stepped out, onto the sidewalk. "Okay, go ahead."

"Frederick and I just came in and I picked up a message on the answering machine. Charles, who played the lead role in the interview this morning, called to say that Mr. Cipriano was very talkative, and he thought they were able to lead him down the path you had requested. An audio tape of the interview has been over-nighted to your office building. It's guaranteed to be at the security desk tomorrow by noon."

A happy Roger walked back into the bar. "What'd I miss, Terri?" he asked the comely bartender.

"Nomar homered. Another Heinie, Rog?"

"No thanks. I should probably be getting home."

"You sure? I'm off in half an hour."

21

Roger walked into Frederick Poole's office and sat across the desk from him. His earlier phone call had assured Frederick that the meeting was urgent and could not be delayed. He was quick to get to the heart of his visit.

"The decision to set up the clerk's interview was difficult, Frederick, and I understand that. But it was also the right decision. I have listened to a recording of Saturday's meeting. Otto's acting friends from New York were terrific, and I think we may have struck gold. Judge Valdes just may be toast."

Frederick rolled an unlit cigar between his palms. He did not appear buoyed by Roger's words. "It's not right that good things come from evil behavior. The end rarely justifies the means, Roger. Why am I wrong in this case?"

"Because the interview with the law clerk has provided evidence that Judge Valdes placed a huge amount of the decision making responsibility for our case in his hands, that she was derelict in her duties and that she has ignored her oath as a judge of the Massachusetts courts." Roger shuffled in his chair, and then continued. "Also, according to her law clerk, she disappears from the courthouse during working hours, and for hours at a time. He says it's to go to museums and that kind of thing. I want to know if that's what she's really up to. I want to know if she's meeting anyone connected in any way to the plaintiffs in the Theopoulis case. If she's involved in something besides looking at old statues and similar crap, and her activity is conduct unbecoming a judge, we have to know that.

"Frederick, if we learn of any reason that she should not be on the bench, we have an obligation to pass that information on to the appropriate parties. We would be doing no more than zealously representing a client. We have an obligation to Cosmos Theopoulis, and, I will suggest, also to the bar."

"Roger, what happens now with this young man, this law clerk, who we've tricked into giving us this information? Do we just throw him to the wolves? From what Otto has told me, he thinks he's likely to be chosen for a lucrative job with some international bank. Do we just abandon him, now that his voice is on a tape player cassette?"

"No, of course not. We try to get him to cooperate with us. For his sake and ours. We use his information, his admissions, to get this case flipped."

"Why would he even consider cooperating with us? We have basically made a fool of him, and, we have no reason to think he won't be loyal to Judge Valdes."

"He'll cooperate because, Frederick, it will be in his interest to talk about the way Valdes conducts herself, in and out of the courtroom. Once this shit hits the fan, Cipriano will need some protection from the brown-out. Simply put, unless we discover something better, we offer him a role like a cooperating witness would have in a criminal trial. If he tries to deny the truth of what he said about her in the Montreal interview, he runs the risk of being accused of slandering her for his own benefit. His future as a lawyer would evaporate. My guess is he'll do most anything to avoid that."

"Perhaps, Roger, perhaps. Of course, if he doesn't cooperate, it could be our careers evaporating. We will be portrayed as having used this young man, having set him up for our own benefit, to get information from him to use against a judge who ruled against our client's interest."

"Well, now that we have that information, let's use it," Roger said. "I insist that we, as members of the bar and counsel to Cosmos Theopoulis, employ an investigator to look into the private life of Judge Zelia Valdes."

Frederick shook his head as he placed the cigar on his desk. "This again, Roger? I've told you my feelings. Yes, you can make one hell of an argument to look into her out of court activity, but let's consider doing this the right way. I'll agree to a complaint with Judicial Oversight. We both recuse, back away, and let the rest of the members do the dirty work, not us."

"C'mon, Frederick, that won't accomplish a damn thing. They'll look at a complaint from us as sour grapes, nothing more. You know how biased the committee is in favor of the bench. And, even if they're at all interested, it will take them forever. This case, and our careers, will be history before they interview their first witness. No, it has to be our baby. And it has to be now."

Frederick harrumphed. "You have raised important issues. I was kind of hoping there was no possible misbehavior on the judge's part. But, perhaps, there could be." Frederick paused as Roger stared directly at him, then said, "Okay, I guess I'll go along."

"I know just the agency for this job," Roger said as he stood and started to turn toward the door, then turned back. "Also, Frederick, I know you don't think your firm has had any court business in front of Valdes, but I'd like you to check its records anyhow. It's possible there was something that you would have no reason to know about. I don't want anything slipping between the cracks."

A small, almost tiny, Jamaican woman dropped a wire basket loaded with fresh cut potatoes into a bin of hot lard, creating a crackling, boiling maelstrom and a puff of smoke. The aroma from the smoking Fryolator drifted from the tiny kitchen throughout the narrow diner. A mini-mountain of French fries piled onto grease-stained towels next to the deep fryer would be replenished regularly over the next three hours.

"Porky Pig's" had morphed into "Double P's" as a result of a copyright suit brought by Warner Brothers against the luncheonette owner in the mid-eighties. Located on a short, dead-end street near Boston's old city hall, Double P's was filling up with the early lunch crowd. A mixture of pin-striped suits and jeans with tool belts took up the swivel stools at the long counter. A half dozen booths along the opposite wall were filling up. The last and seventh booth, furthest from the door and across from the kitchen, was available only to the proprietor, known as Porky, and his invitees.

Porky's reputation went far beyond French fries. He had another specialty - a service that drew the occasional caller to the end booth. His business card read: **Private InvestiGation Services**. It was the unanimous opinion of **PIGS'** clients that its service was the most effective in the city. There was nothing sacred to **PIGS**, no dirt beyond the prying eyes of Porky's cadre of legmen. If the fee was available, so was the information. Often valid, often manufactured, often mixed.

At ten minutes to noon Roger Metcalf walked into Double P's. He glanced to the booth at the end of the room and spied Porky, the *Daily Racing Form* open in front of him. Porky's multiple chins cascaded into the open collar of an Hawaiian shirt. His fleshy, hairless arms extended from short sleeves and rested on the racing sheet. Porky stopped studying the past performances of the entries on today's Patriot Downs race card and looked up at Roger, who had arrived at the booth, briefcase in hand.

"Hey, Counselor. How they hangin'?"

"So, so, Porky. You?"

"Can't complain. Nobody'd listen anyhow. You in for lunch, or business, or both?"

"Business." Roger nodded at the empty bench across the wooden tabletop from the fat man.

"Yeah, sure. Sit down," Porky said.

Through the pass-through window in the kitchen wall, the Fryolator cook, draped with a white apron down to her Nikes, watched Roger slide onto the bench across from Porky. In just moments she placed a plate of French fries between the two men, along with a split bowl holding ketchup and barbecue sauce. The fries were automatic when anyone sat with the boss.

"Thanks, Missy," Roger said. He looked across the table at Porky. "How long has Missy been cooking for you?"

"Thirty years or so. She's the first and only person to touch that original Fryolator. Nobody makes fries the same way. Only Missy and me know the secret ingredient she puts in that oil, and we ain't talkin' - but it's magic, Rog. People love 'em." Porky gestured down the aisle with a hand. "See all these folks? They're all munchin' on Missy's deep-fried taters."

Roger dragged a pair of fries through the ketchup and bit off half.

"Hey, be sure you don't double dip," Porky said, and, accompanied by a loud laugh, slapped the table with his hand. "Got that from a Seinfeld rerun. He's one funny dude, him and that George guy and the rest of 'em. Ever watch 'em, Counselor?"

Roger pinched a napkin from a container and answered as he wiped his mouth. "Sure. Hasn't everyone?"

"Ronald Reagan used to say 'trust, but verify' when dealing with the Commies. You want to double dip? Show me a note from your doctor." Porky heaved into another laugh, this time causing a few diners at the counter to turn in his direction. When he settled back down, he said, "So, Counselor, I bet you didn't come in to be entertained. What's cookin'?"

"Important job, Porky. Not the usual divorce or phony worker's comp claim. Very important people involved. Lots of money."

Porky picked up a fry and asked, "This got to do with that case that's all over the papers? The race track owner, greedy kids, all that shit?"

"That's it."

"Lots of money is kind of an understatement from what I read." Porky pointed at the *Daily Racing Form*. "Even the track sheet's got the story. Anything to appeal?"

"Maybe."

"It seems like those greedy kids maybe got themselves megabucks just for being born. Want a Coke?" Porky said.

"No thanks." The tempo in the luncheonette had increased in just the few minutes since Roger had arrived. Noontime chaos at Double P's provided an added measure of privacy at the back booth. Roger hunched his shoulders and moved into the table, his forearms alongside the plate of fries.

"Porky, we need your top-shelf, top-secret help on this one. This case means one hell of a lot to my future, not just my wallet. We have to tip this case on appeal. I have to win."

"Just what do you need from PIGS, Counselor?"

"The judge, Porky. I need Judge Zelia Valdes deep fried, just like your taters."

Porky paused a few moments, then sat back on the bench and said, "Tall order, a judge. You sure?"

"Anything you can dig up. Anything the least bit unusual. Of course, the nastier the better, and the sooner the better."

Porky grunted and moved back in his seat. "Never know what's out there, Rog. Never know. I got the president of the Back Bay Historical Society - a granny - in the sack with a thirty-year-old city councilor a few years back. Councilor was supposed to be a big time pole smoker, too. Go figure."

"I don't want to tell you how to run your business, Porky. But I have a tip I want you to follow up on."

"Shoot, counselor. Always like to get tips."

"Judge Valdes is supposedly a big art fan. I have information that every now and then she leaves the courthouse during working hours to visit museums around the city. I'm thinking there could be something else she's up to."

"Thinkin' maybe there's a little afternoon delight in her life?"

"Could be. If she's sneaking around to meet someone, instead of staring at some paintings, I want to know who it is, what they're doing and what they're talking about."

Porky was proud of his ability to gauge degrees of desperation. He priced his services accordingly, and seldom lost a client. "No problem, Rog. I'll put my best team on her. You want a twenty-four seven tail, it'll cost. I'll need twenty-five large for a starter."

"You'll have a check within the hour."

Three hours after Keene and Metcalf's retainer check to PIGS cleared, Roger was in his office, feet propped up on a credenza set in front of a window, phone in hand. Four city blocks away, in a glass office tower Frederick Poole answered his direct phone line.

"It's Roger, Frederick."

"Just a moment." Poole looked across the desk and nodded to his secretary who folded her steno pad, stood and left the office. "Did you meet with your investigator, Roger?"

"Yes. He has no qualms about an assignment that involves a judge."

"I'd be surprised if most of these people would have qualms about shadowing the pope. So, the investigator is on the payroll, through a bogus file you've created, of course. God knows we need a few layers of deniability between him and us."

"I want you to be okay with this, Frederick."

"You convinced me it made sense this morning, Roger. Particularly after you mentioned you discovered Judge Valdes's mysterious mid-day sojourns from the courthouse."

"*We*, discovered, Frederick."

"Yes, of course, *we* discovered. I suppose we have no choice. I've even convinced myself of the absurd notion that it may even be malpractice not to look into this."

"We're well within our ethical bounds."

"Ethics have already been sacrificed, Roger. We have a client who has paid us a bloody fortune and is on the warpath. I guess we have no choice, but I don't like it. I don't want to think about it."

"It's what we've agreed to do - whatever the hell it takes to make this case turn out the way it has to, or our careers are reduced to ambulance chasing, at best."

"We still have time to pull the plug on this, Roger. I'm having second, third and fourth thoughts. I think we may have gone way overboard. We could find ourselves disbarred. Me, a former president of the Bar Charities Association. You, a rising star, and on the Ethics Committee. Both of us members of Judicial Oversight. What wonderful role models we make for the young men and women in our profession."

"Stow the sarcasm, Frederick. This case means everything for me. You may be in the twilight of your career, but I'm far from it. God, we're already a laughing stock. A reversal of this judgment will end all of that, will make us heroic, not imbecilic."

"You're exaggerating."

"Frederick, I haven't shared everything Mr. Theopoulis has said to me. I realize that he's an excitable son of a bitch and lawsuits bring out the worst in a lot of people. But this man is a loose cannon. The fact is not only has he threatened to sue us for malpractice..."

"He hasn't a prayer," Frederick interrupted.

"Perhaps not, but he has also vowed to ruin me and you, any way possible. God knows what he's capable of. This case will be our albatross, but I'll be carrying it twenty-five, thirty years longer than you."

"I've faced adversity, Roger. Believe me, life has not been a cake walk. I'll survive this. You'll survive this, even if we go down in flames on appeal." Frederick stood from his chair and slowly shook his head. "No, no. Just talking to you now makes me think we have to reconsider this."

"No! We can't tiptoe around this fucker. We agreed to this course of action!" Roger stood, shouting into the phone. "You agreed! When we first discussed this case your eyes lit up over the millions in fees and the publicity that would be generated. Let's not forget that. We cannot stop now!"

Frederick sat, placed the phone on its cradle and his head in his hands.

22

On the first Saturday of July, a thin man stood in the west cloister of the Isabella Stewart Gardner Museum. He did not appear to be interested in the works of art on display, he did seem a bit agitated. He fiddled with the zipper on his black windbreaker, always worn on the job, regardless of the weather. He wanted to go outside and light up a Lucky Strike, but was concerned that the woman he was tailing would drift away, like the cigarette smoke he craved.

Basil Simeone was also annoyed because his view into the east cloister and of the attractive woman he was watching was partially obscured by stone pillars rimming the courtyard. The sixty-year-old private investigator reached a hand into his jacket pocket and palmed a pack of Luckies. With his other hand he stroked his Vandyke beard, colored, like his neck length hair, to a deep black. He knew a cardinal rule of his profession was to blend into the background, perhaps seen, but not noticed, certainly not remembered. But he liked the beard, and the hair.

Basil had tailed Judge Zelia Valdes during daylight hours the prior Tuesday, Wednesday and Thursday. She had ventured nowhere other than the Suffolk County courthouse and the vendors in her Beacon Hill neighborhood - mini-grocery, antique store, Starbucks. Yesterday, with the courthouse closed for the July fourth holiday, Basil left the judge on her own. Just as well, he thought. It would have been a nightmare to keep tabs on her with the extra tens of thousands in the city for the Pops concert and fireworks along the banks of the Charles. This morning Basil followed a cab that picked the judge up at her condominium building and drove her to the museum, a Venetian style palace in the Fenway section of the city.

Now, late morning sunlight was streaking into the museum's atrium. Zelia, wearing a white blouse tucked into jeans, was appreciating a sarcophagus, its side panel displaying Revelers Gathering Grapes. Her appreciation of the piece was interrupted by a quiet voice.

"Good morning, Judge," Eddie Smelton stepped beside Zelia. A smile appeared on his round face. "It's turned into a nice day."

The judge turned to the museum docent. "Oh, Eddie, good. I was hoping to find you."

"You know my responsibilities, Mom and Isabella," Eddie said as he brushed a few crumbs from the lapel of his navy blazer. "I'm not hard to find."

"Eddie, I'm wondering if your mom would like a visitor today." Zelia paused a moment. "I haven't sat and spoken with her in a while."

Eddie stooped to pick up a discarded gum wrapper, then answered the judge. "I'll be happy to call her and let her know you'll be visiting. You're the only visitor we ever have, and you know you're always welcome."

"Thanks." Zelia smiled and looked at her watch. "One o'clock okay?"

"Sure." Eddie shrugged, smiled and said, "She hasn't got any plans."

"I've been meaning to ask you something, Eddie. It's really none of my business, but the curiosity is killing me. The last few times I've visited with your mom, she's been wearing a jersey with the word braves and a tomahawk stitched across the front. She also wears a baseball cap with a capital B on it. It's real cute, but, if you don't mind my asking, what's it all about?"

"I don't mind your asking, Judge. Mom was a big fan of the old Boston Braves baseball team. Growing up, she lived on Commonwealth Ave, close to Braves Field. She and a bunch of other kids hung around the field and the players a lot. They were called the Knot Hole Gang and they got cheap tickets to the games. It almost killed her when the Braves moved out of Boston in the fifties. About six months ago I found a place that sold old baseball stuff and bought the Braves things for her. She wears them most every day now."

"A true fan," Zelia said.

"I'm proof of that. My full name is Eddie Stanky Smelton. I was born the month after the Braves traded Eddie Stanky. He was their second baseman, and one of Mom's favorites."

Basil had to slow his Saab at the entrance to Storrow Drive to avoid colliding with the roadside railing. As he down-shifted, he kept his eye on the Yellow cab the judge had hailed outside the museum. Her abrupt departure from the Gardner had caught him off-guard, requiring a sprint to the gas station where his car was parked. The private eye had then run two red lights in his pursuit of the cab, finally securing a comfortable following distance just beyond Fenway Park. Once onto Storrow Drive, that ran along the Boston side of the Charles River, Basil settled into the right hand lane, the cab the third car ahead.

Zelia was uncomfortable going to Eddie's home on a Saturday. She wished her visits to be as little known, as private, as possible. Her weekday visits had been risky enough, but she feared that more of the neighbors were likely to be around on the weekends and might notice her arrival or departure. It was a crowded neighborhood, mostly filled with multi-family houses on small lots, alongside a few small, single family houses, such as the Smelton home. She figured residents knew each other and were likely to watch out for one another. Some would be just plain nosy. The last thing she wanted was to raise anyone's curiosity.

But she was willing to chance the Saturday visit. Because of a busy court calender, opportunities to visit the Smelton's home during weekdays had been limited lately. She knew the good work of visiting an elderly, house-bound, demented woman wasn't the only motivation for her trips to the Smelton home. She worked at ignoring the other, non-charitable, motive.

The taxi driver crossed the Charles River over the Anderson Bridge and drove into always bustling Harvard Square. After sitting virtually still in traffic for ten minutes, the cab finally made its way to Massachusetts Avenue on the other side of the square. It then traveled along the busy commercial boulevard towards the working class neighborhood of North Cambridge. Fifteen minutes later the driver pulled to the curb in front of one of the few single-family houses on Rindge Avenue. At just before one o'clock, Zelia climbed out of the cab at a brick walk leading to a small green-shingled house. She stepped through an open gate in a chain-link fence and made her way down the walk a few feet before she veered off the bricks and onto a sloped side yard. Avoiding an upended wheel barrel, she arrived at the cellar door built into the concrete foundation. Zelia pushed a button set in the doorframe and, just moments later, she heard the familiar buzz and the door lock clicked and opened.

The cellar was illuminated, barely, by a pair of high, half-size windows butted to the ceiling. It was familiar territory to Zelia. She crossed the cement floor, dominated by an ancient oil burner, and climbed a narrow staircase. As always, the closed door at the top of the staircase was unlocked. Zelia opened it and stepped into the kitchen. Straight ahead, on the other side of a table and chairs, a hallway led to the rooms at the front of the house. She skirted the kitchen furniture and walked quietly, stopping half way down the hall at a curtained, double-door on her left. It was halfway open. She poked her head into the room.

Eddie's mother, scraggly white hair to her earlobes beneath her Boston Braves baseball cap, sat in a wheelchair parked in front of the room's only window. The elderly woman faced Rindge Avenue as it wended its way westerly from Massachusetts Avenue. Mrs. Smelton was softly singing the words of a nursery rhyme - *'Oranges and Lemons,'* ♫ *say the bells of* ♫ *St Clement's.* As always, the rhyme brought Zelia back to her family, as she had sung and hummed the rhyme and melody to her David often during his infancy. There was a table beside the wheelchair holding playing cards face up and laid out in no discernable pattern. As Zelia took a step into the room, she heard a beep from an automobile horn and watched Mrs. Smelton raise a wrinkled hand. It was a gesture she made to each driver who acknowledged her existence. Zelia heard the soft, singsong voice again: *'You owe me five farthings,'* ♫ *say the bells of St Martin's* ♫*.'*

"Hello, Mrs. Smelton. Nice to see you again," Zelia said.

The elderly woman turned her chair toward the door, just enough to see Zelia. "Oh, hello, Dear. Come right in."

Zelia walked across the room, took a box of penuche fudge from her shoulder bag and placed it on the card table. She then moved a straight chair over a few feet, draped her raincoat across its back and joined Mrs. Smelton near the window.

For almost an hour there was a disjointed discussion between the two women. Their conversation, interspersed with short beeps and returned waves, included Ted Williams not tipping his cap as he rounded the bases after home runs, various painting masterpieces, Braves third baseman Eddie Mathews, and former, long-deceased, US Senator Joe McCarthy - "You know, Dear, even though Milwaukee stole the Braves from us, I think the senator from Wisconsin - I hope he's still alive - is right. I think there are Commies just about everywhere, and I'm worried about that."

At five minutes before two o'clock, Mrs. Smelton said that it was "sleepy time" and she looked forward to another visit, "but after the Jewish holidays or Ramadan, whichever comes first." Eddie's mother was raised a Catholic, and had never set foot in a synagogue or a mosque.

Mrs. Smelton maneuvered her wheelchair away from the window to a darkish spot at the side of the room. *'When will you pay me?' ♫ say the bells of Old Bailey. ♫ 'When I grow rich,' ♫ say the bells of Shoreditch.* She smiled over at Zelia, now standing in the doorway, and said, "I'm thinking you may have a good point about our friends. They may be a little homesick. But, for now, you can still visit them here, right across the hall. Thank you for the penuche, and remember, dear, *Spahn...*"

Without knowing what it meant, Zelia joined in with the balance of Braves' fans' old invocation to the baseball gods, which she had heard from Mrs. Smelton time and time again, *"...and Sain, and pray for rain."*

Carrying her raincoat and shoulder bag, Zelia turned from the room and stepped across the narrow hallway. She stood in front of a door fabricated from steel and laminated in oak paneling. The door had been installed a few years ago when the room was outfitted with humidity control and fireproofed. Zelia pushed down on the brass handle and, silently, the door opened. As always, she felt the incongruous combination of foreboding and ecstasy. She experienced a shiver, and stepped inside.

23

The storekeeper behind the worn counter poked a few keys on the electric cash register and the drawer popped open, its path stopped midway by his pot belly. He placed three twenties in the drawer, withdrew a ten and a couple of ones and handed them to the man with the Vandyke beard. Basil Simeone pocketed his ten dollars change.

"Unbelievable, fifty bucks for a carton of Luckies. I can remember when a pack cost half a buck. They're screwing us for exercising our right to smoke," Basil said. "Watch, pretty soon they'll be taxing the damned hamburgers at McDonald's. Burgers will kill us before these smokes do."

Two days earlier, on Saturday, Basil had sat in his Saab for two hours waiting for Judge Valdes to leave the green-shingled house across the street from Thornton's Neighborhood Grocery. His curiosity in high gear, the private detective had returned to North Cambridge to continue his investigation. He tucked the carton of Luckies under his arm, turned and watched through the storefront window as a kid skidded his bike to a halt in front of the store. Moments later the 12-year-old was through the door and picking a *Herald* off a stack. A wave, accompanied by "Hi, Mr. Thornton.", and he was back out the door and across the street to the green house. Basil watched the youngster drop his bike on the inside of the open gate in the fence, cut across the side yard, and then drop out of view.

"Haven't seen you around these parts before. Need directions or anything?" the storekeeper asked.

Basil ignored the question and asked his own.

"That kid, the one who took the newspaper, he delivers across the street every day?"

"Tommy? Yep. Four o'clock on the dot. Comes in for old Mrs. Smelton. She's stuck in a wheelchair. Just sits by the window all day and waves to the cars that honk their horns coming up Rindge Ave."

Basil stroked his beard. "Oh, now I get it. Was wondering why everyone blows the horn."

"We don't mind it. Poor old gal hasn't got much else in her life. She puts the lights out at eight sharp every night and the noise stops." The storekeeper began to shelve some cans of chicken noodle soup and went on talking to the stranger. "Yeah, Tommy brings the paper over to her like clockwork. Just the other day he said she's starting to smell a little."

"That's too bad," Basil muttered as he glanced at his watch. "The old lady ever get out of the wheelchair?"

"Oh, no, nope. And, the poor soul is scared out of her wits that she'll get caught in a fire."

"Yeah? Why do you say that?"

Thornton rubbed the stubble on his chin for a few seconds, beginning to wonder about the stranger's curiosity. Deciding that he probably just liked to talk, he answered the question.

"Her son, name's Eddie, comes into the store pretty often. He's a real nice guy, kind of a gentle guy, you know? Seems to have been born to take care of his mother. A few summers back there were construction guys over there for two, three weeks. Hell, they had trucks parked on the street all day long. Neighbors, mostly my customers, complained they were taking up all the parking spots. Anyhow, these guys, they'd come into the store for cold drinks and snacks. I asked one of them what they were doing at the Smelton house. Well, long story short, Eddie was having a room fireproofed 'cause his mother's scared as hell of being roasted in a fire during the night."

"She sleeps in the fireproofed room every night?"

"I suppose so. They wouldn't spend all that money and then not use the room, would they?"

"Guess not," Basil said. He considered asking the storekeeper about visitors to the house across the street, but thought better of it. He didn't want to seem too nosy and run the risk of the old guy mentioning him to Eddie. Basil took a few steps toward the door, shook the last cigarette from his pack and lit up with a Bic. He tossed the empty pack into a cardboard box half full of trash and pulled the door open, awakening a small cluster of bells.

The private eye crossed Rindge Avenue to the sidewalk fronting the Smelton house. He looked closely at the sloping side yard where the newspaper kid had disappeared. He saw the door into the cellar and noticed that it was ajar. Basil walked up the street a block to where he'd parked his Saab. He climbed in and moved the sedan closer to the house for a clearer view of the cellar door at the Smelton home. Within a few minutes Tommy emerged carrying a large cookie in one hand, and slammed the door closed behind him with the other. The youngster then checked to be sure it was locked.

At three-fifteen the following afternoon, the waiter working the counter at Double P's nodded goodbye to the pair of hairdressers, the day's final customers, as they stood and walked to the door. He locked up behind them and headed for the mop closet. In the luncheonette's rear booth, Basil Simeone sat across from Porky. With the help of his notes, he was reporting last week's work, finishing with his description of Judge Valdes's Saturday visit to North Cambridge.

"It's about one o'clock when she got there. When she finally came out of the house, through the same cellar door she went in, it's almost two hours later, ten of three."

Porky scratched a few days growth of beard. "Got anything else?"

"Yeah. Yesterday, while the judge was at the courthouse, I checked the books at the Middlesex Registry and at the Cambridge City Hall. The house is owned by an Eddie S. Smelton. It used to be owned by Constance and Andrew Smelton. There's a death certificate on record for Andrew, and a short time after that, a deed from Constance to Eddie. Just a week ago, there was a good size home equity mortgage recorded. The mortgage was signed by Eddie." Basil glanced at the notebook. "The city census for this year has Eddie S. Smelton, fifty-two, docent, and Constance Smelton, eighty-two, retired, living at the address."

"Docent?"

"That's a guide for paintings and stuff in a museum."

"That it, Basil?"

"There's more. It all seemed really weird, you know, the judge leaving the museum to head over to North Cambridge. All the horns blowing when cars drive past the house, like I just told you."

"Yeah," Porky chuckled. "Yeah, Basil, that's weird. What else?"

"Well, yesterday afternoon, after Jonesy showed up to keep an eye on the judge, I went back to North Cambridge to see what the fuck's goin' on. According to the guy that runs a little grocery store across the street from the house, the Smeltons are mother and son. The father died years ago. The old lady can't get out of her wheelchair. She sits by the window all day looking down the street and waves at the cars that honk at her. That's why they honk - to say 'Hi, how you doing?' The honking stops at eight every night and the lights in the room go out."

"Okay. Anything else?"

"Yeah. The store guy told me something that seemed kind of strange, at least to me."

Porky jabbed a toothpick into his mouth. "Try me, Basil.

"Three or so years ago there was a lot of stuff going on over at the house, electricians, sheet rock guys and other kinds of contractors. The store guy says a construction worker came in one day and told him that the old lady was paranoid about getting caught in a fire, being in a wheelchair and all." Porky nodded in a gesture of understanding while Basil flipped a page in his notebook. "Said her son had her bedroom fireproofed, you know, like with firewalls or whatever. Whole thing must have cost a fortune."

"Wonder where the fuck they got that kind of bread." Porky said. He plucked the toothpick from his lips. "That's it?"

"Yeah."

"Anything seem like a coincidence to you?"

"Yeah, this Eddie Smelton works in a museum, and the judge starts out the day at a museum, and then goes to Smelton's house. That what you mean, Porky?"

"You're real sharp, Basil. That's why you get the big bucks. Remember what I told you about coincidences in this business?"

"Yeah. There ain't no such thing."

"Know something else, about the Gardner Museum?" Porky dipped a fry in barbecue sauce, dripping a few drops into his cupped hand as he brought it to his mouth.

"I know about the big heist there about ten years ago. A lot of real famous paintings lifted. I saw pictures of them in a crime magazine a little while back."

"That's right, Basil." Porky licked the sauce off his hand. "The FBI would kill to crack that case. Big reward still out there. Five Million."

Basil whistled softly. "Decent day's pay." He started to stand from the booth. "Want me to stay on the judge?"

"Yeah. Enjoy the scenery. Talk to me next week."

24

The following Saturday Basil peered over the top of his *Herald* as Judge Valdes stepped out the side cellar door of the house on Rindge Avenue. Her visit had lasted a little over an hour. Basil was in his Saab about thirty yards away. He lowered the sun-visor and watched Zelia walk to the sidewalk fronting the house and glance down the street. Shortly, a Cantab taxi pulled to the curb. The driver was quickly out of the cab and opening the rear door for his passenger.

The sense of danger derived from visiting the Smelton home for the second Saturday in a row had made Zelia more alert. On the way over to North Cambridge, this time traveling directly from her Beacon Hill condo in a Yellow cab, she had noticed a black car in the passenger door mirror. It seemed to be behind her cab for most of the twenty minute ride. She thought it may be a Saab, as it looked similar to a car she had considered buying a few months ago. Now, returning home in the Cantab taxi, she also had a view to the rear from the cab's mirror. With a start, she noticed a similar black car. After a couple of turns onto small side streets, her cab turned onto Massachusetts Avenue. She slid up to the front of the vinyl seat, closer to the open Plexiglas window separating her from the driver. She addressed the back of a head rimmed with gray hair.

"Excuse me. Could you pull over at the next phone booth, or at a store where I can find a phone?"

"Don't need to do that lady, here you go." The driver pulled a cell phone from his shirt pocket and reached his hand backwards and into the partition opening. "You can use this one. No charge. A perk for choosing this Cantab."

Zelia frowned. "No offence, but I prefer a pay phone."

"Okay. Your dime. They gotta have a pay phone in Frank's."

As the cab pulled to the curb in front of Frank's Steak House, Zelia turned and watched the black Saab go by and continue down Mass Avenue. Her quick glance at its driver recorded a thin, angular face, long black hair and, was that a beard? She was quickly out of the cab and across the wide sidewalk. Once inside the windowed vestibule, Zelia saw a pay phone. She went through the charade of making a phone call and returned to the cab.

"Thanks, let's go."

"That was fast."

The Saab was stopped a short distance ahead, on Mass Ave, in front of St. John's church. As the cab approached the black sedan, Zelia assumed the driver was waiting for her. As soon as her cab passed the black sedan, she watched in the passenger side mirror as the Saab pulled into the following line of traffic, confirming her suspicion. She would have rather been wrong. "One, seven, nine," she mumbled, storing the first three numbers of the Saab's license plate in her memory.

"Driver, I know it will sound weird, but I've got a funny feeling that the black Saab a few cars back is following us. Can you take a couple of side roads to test my theory?"

"Sure, ma'am. You want me to call the police?"

"No, no. I'm probably just a little paranoid."

When the cab reached Harvard Square, the cabbie drove up and down a pair of side streets, caught the tail end of a green traffic signal on Cambridge Street, and made a right hand turn as the light went yellow. Two blocks down, the cabbie pulled over to the curb.

"He was following us on the side streets 'till the traffic light, then we lost him," the driver said.

Zelia was shaken by the pursuit. In a calm voice that belied her concern, she directed the driver to drop her at a convenience market on Charles Street, a few blocks down the hill from her Beacon Hill home. Fifteen minutes later, the cabbie pulled open the rear door.

"Look, lady, it's none of my business, but that Saab was sure as hell following us. You got somebody at home? If not, I should maybe drop you at a friend's or somewhere else. Who knows, this creep could show up where you live."

Zelia climbed out and stood on the sidewalk. She was a few inches taller than the driver. She had read the trip meter and held out a pair of tens for a nine dollar fare.

"No, thanks. I appreciate your concern, but I'm sure I'm okay." Zelia felt she could trust the driver, and she liked him. "Can I request you when I need a cab? Is that possible?"

"Sure it is." He pulled his wallet from a rear pocket and handed Zelia a few business cards. "Call me anytime, ah..."

"Zelia."

"Yeah, Zelia. Nice name. Call me anytime. Just ask for Walter. If the dispatcher tells you I'm off duty, call my home number. It's on the card, too. I'm either in the cab or at home, right across the river near Lechmere Square. I've always got my cab with me."

Zelia smiled, thankful for the consideration and a little island of security in what suddenly had become a very choppy sea. "Thanks again, Walter," she said and handed him the bills, "and keep the change."

The effort necessary to climb steep Pinckney Street went unnoticed by Zelia, her thoughts zeroed in on the man tailing her. Who? Why? Sure, she was a judge, but if there was a sacrosanct area in this society, it was the judiciary. As she placed her key in the outer door of her condominium building, she admitted to a fear she had known for some five years. Was her involvement with the Smelton family finally emerging from the shadows? Had the Smelton family secret been discovered? Looking at her reflection in the glass panel of the door, she saw the face of a frightened Zelia Valdes.

After double locking her front door, Zelia sat in a winged, high back chair in her front room. Her snow white cat hopped onto her lap, bringing a brief sense of normalcy as she stroked its back. She was usually comfortable being single, being alone. It was a status she knew she could change at will, but, at least up to now, it was a condition she preferred. But finally, she needed someone to turn to. She was convinced her worry was reasonable. She was being followed. And whoever it was had seen her enter and leave the Smelton home. She couldn't ignore this. And, she realized, it wasn't just she who could be in trouble, in danger, but so could Eddie and his mother.

Even before today's incident with the Saab, Zelia knew she needed help, most of all, she needed advice, counsel. Was she doing the right thing? Of course, she had thought of Jack Ralston first. He would be there for her in a moment. But she loved Jack too much to involve him in this area of her life. It would be grossly unfair to him. Jack was in the midst of one of the most admired and important legal and public service careers in the city. To present him with the dilemma of choosing between his love for her, and exercising unfettered judgment on what was the right thing for her to do was out of the question. No, she would not subject him to that.

Fortunately, there was someone else. A man who had played a huge roll in her life. A person she also loved, but in a different way, and whose judgment would not be in danger of being swayed by personal feelings. Zelia knew she could rely on him, as she had in the past. A phone on a nearby desk was within her reach. Her call was answered in the leafy Boston suburb of Wellesley.

"Bettinger residence."

"Could I speak with Judge Bettinger? Please tell him it's Zelia Valdes."

Moments later, the former Federal Appeals Court judge and recently retired head of the Massachusetts Public Defender's Office was on the phone. "Zelia? It's nice, and unusual, to hear from you. Is everything okay?"

"Thank God you're home, Judge. I don't really know how to answer your question. I won't keep you on the phone, but I'd like to see you soon. Could you arrange to see me, preferably today or tomorrow?"

"Of course I'll see you. Today is possible if need be, but I have guests, and so I'd prefer tomorrow."

"Oh, tomorrow would be great."

"How about..."

"William," Zelia interrupted, "pardon my being so secretive, but I just don't know what to think right now. Without mentioning where, can we meet at that little restaurant we used for informal office functions? You remember the place?"

"Yes," there was concern in William's voice. "I know the place you mean."

"I know it's open on Sundays."

"Zelia, you've really got me concerned now. Do you need protection? I can have the Boston police at your apartment in two minutes. And, as a judge, you know you have the State Police at your beck and call."

"No, William. I'll be fine. But I would like to see you tomorrow."

"Yes, of course. What time?"

Zelia recalled her noontime swearing in at the governor's office. "Do you recall the time of day I was sworn into the superior court?"

"Yes. It was ..."

"Is that time of day okay with you?" Zelia interrupted.

"Yes. You're sure I can't do anything for you now?"

"No. I'll be fine. I'll see you tomorrow. Thank you, William."

Zelia placed the phone back on its cradle. Her hand was shaking. She set her head against the chair back and considered her decision to involve her former boss and mentor at the Public Defender's Office.

William Bettinger was held in the highest esteem by the judicial and political hierarchy in both state and federal circles. During his tenure at the First Circuit, United States Court of Appeals, his name had appeared on a short list for appointment to the United States Supreme Court on two occasions. When the election of a new president dashed any realistic hope for the country's highest court, the independently wealthy widower surprised the legal community by resigning from the bench to accept the position as chief counsel of the Massachusetts Public Defender's Office. It was in that office eight years ago that Zelia Valdes fell under his avuncular charm. His concern for her after she had lost her family had touched her like little else in her life. His guidance and mentoring had been invaluable. Since that fateful day, William Bettinger was one of the few persons to whom she had even spoken the name of her Davids, her lost loves.

Zelia stood at her desk and looked through a large front window. An enclosed garden was separated from the brick sidewalk by black iron fencing. She was near tears. She was certain her future was in jeopardy. She was frightened.

25

Sunday morning was perfect - sunny, dry and warm - as the summer humidity was waiting for mid-day to overtake the city. Zelia walked from her condo to attend the nine o'clock Mass at the Paulist Center, on Park Street across from the Boston Common. Although her faith was far from bedrock, the Center had helped to bring her back to life after the loss of her husband and son. She had great respect for the Center. The short walk was usually a pleasant experience, particularly in nice weather, but this trip was a burden. Zelia could not shake her concern about being followed. She studied other walkers as she made her way over the hill from her condominium to Beacon Street, and on to the center.

Before Mass, as the informally dressed worshipers filed into the Chapel of the Holy Spirit, Zelia continued to look about for the man she was sure had been following her, but no one was worth a second glance. Her attention was finally focused on a young woman wearing jeans and a red tee shirt who began to play a piano introduction to the opening hymn. The congregation - a mixture of young and old, white and shaded, stodgy and curious - began to sing *Hear I Am, Lord*, and Zelia wondered if the Lord of Sea and Sky might be available to assist in the battle against whatever crisis had befallen her.

The combination of the setting and the music prompted Zelia's inner feelings to take center stage. She had convinced herself that the unreal situation that had dropped into her lap over the last few years, and, yes, her handling of that situation, was being nudged toward a public, sunlit area, and the heat from that sunlight was about to ignite an explosion. What was left of her spirit, of any hope she harbored for the future, which had been carefully salvaged and nurtured with the help a few wonderful friends, was threatened.

When the procession of priest, deacon and a pair of altar boys reached the altar enclosure, as if directed by an unseen maestro, the congregation quieted and ceded the vocal to a fellow worshiper's strong, melodious voice heard from the rear of the chapel. None turned to discover the source of their pleasure, but rather smiled and enjoyed the uplifting solo that flirted with perfection. Zelia, along with a few others in the congregation, shed tears.

Following the service Zelia had no desire to stop on Charles Street for coffee and a pastry, which she often did, but rather headed directly home. After changing into slacks and a tailored dress shirt, she sat at her kitchen counter and sipped coffee. She wondered if, perhaps, paranoia had overtaken her. Then she recalled someone once joking that being paranoid doesn't mean you're not being followed. She was anxious for noon to arrive, to rendezvous with William. At eleven-fifteen she called Walter's cab and arranged to be picked up at the bottom of the hill. Twenty minutes later Walter's brown and white taxi, gleaming with beaded water from a fresh wash, rolled to the curbside in front of the convenience store on Charles Street.

Walter stepped out and smiled broadly. "Good morning, Zelia. You're lookin' a little less worried today." He held open the rear door.

"Looks can be deceiving, Walter," Zelia quickly climbed into the cab. "Keep your eyes open for our friend. He probably doesn't take Sundays off."

"Where we headed?"

"Guys and Dolls Bistro, Harrison Ave, South End."

"I know it. How long do you figure you'll be?"

"I'm not really sure. Maybe about an hour. Could be more."

"I'll wait for you. I'm off at noon, and so's the meter."

"No, Walter. I don't want you to have to hang around for me. Thanks, but I can call you when I'm done."

"It's okay. I can read my book while I'm waiting, or put some wax on the cab. I'd just go home and do the same thing. Sundays are always slow."

"Okay, Walter. Thank you."

Zelia found William seated at a table against the far wall in the half-full dining room. She was pleased to see that the tables on either side of him were empty. He stood as his hand brushed back a full head of white hair, came around the table, and greeted her with a long hug. When he released her, Zelia took in his open neck, sky blue dress shirt, gray slacks and black linen blazer.

"How is it, William, that you always look so crisp and refreshing, like a cool drink on a hot summer day?"

"Let's not talk about me, Zelia Valdes. I'm very concerned about your problem, whatever it may be," the tall, gray-eyed Bettinger said, "but I will say it's not being taken out on your appearance. You look wonderful."

Zelia sat beneath a life-size mural of gaudily dressed gangsters cheering home their favorites at a racetrack. William sat across from her and hailed a nearby waiter. Small talk filled the void while waiting for a pair of Bloody Marys. Once delivered, Zelia stirred her drink and took a sip.

"William, I don't want to be melodramatic about this meeting, but I am going to ask that you advise me legally. In other words, I am speaking to you now as my lawyer. Is that agreeable?"

"Are you about to tell me something that I might otherwise be forced to repeat from a witness stand?"

"It's possible, and I'd never want to hand you that dilemma."

"I'm still a member of the Massachusetts bar and am honored to be your lawyer. The last thing I'd ever want is to be forced to testify against your interest, even though I can't imagine that circumstance. Okay, Zelia, the attorney-client privilege is firmly in place. Now, tell me what you could possibly be involved in that might require my legal advice." William leaned back in his chair.

Zelia took a couple of deep breaths, and then responded.

"When I lost my family, my two Davids, nine years ago, my life ended. I had no desire at all of bringing it back in any meaningful way. As you know, William, I seriously considered suicide. You were there for me. It is not an exaggeration to say that you rescued what little was left and put me back together."

"That's an enormous and unnecessary compliment, Zelia. I know of your gratitude. I am also aware of your strength, your determination.

Watching you go on from that unspeakable tragedy to a life of selfless public service is more than full payment."

"Your generosity always amazed me, and still does. Now, William, I'm going to call on you again." Zelia paused while she stirred her drink with a celery stalk. "I discovered just yesterday that I'm being followed."

"Followed?"

"Yes, at least I was yesterday. I'm certain of it."

"Was that the first time this has happened?"

"I can't say, but I'm beginning to think I may have seen this man in other places, on other days. Then I think it's just my imagination. But yesterday I know he was there, and I know he was following me."

"This is a police matter, Zelia," William said, alarm in his tone. "The State Police should be called. It is most likely related to a case you've heard, possibly has to do with a sentence handed down. Is there anything on your calendar that you think was likely to have prompted this?"

"Everything, I suppose. You always told me that every case is critical to every party involved. I certainly saw that at the Public Defender's Office, and as a prosecutor before that. And I've seen from the bench that there are no indifferent cases, they're all emotional."

William sipped his drink, and then carefully set it in the center of his cocktail napkin. "I've read in the paper of the Theopoulis family case, saw that you were presiding. Scads of money involved. Enough to make some people desperate."

"I spent the better part of a sleepless night sifting through matters I've sat on. Yes, the Theopoulis case has huge amounts of money involved, but what would anyone following me be looking for? My life, my personal life, isn't relevant to the case."

William scratched at his forehead. "No, of course not, unless..."

"Unless what?"

"Well, unless there was some thought of, well, blackmail." Bettinger raised his hands toward Zelia. "I certainly don't mean to suggest that..."

"It's okay, William. Even if the possibility of blackmail was a motivation before or during the case, that was then. My involvement with the case is over. If they discovered, or rather, let's make that invented, some horrific behavior in my past, what good would it do them now?"

"I can't say exactly, if at all. But there can be substantial post-trial activity – motions for reconsideration, arguments on appeal, these are matters that come immediately to mind."

"Of course," Zelia said. "I'm just not thinking straight."

"Desperate people will look for anything they think they can use. And lawyers, even the most ethical, can't always control their clients."

"William, the truth is, in addition to wondering who may be doing this, and why, I'm very concerned about where I went when I was followed. This takes a little explaining." Zelia sipped her drink, took a breath, and then continued.

"One of the clients I represented at the Public Defender's Office was named Eddie Smelton. Eddie was accused of shop-lifting neckties in Filene's Basement. My representation of Eddie created a curious dilemma after the case was over. I went to you with a question about it back then. I don't expect you to recall what, I am sure, seemed a run-of-the-mill ethical matter."

"And you're right, I do not recall."

"I asked you if an attorney-client relationship could be created if it was only the purported client who assumed that the relationship existed. If the client then went on to reveal certain things about his criminal activity, was the attorney then bound by the rule of confidentiality of private communications regarding the information volunteered?"

William nodded. "It's coming back. I think my response was along the lines that there can not be a unilateral decision made by the would-be client that he or she is represented, unless the client has a reasonable belief that the relationship is in place. Then we got into what makes that belief reasonable in the mind of the client, including whether or not the relationship can be inferred from the conduct of the attorney and client, and other elements."

"Yes, and those elements could be prior representation, a request for legal information, and other things, such as how sophisticated the client is."

"Sounds right, Zelia. Rings a bell."

"Now, let me fill you in on the details of that situation with Eddie, and what has gone on ever since."

"What do you mean, 'gone on ever since'?"

"First, a little background. Fine art has always been a passion of mine, from the time I was a little girl in Miami. I was an art history major at Wellesley. I spent most of my spare time from my studies at the various museums around the city. Of course, the Museum of Fine Arts got a lot of my time, but I fell madly in love with the Isabella Stewart Gardner Museum."

"That's easy to understand. It's one of the city's jewels."

"Any afternoon, William, rain, sun, snow, I was likely to be found at the Gardner. I was drawn particularly to the masterworks - Rembrandt, Vermeer. I was simply mesmerized by them, and they were set off so beautifully in that wonderful building."

"You must have been devastated by the theft of those masterpieces in, what, 1991? And, they're apparently lost forever, after being missing for so long," William said.

"It was 1990, and yes, I was devastated. It was a sad day for the art world. Things of great importance and beauty were taken away from the public."

"What, Zelia, could this possibly have to do with anything?"

Zelia looked up from the table, her attention drawn by the approaching hostess carrying oversized menus.

"Hi folks," the waitress said as she approached the table. "There's a party of six waiting for a table. Would you mind moving over to the table to your left so I can push these other two tables together with yours?"

Before William had a chance to respond, Zelia answered. "Actually, we just remembered that we have to be somewhere. We'll be going right along if you'd please have our waiter bring the check."

Minutes later Zelia walked arm and arm with Judge Bettinger up Harrison Avenue. "I'm sorry about the sudden decision to leave the restaurant, William. I didn't expect it to be crowded so early on a Sunday. I thought we could have a private conversation."

"It's a perfect day for a walk with a beautiful woman. By the way, what's with the cab driver you stopped to speak with?"

"That's Walter. He's Boston's version of a guardian angel. I was in his cab yesterday when I realized I was being followed. He volunteered to be available when I need him. I have no car, so it makes sense. He's really very nice."

"Go on with your story, please, Zelia. I cannot imagine how loving art played into your being followed by someone."

"This may be a stretch, but I feel I can discuss what I learned from Eddie Smelton with you because you and I were both part of the office then. The client wasn't just relying on me, but on the whole of the Public Defender's Office. Do you agree?"

Without hesitating, William said, "I'll accept being bound, along with you, under the attorney-client privilege regarding anything Mr. Smelton told you. Go on, please, Zelia."

"Eddie was back then, and still is, a docent at the Gardner Museum. His mother has been confined to a wheelchair for fifteen, twenty years. Eddie cares for her during virtually all of his non-working hours."

The couple stopped at a curb and, unlike most others sharing the sidewalk, waited for the walk signal to flash.

"All this is related to your being followed yesterday?"

The signal changed and Zelia and William started across the street.

"I'll get to the point very soon. Forgive me for the background. I need to give you whatever information I have so you will understand what I have done."

"What do you mean, Zelia, 'what I have done'?"

"Hear me out, please, William, and you'll understand my concern."

The couple suddenly stopped and froze as a pair of skateboarders whizzed by on either side of them. Danger passed, they continued to walk.

"The jury acquitted Eddie of the shoplifting charge after deliberating for only fifteen minutes. The problem started after the trial."

"After? How could that be?" William asked.

"Apparently, Eddie was impressed with my lawyering. He said that, because I was his lawyer, he wanted to show me something important he had in his house, and then he would ask me about it. Eddie is a likable guy, William. And even though he has a great knowledge and appreciation of the art at the Gardner, he seems very naïve in other, more ordinary areas. Yes, the shoplifting case was over, but I didn't want to hurt his feelings, so I agreed to meet him at his house later the same afternoon. It never occurred to me to tell him that my legal representation had actually ended with the jury's verdict."

Zelia and William stopped walking and sat on a slatted bench facing the street. Zelia noticed Walter wave from his cab as he pulled into the curbside a few car lengths ahead.

"Your guardian angel doesn't seem to trust me," Bettinger said.

"Overly protective, I guess. Back to my story, to my visit to Eddie's home in North Cambridge. It has dominated a huge part of my life, William. I'm sure you will understand why that is once I've told you what happened.

"It was a cold December day, late-afternoon, when I arrived at his small home. Eddie and I sat in the kitchen with cups of tea. His mom was asleep in one of the front rooms. Then in a very meek voice, Eddie told me he actually had stolen some things, but they weren't neckties from Filene's Basement."

"The plot thickens."

"Does it ever. Does it ever. Eddie asked what the time limit was, meaning the statute of limitations, for stealing. I told him it depends, like most things in the law, on the circumstances. That there are different kinds of stealing, and other related crimes, such as possessing and selling stolen goods, etcetera. He then asked if what he had stolen was worth a lot of money, would that make a difference, and I explained the difference between misdemeanor and a felony theft. Then, William, he asked me if I wanted to see what he had stolen."

William turned to Zelia. "Normal curiosity would have you wanting to find out what he was talking about."

"Yes, and I was curious. I didn't know if Eddie had stolen a candy bar from the Seven Eleven, or a diamond necklace from Shreve's. We left our teacups on the kitchen table and I followed him down a short hall leading to the front of the house. Eddie stopped at a door on the right side of the hall, pushed it open, turned on a light switch, and stood aside. I stepped into the room." Zelia paused and drew a deep breath. She looked directly into William's eyes. "The moment is singed in my memory. I was stunned. A painting was hanging on the wall ten feet across from where I stood. It was Rembrandt's masterpiece, *The Storm on the Sea of Galilee*. William, I was in the presence of the stolen Gardner Museum masterpieces. They were hung on the walls of the room I had walked into. The room had been turned into a makeshift gallery."

Bettinger stared back at Zelia, his mouth agape, and then spoke in a whisper, virtually mouthing the words.

"The stolen Gardner Museum paintings? In a house in North

Cambridge? Oh, my God." William suddenly understood Zelia's burden. "You've known the whereabouts of the stolen masterpieces for years, and you've stood silent, because of the circumstances under which you discovered them."

"What should I have done, William? What could I have done? Eddie thought I was his lawyer and I assumed that I, at least probably, was his lawyer. Therefore, whatever he brought to my attention was done in confidence."

"Did you attempt to persuade this Eddie fellow to, at the least, get the art back to the museum?"

"Of course."

"Oh, I'm sorry, Zelia. That question was out of order. I know that's exactly what you would do."

"Don't apologize, William. This isn't your standard ethical dilemma. In my attempt to persuade Eddie to make anonymous arrangements to return the art, I offered to help, to do whatever was needed, financially or otherwise. I've been maintaining that offer since I discovered the paintings five years ago. Eddie continues to have none of it. When he brought the paintings home, as he put it, his mom's life suddenly changed, had meaning. She was happy. Eddie told me that she spent the early mornings and the end of her day in the room with the paintings. In the meantime, she sat in her wheelchair at a window in her bedroom and waved to the occasional driver who recognized her existence with a beep of his car's horn. William, that very same routine continues today, thirteen years later."

William stood, his attention riveted on the seated Zelia, and said, "His mother? He stole millions and millions of dollars in masterpieces so his mother could have a private art show?"

"Yes, I know it's hard to believe, but it's true, William. He told me he intends to return all of the artwork to the museum, but only after his mother no longer lives at home with him, either because he is unable to care for her or, of course, her death."

"My God. This is incredible."

"Eddie told me it was very easy to accomplish. He said that it was as if he was invited into the museum that night. He acted as if the robbery itself wasn't a major happening in his life. Perhaps because he was so familiar with the museum, and he never thought his mother would refuse to agree to let him return the paintings. She is a demented art lover. She had dementia then, and it's much more severe now.

Judge Bettinger was quiet a moment, and then said, "You know, Zelia, it sounds like the docent may have hand-picked what was taken from the museum for his mother."

"Perhaps that's why so many other, priceless pieces were untouched."

"I think that's very likely." William raised his hands and rubbed his temples.

"Are you okay, William?"

"Yes, yes. I still get migraines on occasion, and this is one of them. I'm sorry, Zelia, but I'm not sure I can absorb anymore this afternoon. These headaches are debilitating, and prevent me from thinking clearly. God knows, we need clear thinking. Is there a good time and place to see you during the week?"

Zelia stood, disappointed that her meeting was ending so abruptly. "Could you come by my chambers at the Suffolk courthouse? Fifth floor, second session. It's as private as I want it to be. I usually end the trial day about four o'clock."

"I'll be there Tuesday at four, if that's okay."

"I'll expect you then."

William cast a glance toward the nearby taxi. "I see your friend is still waiting. My driver is waiting back at the restaurant for me. I'll walk back by myself. Be careful." He bent into Zelia, kissing her on the cheek, "Call me whenever you'd like, and give serious consideration to police protection."

Walter's taxi turned onto Charles Street just as a downpour swept up from the Charles River, soaking Beacon Hill.

"What do you say I take you right to your doorway, Zelia. You'll get drenched walking up Pinckney."

"Okay, Walter. Thanks. My address isn't exactly a secret anyhow."

A minute later the cab had climbed the side of Beacon Hill and pulled into the curb in front of Zelia's brownstone condominium building. She looked into the front of the cab and noticed that the trip meter wasn't on. "What are the damages, Walter?"

"Don't worry about it now. I'll figure it out and charge you the next trip. I'm off company time, so it's only my business."

"Okay, but don't cheat yourself. I'll be calling again. You're my exclusive transportation."

Zelia stepped out of the cab and raced through the rain, up the steps to her front door. As she inserted the key, she turned back and waved at Walter, signaling him that she was home safely. Further up Pinckney, she noticed a pair of windshield wipers making an intermittent sweep. They were attached to a black Saab.

26

Basil Simeone arrived at Cambridge City Hall at mid-morning. A janitor directed him to the Building Department where he spotted a hanging sign marked PERMITS. Moments later a clerk, identified as Al Sullivan by his name tag, placed a bundle of papers on a counter in front of Basil. Reading upside-down with experienced ease, Sullivan detailed the single-spaced document on top.

"Renovation permit, issued in February, 1998, firewalls and electrical work, twenty-three thousand, permit fee, one twenty-six fifty. Is that what you were looking for?"

"Yeah ..." Basil looked up at the clerk, spotting the name tag, "Al, I think so. Is the contractor listed?"

The clerk turned the permit over and read, "Trowbridge Construction. Porter Square."

"Still in business?"

"Sure are. They're in here squawking all the time," the clerk leaned across the counter and added in a quiet voice, "and, they never give the real cost of the work. See, the permit fee is based on the cost of the job, five-fifty a thousand. I'd bet dollars to doughnuts that this job cost was at least double the twenty-three grand. Probably charged the homeowner what the permit fee should be, and pocketed the difference."

"Shit, Al, can't trust anyone these days. What are these other papers?"

The clerk moistened the tip of an index finger and turned up the papers attached to the permit. "Mostly inspection certificates, specs. Take a look. Here's the floor plan for all the construction they did."

"I've been out there," Basil said as he scratched his Vandyke. "Lotta dough for that place."

An hour later, Basil had finished interviewing the manager at the tiny office of Trowbridge Construction Company. Cheryl had been friendly and cooperative. Right off the bat she confided that she loved Vandyke beards and had just broken up with her boyfriend. She was happy to retrieve the old file and provide information on the North Cambridge fire-proofing job. Basil, who had identified himself with one of his usual aliases - adjuster for Metro Home Insurance - left the office with a copy of the invoice for labor and materials, and Cheryl's phone number, which he was quick to discard. Tinted red hair did nothing for him.

After walking over to a Dunkin Donuts shop across the street from the contractor's office, Basil returned to his Saab, which he'd parked in the nearby Star Market lot in Porter Square. The investigator placed his coffee cup in the dashboard holder, opened his notebook, and pressed the red button on his tape recorder. The mini-cassette he'd drop off at Double P's would play back the following words:

This is really kind of weird, Porky. It's Monday morning, eleven o'clock. The judge is at the courthouse in the middle of a trial, so I ducked out and went over to the building department at Cambridge City Hall. I was following up on what that grocery store guy told me about the work that was done a few years ago on the house in North Cambridge that the judge visits.

In 1998 the owner pulled a building permit for renovations. The permit says firewalls and electrical. That's all. No explanation. The work is listed as costing twenty-three thou, but I know that contractors always low-ball the real cost 'cause the permit fee is cheaper and they can make a few extra bucks. I checked the paperwork real close and saw that it listed the contractor, Trowbridge Construction. Their office is over in Porter Square. So I went there to see if I could learn exactly what the hell they did at the house.

The job took three weeks and was very unusual. Heavy duty firewalls installed in one of the rooms in the house, and an air-conditioning system for the same room. Pork, the rest of the house could have burnt to the ground, and this room would've been left standing like Clinton's cock. The floor plan shows it as a converted dining room. It was finished with hardwood floors and ceiling and wall lighting.

According to the invoice, the job ran just under fifty G's. But here's the kicker - the entries on the payment ledger show that the job was billed to, and paid by – you're gonna love this – the one and only Zelia Valdes, the very same judge I've been tailing. By the way, it took Ben Franklin's help to get the info out of the contractor's office. When that shows up on my bill, you'll know why.

27

Kate Rosenfield smiled when she saw the caller ID screen on her phone. She only knew one person at the Suffolk County courthouse. "Hi, Tony, what's going on?"

"How about lunch in town?" the law clerk responded as he sat at a desk in a small windowless room off the fifth floor lobby. Tony had paused from redrafting a proposed ruling on a bench trial while the judge was in the courtroom hearing arguments on motions.

"You're on."

"Great. I got a letter from the London bank I want to tell you about."

"Really. What's it say?"

"I'll tell you in person. There's a little lunch counter down by the old city hall. It's called Double P's. Best French fries in the city. Take the Red Line to Downtown Crossing. I'll meet you at the Washington Street **T** exit. Can you hold off 'till a little after one?"

Tony and Kate entered the narrow luncheonette and sat across from each other at a booth halfway down the aisle.

"So, this is the famous Double P's?" Kate said, looking around the eatery.

"Yeah, at least its French fries are famous. I used to come in with guys on my high school hockey team once a week for the fries and a few hot dogs."

"Sounds good to me. My stomach likes to go slumming on occasion."

A slight woman, white hair nestled in a brown hair net, appeared at the table. "What'll it be?"

"Two dogs for me, one for my friend, fries for both of us, and a Coke for me, Missy."

"Coke, too," Kate said, and Missy started toward the kitchen. "You know the waitress?"

"Actually, she's mostly a cook. Been here as long as I've been coming in."

"So, tell me, Tony, has the London bank offered you the job?"

"I think they're about to." Tony slid a folded letter across the table and smiled while Kate read the first paragraph.

"Congratulations! That's great!"

"Not yet, Kate. The letter says this Mr. Mortimer wants to see me again. This Friday, lunch at the Ritz-Carlton, here in Boston."

"I see they're still going first class. Lunch has got to be just a formality, Tony, to go over some details. You're home free." Kate paused a moment, then asked, "Will you take the job?"

"I think so. The letter says I'd be based in Boston. At the interview they talked about the salary range. To be honest, I never dreamed I'd ever see the low end. I've kind of decided a career in international banking law looks pretty good. I'm really excited about this, Kate. If they offer the job, how can I turn it down?"

"They will, they will." Kate stood, leaned across the table and gently squeezed the sides of Tony's head, drawing him up and towards her. She kissed his lips and sat back down.

"Thanks, Kate," a flustered Tony said.

A few minutes later, Missy arrived at the table carrying two oversize plates holding hot dogs tucked into buns and drowning in a sea of French fries. "Cokes will be right up."

"We have to speculate on what will happen at lunch on Friday, and then figure out a strategy that will wrap this bank right around your finger," Kate said.

"I figure...." Tony paused as he looked up at a tall man with a narrow black beard making his way down the aisle.

"What is it?" Kate asked as the man passed the table.

"Ah, nothing. Just that that guy looks kind of familiar. I remember the beard. I've seen him around the courthouse or somewhere. Okay, Kate, how am I going to handle phase two of my interview?"

"You know, Tony, at this stage, I don't think you prepare. Just put on your best suit and charm the hell out of them. I'll be at home from noon on Friday. You have to call me after your luncheon."

Tony smiled and pushed the end of a hot dog into his mouth.

Roger Metcalf arrived at Wiggins, Lewis & Poole at about one-thirty, twenty minutes after Frederick's phone call, and took a chair across the desk from him. He loosened his tie and asked, "Okay, what have you got that has me racing over here?"

"You asked me to check if our firm had ever been involved with Judge Valdes in any way, Roger. Because we do not represent clients in the state criminal courts, I was surprised to find out there was an exception. It was a matter that involved both Judge Valdes and her law clerk, Mr. Cipriano."

"Really? How could Cipriano have been involved?"

"In a way, his involvement was after the fact. It was about six months ago and concerned the daughter of an important client. She had been involved in a minor drug situation a number of years ago. The charge was disposed of by pleading to something insignificant to her then, but it resulted in a criminal record. When she applied for a position at the National Security Agency last year, she was told that her criminal history disqualified her. However, apparently the NSA wanted her talents badly enough to give her the opportunity to do whatever was necessary to clean up the record."

"Petition to expunge?" Roger asked.

"Yes, that's what it's called, and the firm filed the petition on her behalf."

"And why is this important in the Theopoulis case?"

"I'm not sure it is, Roger, but here goes. My information comes directly from the paralegal involved in the matter. Judge Valdes allowed the petition to expunge the criminal record, which was unopposed, but for some unknown reason, she never signed the accompanying court order. Best guess is someone in the court clerk's office dropped the ball. In any event, the judge's signature line was left blank when the court order was mailed out to our office. We were in a hurry to provide the document to the client, so, when we noticed the order wasn't signed, we sent the paralegal over to the courthouse with the document to secure the Judge's signature on it.

"Court wasn't in session, so an assistant in the clerk's office called the judge's chambers. This was on a Wednesday. Judge Valdes wasn't there, but her law clerk, Mr. Cipriano, was. He came to the counter and explained that Judge Valdes was in Florida, and would not be back in the courthouse until the following Monday. Our paralegal showed him the unsigned document and explained that it was very important to a client for a signed order to be available immediately. Waiting until the following Monday could be a disaster. She mentioned that her head was likely to roll if she returned without the signed order.

According to our paralegal, Mr. Cipriano looked at the document and said he remembered the hearing. He told her that the case docket had been impounded because the paperwork referenced a government agency that required confidentiality, and that the hearing was held in a closed courtroom. He recalled that Judge Valdes verbally allowed the petition to expunge after the brief, uncontested hearing. Our paralegal said Cipriano could not have been nicer or more cooperative. She recalls his saying 'no harm, no foul.' "

Roger stood up and smiled. "I think I know what you're going to say, and I think I like it."

Frederick looked up at Roger, hesitated, and then slid a document across the desk. "Here's a copy of the court order from our files. Mr. Cipriano signed, that is, forged, the judge's signature on the original, official document. That is now buried somewhere in the bowels of the National Security Agency. The paralegal is very concerned about this. She said she hopes the law clerk won't get in any kind of trouble because he did her a favor."

Roger reached for the document and looked at the forged signature. He then asked, "Frederick, does your firm have access to a hand-writing expert?"

28

A bemused expression lit William Bettinger's face when the piercing alarm sounded. He came to a quick halt, just beyond the arch of the metal detector.

"Any keys, coins, other metals?" asked the courthouse security guard.

"Ah, keys, I think, ma'am." Bettinger answered, searching his pockets.

As the guard approached Bettinger, detector wand in hand, a mostly bald man carrying a briefcase walked the same path through the detector. He paid no heed to the alarm his appearance had triggered, but stopped behind Bettinger who was stretching his arms outward.

"Cheryl," the bald man addressed the guard, "you don't have to be concerned about this guy. He's no terrorist."

The guard recognized the man toting the briefcase, a regular at the Suffolk County courthouse. "You vouch for him, Mr. Kirk, it's good enough for me."

"Not to worry, he's okay." Kirk turned to Bettinger. "What brings you to our humble courthouse, Bill? Making a comeback?"

"Hi, Ed. Thanks for the character reference. No comeback planned, just a quick stop to say hello to an old friend."

Kirk patted Bettinger on the back. "Gotta run before the clerk's office closes on me. Nice seeing you, Bill. Call me for lunch and, next time, leave your gun at home."

The elevator deposited Judge Bettinger into a crowded fifth floor lobby. It was a few minutes after four o'clock and a pair of courtrooms had just emptied of lawyers, litigants, witnesses and jurors, their business concluded for the day. Bettinger crossed the lobby and entered the courtroom marked 2nd Criminal Session. He walked to the front of the room and knocked on the door to the judge's chambers. A young man in shirtsleeves opened it. Beyond him, standing behind her desk, Judge Valdes smiled and welcomed her visitor.

"Hello, Judge. Say hello to my clerk, Tony Cipriano. Tony, this is Judge William Bettinger."

Tony recognized the name, recalling that he had actually studied decisions from the First Federal Circuit authored by Judge Bettinger. He shook the judge's extended hand.

"It's nice to meet you, sir. I'm just on my way out." Tony turned back to Judge Valdes and said, "I'll be in at eight tomorrow for those early arguments, Judge."

"See you, Tony," Zelia said, and then paused momentarily. "And, Tony, let's keep Judge Bettinger's visit under wraps, okay?"

"Sure, Judge. No problem."

The door closed behind Tony.

"Seems like a nice young man."

"He is, and a very good law clerk," Zelia said. "A little moody sometimes, but aren't we all? I was hoping Tony would be gone before you arrived, but I'm comfortable that he'll keep your visit quiet."

"I don't see a problem even if he mentions it. It's hard to think anyone should be at all interested in my stopping by to say hello to my protégé."

Zelia sat at her desk, William taking the chair across from her. "I think my paranoia is growing, William."

"Why do you say that, Zelia?"

"It could be my imagination, but when I went home on Sunday after our meeting, I think I saw the same car that followed my cab on Saturday."

"My, God, Zelia. Are you sure?"

"Pretty much. There was someone sitting in it, with a clear view of my condominium."

"By any chance did you notice the plate number?"

"No. The car was facing my apartment, and it didn't have a front plate. Wait, William, on Saturday I did get the first three numbers of the car's plate – one, seven, nine."

"That's a good start. Massachusetts tags?"

"Yes I think so. I would have noticed if not."

"I'm on the verge of calling the State Police. Can you give me any good reason not to do that?"

"I want you to hear the full story, William." Zelia said as she pushed a paperweight around the surface of her desk. "Then we can decide what to do."

"Go ahead and tell me, Zelia. Exactly what is the full story?"

Zelia took a deep breath. "As I told you, near Christmas of 1998 I discovered the masterpieces taken from the Gardner Museum at Eddie's home. My problem, of course, isn't only that I could have just picked the phone up and have the paintings recovered, but haven't done so..."

"It's not that simple, as we discussed," William interrupted, "in my opinion, on balance, you certainly appear to have exercised proper professional discretion."

"I hope you're right about that. However, William, my involvement is far more complicated, more involved."

"What could you possibly mean?"

"What I mean is that for almost five years I have visited the Smelton home often, sometimes staying for hours."

William shook his head, as if to rid it of some nonsense that had filtered into his consciousness. "What are you saying, Zelia?"

"When I discovered that Eddie had the paintings, as I told you, I felt obligated to convince him to make arrangements to return them."

"No problem there."

"Not yet," Zelia said. "I assured Eddie the return of the paintings could be accomplished anonymously, but he'd have no part of it. He was adamant about it. As I told you, Eddie said the paintings were for his mother, and, basically, she called the shots. If she wanted them to go back to the museum, he'd agree. If not, the status quo was the rule."

"It's unreal. The fate of some of the greatest art in world history in the hands of a demented person," William said.

"Exactly. So I set out to convince her to do the right thing."

"And?"

"And, I've been trying to do that for the last five years, hoping for the moment the stars in her universe align, and she'd agree to let Eddie arrange to return the paintings. Every now and then, I'd see Eddie at the museum and he would tell me his mom would like me to visit. That she seemed to be mellowing about returning the paintings. Or I would ask Eddie if it was okay for me to see his mom and talk to her about returning the artwork. I'd rush over to North Cambridge, only to have my hopes dashed, time and time again. The reality is, William, I think Mrs. Smelton has been, and still is, playing games, or maybe she just goes in and out of reality. I doubt that she will ever agree to have the paintings returned to the Gardner."

"You're probably right, but I still haven't seen any problems with your conduct. To the contrary, you do seem to be doing the right thing."

"There's more." Zelia, again, drew a deep breath. "Once I realized it was unlikely that I would make any immediate progress with Mrs. Smelton, I argued that the house should be fitted with smoke detectors, and the room serving as a gallery fire-proofed. I also suggested air-conditioning for humidity control, and a burglar alarm. Eddie and his mother refused to consider a burglar alarm, afraid that it could be triggered accidentally and frighten Mrs. Smelton, but I was delighted that they agreed to the other suggestions. I wanted to be sure the art was as safe as possible, that nothing happened to the paintings before Eddie eventually returned them to the Gardner, whenever that was going to happen.

"The contractor was told the room was being converted to Mrs. Smelton's bedroom because she had a fear of fire. It's ironic. Even though Mrs. Smelton refused to put a lock on the room's door, the outside doors to the house are locked. The paintings are probably safer with her than they ever were at the museum, from fire or theft. Prior to the break-in, the Gardner had a reputation for being somewhat lax about security. I wouldn't be surprised if its fire alarm system wasn't exactly up to speed either."

"That construction project had to have been very costly. If the Smeltons were not well off, how did they ever pay for it?" William asked.

"You're right about the cost, and they didn't have that kind of money." Zelia was silent for a few moments, and then continued, "But I did. I paid for the contractor."

William's eyebrows lifted, "You paid?"

"It made sense, William. Some of the world's greatest paintings were hanging in an old, wood-framed house. I wanted them protected because, at some time, they were supposed to be returned to the museum. God knows, the house could have burned down in the meantime." Zelia held back her involvement in designing the room that hosted the masterpieces. Why add fuel to this fire, especially when the next flare up could end the conversation.

"I'm still not finished." Zelia turned the paperweight in her hands and offered a small smile. "I hope you have your aspirin ready."

"At my age, I should be shockproof. Try me again."

"Once the project was contracted out, Eddie was concerned that the workmen would come across the paintings and other art objects he had taken from the museum. It's a very small house. Only one floor of living space. There's no real attic, just a crawl space, and the workmen would be coming in through the cellar. There really wasn't sufficient space to hide anything. The three of us had a discussion about what to do. Eddie thought it would be okay to store them in a rental locker during the construction project. That kind of gave me the willies, but more importantly, his mother would have nothing to do with it. She said it was a crazy idea. That she read that the FBI sweeps those places on a regular basis- wily old lady, eh? Then she asked me if I could store them in my home while the work went on." Zelia paused, watching a silent William's eyes grow wide. "Yes, William, I agreed to store the stolen Gardner paintings in my condominium. Eddie said okay, but only after I gave him my solemn vow that I would return them to the Smelton home when the project was completed."

William seemed frozen, his expression and his body. He stared across the desk at Zelia, saying nothing. Zelia went on.

"In the black of night, Eddie and I moved the art over to my condo, and then, about a month later, back to his home. I actually wore latex gloves so my fingerprints would never be found on the artwork, or the van Eddie rented. I felt like a member of a gang, William. Eddie was extremely careful with the paintings. To keep them safe, he wrapped and sealed them with special materials. I kept everything in my spare bedroom. I had actual possession of the stolen masterpieces. I could have turned them over to the authorities, but I felt I had to honor my word to Eddie and return them to him, and I did. And they are still there, in North Cambridge."

William finally spoke. "Principle, Zelia, does not get watered down because the stakes get higher."

"Finally, William, and this bothers me more than everything else combined, my visits to the Smelton home have not been selfless. Twenty years ago, David proposed marriage to me at the Gardner Museum. We were standing in front of Vermeer's painting, *The Concert*. It's one of the paintings Eddie took from the Gardner. Now, I sit and look at that painting every time I visit the Smelton home. It gives me solace. I love that painting, and I have taken full advantage of having personal, private access to it. When I'm sitting by myself in front of *The Concert*, I feel as if I'm alone with David and our son. I sense their presence in the quiet of that room in North Cambridge.

"I have found the visits to Eddie's home the most important moments in my life. They have had a calming, euphoric effect on me. Being in the presence of the Vermeer, without sharing the moment with anyone except my Davids, has given me a level of contentment I have found no where else since that horrific day in my life. If I dared think about it, William, I'm sure I'd find some happiness that Eddie took those paintings, at least the Vermeer. I have personally benefited from this theft. I cannot justify my taking advantage of this access, neither can I stop. The truth is, William, I'm not sure how much I ever truly wanted Eddie to return the paintings."

"Zelia, I recall feeling very fortunate when you applied for a position at the Public Defender's Office because you had years of experience on the other side of the courtroom as a prosecutor. You explained to me that you did not want to go back to the district attorney's office at that time in your life because you didn't think you could be fair. When virtually anybody in your position, a victim of a crime with the most unthinkable consequences, would return to the role of prosecutor with a vengeance, you went in the opposite direction. Do you remember what you said when I asked 'Why the Public Defender's Office?'"

"I remember exactly. I said that my dear David, my dear husband, believed the most important benefit this country bestows on its citizens, whether naturally born or washed up on its shores, is a system of justice that is fair. He felt that equal justice for all of our citizens - rich or poor, educated or illiterate, good person or not - was the legacy of all who fought and died in our wars. That without equality in the law we might as well all be in chains - Cuban chains, Soviet chains, it made no difference, because there would be no freedom, no liberty."

William stood from his chair. "You obviously agreed with your husband, Zelia. You are one of the most decent, honorable persons I have ever known, and I have had the good fortune of knowing many. I have never been more proud than I was on the day you took the oath and became a judge."

"Perhaps it's time for second thoughts."

"Never. Through no fault of your own, you have been placed in the center of some unbelievable circumstances. The bottom line is you persuaded Mr. Smelton to let you talk to his mother to attempt to persuade her to let go of the artwork. You did the best you could, but the woman is demented. No one was going to change her mind. The paintings are not going to be returned to the museum until she dies. The fact that you are able to appreciate the stolen art, regardless of any benefit it gives you, is not a crime. That access takes nothing away from anyone."

"And my storing the paintings in my home? And then returning them to the man who stole them, not to the museum?"

"I understand why you did not break your vow to Mr. Smelton, why you returned the paintings to him. Although your having stored the paintings could be a problem if it became public knowledge, under all of the circumstances, I do not think it was illegal behavior. Also, if you hadn't agreed to store them, only God knows what might have been their fate."

"I've done nothing, said nothing, about this infamous crime for five years. How can that possibly be in the interest of justice?"

"Mr. Smelton's mind-set has been that you were his lawyer, from the day you were appointed in the Boston Municipal Court to defend him from a shoplifting charge, through the day you stopped practicing law and became a judge. That time frame includes your learning of his burglary of the Gardner Museum and his continuing possession of what he stole. Considering the circumstances, as you have described them, he had a reasonable belief that the attorney-client privilege was still in place when he told you about, and showed you, the stolen property. Those were confidential, privileged communications, and you did not have the right to reveal to authorities what you learned then, and still do not.

"If you had reason to think that his prospective conduct involving the robbery would have been likely to result in death or substantial bodily harm to anyone, Zelia, that would have been different. That would have obligated you to speak out. But that was not the case. Your decision to be bound to secrecy by the attorney-client privilege is not assailable."

Zelia pushed back from her desk and stood. "You know, William, with the public, perception is reality. If this bizarre story is ever discovered, it's front page news."

William stood and moved to Zelia. "I know that. But we have no reason to think that this person following you has any idea about what is in the Smelton home. Let's see if we can find out anything about him. You have given me a lot to think about, Zelia Valdes."

Zelia turned to William who reached his arms out, encircled her, and held her close.

29

Tony brushed his hair back with a hand as he walked into the kitchen and over to a wall mirror. His mother was at the table fingering a set of rosary beads. Anna no longer mumbled the *Hail Marys* associated with the rosary. Shortly after immigrating to the US she told the parish pastor that she felt funny saying the prayers in her native Italian when the congregation was praying in English. Father assured her that just thinking about the Blessed Mother while holding the beads would work as well at getting souls out of purgatory. Anna then discovered that the string of purple glass bits made good worry beads. She looked up at her only child.

"Are you sure it's okay to take a holiday on a weekday from the judge to go to this interview?"

"Yes, Ma. It's called a personal day. That's why they have them. For important things, like job interviews."

Anna nodded her head, accepting her son's answer. "I know the Blessed Mother will guide you the right way, Tony. She will protect our little family the way she always has. I only wish it was May, the month of Mary."

"I'm sure the Blessed Mother can help us out in July, too, Ma." Tony took a final glance in the mirror and then stepped to the table, pulled out the chair next to his mother and sat. He took her hands in his, raised them to his lips and kissed them. "Ma, you know I'm thinking of you and Dad all the time, including today when I have this interview.

If I get the job, it'll be for the best. It could give you the chance to get into a nice little house with everything on the first floor. A house that you and Dad can be real comfortable in. I've been looking in the *Globe* on Sundays, and there are some nice small houses not too far from here, down in Quincy or Braintree, near your cousin, Rosa, that we might be able to afford."

"You've already looked?" Anna took her hands back, raised them and squeezed her head. "You didn't tell us."

"I didn't want to get your hopes up, but I want to know what might happen if things work out." Tony relaxed in his chair. "By the way, where's Dad?"

"Like he does on every Friday, your father took the subway to visit with his Army friend, Vito, his partner from the war."

"I forget. Where does Vito live?"

"On the other side of the city, in East Boston. His neighborhood is next to where the horses race. He lives in a house like this one, but on the second floor, not as many stairs to climb every day. Your father and Vito sit on the back porch and watch the horses run around while they clean Vito's guns. I don't know why they clean the guns. I don't think Vito ever shoots them off and gets them dirty. Your father says Vito snuck them home from Korea as souvenirs. I know about them because once your father came home from Vito's house with gun grease all over his trousers. I made him tell me what it was so I could clean it off."

"You know, Ma, I never understood what Dad and Vito did in the war. Why do you say they were partners?"

"Your father is a quiet man. He doesn't like to talk about anything. But Vito talked to me about the war on the day you were baptized. He was at the church hall party for all the new babies, and we talked a little."

Tony was intrigued. His father had volunteered for the Army soon after he had immigrated to the United States in the fifties. Tony knew he had served in Korea, but he never talked about it, and Tony never asked him about it.

"What did Vito tell you?"

"He said that your father saved his life by shooting an enemy soldier who was going to shoot him, and that he would do anything for your father to repay him. And he said that your father was very brave and the best shooter in the Army. That they would go into the bushes and trees together to look for the enemy soldiers. Vito would tell your father where they were, and your father would shoot them."

"Wow. Dad was a sniper?"

"Don't call your father things like that," Anna scolded her son. "I told him to go to confession and tell the priest what he did. He said the chaplain priest in the Army already said it wasn't a sin because of the war. That it was allowed to shoot at the enemy. That's what he said. No, Tony, your father was not a sniper or anything even like that."

Tony smothered a chuckle as he stood and walked the few steps to the kitchen counter. "You know, Mom that explains something I could never figure out."

"What could you never figure out?"

"When Dad takes a nap in his chair, sometimes he mumbles between snores. I just figured out what it means. He mumbles 'trigger squeeze.' I read in a magazine that you don't pull the trigger on a rifle. You kind of squeeze it. Dad probably dreams about the Army, about being in the war. A lot of soldiers never forget that part of their lives." Tony reached into a box of Cheerios and grabbed a fistful.

Anna had talked enough about shooting at enemy soldiers. Regardless of what the Army chaplain said, she still feared her husband's war service may keep her from meeting up with him in the afterlife. No one but Frankie would listen to her all the time, and heaven was forever.

"Tony, you look so handsome. They have to give you the job. And you take that job if you think it's right. Only if you think it's right. If you do, they will be very lucky to have you."

Tony shoved the Cheerios into his mouth, and then walked over behind his mother. He squeezed her shoulders, kissed her on the top of her head, and started for the staircase.

Tony boarded the train at the Ashmont **T** station at noontime. His trip in town would take about twenty minutes, leaving plenty of time to walk from the Park Street station, through the Boston Common and Public Garden, to the Ritz Carlton Hotel.

Arriving at the Park Street stop in a confident, upbeat mood, Tony took the stairway up from the cavernous subway station two steps at a time, emerging into sunshine on the edge of the Common. Beginning to sweat from his effort, Tony wished he had used the station's escalator as he started walking across the city's venerable public park, thankful for a slight wind on the mid-summer day. Tony was buoyed by Kate's confidence, and the headhunter's letter that suggested the follow-up meeting was nothing more than a formality. He was calm, actually looking forward to the meeting that he was sure would alter his future for the better.

Norman, legendary greeter at the Ritz-Carlton's Arlington Street entrance, held the door open for Tony at five minutes before one o'clock. A few minutes later, the maître d' hôtel seated Tony at a table in the newly restored upstairs dining room. The table was set for three and located towards the rear of the white and gold restaurant. Tony figured its extra distance from the other tables was a request from Mr. Mortimer, perhaps to insure privacy. He had wondered if Mortimer would be accompanied again by the woman from the bank's legal department. The third place setting on the table seemed to answer that question. As he looked up at the chandeliers and around the room, Tony turned a silver butter knife on the tips of his fingers. Small trees in large pots dotted the lush carpet, and oversized flower arrangements adorned white linen tablecloths. Well-dressed men and women sat in deep chairs offering views of the Public Garden. A few briefcases leaned against the inside of table legs, their owners hoping that lunch at the Ritz would rope in a new client.

Tony looked at his watch. It was ten minutes after one. He began to wonder where Mr. Mortimer and his colleague, Beatrice, were. Unexpectedly, a pair of familiar faces appeared at his table. Tony stood halfway up and spoke a weak, tentative hello to the men, both wearing dark suits, white shirts and neck ties. Without responding, Roger Metcalf drew out the chair to Tony's right and sat. Frederick Poole took the remaining chair across the table. Tony sat back down, baffled by the presence of the two lawyers from the Theopoulis case.

"Ah, hi, Mr. Metcalf, Mr. Poole. I'm glad to see you, but I'm afraid I'm meeting someone here for lunch. I..."

"We reserved this table, Tony," Metcalf interrupted. "We're here to discuss your Montreal interview with London Group EquiBank."

"What do you mean?" Tony quickly responded, eyeing Metcalf, then Poole, then back to Metcalf.

"You didn't go to a job interview in Montreal, Tony," Metcalf said.

"What? What are you talking about?" Tony moved back in his chair, as if repelled by an unknown danger. "What the hell is this?"

"Just take it easy, young man," Poole joined in. "The truth of the matter is that the Montreal meeting was something we arranged."

Tony's respect for the two lawyers evaporated. His stomach dropped. "You have to be shitting me."

"No," Metcalf said as he waived off a waiter, "we're not shitting you. Hear us out. It was very clear that Judge Valdes's attitude and decisions throughout the Theopoulis trial were beyond biased. Then her rulings on the fraud counts took the cake. We needed to know how these things happened, and you didn't disappoint us. You told us just what we wanted to hear in that Montreal interview."

"What the hell are you talking about?" Tony said.

"I'm talking about how you bragged about the discussions that went on between you and Judge Valdes, how she mentioned she had no respect for our client, Cosmos Theopoulis, and that she left a huge chunk of her responsibility to you, including preparation of the jury instructions. You, a clerk, not even a year past the bar. And you just lapped it up. Loved being the big shot didn't you."

Tony shifted in his chair and looked around. The room was filling with diners, but he realized he was alone. He was angry and frightened. He began to fiddle with a fork.

"That's bullshit, and you know it is. Judge Valdes respects everyone who comes into her courtroom, and I never had the final say on anything. Judge Valdes examined everything I did in that case, like she does in every case."

"From your very mouth, young man, not only is it clear that Judge Valdes was biased and predisposed against our client, but also that you had a considerable role in deciding the Theopoulis case," Poole said.

"I was just, you know, pumping up my resume at that interview, or whatever it was. Trying to sell myself. Yeah, maybe I exaggerated a little. Big deal, everyone does."

"You're playing in the big leagues, Tony. This is fucking hardball, not wiffle ball. You can end up paying a huge price for your little exaggeration," Metcalf said.

Poole took a black cassette player the size of a deck of cards from his suit coat's inside pocket and placed it on the table next to a vase of flowers. "I wish we didn't have to be here, young man. I surely do wish that."

Tony stared at the diamond embedded in Poole's right cufflink as the lawyer pressed the play button. A few edited minutes from the Montreal interview filled the corner of the elegant dining room. As soon as the recording stopped playing, Roger slid a business card across the linen tablecloth. "Call my office next week, on Thursday. If you're using your brain, you're going to tell me you'll play ball with us."

"Play ball? Why should I even give you the time of day? If you pulled off what you claim you did, it's you who'll be in the shit, not me." Tony half rose from his chair.

"Hold on, young man," Frederick said as he took a two page document from the same inside pocket, unfolded it and placed it at the center of the table. "Before you go off in a huff, you may want to look at this."

Tony immediately recognized the top page as a copy of the court order upon which he had signed Judge Valdes's name. Over the last few months he had occasionally thought about what he had done, deciding that he might have been foolish in his desire to help out the young paralegal. He'd been more comfortable about it as time passed, thinking that the further away the deed, the less likely it would be discovered, which seemed a real long shot in any case. Now, without warning, the document had surfaced. He picked up the court order and examined the attached page. It was a short, notarized statement from a handwriting expert opining that the signature on the order was not written by Judge Zelia Valdes.

"Yeah, I recognize that. So what if I helped someone out. I didn't do anything wrong. I was at the hearing when Judge Valdes announced from the bench that the petition was allowed. There wasn't even any opposition. If she was in court the day her order was brought back in for her missing signature, she would have signed it."

Roger Metcalf pointed a silver fork at Tony and said, "You don't know that. For all you know she didn't sign it because she changed her mind. Maybe she got more information, like a probation report, that showed more criminal activity by the petitioner."

"That's bullshit speculation."

Metcalf picked up the copy of the court order from the table and held it, face up, in front of Tony. "You know what I think? I think you were hoping you could use that forged signature as a ticket to a 'no-tell motel' for something in return from this paralegal who, I understand, is one sexy little piece of ass. That's what I think."

Tony's sense of doom was confirmed by the next sentence out of Metcalf's mouth. "Cipriano, you will absolutely be disbarred if your forging the signature of a superior court judge on a court order is disclosed to the Board of Bar Overseers. Cooperate, and this document never sees the light of day."

Catatonically, Tony picked up Metcalf's business card and slid it into his shirt pocket. Without a further word, he rose from the table and walked away.

"This makes me sick to my stomach," Frederick said as he stared after the departing Tony.

"We've gone over this. We have no choice. And, it looks like it will pay off. He's pretty scared. He'll cooperate."

"Hooray for us."

Roger stopped a passing waiter and ordered two vodka martinis, then turned back to Frederick and said, "This Montreal charade may be critical, and could save our asses in the long run, but I'd still love to find a smoking gun. Some rotten conduct with Valdes's prints all over it."

"I would imagine our private investigator, Piggy, or whatever it is you call him, is doing his best to deliver just what you're looking for."

30

Walking out of the restaurant, Tony saw his career in international banking disappearing, but then remembered there had been no career to lose. The whole thing had been a setup, and he was the mark. Once downstairs and through the hotel lobby, he began to walk along Arlington Street without a destination, in the direction of the Charles River.

Tony took the footbridge over Storrow Drive and arrived at the green apron of lawn that bordered the river. It was just after one o'clock when he reached the esplanade. He was in another world. He could not believe the situation he was in, and was thinking he may never get out of it. He began recalling every word that was said in Montreal. Now, those words haunted him.

Wandering aimlessly, tie undone, suit coat slung over his shoulder, Tony found himself at the Mass. Ave. Bridge and crossed over the river and into Cambridge. He walked a footpath along the Charles in the direction of Harvard Square. A large clock on the face of a building read quarter after two. Suddenly, Tony thought of Kate. Ignoring the mid-day heat, he began to sprint across the grass lawn, then across Memorial Drive. He slowed as he arrived at a hotel entrance. In moments, he was in a phone booth.

Thirty minutes later, a mystified Kate rushed into the lobby of the Hyatt Regency Hotel and hugged a desolate Tony. Minutes later they sat at a table in the mezzanine lounge. The bartender delivered a bowl of popcorn and a pair of mugs filled with draft beer to his only customers and returned to tidying up the bar. Kate reached over and took Tony's hand.

"What happened, Tony? You sounded desperate on the phone, and, I've got to say, you look like hell." Kate raised some popcorn towards her mouth.

"It was all bullshit. There was no job interview in Montreal."

The popcorn stopped in mid-delivery. "What?"

"It was all a setup. The company interviewers, the headhunters, they were all phonies."

"That's unbelievable. Why? Why would anyone do that?"

"Remember the Theopoulis case?"

Kate thought a moment. "Yes, sure. The case you told me about."

"My lunch appointment today..." Tony shook his head.

"Yeah?" She chewed the popcorn.

"...it, and the Montreal interview, and the letters, all arranged by the Theopoulis attorneys, Metcalf and Poole. I told you how I bragged at the job interview about being a big shot on the Theopoulis case, making decisions about witness credibility, telling the judge what I thought and all that crap."

"That was no big deal, Tony," Kate said.

"The hell it wasn't. They secretly taped the interview. That's exactly what they wanted to hear. They played part of it back for me, Kate. I had to be the biggest asshole in Canada."

"Why did they do this? What are they looking for?"

"They got their asses handed to them by Judge Valdes. Their client got whacked by the jury for a fortune, and the judge tripled the amount. One billion dollars. That case is the only thing that's been talked about around the courthouse since the verdict. It's been the talk of the Suffolk County Bar for weeks, months."

"Well it's spilt milk. They better get over it and get on with life."

"It's not over yet, Kate. Everything is on appeal. The trial rulings, all kinds of decisions on motions, the judge's jury instructions, which I helped prepare, by the way. Metcalf and Poole are looking for anything they can find to reverse the judge's decision, or at least get the case sent back for retrial. I guess they zeroed in on me as a way to get to the judge."

Anger turned Kate's face crimson. "This is pure bullshit. What can they possibly do to you?" she demanded.

Tony was quiet a moment. The whir of the glass washer underneath the nearby bar broke the silence. Tears began to well up in his eyes. "As it turns out, plenty."

"What? Why do you say that, Tony?"

"About six months ago, I did something at the courthouse that I thought was no big deal. I actually thought it was the right thing to do at the time. I was wrong. Big time wrong."

Tony explained what he had done, and how Metcalf and Poole had threatened to use the forged signature of Judge Valdes on the court order. "They said my legal career, my future, is on the line if I don't cooperate, Kate. They threatened to turn the forged court order over to the Board of Bar Overseers, and said I'd be disbarred. I've been suckered and made a fool of. And just think of what I've done to Judge Valdes." Tony paused a few moments, then heaved a sob. "And, to my mom and dad."

"Hold on, Tony. You can't just roll over. Big deal, the judge forgot to sign a piece of paper, and you did it for her, as a good deed. And you did some puffing at a job interview. Think of what these two big shot lawyers have done. To begin with, they've committed fraud, first class fraud. And, this phony interview crap is also probably a crime. Then, they turn into extortionists - threats against you if you don't lie, or at least exaggerate, about the judge. No, we're not going to let them get away with this. We will figure out how to handle it. You're the one who's getting shafted. C'mon, let's get out of here. We have to figure out what we do about these sons of bitches, and I think that means getting the judge in the loop."

Tony heard "we" louder than the rest of Kate's words. Suddenly, his spirit was lifted. Tony paid the tab. He and Kate left the bar. The beer, and all but two kernels of popcorn, were untouched.

Tony's call to Judge Valdes was put through to her chambers just after four o'clock. An excited and, the judge sensed, very nervous Tony emphatically said it was critical that he and a friend meet with her as soon as possible. He asked her to take him at his word, with no further details over the phone. A very curious Zelia agreed to meet with them at her condominium. She informed the court clerk's office she was leaving and walked quickly from the courthouse to her nearby home.

Thirty minutes after leaving chambers, Zelia Valdes stood at her living room window, looking out at Pinckney Street. She wondered what caused Tony's urgent call, and was honing in on a possible connection with a pair of things that were turning her life into an obstacle course – the paintings hanging on the wall at the Smelton house, and the creep following her. Then, with a degree of comfort, Zelia decided that if anyone was on to the Smelton home's private museum, he or she must have kept quiet about it. Otherwise, pretty much all of North Cambridge would be roped off by now, and the news outlets would be talking about nothing else. Zelia's musings were interrupted by the front door knocker. A minute later her law clerk and his girlfriend sat next to each other on the living room couch. Standing, Zelia looked at Kate.

"Could you tell me again exactly why you're involved in this matter?"

"She's..." Tony began to respond.

"Not from you, Tony. From your friend, please."

"Well, it's just that I've known Tony for about nine or ten months, and we've gone out a number of times, and, well, we're good friends. When he told me what happened today, I wanted to help in some way. Do something. I mean, what they're trying to do to him, and to you, Judge, is outrageous."

Tony chimed in. "Judge, Kate's going to be taking the bar exam herself, and she's been very supportive of my job search and I know she's just trying to help." He paused momentarily. "And, I need her. She's been great."

"Okay. I'm sorry if I seem overly cautious." She looked at Kate. "It's nothing personal. I have a lot of respect for Tony and I'm sure he chooses his friends and confidants wisely." Zelia turned back to Tony. "You chose not to tell me anything on the phone, Tony, so, what's up?"

"Judge, I'm really embarrassed."

Zelia raised her hands toward Tony and Kate. "Hold it just a second, both of you. As much as I want to hear what this is all about, you should realize that there is no privilege of any kind here. If I'm ever asked to repeat this conversation, under certain circumstances, I may have to comply."

"Understood." Tony said.

Kate nodded, then said, "Anyhow, Judge, it's not Tony who's doing the wrong thing. It's a couple of lawyers."

"That's not completely true, Judge," Tony said. "This whole thing's unbelievable, and there's something I did that I know was wrong."

Zelia found a cigarette, lit it, and sat in an armchair facing the couch.

"Okay, what's the story?"

As soon as Tony and Kate left the condo, Zelia was back at her living room window, now with a phone to her ear, waiting for her ring to be answered. What she'd heard from Tony was hard to believe. One of the most prominent lawyers in the city and another who was on track to that distinction were involved in a scheme that could well end up on the desk of the US Attorney. Tony was being used as a pawn. Justice itself was the target of the scheme. Zelia hoped she would have some definite information to tell Tony when he called her in thirty minutes for instructions. *Please be there, William.*

William Bettinger answered his phone.

"Hello, William. I'm glad you're at home, and afraid I may have to seek your advice again. I don't know where else to turn."

"You know I'm always available, Zelia. Is this about what we've been discussing?"

"Actually, I don't know. It could be. Maybe everything is connected somehow or other. Could you possibly spare some time, a half an hour or so, tomorrow?"

"I'm sure I can see you, Zelia. I have a nine o'clock appointment here in Wellesley that I'd have difficulty canceling, but, I can see you at my home earlier if you can make it."

"Seven-thirty, if that's not too early."

"That will work."

"And, William, I'll have my law clerk, Tony, and his friend with me."

Zelia watched through the window as Kate picked a bright orange parking ticket from her windshield before the red Jaguar drove off down Pinckney Street.

"You're right, Tony, Judge Valdes is very bright, and very nice," Kate said as she turned onto Charles Street.

"She didn't seem too nice when I mentioned signing her name on the court order."

"Well, she wasn't very happy about having her name forged, that's for sure. But she knows we never always do the right thing, and you were doing someone a favor for a good reason. She understood that."

"Thank God she remembered the petition, and that she would have signed the order if anyone ever gave it to her to sign. I may not be out of the woods yet on that, but I sure as hell feel a lot better about it, knowing she's got my back."

"I wonder if she'll be able to reach Judge Bettinger," Kate said.

"I hope so. I met him once and he seemed like a nice guy. He was a very important judge a while back. I just want to get this thing over with."

At Frederick Poole's Back Bay condominium, Roger Metcalf was standing as he watched Otto uncork a 2001 Merlot. Frederick pushed his empty glass across the dining room table for a refill.

"Roger, I asked you over for dinner with me and Otto, because we are obligated, I think, to reconsider what we have hatched. I'm not sure we can put this toothpaste back in the tube, but we have to try. I've thought of nothing else since our meeting with that young law clerk today. We have to make this right somehow."

"You should have saved the invite to dinner, Frederick. The die is cast, and we're not going to stop now." Roger walked across the room and sat with the two men. He looked in the direction of the wine. "And, I sure don't mean to lecture, Frederick, but we're going to have to be as sharp as tacks until this charade with Valdes's clerk is over."

"Oh, come on, Roger. Now that we've sunk to new lows, a little inebriation can't hurt. Perhaps, Otto, we should decant some Ripple. It would be in keeping with our tawdry little scheme, don't you think?"

"You know, I actually entertained the possibility of a nomination to the Federal District Court," Roger said. "Judge Powers is about to call it quits. Rumor is Weingarten's got inoperable something or other. I thought this Theopoulis case would not only make me rich, but maybe famous as well. Well, I sure as hell got my share of ink, but it's for losing the biggest verdict anyone around these parts can remember. That'll look great on my resume." Roger chuckled as he shook his head, and then continued talking.

"Believe me, Frederick, if you'd overheard the phone conversation I had with our client this afternoon, you can bet your ass you'd have no regrets at doing whatever the hell we have to do to get this judgment thrown out. Theopoulis started by screaming about the malpractice action he's about to bring. And, did you know that little prick is the biggest contributor to both of our United States senators? That he talks to them on a regular basis? These are the same senators that recommend names to the president for the federal bench.

"And you know something else, Frederick? For some reason this miniature Greek bastard seems to loathe you, who he's hardly met, even more than he hates me. He vowed to do whatever he can to see that we're both ruined if this case doesn't get flipped on appeal. We have no choice here, Frederick. We have to continue to fight back against this judge, or our professional lives are over."

"It's just that I have never, ever been party to such a fraud, Roger. A fraud on that poor young man who is just starting out in his professional life, in his career in the law. A fraud on the court, a fraud on human decency." Frederick tried to hold back sobs.

Otto reached over and squeezed his hand. "It will be all right, Frederick. Everything will be fine. We have only done what was absolutely necessary, what we had to do. You'll see."

31

There was light traffic early Saturday morning. Walter's taxi entered onto the Mass Pike in Boston and sped west, toward the exclusive suburb of Wellesley. Zelia sat up front, sipping from a cardboard cup of steaming coffee.

"Donut, Walter? Glazed."

Since recently discovering Zelia's line of work from a fellow cabbie, Walter had over-apologized for not being "properly respectful" and insisted on calling her by her title.

"Yeah, sure, Judge, thanks. Didn't eat anything yet. You haven't needed me this early before. Got to be important, I guess."

"You're right about that," Zelia said as she handed a donut wrapped in wax paper to Walter. "Very important."

When Walter's cab arrived in front of William Bettinger's home, Tony and Kate were waiting in the red Jaguar at curbside. At Zelia's direction, they followed the cab up the gravel drive that ended in a circular area, completing a keyhole appearance. The taxi and Jaguar pulled to a stop in front of a short set of granite steps at the front door of the white-shuttered brick colonial. Walter pulled a paperback from the glove compartment as the others waited for the front door to open.

In short order the three callers joined Judge Bettinger in his living room. They all declined his offer of coffee. Tony and Kate sat ramrod straight on a Victorian style sofa in front of a coffee table. Zelia sat next to them in a chintz covered chair.

"Tell me, what's going on?" Bettinger said, facing his visitors from a wing chair across from them.

"Well, Judge," Zelia responded, keeping a level of formality evident for the benefit of Tony and Kate, "based on what I heard from Tony and Kate last evening, I would say there is a powder keg ready to explode on the Boston legal scene."

Judge Bettinger moved to the edge of his chair. "Who's involved?"

"The key players appear to be Tony, yours truly, and attorneys named Roger Metcalf and Frederick Poole." Zelia breathed deeply and looked at Tony and Kate. "Tell the judge what you told me, and let's see where we go from here."

Twenty minutes later, Bettinger stood by the fireplace mantle.

"I've listened to things that are nothing short of astounding, and very disturbing, but I've been around long enough to have a pretty good idea when the truth is being told, and I do believe you. What you have told me of the conduct of these two lawyers is beyond outrageous. It is absolutely disgusting. It is astounding to me that Frederick Poole is involved, but, as I said, I believe what I have just heard."

Bettinger looked at Zelia in a manner she recalled from her days in the Public Defender's Office. It meant it was time to get to work on a problem. "We'll have to do something, and soon. This will only get worse if we don't address it. I have a downtown office I use for mediation sessions. It's in the Three Post Office Square Building, fifth floor. I can be there this coming Tuesday at one o'clock. Is that okay with you Zelia?" She nodded. "Tony?" He nodded. The judge glanced at his watch. "Okay, enough for this morning. And, Zelia, could I speak privately with you for just a few minutes?"

As the front door of the judge's home closed behind Tony and Kate, Bettinger led Zelia into his study. He stood behind an ornately carved desk, leaned into it and pulled a manila envelope from the center drawer. Zelia remained standing.

"Something seems ominous, William. What is it?"

"I had some contacts at the FBI do some research using the information you gave me about the person tailing you. They came up with this." William slid a 5 x 5 glossy photo from the envelope, handed it to Zelia, and then continued, "The man following you in the black Saab is most likely this character, Basil Simeone. He's fairly well known in the Boston private investigating community. Works free-lance for a number of licensed agencies, but mostly for one called Private Investigation Services."

Zelia studied the head shot of Simeone a moment and said, "I think that's the man I saw in the Saab, Vandyke beard and all."

"According to the person who prepared this report," William continued, "the agency Simeone usually works for is known to be ruthless, as well as very expensive. It's operated by a man who has been investigated himself over the years for a variety of criminal acts, some of them quite gruesome, but some way he keeps avoiding arrest."

"William, just what could be going on? This all seems like a dream. A nightmare."

"Until a half an hour ago, I could only speculate that it was the Theopoulis case that's behind your being followed. After hearing from your clerk, there is no doubt in my mind that's the source of your troubles. If they are willing to pull off that elaborate, bogus employment interview, they'd certainly not blink at hiring an investigator to follow you around. They're fishing for whatever they can find. There is an all out attack on your integrity. Both your personal and professional lives are being looked at by this unethical detective agency."

"This is hard to believe."

"We have to believe it. We are dealing with desperate men. These lawyers see their big-time reputations and futures sullied, if not ruined, by an important case they lost. Now, they seek to hang that defeat on you with the aim of having it reversed or remanded on appeal. They're searching for anything they can use."

"They have no right. God, it was a civil case that they would have lost in any courtroom. I heard the evidence, William. Their client is lucky I didn't refer this matter to the district attorney's office for criminal investigation and, at the least, a likely perjury indictment. The decision was the right one."

"Of course, Zelia, I totally trust your judgment. What really concerns me at this point is if this investigator, Simeone, has discovered, or is likely to discover, what's hanging on the walls at your docent friend's home."

Zelia stepped to a window that faced a flower garden. A large grouping of light blue hydrangeas was in full bloom. The judge joined Zelia at the window. Her arms were folded tight to her chest. Her eyes were downcast. Silently, he placed an arm around her.

32

Tony skipped lunch on Tuesday and went directly to the Three Post Office Square Building in the city's financial center.

"The last time I sat at a conference table I got into trouble."

"If there's any justice in this city, Tony, that jinx is going to be broken." Judge Bettinger sat across from Tony at the polished mahogany table. The two men were alone in the judge's private office space in downtown Boston. "Judge Valdes is on her way?"

"Yes, sir," Tony said. "She thought it would be better if we left the courthouse separately. She said she'd be ten minutes behind me."

"And here I am." Closing the door behind her and taking the chair next to Judge Bettinger, Zelia mentioned that she would be charging a jury in forty-five minutes, at two o'clock.

"Then let's get right to it," Bettinger said. "Since our meeting Saturday morning, I've talked with one of the more experienced attorneys in the city. He's a former assistant U. S. attorney here in Boston and a trusted old friend. He is very upset at the conduct of the Theopoulis lawyers. He was quick to offer his services in any way they're needed, and without a fee. If you agree, Tony, you will meet with him. He'll be available at six this evening."

"I will, Judge."

"Good." Bettinger slipped a half sheet of paper to Tony with the name, office address and phone number of the lawyer. "I suggest you take whatever advice he gives you. I expect he will ask you to accompany him to the Justice Department. Based on what I've told him, he thinks it's possible the US Attorney's Office will get involved, but he's not certain. He feels that influence plays a big role with the present US Attorney, and these lawyers are likely to have a lot of influential friends.

"If Justice does get involved, the US Attorney will most likely apply for a warrant authorizing a wiretap on the phones of both Attorneys Metcalf and Poole under section eighteen of the US Code. What these men have been doing has to be included in the laundry list of offenses in that section. I'm familiar with the disposition to issue warrants from the federal bench here in Boston. I don't expect any problem, even though the targets are practicing lawyers."

"Did your friend suggest exactly what the Justice Department might be looking for?" Zelia asked.

"He can't speak for the Department," William said, "but he thinks for starters, extortion, mail fraud, and racketeering are likely candidates."

"Jeez," Tony said, "just the sound of the charges scares me half to death." He shifted in his chair, then continued, "When I met with Attorneys Metcalf and Poole at the Ritz-Carlton, Metcalf told me I was playing hardball. I guess he's right about that."

"He is," Bettinger said, "but don't be intimidated. We are going to turn the tables on attorneys Metcalf and Poole with a little, but legal, charade of our own. I'm hoping they'll get a taste of their own medicine. Tony, when you call Attorney Metcalf on Thursday, you tell him something along the lines that, after thinking things over, you have decided to cooperate. That you're upset with Judge Valdes for putting you in this spot, that kind of thing. I'm sure he'll want you to meet with him, and soon. Volunteer to him that you'll even let him record that meeting with you if he wants to. Let's hope he bites."

"Why do you want Attorney Metcalf to record the meeting with me?" Tony asked.

"I think I'll wait until we meet again, which will be after your phone call to Metcalf, to answer that. It will be clearer then. By the way, I have discussed this plan with my friend, soon to be your lawyer, and he agrees with it.

"Also, Tony, my guess is Metcalf will have an affidavit at some point for you to sign, and maybe ask you to submit to a formal deposition. Let him think you don't really care what he does to Judge Valdes, as long as he keeps quiet about your forging the judge's signature."

"What exactly do you think these lawyers are hoping for, Judge?" Zelia asked.

"That Tony gives them enough to show that you were biased against Theopoulis, that your judgment was predisposed in some way, that you were swayed by out-of-court opinions about the parties, perhaps even from your law clerk. They need to produce some kind of evidence that you, at least in part, based your findings on something outside of the trial evidence. That is an enormous burden to meet. I can not imagine they're ever being successful, but I fully expect them to try."

"My decision was justified. It was absolutely called for," Zelia said.

"As I have said, you don't have to justify your decision at this table, Zelia."

"I know that, Judge. It's just that this is so damn maddening. These lawyers don't have to go around ruining people's lives. For God's sake, if they think they got a raw deal, wait and have me reversed on appeal. That's why we have appellate courts."

Judge Bettinger stood. "Now they're going to find out they've really stepped in it."

The following Thursday, Frederick Poole left his office shortly before noon, having decided to spend the afternoon at home. With tie loosened and shoes discarded, he was stretched out on a chaise lounge on his deck, under the sun, sipping a Long Island Iced Tea. Frederick was thinking that chances were pretty good that Wiggins, Lewis & Poole would be making its way through the early years of the new millennium without a Poole at the helm. Until last week, he had not seriously considered retiring. Now, that possibility was galloping.

"Frederick, it's Roger Metcalf." Otto carried a portable phone across the patio, the heels of his loafers clicking on the flagstone floor.

Without acknowledging his partner, Poole turned his head from his view of the river and reached an arm up from the chaise lounge for the phone. "Hello, Roger. What have you got to tell me?"

"Cipriano called this morning. He said he'd play ball. He's pissed at Judge Valdes. Says she's turned into a real bitch lately. He thinks she's about to end his court appointment, and he's bullshit about that. He said he's also really upset with Valdes because she placed so much responsibility in his hands. He complained that she was downright lazy." Roger paused a moment for a breath. "Goddamn, Frederick, we couldn't have asked for more."

"Do you believe him?" Poole stood from the lounge chair with a slight wobble.

"I heard what he said, Frederick, and I don't give a shit whether or not it's true as long as he cooperates and signs whatever we stick under his nose, and he'll do that to save his ass. He even said he didn't care if I recorded him this time. He's coming into my office on Monday morning. He's in our pocket, Frederick."

"My God, Roger, what this law clerk has told you could mean that our little scheme may have actually been a public service. Maybe Judge Valdes does not belong on the bench after all."

33

The kitchen clock read six-thirty. Anna Cipriano approached the table, sat heavily and placed her dishtowel in front of her. She stared at her son as he fiddled with his fork and plate. "Did I do something wrong with the sausage, Tony? You usually eat more for breakfast."

"No, Ma. It's great, like always. I guess I'm just not real hungry this morning. I'm not used to getting up at the crack of dawn for this job."

"Why do you have to leave so early?"

"There are a lot of things we have to get done before court starts at eight-thirty."

Tony stood, taking his suit coat from the back of his chair. As he slung it over his shoulder he said, "Dad must be in the bathroom. Tell him so long for me." Tony leaned down to kiss his mother, but she backed off, holding the palm of a hand up at him.

"Don't go running off like everything's just hunky-dory. Sit down and tell me what's the trouble the last few days. Even your say-nothing father told me he noticed you looked like there's something wrong. What is it, Tony? Did you run out of pills again? Those zo-something pills? Did you have a fight with the girl you talk to on the phone so much? Is it the new job they're going to offer you? Maybe you think too much traveling?"

Tony continued to stand. "No, Ma, it's nothing. I'm taking the pills again, and everything's fine with Kate. I'm just trying to make the right decision, that's all. Don't you and Dad worry. Pretty soon I'll decide. Really, Ma, I gotta go. Okay?"

He denied his mother the opportunity to continue with the questions, pulling the kitchen door open and racing down the back staircase.

Tony was surprised that the train was crowded so early in the day. He distracted himself from thinking about what lay ahead this morning by examining his fellow subway passengers. Many were in shirtsleeves or shorts. He liked the variety of ethnic backgrounds who took the Red Line into the city. Tony envied their anonymity, and the predictability that he presumed directed their lives. He wondered why anyone would ever want to be the center of attention. As the train pulled into Downtown Crossing and came to a halt, the collection of riders rocked to and fro in unison. At least half of the passengers got off the train with Tony. They jammed the narrow escalator leading up to Washington Street and stepped into a summer day, already warming.

After Tony's meeting with Judge Bettinger last Tuesday, he had met with the lawyer the judge had recommended and accepted his offer of pro bono representation. On Wednesday Tony accompanied his lawyer to the US Attorney's Office. After an hour long conference with a pair of Justice Department staff attorneys, Tony and his lawyer were told that an investigation by the Department of Justice into the conduct and activities of Attorneys Metcalf and Poole would most likely be authorized, along with a warrant application to wiretap the lawyer's phones.

On Friday, Tony's lawyer received word that the warrant was issued by the Federal District Court. Tony's meeting with Roger Metcalf was scheduled for nine o'clock this Monday morning.

When Tony arrived at the Three Post Office Square Building at eight o'clock, Judge Bettinger was standing in the conference room watching as FBI agent Richard Burke tested a dime-size battery before placing it in a recording device disguised as a money clip. Burke looked up from his task at the two men and Bettinger introduced him to Tony. As Tony declined the judge's offer of coffee, Burke stood and shook his hand.

"Okay. She's working just fine," Burke said. He handed the money clip, to Tony, who managed to drop it onto the conference table. Burke quickly picked it up, tested it, and handed it back to Tony. "It's still okay. There's one hour's worth of recording time. You can stop and start it by pressing on the button with Mr. Greenspan's face on it, but if you're going to do this without taking it out of your pocket, you have to keep track of whether it's on or off. If the button is indented, it's on."

"Tony, you don't want to be there even close to an hour," Bettinger said. "I hope you're not there even half of that. So turn the recorder on just before you go in and leave it on. That way you won't have to think of it. Remember, you have a built in escape hatch. You have to be at the courthouse by ten o'clock. A sentencing hearing is scheduled at that time. You tell Metcalf up front you have to leave by nine-thirty."

"Remind me once more, please, Judge, exactly what we want Attorney Metcalf to say. Also, you were going to tell me why we want him to be recording our meeting."

The judge sat at the table and was joined by the others. "Simply put, Metcalf has to say things that will make it clear that he and Poole set up the bogus Montreal meeting in an attempt to gather information relating to the Theopoulis case, information to be used to influence the outcome of the pending appeal. We hope to be developing evidence to be introduced at a criminal trial if this matter results in indictments from the Justice Department investigation. We are also trying to get the Board of Bar Overseers on the case. We want these lawyers to be disciplined for unethical behavior."

"But, I thought you couldn't record conversations in Massachusetts for use in any legal proceedings. In fact, isn't it a crime to do that? I thought that's why they set up my job interview in Canada."

"The Massachusetts wiretapping law only applies to secret recordings, Tony. If we can show that attorney Metcalf is recording the conversation himself, he obviously can't argue that he didn't know it was being recorded. Metcalf's tape can then be subpoenaed by the Justice Department and the Board of Bar Overseers. If he refuses to produce it, he can be held in contempt, and your recording can be offered into evidence as a copy. This may be a stretch, but it's worth the effort. That is why we're hoping he's got his recorder going, and you're able to get him to actually say that he is recording the meeting.

"Tony, Agent Burke knows this city and its legal and political landscape as well as anyone does. You may know this already, but he'll give you a little background on these lawyers."

Looking across the table at Tony, Burke smoothed his maroon and gold-striped tie. "As you know, these are very high stakes for these two pillars of the legal community, but money's not the only issue. It's also reputations and careers. Cosmos Theopoulis is as connected as you can get. He's vowed all over the city to ruin Attorneys Poole and Metcalf if the judgment in this case stands, and maybe he's able to do that.

"In short, Frederick Poole sees his impeccable reputation in legal circles and in Boston society going to hell in a hand basket. He's proud of his family's contributions to the Boston Bar and to city charities. He treasures his and his family's standing in the city. He has friends in very high places.

"Interestingly, Poole is unashamedly gay. He has a live-in partner. He doesn't shout about his sexual persuasion, or hide it. It's safe to say he would consider a slap to his reputation as a step backwards for the gay community, which he would love to see come out of the shadows in the city he truly loves. Conclusion? I'm more than a little surprised he's involved in something this slimy. My guess is he made the wrong decision to get in, and just can't get out.

"Roger Metcalf is a different story. He's from a humble, hardscrabble background out in Springfield. Married, a couple of kids, but he's reputed to screw around big time, known as quite the ladies' man. Metcalf is also known as a courtroom brawler, but one hell of a litigator. Some say he's a little too slick. A lot of his fellow lawyers think it's pretty ironic that he's on the Bar Ethics Committee. Even though he's young, he's known to be angling for a judgeship. Doing the requisite political groundwork. This Theopoulis case knocked him cold, and he doesn't have the financial resources that Poole does. Just started his own firm a year or so ago. Long story short – this case could spell professional and financial disaster for him."

Tony moved his chair closer to the table. "Mr. Burke, am I in any physical danger?"

"Nothing's impossible with this kind of money involved, but my best guess is no, you are not likely to be roughed up in any way. That's not how high profile people accomplish their goals. They're willing to use bribes, blackmail, that kind of white collar activity, but they're not into breaking legs. This morning you're going to be in a major Boston office building at the start of the business day, not a downtown alley at two in the morning. I'm sure you'll walk out under your own power."

It was just before nine o'clock when Tony stepped out of the elevator and into the reception area of the office of Keene & Metcalf. He took a deep breath and straightened his tie. When he'd left Judge Bettinger's office fifteen minutes earlier, the judge told him to remember that he was dealing with a thug in a fancy suit and nothing more. But Tony couldn't quell the butterflies. He reached into the inside pocket of his suit coat and pressed his thumb against the recorder button, engaging the device. The receptionist was settling into her desk. She looked up with a smile as Tony approached. He said his name and that he had an appointment with Mr. Metcalf.

"I don't see your name," the receptionist said as she glanced at her computer screen. "I'll buzz him."

Just moments later, Roger Metcalf came around a corner. "Good morning Mr. Cipriano. Thanks for coming in."

"I have to be over to court before ten o'clock. There's a sentencing hearing and the judge told me to be available." The words tumbled out of Tony's mouth at high speed.

"It's only a ten minute walk to the courthouse. You'll be there in plenty of time, but we'll skip the coffee and doughnuts. This way." Metcalf turned the corner and led Tony down a hallway, past open doors to the copy center and a small conference room. He then stopped at his open office door, stood aside and followed Tony in. He closed the door.

"Sit down, and let's get to it," Metcalf said, and he sat behind his large desk.

Tony sat in a leather armchair in front of the desk. There was a single manila file on the desktop. Metcalf stared at Tony. He spoke in a moderate and clear voice.

"When you called last Thursday, Mr. Cipriano, you told me you no longer cared what happened to Judge Valdes, or the Theopoulis case. You seemed to have decided that the Judge had, basically, used you. Do you still feel the same way?"

Suddenly, Tony remembered that he wanted to get Metcalf to actually say that he was recording the meeting. With the exception of the manila folder and a pen and pencil, the desktop was bare. What the hell, he thought, might as well just ask. "Are you recording us, Mr. Metcalf? I mean, it's okay with me if you are. I was just wondering."

Metcalf smiled at Tony, reached into an open desk draw and withdrew a hand recorder, the "on" button glowing red. "Yes, I am. You said it was okay." Roger held up the recorder, "I took your word for it."

"It is okay," Tony said. "I don't intend to deny any of the things I said at the make-believe job interview set up by you and Attorney Poole. I'm willing to tell you all about working with the judge. From what I can tell, she doesn't know what she's doing half the time. She may be okay sitting in the criminal sessions, but she should keep away from civil cases. She put so much pressure on me I almost quit, but I needed the job."

"Are you saying that you had a substantial amount of the responsibility in the Theopoulis case?"

"Exactly. Which is what I said in the Montreal interview."

Roger picked up the pencil, tapped its eraser on the manila folder and said, "You should know, Mr. Cipriano, that there are many degrees of separation between Mr. Poole, me and that bogus interview in Montreal. If it is ever suggested we were involved, we are vested with what is referred to as plausible deniability. But, if you cooperate, which is in your interest, and the interest of justice in this case, that meeting will never be the subject of any discussions again. It will never have taken place."

Metcalf opened the folder which contained a three page, single space document and said, "This affidavit sets forth facts about Judge Valdes's handling of the Theopoulis case. Facts that came out of your mouth at the Montreal meeting, plus, as we say in our business, reasonable inferences that can be drawn from those facts. We want your signature on this document, Mr. Cipriano."

"What do you plan to do with the affidavit?"

"There are alternative uses. We will first use it to try to settle the case on far less onerous terms than the judgment entered by Judge Valdes. Maybe that will be possible when the plaintiffs understand we have real ammunition for the appeal. However, it's possible, and knowing the parties involved, likely, that the case will not settle. If that happens, the affidavit will be filed with our appeal and with post-verdict motions to have the judgments set aside.

"Of course, you also have our assurance that we will not report your conduct, particularly your forging of Judge Valdes's signature on the court order, to the Board of Bar Overseers, or anywhere else."

"Judge Valdes used me, and now my life's all screwed up. I don't care who wins or loses the Theopoulis case, or how much they win or lose. Give me a pen."

PART THREE

FINALLY

Tom Kenny

34

A daydream involving his former colleague, now Judge Zelia Valdes, ended when a paralegal at the Public Defender's Office arrived at Jack Ralston's open office door. Her message was that Jack had a call from a staff attorney, Amy Westfield, on the flashing line. "She says it could be important."

Reaching for his phone, Jack wondered why Amy, the lawyer covering afternoon arraignments at the Boston Municipal Court, insisted on talking to him. The BMC dealt with misdemeanors and lesser felonies. As chief counsel, Jack's bailiwick was overseeing the office's defense of major criminal indictments in the Superior Court, an occasional trial to keep his edge, and hiring and firing. Phone to his ear, he chewed on a stick of beef jerky while Amy explained why she asked to speak directly to him.

An arraignment resulting in a defendant's release on personal recognizance had concluded fifteen minutes earlier. The defendant was a woman charged with possession of marijuana with intent to sell, an everyday charge at the BMC. Then Amy mentioned that the accused was a former client of the PD's office named Julie Santos, and had asked specifically to talk to Jack. The name clicked right off. Jack recalled representing Julie a few times, ten or so years ago, on garden variety soliciting charges. Her pretty face, which he remembered as always wearing a smile, popped up in his mind's eye.

"Yeah, sure, I remember Julie. But what's the big deal? We aim to please, but she doesn't get to pick her lawyer on a simple possession with intent case."

"Oh, I explained that to her, sir, and I normally would never bother you with this kind of case. The reason I asked to be put through is because I figured you'd want to know what she told me."

"Okay, Amy, shoot."

"The client says she really trusts you and she's afraid of going to jail because she has a five-year-old son, and she's worried that the state will place him in a foster home. She thinks she has some good information that maybe she could use to bargain with the DA's office. It's something about a huge crime that happened around ten years ago and has never been solved. She's wondering if maybe she can do some horse-trading."

"You've got my attention. What's she talking about?"

"I kind of remember it, even though I was in high school at the time. It was at a museum. The Gardner Museum robbery?"

"Gardner Museum? You sure that's what she said, Amy?" Jack asked as he stood from his desk.

"Yes, sir. That's what she said."

"Don't let Julie out of your sight, Amy. I'm on my way over. Ten minutes."

His suit coat left hanging in the office, Jack arrived at the old building housing the Boston Municipal Court in under ten minutes, oblivious to his sweat-soaked shirt. As he'd walked, mostly jogged, the half mile to the courthouse under the hot August sun, he'd thought back to his first encounter with Julie Santos.

He had been assigned to the Roxbury District Court. When he arrived on that snowy winter day, the young and comely Julie was wrapped in a short wool coat with a big fur collar, awaiting arraignment on a solicitation charge. Jack thought back to the smile on that glowing face that greeted him in the court's holding cell, and those big brown eyes, and to realizing that this wayward young woman was polite and smart. He also recalled that she was a straight shooter - no excuses. *Goddamn,* he recalled thinking after his fifteen minute meeting with his new client, *what the hell is Julie Santos doing on the stroll? What a waste.*

Jack made his way down a wide corridor, its once white walls long ago stained the brownish-yellow hue patented by the tobacco industry. The area was loud with the babble of lawyers in animated conversations with their clients. Amy greeted him across the hall from the door to a conference room. She handed Jack a two-page police report, which he scanned, folded, and put in his pants pocket. He then complimented Amy for recognizing the importance of the situation. The young lawyer smiled and readily agreed to keep the information to herself. She pointed to the door across the hall. Jack stepped over and pushed the door open.

Julie Santos wore a red, short-sleeved polo shirt and short tan skirt. She was sitting at a metal table in the bare-bones conference room and holding a can of Coke. Jack was a little taken aback. Julie looked exactly as he remembered her from almost a decade ago. Spotting Jack, Julie set the soda can on the tabletop, ran a hand through her short hair and smiled that smile.

"Hey, Mr. Jack Ralston, how you been?"

"I've been good, Julie. It's been a while." Jack returned the smile.

Julie stood. "You haven't changed. Good-looking as ever. Still got all your hair. The girls were always jealous 'cause I got the hottie for a lawyer."

Jack stepped into the room and closed the door behind him. He reached across the table and shook Julie's hand. "Thanks, but I'm getting a little gray and I've put on a few pounds." Jack patted his belly. "It's you who hasn't changed. Other than today's problem, how's it been for you?"

Julie sat back down. "Real good. Since my boy, Brandon, came along five years ago, I've been on super good behavior, except for this little misunderstanding between me and the boys down at District Two."

"Possession with intent. I never figured you for narcotics, Julie. You used to tell me drugs were out of bounds. What happened?" Jack sat at the table.

"Believe it or not, I was doing a favor for my cousin because she had to go into City Hospital for some tests. She'd promised a college kid over at Northeastern a delivery, told me she really needed the cash. That's the truth, Jack. I never intended anything but a favor." Julie rolled the can of Coke between the palms of her hands. "Problem is, the kid she promised the weed wasn't exactly in college. He was a narc."

Jack pulled the folded police report from his pocket and placed it on the table. "Serious stuff, Julie. Judge Meagher is hell on pushers, even if they're pleading out."

"I'm really scared, Jack. If I get convicted of this weed charge, plus my old criminal record, I could be looking at time in the house, or maybe even at Framingham. I can't do any time, Jack. I got my boy at home. Child services would take him for sure. I might never get him back. That can't happen. Things are going real good. Got a decent job at the Colonnade Hotel. I just made assistant supervisor in housekeeping. I really got my act together for my Brandon."

"Talk to me. Tell me what you've got, what we can barter with the DA. He won't just roll over. Even for good old Jack."

"I kind of mentioned it to the kid from your office when I was arraigned. You see, it was a while ago, real early nineties, I was working the bar at the Frisky Goose over in the Zone. This kind of nerdy, but nice guy used to come in once a week, on Tuesday afternoons. He was a decent guy, quiet and all. Never looked for any booth action from any of the girls. Just liked to come in for a drink and a little company at the bar. Watch the girls dance." Julie scraped her chair in closer to the table. "Well, back then, me and another one of the girls scored a regular date with a couple of overnight guards at the Gardner Museum over in the Fenway."

"The Gardner Museum," Jack repeated, wanting to be sure of what he heard, "over in the Fenway."

"Yeah, that's where they were at. We used to call it our mansion call, you know, like house call, because it was at this mansion that we provided the fun for these johns. Every Sunday morning, right after the Goose closed, we'd cab it over for a little party."

"Right in the museum?"

"Yeah. They'd leave a door off an alley unlocked and turn the alarm off. About one-thirty or so we'd just walk right in and then go upstairs to the room with the rugs on the wall."

"That's amazing."

"Didn't seem like a big deal."

Jack shook his head, produced a wry grin. "Doors unlocked? The Gardner had a reputation for being casual about things back then, but this takes the cake. Do you have any idea of the value of the stuff hanging on the walls over there?"

"Lots."

"Lots, plus. What's the nerdy, nice guy from the Goose got to do with anything?"

Julie took a sip of soda, and then said, "I mentioned the museum parties to him once, just making small talk at the bar. He asked how we got in, how long we hung around, that kind of stuff. I told him. Seemed harmless enough. Real casual like, Jack. I mean, he wasn't grilling me or anything. Then, just two weeks after I had this talk with the guy, they had that huge robbery that was all over the news." Julie paused a moment. "Jack, it was on one of the nights while me and Maggie were at the mansion with the guards. If they got the time right, we were there when it happened."

"You were there, in the museum, entertaining your customers, while it was being robbed?"

"If it happened around one-thirty, when the Globe said it did, yep. We were in the room with the rugs on the wall then. I remember it was Saint Patty's Day. The guards had a buddy with them. They gave us a bonus for the extra john. He brought some of those funny green hats the little Irish guys wear, and, after a while, that's the only thing any of us were wearing."

"If you and your pal were there at one-thirty, Julie, then all the newspapers got the story wrong, at least the time of the robbery. It would have to have happened later than they all reported."

"Go figure. I know when we were there, Jack."

Jack stood and paced the small room. "And two weeks before the heist you told this guy how to get into the museum in the middle of the night, without setting off an alarm?"

"I didn't think he'd rob the damn place."

Jack sat back in his chair. "When did you put two and two together, Julie?"

"Right after I found out about the robbery. Found out in the *Globe* on Monday morning. Right off, I thought of my bar talk with the nice guy customer. Then, after he never came back to the Goose, at least when I was working the bar, I kind of figured he might have been involved somehow. But back then I wouldn't think of ratting out anybody for anything. And the guy was kind of sweet, a good guy. Now, with Brandon, and this weed thing, well, I gotta do what I gotta do. Plus, I was thinking about that law of limitations or something like that. Will the nerdy guy maybe be okay, even if they collar him, Jack?"

"Statute of limitations? It's run on the theft." Jack rubbed his chin.

"Possession of stolen property? Maybe, maybe not. Depends on the facts, on the circumstances, but I can't imagine this guy, or whoever robbed the museum, still has the paintings."

"It'd be great if you could try and keep the nice guy out of the picture. You know, Jack, maybe try and get the paintings back, without saying who might have stolen them?"

"Julie, that would probably require Houdini. But it's a little early in the game to throw in the towel. Who knows what will happen, if anything."

"I'm not in any trouble for this stuff, am I?"

"No. Not after all these years. If you had any problems here, they're long gone." Julie relaxed a little in her chair. Jack stood. "Got a name for the nice guy?"

"Ah, no, no, I don't. If he ever told me what it was, I forget. I just called him Mr. Nice Guy, because that's what he was. But, Jack, I'm sure I'd remember him if I ever saw him again."

Jack groaned, "Julie, there are a few billion people in this world. And guys that steal millions of dollars worth of paintings could be anywhere. Got any clues?"

"If he's still got a job, maybe it's the same one he had back then."

"You knew where he worked?"

"Yeah. He worked at the Gardner museum."

"You're kidding me."

"No, that's what he said. That's why I figured he was so interested in me and Maggie going over there. He told me he was a guide or something like that, at the Gardner. He had a fancy word for it."

"Docent, I'll bet. He must have been a docent. That's a kind of guide in a museum."

"Yup. That's what he said he did. Said it was like a tour guide, but for art stuff, instead of foreign countries. Think he could still work at the museum?"

Jack chuckled as he sat back on the metal chair. "My guess is that he's in a villa on the Côte d'Azur."

"Say what?"

"France, Julie. He's probably at the beach in France."

Jack looked at his watch. "Julie, you've got to promise me something, and I really mean it. It's for your own good. You don't mention this Gardner Museum story to anyone, period. Okay?"

"Sure."

"Have you ever told anyone what you just told me about this docent guy?"

"Nope, not a soul. Never."

"Not even Maggie, your friend from the Frisky Goose?"

"Nope. I never mentioned the docent guy to anyone, even Maggs."

"Is she still around the city?"

Julie paused a moment. "No. Good ol' Maggs. She OD'd just a few weeks after the museum got hit. Do you think you can help me with my little weed problem, Jack?"

"I'll sure as hell try." Jack stood and opened the door, then turned back to Julie. "I'll send Attorney Westfield back in. You'll have some paperwork to fill out. Where will you be tomorrow?"

"My job, at the Colonnade."

"I'll be in touch, Julie, and remember…" Jack mimed a zipper pull across his lips.

35

Jack Ralston sat at the computer in his North End apartment. After thirty minutes of searching the Gardner heist on Google, he donned his rain gear, grabbed a plastic supermarket bag from a kitchen drawer, and left his apartment for the fifteen minute walk to his downtown office. His dog, Thurgood, was at his side.

"Police leave anything for me yet this morning?" Jack asked, shedding his wet raincoat and Bruins baseball-style cap as he walked across the reception area of the Public Defender's Office. He hung his gear and Thurgood's leash on the coat rack and the black and white mutt, that had shaken itself silly on the building's cement portico, walked into Jack's office and curled up in a corner.

A white-haired secretary stationed beside Jack's office door held up a plump manila envelope dropped off fifteen minutes earlier by a BPD detective. "Sam Ketchum says you owe him for the overnight delivery. I see you've got your service animal with you."

Five minutes later, Jack came back out of his office carrying the envelope. "Back by noon," he told his secretary as he grabbed his raincoat and cap. "Thurgood will be okay 'till then, but if anyone wants to walk him, they'll have a friend for life. He's already pooped and loves the rain. Leash is on the rack."

The Colonnade Hotel sat on the edge of the South End, tucked in behind the Prudential Center complex of upscale apartments and shopping malls. Jack's cab dropped him at the hotel entrance where he was greeted by a regally outfitted doorman holding an umbrella. Within five minutes, Jack had persuaded an assistant hotel manager that Julie Santos needed an early coffee break.

Walking up Huntington Avenue in a light rain, Julie admonished her lawyer. "Damn, Jack. You'll get me in all kinds of trouble, taking me away from the hotel in the morning. I got an even dozen rooms need cleaning."

Ten minutes later, Jack and Julie were sitting across from each other in a Burger King. Two Styrofoam cups of coffee sat beside the now empty manila envelope Jack had carried into the fast food restaurant. He watched Julie's face as he slid 5 by 7 photographs across the table. She rejected the first five, saying they were not at all familiar. She hesitated on the sixth.

"You testing me, Jack?"

"What do you mean?"

"These pictures are supposed to be of these docent guys at the museum, right?"

"Yeah, they came from the museum's personnel office."

"Well, this guy," Julie poked photo six with an index finger, "he's one of the johns me and Maggs used to party with."

"Really? They must have thrown in photos of others along with the docents."

Julie turned photo six face down and placed it on the pile next to the envelope. She read the name hand-printed on the back. "Smathers, Norman. We used to call him naked Normy. Never saw him with a stitch on. He'd have his uniform off before we even got up to the rug room."

Julie then asked, "By the way, how do you go about fencing something like those paintings, anyhow?"

"It's got to be close to impossible," Jack said. "One theory is that there may have been a buyer in mind and the paintings were hand-picked. They left a slew of real valuable ones hanging on the wall. There's never even been a rumor that the paintings were on the market. If they were put up for sale, someone would have heard about it."

Three photos later Julie smiled and nodded as another head shot was slid towards her. "Yup, that's Mr. Nice Guy."

"Sure?"

"Absolutely."

Jack turned the photo over. "Smelton, Eddie S," he read aloud.

"Eddie, that was his name, Eddie the docent. I remember now. He did tell me his first name once."

Jack looked back at the head shot and, in his mind, repeated Julie's words - *"Eddie the docent."* The words triggered a memory, but he couldn't quite nail it down. He flipped the photo over and read the rest of the information. "Status, active. Active? Hell, that can't be right, or can it? If it is, Eddie could be giving museum tours this very minute."

Then Jack remembered. *Holy shit. It was after dinner last fall. I was walking down Charles Street with Zelia. She told me about the guy at the bar - Eddie, the docent. Knew all about masterpieces. What the f...*

"Earth to Jack," Julie interrupted Jack's brief hiatus from their conversation.

"Oh, sorry about that, Julie. Something popped into my head." Jack paused a moment, and then said, "Julie, you must know there's a big reward, in the millions, for the return of those paintings."

"Yeah, I know. I've been tempted, but I don't really know if the nice guy was involved, or if they'd ever catch him. Anyhow, I'm just not a rat. I don't have that in me, Jack. Especially if it would get a good guy in trouble. I'd probably get screwed out of any reward anyhow, and end up in trouble myself. What I really want, Jack, is to be sure I'm with my Brandon as he grows up."

"Julie, I don't really know how this is going to play out. I'm going to do my best to protect you and make the best deal I can on the drug charge. I may have to talk to what we call third parties on your behalf, but I can't talk to anyone about what you've told me without your permission."

"Jack, you can tell anybody anything I've told you. I trust you to protect me, but how about the docent guy. I really don't like fingering him."

"Well, like I said yesterday, Julie, the statute of limitations has run on the robbery. If this Eddie guy was involved, he's probably out of the woods there, but if it could be proved he kept control of the paintings for a while, they might try to charge him with possession of stolen property. Anyhow, I'm beginning to think this whole thing may be Alice-in-Wonderland. Why the hell would he still be working at the museum if he stole the paintings?" Jack began to collect the photos and place them back in the envelope."Whatever, I'll try and find out."

"Jack, I got real lucky with a great guy. We've been going pretty strong for over a year now. He gets along real good with my son, and Brandon's nutty over him. I think it's gonna work out with us for the long term. I can't screw it up, Jack."

"I hear you, Julie. I love that you got it together, and I'll do what I can to protect that situation. I promise."

The beginning of a tear was accompanied by, "Thanks, Jack. I know I can count on you doing your best."

"Just remember to keep your lips sealed about this, Julie. Do not mention it to anyone, including your boyfriend. Period. Got it?"

"Yep, I got it. Can I go back to work now?"

William Bettinger leaned back in the high-back leather chair and cradled his head. As on most days since leaving the Public Defender's Office, he was enjoying a light lunch in the study of his suburban home. A half-eaten chicken salad sandwich and a glass of lemonade sat on his desk. He was looking through a window at deep red rhododendron bushes and thinking of Zelia Valdes. He decided that, maybe - actually, forget maybe - he was just an old fool in love with a woman half his age.

Bettinger took a pint bottle of vodka from a desk drawer and poured a stream into the lemonade. He hoped the scent-free liquor would keep Honora, his long-serving cook and housekeeper, from picking up on his habit of spiking the summer drink. As he sipped, he weighed the possibility of Zelia being romantically interested in an old man. For the last two weeks he had thought of little else. The sound of the phone shook him. He answered and recognized the voice of his replacement, whom he had hand-picked, at the helm of the Public Defender's Office.

"How are you, Judge?" Jack Ralston asked.

"Just fine, Jack. It's nice to hear a familiar voice. Keeping things under control at the office?"

"As much as I can. Actually, I'm calling to ask your advice on a very unusual matter that came to my attention yesterday. If it turns out to be the genuine item, it will be headlines in the *Globe*."

Bettinger rolled his chair into the desk and reached for a pen and yellow legal pad. "Go on."

"Well, Judge, late yesterday afternoon I got a call from one of our lawyers over at the BMC. She had a former client of the office, a woman I represented on soliciting charges years ago, being arraigned on a minor drug charge."

Ten minutes later William Bettinger was pacing his study, his mind racing, close to panic. *Who could ever imagine such a thing! A fluke of the highest order - a bar girl and a Gardner Museum docent? And the second it leaks that there's a real lead in the Gardner case, there'll be chaos in the Boston press. My God! Zelia's prints, her DNA must be all over the docent's house. She's sure to be dragged into any investigation. She'll never recover. I can't let that happen. Thank God Jack called me. At least he's promised to wait until I get back to him before he blows the whistle. I hope I've bought enough time.*

36

A recent phone call Roger Metcalf received from the bellicose Cosmos Theopoulis had resulted in a pair of sleepless nights for the litigator. Roger began to think it could make sense to tell Cosmos about the bogus Montreal interview, and what had eventually been gleaned from the charade. He had to at least try to calm down the little bastard before he started to make life even more miserable.

When Roger put a call into Frederick Poole to discuss sharing the interview information with their client, a secretary informed him that Mr. Poole was out of the office because of an illness. Roger called Poole's home and learned from Otto that Frederick was drunk, and had been for three days. Otto was certain that his partner would agree with whatever decisions Roger was making about the Theopoulis case. In any event, Frederick was not capable of making any himself. Roger hung up and immediately called over to Patriot Downs. A half an hour later the unforgiving client was standing in Roger's office.

"Okay, here I am. What's the big news? And it better be worth my racing over here in this goddamn heat wave." Cosmos stood just inside the closed office door. The small man rubbed his forearms below the short sleeves of his open neck shirt. "Shit, Metcalf, it's hotter than hell out there, and like the North Pole in here. It's too damn cold."

"You'll feel nice and warm in a minute. Have a seat and listen to some tape recordings. It's critical that you keep this information to yourself for now. It's for your ears only. I promise you I'll use it to reverse this goddamn judgment and, if I'm right, you'll never have to deal with Judge Zelia Valdes again. Maybe nobody will."

"Skip the bullshit, Metcalf." Cosmos remained standing. "What information?"

"It has to do with Judge Valdes's law clerk. His name is Cipriano. Sit down for a few minutes, Mr. T. I think you'll like what you hear."

Cosmos remained standing, leaning back against the office wall. After Roger gave a brief description of how the law clerk had been duped, Cosmos listened to selected portions of the tapes for a few minutes, then sat down. He listened for another fifteen minutes, and then looked across the desk at Roger.

"Looks like you may have finally done something right, Metcalf. The problem is, even though you and your fruity law partner may threaten, you won't use this crap about the law clerk and the phony job interview. You know it would cost both of you your law licenses. A nice little trick you played on him, but most likely it's illegal and, even in your business, unethical. Not that I give a shit, but somebody else might."

"Let me worry about my law license, Mr. T. This law clerk is in our pocket, and that means that Judge Zelia Valdes is in our cross-hairs."

The Monday after hearing the tape of the law clerk's employment interview, Cosmos Theopoulis was sitting in the glass-walled broadcast studio of WAKM Radio in a Boston suburb. A Tufts college intern drew an appreciative smile from Cosmos as she adjusted the boom mike hanging in front of his face. Taking a seat across the table from Cosmos, Hank Cahoon, the drive-time ratings king of Boston talk radio, noticed Cosmos' smile and quickly claimed credit for hiring the station interns, then added, "and every damn one of 'em is *Hustler* material, or, you can bet your ass, Cosmos, they don't get into this room."

"Better watch it or her lawyer will be all over you like flies on horseshit, won't he, honey?" Cosmos said, then smiled and winked at the undergraduate.

"Okay, Cosmos, we got two minutes to airtime," Cahoon said. "Let's go over the ground rules. Real simple. Watch your language. Even with the eight second delay, a lot of crap gets out on the airwaves. And try not to scream at the callers. Give 'em a ration of shit if you think they deserve it, but too much noise turns the listeners off. Got it?"

"Yeah, I got it."

Cahoon was delighted with the scheduling of Cosmos as his studio guest. A mutual acquaintance - the horse racing columnist at the *Herald* - had called at Cosmos' behest late last week. The emissary had explained that Cosmos claimed to have a red-hot disclosure that would prove that the judge who "fucked him out of a cool billion" was a fraud. The Theopoulis family feud had been well-reported in the Boston press during the trial. Cahoon knew that bad blood, particularly involving the wealthy and powerful, was lapped up by the public and, in particular, by his loyal listeners. His audience was always eager to see the mighty brought to their knees. This, coupled with the shock-jock's general dislike and distrust of the Massachusetts judiciary, assured Cosmos of a spot during the early week drive-time. Cued by the radio show's producer, Cahoon drew in his overhead mike.

"It's show time. Our guest for the next hour is Cosmos Theopoulis. For any of you dolts who don't know, Cosmos not only owns and operates the Patriot Downs racetrack in East Boston, plus a dozen other businesses around the country, he also has the distinction of being on the wrong side of the largest civil court judgment in Massachusetts history. That occurred because one of our state's liberal trial judges, Senorita Zelia Valdes, tripled a jury award of three hundred and thirty-three-million dollars. That's right, tripled. With her help, it ended up being a very cool one billion dollars that Cosmos now owes. That's right, folks, billion, with a B. Cosmos says he has information about the lady judge that will eventually nullify the verdict and disqualify Valdes from being involved any further with his case, and should cost her her gavel. Cosmos, talk to my listeners."

Other than his future, or lack of future, in the legal profession, virtually nothing else had crept into Tony Cipriano's head since his meeting at the Ritz-Carlton with Attorneys Metcalf and Poole. He was sure he had been convincing in his subsequent meeting at Attorney Metcalf's office, but that was about a month ago, and Tony was surprised that he had not been contacted since then. Judge Valdes suggested the Theopoulis lawyers were most likely planning their strategy, and another shoe was likely to drop soon. Also, she said, as in a lot of cities, not much got accomplished during the dog days of August.

Even though the US Attorney had agreed to investigate Metcalf and Poole for possible criminal activity, there was no feedback from the federal prosecutors. What, if anything, had been accomplished, and whether the Justice Department would decide to take formal action against the Theopoulis attorneys, was simply unknown. The Board of Bar Overseers seemed to be hemming and hawing over getting involved. Maybe they were just waiting and, perhaps hoping, that any Board action could piggyback the feds. On Friday, a criminal case had unexpectedly ended in a plea, leaving the last Monday of the month with an empty docket. Judge Valdes told her law clerk to take a hike until Tuesday.

Kate realized Tony was obsessed by the Theopoulis mess. Since the initial burst of eagerness to right the wrong after meeting her at the Hyatt Hotel in Cambridge, and the follow up activity led by Judge Bettinger, Tony's involvement had come to a halt, and he seemed to be spiraling downward. Hoping to help pull him out of the doldrums, over the weekend she'd suggested a Monday drive to her family's summer home on the South Shore and vegging out on the waterfront deck. The house was empty and would provide a brief change of scenery, as well as a temporary hideaway from the real world. Tony agreed and Kate's red Jag picked him up at Columbia Point in Dorchester at noontime.

After stopping at Hingham Harbor for lunch, Tony and Kate drove to a North Scituate neighborhood of summer homes, arriving in mid-afternoon. Following a tour of Kate's family's house, which Tony calculated provided about ten times the living space of his family's Dorchester walk-up, he and Kate decided to walk the beach. In spite of her best efforts, the conversation kept drifting back to the problem at hand. A cool summer wind off the water, and Kate's not so subtle hints that returning to the house might make for an interesting afternoon, could not rock Tony's relentless stream of consciousness: *my career is history, all those nights and hours of work for nothing, humiliation, laughing stock, stupid, asshole, braggart, liar, a joke, and my parents, what have I done to my parents?*

At about four o'clock, Tony hitched his shoulders up against a salty spray whipped up from the ocean's edge. "Sorry Kate, but I should get back. Let's get going."

"If we leave now, Tony, by the time we get back near the city we'll just hit rush hour traffic."

"We should be okay. The traffic will be heading south, coming at us."

"The phone lines are all lit up for Cosmos Theopoulis. Let's go right to a call. Maude from Malden, say hello to Cosmos."

"Hello Cosmos. I feel so bad for you. Believe me I know these judges think they're God almighty. One of them did a number on my daughter in the probate court last year. Make you think it was her screwing around, not her scumbag husband. Let me ask you a question."

"Please do, Maude," Hank Cahoon interjected. "This show is about my guest, not your whacked-out daughter, who probably deserved whatever she got."

"Oh, you're such a card, Hank. Love ya. Here's my question, Cosmos ..."

Kate pulled the Jaguar into the passing lane on Route 3. She and Tony were about five miles south of Columbia Point, traveling north in light traffic. The south-bound lanes were crowded with rush hour commuters on their way home.

"You were right, Tony, most of the traffic's heading out of the city. Press the second button and put Hammerin' Hank on the radio, will you?"

"He's the talk show guy, right? My dad listens to him all the time. When I'd be leaving for my night law classes, he'd always be at the kitchen table listening to this Hank guy on our old radio."

"He's pretty good when he's muck-raking the local politicians, and kind of funny now and then. Maybe he'll put you in a better mood. I've got to tell you, Tony, you've got me more than a little worried."

Tony pressed the radio tuning button.

"Here's my question, Cosmos – why are you so certain that this inexperienced law clerk, this kid, actually decided your case and cost you a billion? Don't these clerks just help judges out with research and looking up cases, and that kind of stuff?"

"I don't know what the hell they're supposed to do. But I know what this one did. Because we had a lazy judge who didn't know her ass from her elbow about this kind of case, she had this totally inexperienced kid just out of law school make decisions, like, who was lying on the witness stand. He was doing all the stuff she was supposed to do herself.

How do I know? Because I heard him say so on tape recordings. That's how I know. I got screwed royally, by this Judge Zelia Valdes, and by her idiot law clerk, who thought he was a big shot."

The final fifteen minutes of the Hank Cahoon talk show was filled with a few advertisements and a lot of haranguing about Judge Zelia Valdes and her law clerk. Then, Hammerin' Hank asked Cosmos if he had any final comments.

"Yeah, I did what I was supposed to do for my dear brother, what I promised him on his death bed I'd do, and I end up getting screwed in a lawsuit. On my parents' graves, I will make this right. I will not stop fighting for what's right in this case 'till the day I die."

37

Why anyone would vacation in Florida in August was beyond Basil Simeone's ability to comprehend. But that's where Judge Zelia Valdes was this week. Porky had handed off the judge's surveillance to a private eye in Miami, and Basil was on his own until she returned. He decided to take advantage of his freedom from tailing the judge.

On this final Monday afternoon of August, wearing his usual black windbreaker and black jeans, he sat in his Saab a short distance up the street from the Smelton home. Breaking and entering was never his favorite part of being a private investigator, but sometimes it was necessary. The weather was overcast, but dry. Basil would have preferred a rainy day, one more likely to keep the Rindge Avenue neighbors inside their homes. It wasn't rocket science - the fewer people observing, the better.

He figured this risky effort would make points with Porky, who was his main source of income of late. Also, his curiosity was raging. He could not figure out why the lady judge with the fancy condo on Beacon Hill had such a generous bent, paying tens of thousands of dollars to renovate someone else's property. He was looking for the real reason the judge spent her free time in this neck of the woods, and all that construction money on that crappy little house. He didn't buy that it was simply to help out an old lady in a wheelchair who was afraid of fire. There had to be another reason. Maybe a special room with cameras and toys to rendezvous with a guy, maybe even a woman, maybe a whole gang of trans-whatevers. But there was something, or somebody.

Basil watched Tommy leave Thornton's Variety carrying the *Herald*, jump onto his bike and race diagonally across the street. With a sudden swoop, the twelve-year-old dropped the bike on the sidewalk and hurried through the open gate in the fence. In moments he was across and down the small lawn and through the cellar door of the Smelton house. To Basil's delight, Tommy left the door half open, just as he had the last time Basil watched him enter the cellar.

The private investigator glanced around the immediate area. There was no one in sight. In just seconds, Basil was out of his Saab, across and down the Smelton's sloping lawn, through the open door, and into the cellar. Basil turned slowly, taking in the small area barely lit by a pair of narrow windows high in the foundation wall. Glancing to his right, Basil saw a long wooden table piled with a mishmash of tools and odd pieces of wood and wire. It all seemed connected by a gray jungle of cob webs. At the back end of the cellar, an open staircase next to an electric service box led up to the first floor. The door at the top of the stairs was open. Basil looked up the staircase. From his angle, he saw only kitchen cabinets. He then squeezed into a small open area behind the staircase to wait. For a minute or so he heard muffled voices. Then a clear young voice said, "Thanks, Mrs. S. See you tomorrow."

Basil heard footfalls on the floor above. The kitchen door to the cellar slammed shut. He held his breath and watched through the open treads as a pair of sneakers padded down the staircase. The paperboy did not turn back as he walked quickly across the cellar and out the door, slamming it closed behind him. Basil waited a half-minute, then wriggled out of his space and climbed the staircase to the kitchen. He slowly opened the door.

Across the kitchen floor, on the far side of a table, a hallway led to the front of the house. Facing him at the end of the hall, a high window framed the limbs of an oak tree against the gray sky. Basil walked around the table to the hallway. There were two doorways on the left side of the hall, the first, a small single door, the other a narrow double, or French, door. The single door was closed. He could hear a soft voice coming from the room with double doors, open just a crack, its glass panes covered with an interior curtain. The voice had a simple melody to it. Basil could just make out the words - "'*When will that be?' ♪ say the bells of Stepney. ♪ 'I do not know', ♪ say the great bells of Bow.*"

The sounds brought back a distant memory - a nursery rhyme?

Basil pictured the diagram of the house layout he had seen at the city building department. The nursery rhyme had to be coming from the room where the old lady sits at the window.

On the right side of the hall, the first of two doors was open. Basil took two steps and looked in. It was a wide bathroom outfitted with various handicap grab-bars. The tan-colored window shade was drawn. He looked at the door a few feet down, on the same side of the hall. Recalling the floor plan, he was sure this was the room where the old lady slept, the fireproofed room. The door was oversized and finished in oak paneling.

Basil stepped down the hall, his crepe soles silent on the worn rug runner. He stood near the double door on his left for a moment, then heard a voice, louder than before.

"Tommy, don't forget your cookie from the jar on the table."

Basil froze. He had watched the paperboy leave the house minutes ago, and hoped the old lady had just lost track of time, rather than sensed there was someone in the hallway. He waited a solid minute without moving, listening to more of the nursery rhyme. *"Here comes a candle to lead you to bed. ♫ Here comes a chopper to chop off your head. ♫ Chip chop chip chop-the last man's dead."* Then he heard a short beep of a car's horn. "Hi," he heard in response in a soft voice.

Now, sure of the old woman's location in the house, and that she was involved in her window routine, Basil stepped to his right, stopped and pushed down on the oak-paneled door's handle. He breathed a quiet sigh when it opened slowly, silently, into a room with a parquet floor barely lit from the hall's natural light. He stepped over the threshold. There was a soft whoosh of air flowing in the room. Maroon curtains cut from heavy felt sealed a pair of windows from the outside light. Basil noticed an electrical switch on the wall to his right. He closed the door behind him and pressed the switch. Soft overhead lights came alive. Simultaneously, individual picture lights throughout the square room were lit, shining down on five canvases hanging on the walls. Directly across from where Basil stood, he saw Christ and his disciples in a fishing boat, battling through heavy whitecaps in the Sea of Galilee.

Basil stepped to the center of the square room and stood beside a brown leather swivel chair on rubber rollers. He glanced around the room. He was no art historian, nonetheless, he was awestruck. He had seen pictures in magazines of the same paintings. He knew he was in the presence of the stolen Gardner Museum masterpieces. Turning, and staring, he let his discovery sink in. Excitedly, he dug a digital mini-camera he always carried from his jacket pocket. After multiple clicks he had two images of each painting stored in the camera.

The bartender at Frank's Steakhouse on Massachusetts Avenue poured another shot of Wild Turkey into the chunky glass in front of Basil. "On the house," he said, hoping to develop a regular with a taste for the top-shelf offering. The gesture was lost on Basil, his mind fully occupied by his twenty-minute-old discovery. He was comfortable that the old lady in the room across the hall never knew she had a visitor after the paperboy left. As soon as he'd slunk back out of the house the way he'd come in, Basil spent a few minutes sitting in the Saab, calming down. Then he drove around the block and back up Rindge Avenue, toward the house. He honked his horn and the lady in the window waved. Things were normal.

While he sipped the bourbon, Basil attempted to relax, convinced that he had, literally, discovered hidden treasure, treasure with a five million dollar reward attached to it. The bartender was at the far end of the mahogany bar absorbed in a cribbage game with the only other patron. Basil took his camera from his pocket, pressed a button and looked at the images of the paintings. Even though he was certain he had stumbled upon the Gardner paintings, he decided that an Internet search when he got back to his apartment would make sense. He also made the quick decision that there was no chance he'd share the information, or reward, with Porky. He was an independent contractor and, anyway, he wasn't going to need Porky's money. Basil breathed deeply, and tried to organize his thoughts.

I've got to act fast. Lots of things could happen and screw me out of the reward. The old lady has a medical emergency. Shit, somebody could actually steal those paintings from her. Worst of all, somebody else might find them and blow the five-million-dollar whistle. I'd never get over that. He looked up at a Miller Lite clock hanging from a chain, revolving over the bar. It was closing in on five o'clock. *I'll never get in town to the FBI office before the close of business. Don't want to talk to some flunky covering after hours crap. Anyhow, before spilling anything to the FBI, I should call a lawyer. Protect myself. Yeah, I'll call Bobby Feeley. Saw him just the other day at the Bell in Hand. He'll know how to protect my rights, and he deals with the Feds all the time. Holy shit, five million, and the most famous private eye in Boston history.*

Basil slapped a ten dollar bill on the bar and hurried back to his Saab. His hand was shaking as he scrolled down the list of names on his cell phone and found Feeley's office number. To his dismay, a secretary told him that the lawyer was still in court in Rhode Island, and put him through to his voice-mail.

"Bobby, it's Basil. Basil Simeone. I gotta talk to you, and right off. I found something unbelievably valuable while I was tailing that judge I told you about the other day at the Bell. I have to act real fast, like yesterday, or a fortune could be lost. I'm not fucking with you, Bobby. Call me back at this cell number the second you hear this, the very fucking second!"

38

As soon as Basil arrived at his Cleveland Circle apartment, he turned his computer on. In a minute, he'd confirmed that the five million dollar reward was still being offered through the FBI. He then compared his camera images with the stolen paintings pictured on-line. *Wow, sure as shit, this is them.* Basil tucked the camera back into the pocket of his windbreaker and set off for the submarine sandwich shop around the corner.

As he sat eating a chicken Parmesan sub, one of the shop regulars asked him why he was so damned happy. Basil answered with a silent smile. He spent the next two hours killing time at the Circle Cinema. The noise and action from *Pirates of the Caribbean* couldn't take his mind off his discovery. He kept his cell on during the movie - *Why the hell doesn't Feeley call?*

Back in his apartment, the TV failed to get his attention. After a couple of beers while daydreaming, Basil hit the sack, fidgeted for a while, and finally got to sleep. The ring of his cell phone on the bedside table woke him at 7:00 the next morning. He heard Bobby Feeley's voice on the line. "Hey, Basil."

"Damn it, Bobby, where the hell have you been?" Basil sat on the edge of his bed.

"Sorry, man, I was in federal court down in Providence yesterday. I got back to the office late and figured I wouldn't bother you 'till this morning. I set my alarm early to call you. What's so damn important?"

"Listen, Bobby. I can't tell you exactly what's involved yet, at least over the phone. But trust me, it's big, and there's going to be a lot of money involved. A shitload. You have to get me an interview with the feds, Bobby, the FBI, like yesterday. All I can tell you is I discovered some stuff they want, big time. There's a reward, Bobby. Believe me, a real nice reward. I'll take care of you real good."

"Where the hell did you trip over this fortune, Basil?"

"It was in a house, an old lady's house. Don't ask me what I was doing there."

Feeley then explained to Basil he was sure he could introduce him to the right people at the FBI. He was also sure the Bureau could come up with a search warrant if necessary. If it led to anything with a reward attached, Basil would be on record and credited with supplying the critical "but for" lead. How he happened to be in this lady's house was something to sort out later, if necessary. They arranged to meet outside the FBI office at Boston's downtown Government Center at eight-thirty.

Forty-five minutes later Basil left his studio apartment, his digital camera secured in his zippered coat pocket. He skirted a white van parked next to his Saab, pushed a button on the car's remote and heard the familiar short toot and click as the car locks released. As Basil reached down to open the door, he was grabbed on both shoulders, his head was jerked backwards and his face covered with a soft, white cloth. He inhaled chloroform and began to fade.

Basil Simeone's naked body was splayed out like a half-limbed Vitruvian Man. He was face-up on a piece of six by eight plywood. The board was secured to an uneven pair of sawhorses, the high end raised four feet off the ground. It sloped at a slight angle, the top of Basil's head aimed at the concrete floor. Leather straps nailed to the plywood secured his wrists, ankles and forehead. Basil had a view of the top half of the only door into or out of the windowless room.

Light came from a pair of florescent tubes, one flickering, in a ceiling fixture. There was an industrial size soapstone sink against the wall to Basil's right and a drain cover in the middle of the floor. A length of hose connected to the sink faucet ran into a large galvanized watering can.

Accompanied by a grinding sound, the room's gray metal door opened off a drab hall. Basil watched a man with a Mohawk haircut walk in, leaving the door open. The man was average height, and had oversized upper body and upper arms, suggesting that the weight room at a gym was his second home. He wore glasses with a thick, black frame. From what Basil could see, the man was wearing only a black rubber apron. It was draped around his neck and covered him from mid-chest to his knees. The man reminded Basil of a cartoon character. He trembled in disbelief of his situation.

Ignoring Basil, the man walked to a table against a far wall. Basil's eyes rolled to follow the man, confirming the state of his single-piece wardrobe. A variety of cutting instruments and a number of various-sized brown bottles were on the table.

Basil's attention was drawn back to the open door as Porky filled the threshold and walked into the room. Then it hit Basil, and his trembling increased. Over the years, he had heard about "the pig's pen" through rumors burped up from the city's underbelly. The pen was rumored to be located somewhere in the bowels of the Leather District, and to be avoided if at all possible. Descriptions Basil had heard of what happened at the pig's pen were sufficiently freakish to discount the possibility of its existence, until now.

The luncheonette owner waddled over to the plywood. He looked down at Basil, and felt satisfied with the horror he saw in the investigator's eyes. Porky stopped chewing on a toothpick and spat it to the floor.

"You will not be pleased to learn that Bobby Feeley has been my lawyer for a long time. He's not like you, Basil. Bobby is very loyal to me. Of course, he called me last night and played your urgent voice-mail message. This morning I took the liberty of looking through the camera we found in your jacket to see if I could figure out what got you so damned excited. After I saw the pictures, I decided to have Maury, here," Basil gestured toward the sink, "help me out. I don't know exactly where you took those pictures of the paintings stolen from the museum, but I will find out. You will tell me, like you were supposed to tell me yesterday, about what you found. You were on the job, Basil. That was proprietary information you turned up, and I'm the proprietor.

"Maury has just learned a new trick on some weird grapevine he's connected to. He tells me the Khmer Rouge folks over in Cambodia were pretty good at it, and he's dying to try it out."

Basil now heard Porky's voice over the sound of water pouring into the galvanized can, as it asked, "Do you want to tell me where you took those pictures, and who else knows about them, or do you want me to let Maury practice his new trick?"

Except for the Fryolator cook, a man washing the kitchen floor, and Porky, Double P's was empty when Bobby Feeley pushed the door open at three-fifteen. Reaching the rear booth, he tossed his briefcase on the bench and sat across from Porky. "Hear I am, Pork. What's the big news, and did it come from poor old Basil?"

Porky ignored the questions and asked, "You still tight with the feds?"

"Of course. Ever since my brilliant defense of their number one agent, who beat the piss out of a numbers runner in Southie."

"Set up a meeting with them as soon as you can. Today will work. This is it, Bobby. It's the real thing."

"First of all, I know my main man at the Bureau is out of town until Thursday. Son of a bitch is playing golf in Myrtle Beach." Feeley looked up and thanked Milly as she placed a plate of French fries on the table. "Second, Porky, your last real thing cost me scads of unpaid hours and over a grand out of pocket. Ended up with zilch. Remember the shared lottery ticket claim? Or should I maybe say scam? I'm lucky I didn't get disbarred."

"This will pay you back in spades."

"Okay. What's going to make me rich?"

Porky stared at the lawyer for a full five seconds, and then said, "Of course you remember the Gardner Museum heist back about ten years or so ago?"

"Sure I do," Feeley said. "I'm not brain dead, yet, anyhow. That rock and roll gangster claimed he knew where the paintings were hidden. Nothing ever came of it. The paintings are still adios."

"The rock and roll guy was full of shit. Claimed the paintings were in a Brooklyn warehouse. They're not." Porky picked a fry up from the plate.

"Come on, Porky. You're not really going to waste my time with some goddamn nonsense about the Gardner heist, are you?" Feeley took a few fries from the plate and dipped them in barbeque sauce.

"Bobby, this is on the level." Porky's' eyes were riveted on the lawyer. "The feds have a five million dollar reward out there, and I know where the paintings are hidden. No shit. I know where the fuckers are."

Feeley pushed to the back of the bench, shaking his head, eyes raised. "Okay, then where, Porky? Where are the millions of dollars worth of paintings hidden?"

"In Cambridge."

"Cambridge? Like the Cambridge where Harvard is?"

"Yeah, that Cambridge. Actually, they're in an old lady's house in North Cambridge."

"Jesus, Mary and Joseph. You going senile, or what?"

Porky grunted as he reached across his belly and grabbed a wrinkled white paper bag from beside him on the bench. He pulled Basil's digital camera from the bag and held it over the table. "Just press the fuckin' button and take a look at some of Basil's photography, Bobby. Then tell me if you think I'm headed for the nursing home."

Feeley reached for the camera, fiddled with it for few moments, drawing a "Careful, Bobby! Don't delete the fuckin' pictures!" and then stared at the mini-screen as it filled with images of the stolen paintings. Bobby's hand started to shake a little. He'd seen enough TV coverage of the heist to recognize at least a couple of the photos. *Shit,* he was thinking, *could this be for fucking real? Jeez, if it is, I want a piece of this fucking pie.* Porky reached across the table for the camera.

"This is still a fucking long shot, Porky, a real long shot. But, what the hell, you've been good to me over the years - not that I haven't sent a shitload of business your way, too."

"Cut to it, Bobby."

"Yeah, right. I tipped you on Basil and his big discovery. No tip, no stolen pictures, and, I can deal with the feds."

Porky shifted his considerable girth, looked Feeley in the eye, and moved some fingers in a"c'mon" gesture. Feeley got the message. "Okay, Porky, bottom line, twenty per cent, an even million."

"You are fortunate to be dealing with a generous man, Bobby. *Ten percent,* combined finders and legal fee. Five hundred large. The biggest payday you'll ever fucking see. Set up the meeting the second your guy's back in town. Don't waste any time, Bobby. Don't waste a fucking second."

39

Tony Cipriano stood in front of Zelia Valdes's desk. The judge stood beside her chair, still wearing her robe from the just concluded Wednesday afternoon court session. She handed a single sheet of paper back to Tony and folded her arms.

"Tony, there is no way in the world I will accept your resignation under these circumstances. The fact that a disgruntled horse's ass decides to slander your good name on a radio show is not sufficient reason for you to walk away from a problem. You're better than that, a lot better."

"The whole courthouse must have been listening to that show, Judge, because that's all anyone's talked about in the building for the last two days. Slander or not, it's impossible for me to stay on the job. I can't walk down the hall without people either staring at me or turning away. And, I am so sorry I've dragged you into this mess by being so damn stupid, and greedy."

Zelia walked to the front of her desk. She put an arm around Tony's shoulders and turned him toward the door. "Tony, take some leave, sick, personal, whatever. We'll straighten it out with the personnel office when you come back. If you're not going to be at home, check in with me every evening. You still have my home number?" Tony nodded. "Good. This is a mess, and I won't try to sugarcoat it. But we're the good guys in this drama, and we're going to prevail, believe me. Now, get out of here, go somewhere for a few days and do whatever it is that makes you relax. I'll see you Monday. No, wait, that's Labor Day. See you Tuesday morning."

40

William Bettinger knew he was eating more than usual over the last couple of weeks. He also knew his sleeping pattern hadn't been the same since Jack Ralston called with the news about the B-girl and her connection to the Gardner Museum docent. He sat at his kitchen table spooning a dollop of Honora's crème fraiche onto a good size serving of her apple crisp as he complimented her on her kitchen skills. He was speaking over the voice of a Channel 7 evening newscaster. As Honora puttered around the sink, she voiced her opinion that cheating on a diet every now and then was permissible, particularly by seniors.

The retired judge was putting a spoonful of the dessert into his mouth when the TV newscaster reported that the identity of a severed head found in a landfill north of Boston had been discovered. He went on to report, "An examination of dental records has shown the victim to be Basil Simeone, well known in Boston's private investigator community." Then, with a straight face and even voice, the newscaster added his concluding remark: "Police suspect foul play."

Two or three minutes later, Honora was nervously dialing 911. Arriving with their ambulance siren blaring, a pair of EMTs from the Wellesley Fire Department quickly diagnosed Judge Bettinger's upper arm pain as a possible, even likely, symptom of a mild heart attack. Although imminent danger was not apparent, a trip to an emergency room was urged. The judge suggested the Mass General, and the EMTs agreed that the time and distance to MGH was reasonable. As the judge was being strapped onto the gurney, he instructed his anxious cook to find the phone number for Jack Ralston in his office phone directory, call Jack, and have him seek him out at the hospital as soon as he can get there.

At 8:30 on Wednesday night, Judge Bettinger was wheeled from the Mass General emergency room, into and out of a pair of elevators, through multiple corridors, then past a nurses station and into a private room. A nurse gave him a brief explanation of his whereabouts and told him the hospital's chief of cardiology had been located at his home on the Cape. The doctor, who sat on a city charity board with the judge, said he would be at the hospital as soon as possible. The judge was also told that a Mr. Ralston from "his old office" was in the reception area insisting that the judge wanted to see him. Judge Bettinger confirmed the visitor's request and the nurse sent an orderly to fetch Ralston.

Jack came into the hospital room, walked over and stood by the bed where the judge lay, his head propped up by a pair of pillows. "What have you been told, Judge?"

"They're not sure, but they think I may have had a minor heart attack. They're being a little coy about telling me anything until a big-shot doc shows up. I'm sure I'll be okay, but as soon as the EMTs strapped me on to a gurney, I realized I could possibly be laid up in here for a while. That's why I needed to see you, Jack, and I thank you for coming."

"Of course I'll help you out, Judge. What do you need me to do?"

There was a slight weakness in the judge's voice. "Before I get into details, Jack, please check the bathroom to be sure it's empty, and any closets in the room as well."

"Really?"

"Really, Jack, and I pray to God there are no audio recording devices in these rooms. Just humor me, okay?"

"Sure, Judge. No problem." Jack did as requested. He then placed a straight back metal chair next to the bedside and sat. "What the hell's going on, Judge?"

"Jack, I'm laying all the cards on the table, face-up. I may be telling you some things I shouldn't, but I have no choice at this point. I trust your discretion. Whether you do what I'm going to ask of you will be your decision of course, but I'm hoping you'll agree with me."

Ralston couldn't imagine what the judge had in mind. As he scraped his chair a little closer to the bedside, he thought he noticed an increase in the activity on the small green screens monitoring the judge's vital signs.

"You sure you're okay, Judge?"

"Yes, yes, I'm fine. Jack, if you have any cash on you, lend me ten dollars, would you?"

Becoming suspect that the judge's mental state may be impaired, Jack played along and found a ten dollar bill in his wallet. He held it over the bed to give to the judge.

"Keep it, Jack," Bettinger said, "as a retainer. In your private capacity, do you agree to be my legal counsel?"

"Sure, Judge. I'm honored to be asked. Now tell me, please, what's this all about?"

"First of all, this concerns Zelia." The Judge lowered his voice. "She's connected with all this."

"Zelia? Zelia's connected with all of what, Judge?"

"Recently, you called to ask my advice about a client of the PD's office being arraigned at the Boston Municipal Court, on some minor drug charge, as I recall. You told me the client could have been involved in, or at least have information about, the Gardner Museum robbery. I didn't know what to say then, and asked you to put the matter on hold until I contacted you."

"Yes," Jack agreed, "and I've been waiting to hear back from you."

"Jack, I didn't know what to say because, from what you told me, I knew that the client's information could very possibly lead to the discovery of where the stolen Gardner paintings are located. That's where Zelia comes in. What you told me was not good news for Zelia. Actually, it could be disastrous."

"I don't mean to be disrespectful, Judge, but did they give you any, like, strong medications? In all seriousness, it sounds like you're hallucinating."

A small smile creased the lips of the judge. "I understand the question, Jack. The answer is no, and to prove I'm in my right mind, I'm going to tell you where the stolen paintings are this very moment. They're hanging on the walls of a room in a humble home in North Cambridge. The home is the residence of a Gardner museum docent named Eddie Smelton. I expect that that's the same docent you told me the client mentioned to you over at the BMC."

"My God," Jack said.

"Get comfortable, Jack, while I tell you the rest of what I know, and what I'm suggesting we do to try and arrange the softest landing possible for all involved.

During his years as a public defender in the criminal courts of Massachusetts, Jack had heard some of the strangest stories and fact patterns anyone could imagine. They were all about to be topped. He listened, without interruption, as William Bettinger related the most interesting and unlikely tale he had ever heard. If not for the narrator's credentials - a universally respected, retired Federal Appeals Court judge - Jack would have disregarded what was said as pure fantasy.

A superior court judge and her law clerk, a pair of highly-regarded Boston lawyers, a Combat Zone B-girl, a museum docent and his demented mother, and a beheaded private investigator had all been woven into the same fabric, and that fabric was covering up the most notorious art theft in the country's history. But the cloth was starting to unravel. From what Judge Bettinger told him, Jack realized that, in addition to whomever took the masterpieces from the museum's walls, there were two people, both beyond ethical reproach, who were able to pick up the phone and provide information that would solve the Gardner Museum theft. But neither would make that call, both believing that they had no right to do so. And now, he was in the same boat, adrift in a white-capped sea of legal niceties, but Judge William Bettinger had set a course, although tenuous, for him to follow.

After a no-nonsense head nurse unceremoniously threw him out of the judge's hospital room, Jack Ralston left the Mass General and walked up Cambridge Street towards Government Center. The area was busy with city-dwellers enjoying the warm, late summer night. He mulled over his conversation with the judge. There was no longer any question whether or not Julie Santos' bar talk in the Frisky Goose some thirteen years ago had been the inspiration for the Gardner heist. Judge Bettinger left no doubt of that when he disclosed where Zelia Valdes had been visiting the stolen artwork for the last few years. The docent, whom Julie had told about her Saturday night museum parties, and maybe some accomplices, had surely walked off with the priceless paintings. Now, with the judge sidelined, and time being of the essence, Jack knew he carried the burden of convincing those who could make the judge's plan work to cooperate, to make a deal.

By the time he reached the JFK Federal Building, Jack had concluded that his pursuit of the judge's plan would require unusual, perhaps borderline legal, action. Jack knew the judge was being directed by his love for a woman. But his goals still made a lot of sense, and he wasn't the only one who loved, and was determined to protect, Zelia Valdes.

41

The next day Jack's contact at the BPD detective bureau secured Eddie Smelton's work schedule from the Gardner Museum Human Resource office. At ten minutes before five on the sunny afternoon, Jack pulled his Bel Air into the curb on the Fenway roadway in front of Simmons College, a block up the street from the museum. The soft top was up as protection against the still strong sun. Jack lowered all the windows for Thurgood's comfort and climbed out of the car.

A short walk to the corner of Palace Road gave Jack a clear view of the museum's main door and of the delivery alley that ran alongside the building. He checked the Walther P99 holstered under his sport coat. It wasn't often that he carried his licensed hand gun, but the variety of people and places he visited could present dangerous situations every now and then. Jack guessed this could be one such occasion. Julie's description of Eddie as a gentle soul, and Judge Bettinger's description of Zelia's interaction with the docent, didn't knock down the red flag in Jack's mind. He was thinking that a dozen years ago this guy pulled off one of the biggest robberies in world history. Yeah, the gun made sense. Jack patted the holster again.

As Eddie Smelton stepped through the Gardner's main door onto the empty sidewalk, Jack recognized him from his photograph and Julie's description. Walking quickly up behind the docent, Jack got within ten feet and then called out, "Excuse me, Mr. Smelton." Eddie stopped and turned as Ralston approached.

"Mr. Smelton, my name is Jack Ralston. I'm a lawyer with the Public Defender's Office. I'd like a minute of your time to talk about some paintings. Could I buy you a cup of coffee?"

Eddie wasn't too shaken. He knew this day was coming in some form or other. He declined the offer of coffee, but suggested walking the footpaths in the park area across the street from the museum. The two men crossed the street.

"I was a client of the Public Defender's Office once." Eddie said. "My lawyer was really good. She's a judge now."

"That would be Judge Valdes. Zelia Valdes."

"That's right. Because my lawyer was from your office, does that make you my lawyer, too?"

"Do you want me to represent you?"

"I'm thinking I'll probably need a lawyer. Sure. I'd like that to be your office."

"Good. My guess is you are still qualified for representation. I'm happy to represent you," Jack paused a moment, "that's if I don't have a conflict of interest. But, if I need to, I can sort that out later. I'm hoping, maybe, it won't be a problem. May I call you by your first name, Eddie?"

"Sure, that's okay."

"Okay, Eddie, and I'm Jack, if you like. Do you remember a young woman who used to work at the Frisky Goose Lounge on Washington Street whose name was Julie?"

Eddie smiled. "Sure. I liked Julie a lot. She's okay, I hope."

"Yes, Eddie, she's fine, and, quite frankly, how our conversation goes may have some bearing on her staying that way."

"Why would that be, Mr. Ralston? I haven't seen Julie in years."

"I'll get to that in a minute, Eddie. I've learned a lot of things in the last few days. Some of it involves Julie, and some of it involves Judge Valdes. I'm talking about them with you, Eddie, because it seems that you played a part in most of what I know."

The two men reached a wooded area and set out on one of its paths. There were a number of people walking and some sitting on benches. They were all wearing shorts, most with T-shirts printed with logos. Eddie and Jack, both in open-collar, short-sleeve shirts and long pants, walked side by side.

"I took the paintings," Eddie said.

"I kind of knew that," Jack said in an unfazed voice, "but I learned for sure because you just told me, and because I'm your lawyer, I can't tell anyone what you tell me. I'm not allowed to do that, even if I want to, which I don't."

Eddie maintained his calm demeanor. "Attorney-client privilege is what Judge Valdes called it."

"That's what it's called, okay. But don't misunderstand me, Eddie. I want to see the paintings returned to the museum."

"I took them for my mother."

"That's another thing I've been told, Eddie, but not exactly why you did that."

"Do you want to know why?"

"Sure."

"My mom used to work as a cleaning lady at the Fogg Museum over at Harvard. She got to love the paintings, especially the really old ones. Then Harvard fired her. They said she was acting strange, and that she should be tested for early dementia. She wanted to stay at her job. She loved her job. But they wouldn't let her keep it. They said they were afraid they'd get sued if she got hurt, or that she might do some harm to the paintings and other things in their collection. They told her to apply for some kind of government welfare because she was disabled. She didn't want to do that. She doesn't like the idea of being on welfare. She was very upset. She started to stay in bed all day. She was sad all the time. She said she missed the museum, the paintings. She cried a lot. She was afraid to leave the house. Her arthritis got much worse, too. She was really in tough shape.

"Then, one day I brought home a museum catalog from the Gardner. She kept looking at the old paintings in the catalog, and then mentioned a few of them that she really liked. I thought it would be wonderful if she could see the real paintings, but she wouldn't go out, to the museum or anywhere. All of a sudden, I had an opportunity to help my mom. So I took the paintings, and brought them home. Looking at the paintings, having them nearby, made her feel better. She stopped crying. She smiled a lot, was happy. They gave her comfort for all these years. She didn't have anything else in her life. Seeing the actual, real paintings changed her life."

"You're really devoted to your mother, Eddie. I admire you for that."

"Everyone should love their mother, and should be willing to do anything for her."

"But, Eddie, the biggest robbery, probably ever?"

"I never thought of it like that."

"I understand you never had any intention of selling the paintings."

"Oh, no, I'd never do that. That would really be a crime, Mr. Ralston."

The men stopped walking in front of an empty bench. Eddie sat and Jack remained standing, and said, "Back to Julie. She has a five-year-old son. She has a good, steady job. She's got their lives on the right track. She wants to keep it that way."

Eddie looked up at Jack. "I'm glad to hear life's going good for her and she has a little boy. I bet she's a great mother. I always figured she was meant for something better than hanging around bars in the Combat Zone."

"She came to the Public Defender's Office a couple of weeks ago because she got herself into a little jam with the police."

"I'm sorry to hear that. Can you help her?"

"Maybe, and that's one of the reasons I wanted to talk with you. Julie always figured that you were mixed up in the Gardner break-in. She remembers that a couple of weeks before the robbery she told you about the Saturday night museum parties, and how she got into the building without setting off alarms."

"I was surprised when she told me the alarms were turned off," Eddie said, "and that the door stayed unlocked."

"I bet you were. Anyhow, she never said anything to anybody about her suspicions about you because she liked you, thought you were a nice guy, and she didn't like the idea of ratting anyone out. There's been a big reward, millions of dollars, available for years, but she's kept quiet. She still isn't looking for the reward. What Julie wants, Eddie, is to be sure her present legal problem doesn't land her in jail. If that happens, she thinks the state will take her little boy and put him in a foster home, and that really scares her. She's afraid she'd never get him back."

"My God, that would be awful," Eddie said.

"Julie thinks that if she just tells the police that she told you about the museum parties with the guards in March of 1990, even if she only describes you and says how she met you, the district attorney might go easier on her, give her a break. You know, Eddie, make a deal that could keep her out of jail. Nothing's guaranteed, but she may be right. Any information at all about the museum robbery is a big deal to the DA."

"She has to think about her son, Mr. Ralston. I understand that."

"But I've got to be honest with you, Eddie. It's possible that Julie may have to tell the DA she knows your first name, and that you worked at the museum as a docent back in 1990. Julie's information could lead the police back to you."

"She's been quiet about me all these years, Mr. Ralston. Tell her it's okay with me to tell them whatever she needs to if it will help her stay with her son."

Jack took a pack of Marlboros from his jacket pocket and offered one to Eddie, who declined. Jack lit up, apologizing for his habit. "Eddie, along with Julie's situation, there's a second reason I tracked you down. Something else is coming to a head. I know all about Judge Valdes's involvement with you and your mother and the paintings. The immediate problem is that Judge Valdes was followed a few weeks ago when she went to your house. The man who followed her was a private investigator. I say was, because he was found murdered recently." Jack watched Eddie's jaw drop slightly, and then continued. "Eddie, we are very concerned that the private investigator may have told someone that Judge Valdes visited your home, and we don't know whatever else he may have discovered." Jack paused, staring at Eddie. "Did you say the paintings *gave* your mother comfort for a long time?"

"Yes. She's not at home any more. Her health got so bad, I couldn't leave her alone during the day, and she would never let anyone else just come into the house and take care of her. She's really failing. She finally had to go to a nursing home. My mom's at the Pinecrest Manor in Central Square, in Cambridge. Truth is, she hardly knows where she's at. She sleeps most of the time. She went downhill real fast, but they take good care of her at the Pinecrest."

Jack took a drag on his cigarette as he digested what Eddie had just told him - *God, problem solved? Sure sounds like Eddie's mom isn't going back home. The paintings aren't going to be hung at the nursing home. This sounds too good to be true.* Part of Jack's briefing in Judge Bettinger's hospital room was suddenly relevant. The judge had volunteered to foot the nursing home bill if there was some way to get Mrs. Smelton admitted to a facility.

"Eddie, there is money available to pay your mother's nursing home bills," Jack said. "It would not be a loan, but a gift. The person paying the bill would only require that the paintings go back to the Gardner."

"The Pinecrest is expensive, but I took out a home equity loan so I could pay the bill. We don't need anyone else's money. My mom wouldn't like that, and neither would I."

"That's admirable." Jack sat on the bench. "Considering the situation, Eddie, it may be a lot safer for your mom that she is out of the house. I wonder if maybe you should move out, at least for a while. There may be people, some very dangerous people, who would like to get into your house."

"Oh, I'll be okay. I'm not worried."

"I'm almost afraid to ask, but are the paintings still in your house?"

"Nope. I moved them."

"Thank God. Eddie, knowing that you don't need the Gardner paintings anymore for your mom, it may be possible Julie won't have to tell anybody about the museum parties, or that she told you about them back in 1990. Judge Valdes believes you always intended that the paintings would end up back in the museum. If that's so, for any chance that everything will end up the best way possible, the paintings will have to be available to go back soon. It will take some heavy deal-making, but we may be able to clear up Julie's police problem without having her say anything about the museum parties."

"I'd like that, and now that my mom can't look at them anymore, giving the paintings back is not a problem." Eddie glanced at his watch and stood. "I have to get over to Cambridge, Mr. Ralston. I told my mom I'd have supper with her. I want to be sure to be there if she's awake."

Eddie accepted Jack's offer of a ride to the nursing home. The two men walked the short distance to where Jack had parked the Bel Air. Thurgood was shooed into the rear seat. After a minute to get the top down and properly tucked into its well, the surf green convertible was heading toward the BU Bridge to cross over the Charles River into Cambridge. Jack was glad to have more time to talk with Eddie.

"I know you're fond of Judge Valdes, Eddie. Even though she's done the right thing all these years in keeping your connection with the paintings a secret, if her involvement becomes public knowledge it will be a disaster for her. She won't be criticized for being faithful to the attorney-client privilege, but there could be hell to pay for all her visits to your home, hiring the renovation contractor, and, especially, storing the paintings in her home."

"I'd never tell anyone about those things. She was a person of her word to me, and I will never do anything that would hurt her."

"That's good to hear, Eddie. Very good. It's exactly what I wanted to hear" Jack was unable to resist asking Eddie how he pulled off the notorious heist.

"I don't want to know any names, Eddie, but I am curious. How many people were involved in the break-in?"

"Just me. The door off the alley was unlocked, just like Julie said it would be. Nobody knew I was in the building. I was in and out twice in under an hour. Of course, I know the building like the back of my hand. I just took care of business and left."

"One guy. Amazing. Did you deliberately make it look like amateurs were involved? Breaking some frames, and taking some extra things that didn't seem to be of much value."

Eddie smiled. "Good guess, Mr. Ralston. I knew what paintings my mom would like, and took them on my first trip in and out. Then I went back and took a few other things that I figured wouldn't be too important to the museum patrons. I made it look kind of sloppy, I trashed some of the frames and broke some glass on purpose. I was careful that nothing really valuable was damaged. I wanted to cover my tracks. I hoped to keep the police from thinking it was someone who was familiar with the museum, you know, an 'inside job.'" Eddie paused a moment, then continued. "One thing I could never figure out, though, is how and why the guards got themselves handcuffed to the poles and wrapped in duct tape like the newspaper said they were when they were found."

Jack felt the satisfaction of inside information. As he slowed for an intersection, he said, "I think I can solve that puzzle for you. There were three guys in the museum when Julie and her friend arrived on St. Patty's' day. The guards had invited a pal. After the party, when they discovered that the museum had been robbed, they must have been shocked. They most likely figured they'd better come up with a story or they'd be blamed for the robbery. They probably had their buddy, the third guy, cuff them to the poles, tape them, and then he split. At least, that's my guess."

"Where would they get the handcuffs?" Eddie asked. "Our security people at the Gardner don't have things like guns and handcuffs. They're not real police."

Jack turned toward Eddie and smiled. "The security guards had handcuffs for a different reason than usual."

Eddie was silent for a just a moment, then said, "Oh, I get it. The party."

"Yeah, and as it turned out, the final party."

"You know, Mr. Ralston, Julie's had my back for the last dozen years. Maybe it's time to return the favor. Her situation is giving me an idea. Do you think you could help me out with it?"

"Let me know what your thinking, and I'll do what I can."

Once Jack had successfully navigated the convoluted road system that led him onto the BU Bridge, he pulled a business card from beneath an elastic wrapped around the windshield visor. "Here's how to reach me, Eddie. My home number is also on the card. Please let me know your idea as soon as you've put it all together, and I hope that's real soon. If I need to reach you, how do I do that?"

"I don't have a phone where I'm staying, or one of those cell phones, but I visit my Mom every day. Call and leave a message at the Pinecrest."

Eddie held his arms straight up, roller coaster style, and remarked on the feeling of freedom as the Bel Air crossed the bridge into Cambridge. Thurgood, upper torso and front paws draped over a rear window well, peered ahead into the breeze.

As soon as Jack dropped Eddie at Pinecrest Manor, he was on his way back across the river to Mass General. He was anxious to let Judge Bettinger know that the immediate "Eddie" problem had been neutralized. Without using exact words, the judge had made his wishes clear. The primary mission wasn't to salvage the Gardner paintings, or to protect or assist Eddie Smelton or Julie Santos. But rather, it was to insulate Judge Zelia Valdes from any and all suggestions of wrong-doing. That seemed to be happening. Jack trusted Eddie to keep Zelia out of the picture. The docent seemed like a guy who simply loved his mother. Jack felt it in his gut - Eddie would do the right thing. With that piece secured, Zelia's involvement with the stolen art would remain a secret. Jack was cautiously optimistic that he could accomplish much more.

If anyone intended to do anything about the paintings based on whatever they may have learned from Basil Simeone, that problem had gone away - the walls of the Smelton home were bare, and the stolen art was now in places unknown to the world, save Eddie Smelton. Jack had resisted the temptation to ask Eddie about where he stored the paintings. The docent had no reason to tell him, and maybe five million reasons not to tell him. When Eddie was stepping out of the Bel Air at the nursing home, he promised to contact Jack within twenty-four hours to discuss his plan for returning the paintings to the Gardner. Jack was closing in on the ultimate bargaining chip.

Jack parked his Chevy in the Mass General garage. He walked through the hospital's main lobby against a stream of employees and visitors on their way out of the building. Unexpectedly, he spotted Zelia standing at the counter of a coffee kiosk. She was being handed a cardboard cup as he walked toward her, calling her name. She turned in his direction.

"Jack, why are you here?"

"To see Judge Bettinger." Jack followed Zelia a few steps to a small metal table and chairs and sat with her. "Are you here for the same reason?"

"Yes," Zelia said. Her hands trembled around her coffee cup.

"What's wrong, Zelia?"

"The judge is in emergency surgery. They discovered a problem in the catheterization lab. They're doing heart bypass surgery right now. He's been in the operating room since four o'clock."

Jack reached for Zelia's hand. "This is one of the best hospitals in the world, Zelia. The judge will be okay."

"He put my name down as his primary contact. I'm only ten minutes away from the hospital, at home or at the courthouse, but he was in the operating room by the time I arrived at his room. I didn't get to see him, talk to him. That reminds me," Zelia reached into her shoulder bag, pulled out an envelope with Jack's name on it and handed it to him. "One of his nurses asked me if I knew you, then asked if I could deliver this letter from the judge."

"That's a letter he told me he'd write for a project I'm helping him with," Jack said. Without opening the envelope, he placed it on the small table. "I can wait with you, if you'd like."

"Thanks, Jack," Zelia said as she reached over and wrapped his hands in hers, "but, as much as you do for me, at this time I just need to be alone. There's a hospital chapel. Maybe I'll say a few prayers. I haven't prayed since. ..."

42

The 911 call originated from a cell phone at 7:27 on Friday morning. It was immediately routed to the State Police Marine Unit. The caller, a secretary employed at the Charlestown Navy Yard, carried a pair of binoculars on her weekday commute across Boston Harbor on the Long Wharf Ferry. She would routinely sweep the area off the portside, searching for anything of interest. To date, her most memorable discovery was a pair of early morning lovers on the bow of a Chris Craft. Knowing that bodies were pulled from the historic harbor every now and then, she occasionally wondered if she'd ever spot a floater. Today, as she surveyed the calm water shimmering in the early morning sunlight, she did.

Soon after receiving the emergency call, the pilot of a Marine Unit Boston Whaler spotted a bloated windbreaker, a small dark bubble on the harbor surface. A minute later, Sergeant William Daly was hooking the nylon jacket with a long-poled fishing gaff and pulling the body to the side of the 25-foot boat. With a few grunts, he and his fellow Statie muscled the body, male and about six feet long, onto the stern and turned it on its back. Daly did a double take.

"Holy shit! I play hockey with this guy!"

"Used to."

43

On the third Tuesday of January in 1950, a half dozen men wearing dark clothing, caps and rubber Halloween masks walked out of a nondescript building in Boston's North End carrying three million dollars in cash and negotiable securities. Six years later, the Boston office of the Federal Bureau of Investigation was being toasted by the law enforcement world for solving the "Great Brinks Robbery." Now, about a half a century later, Special Agent in Charge, Thomas McBride, was excited by the possibility of leading that same Boston FBI office back into glory. The key to solving the most notorious art heist in the history of the United States, if not the world, just might be sitting across the conference table from McBride. *Hell of way to end the summer* was his happy thought.

McBride had been asked to meet this Friday morning with three men: Andrew Fox, an FBI agent he had been trying to transfer out of the Boston office for over a year, Robert Feeley, a local lawyer of mixed reputation who had successfully defended Fox on an assault charge, and Eugene Krill, a middle-aged private investigator who had no criminal record, but whose reputation as one of the city's most notorious reprobates was well established, and who, after only fifteen minutes, had impressed McBride as one of the most repugnant persons he had ever encountered. This impression was surely bolstered by the strange aroma Krill's ample flesh diffused throughout the closed room. McBride, on the verge of gagging, stood, walked over to the door and opened it wide. As the others at the table watched him, he returned to his seat and took a cursory glance at a document Feeley had placed on the polished surface. It was a single-spaced, one page instrument, with attachments.

REWARD ACKNOWLEDGMENT

Eugene Krill, a/k/a "Porky," has brought information, including photos of paintings (copies of which are appended to this document) to the attention of the FBI and is herewith making a claim for any and all rewards of any sort whatsoever from any and all parties from this date forward until the end of time for the recovery of any property stolen from the Isabella Stewart Gardner Museum on or about March 18, 1990, if the recovery thereof is fully or partially based in any manner whatsoever upon the information provided herein, specifically, but not limited to, the suggestion that the subject property could be discovered at a house located at ...

The text stopped abruptly, and the document was silent as to where "the subject property could be discovered."

Special Agent McBride wasn't concerned with the wording or enforceability of the document. He just wanted, actually, was desperate, to know the location where the appended photos of the paintings known as *The Concert, The Storm on the Sea of Galilee, Chez Tortoni, Landscape with an Obelist* and *La Sortie de Pesage* had been snapped. He snatched a pen from the table and scrawled his oversized signature on the line provided, and then turned to Porky.

"Okay, where are the paintings?"

Porky looked at Feeley who held the palm of a hand up to his client, then reached over and slid the signed document across the table with a request that Agent Fox sign as a witness. This accomplished, he nodded to Porky.

Porky, through a yellow-toothed smile, delivered the information in monotone. "I found an envelope in a booth at my restaurant. It contained the photos and directions to where they were taken written on a separate piece of paper. I followed the directions to see what was there. It's a little green house on the right side of Rindge Avenue about a quarter of a mile up from Mass Ave, in North Cambridge, Massachusetts. I didn't see a number on it. I have lost the paper with the directions on it."

Attorney Feeley quickly scribbled Porky's description of the house location on the signed and witnessed document. He folded the paper, reducing it to a third its size.

"We also have to know who took the photos," Agent McBride said.

"Why does that matter?" Feeley asked.

"Because, Attorney Feeley," McBride withheld an almost automatic tag, *you moron,* then continued in a pedantic tone, "we need to put that information in an affidavit so we can get a search warrant."

Porky shrugged his shoulders. "Don't know who snapped the pics. Like I said, the envelope was left in a booth at my place."

Feeley wasn't about to let McBride start an interrogation. He was anxious to leave. "That's the way it is, Agent McBride. My client's not signing an affidavit that says anything more than what he's told you already. That's all he knows." Still holding the signed document, the lawyer stood and reached his free hand down for his briefcase. "I was due in superior court ten minutes ago."

McBride felt his heart rate go up a few ticks. He needed a search warrant and knew un-attributed photos alone wouldn't be enough, even for the law and order federal judge who would rule on the petition. The Bureau had a number of "reliable informants" on hand who would support the issuance of a warrant, but he needed a signature on the affidavit naming the informant/photographer. He figured there was nothing to lose, and also figured that Feeley would cave. He made a suggestion to the lawyer.

"Okay, if that's your final position, Bob, I understand. We'll see what we can get with the information you gave us. Judge Milton's usually cooperative with the Bureau. He hardly looks at what's included in an affidavit. I'll just need something for the record. I know you don't have time to wait around for our snail-paced government typing pool." McBride slid a sheet of blank paper in front of Porky, who was still sitting, and continued to speak to Feeley. "If you'll just witness your client's signature along the bottom, we'll print what Mr. Krill just told us over his John Hancock. Do it all the time."

"Are you serious?" Feeley said. "You want me to have my client sign a blank piece of paper? C'mon."

McBride reached over and plucked the folded *Reward Acknowledgment* from Feeley's fingers. "No affidavit, no deal, no reward."

The lawyer immediately thought of his ten percent fee. It took just seconds for him to respond. He pulled a pen from his coat pocket and put it on the table in front of Porky, next to the blank sheet of paper.

"Go ahead and sign, Porky. If you can't trust the FBI, who can you trust?"

44

The following Tuesday, the headline in the *Boston Globe* read:

FBI KEEPS LID ON LABOR DAY RAID

Traffic was brought to a halt for over two hours on Rindge Avenue in North Cambridge early last evening while an FBI SWAT team conducted an assault on an unimposing, single-family home in the working class neighborhood. A half dozen heavily armed agents surrounded the green-shingled house while an equal number of agents, also outfitted with protective headgear and body armor, stormed the front door, knocking it in with a battering ram. Fifteen minutes after the house was invaded, a spokesperson said it appeared to be uninhabited and empty of furnishings. City records list Eddie S. Smelton, 49, whose whereabouts are currently unknown, as the owner.

Special Agent in charge of the FBI's Boston office, Thomas McBride, refused to comment on the reason behind the Labor Day raid, saying only that it was based on highly vetted information from a trusted informant. He would not say who or what the Bureau expected to find, citing an ongoing investigation.

Joseph Thornton, the owner of the neighborhood grocery store across the street from Smelton's house, was shaken by the presence of the SWAT team. "I never saw anything like this around here," he said. "This is a nice, usually quiet, neighborhood." When asked about any unusual activity recently at the Smelton home, Thornton said that Mr. Smelton held a "garage" sale two weekends ago and that people were carrying furniture from the house and taking it away in cars and pick-up trucks.

Thornton also said there were strangers to the neighborhood sitting in a car parked up the street from the house over the Labor Day weekend. One of them, according to the storekeeper, came in on Sunday and bought a root beer Popsicle. When Thornton quizzed the stranger, he said he was part of a neighborhood crime watch group the city hired. Thornton said he had never heard of that happening before. Special Agent McBride refused to comment when asked if the FBI had stationed agents in the neighborhood during the holiday weekend.

Thornton has known the family for over twenty years. "The Smeltons have always been good neighbors, never any trouble. Mrs. Smelton is housebound, in a wheelchair, and a couple of weeks ago an ambulance came and took her away. I don't know if she ever came back home. I can't believe they were dealing drugs or something like that. Not Eddie and his mother. All that activity, you'd think Bonnie and Clyde must be hiding in the cellar. I'll never forget this Labor Day," he said.

At press time there was an unconfirmed rumor that the FBI raid was connected with the 1990 burglary of priceless paintings from Boston's Isabella Stewart Gardner Museum. There is an outstanding reward offer of five million dollars for information leading to the solving of that historic theft.

The *Globe's* "**Of Local Interest**" column on page 4 included the following items:

JUDGE WILLIAM BETTINGER, 77, DIES.
Former Federal Appeals Court Judge William Bettinger of Wellesley died this past Saturday at Massachusetts General Hospital following complications from open-heart surgery. The retired jurist and former head of the Massachusetts Public Defender's Office had undergone...

BODY PULLED FROM HARBOR IDENTIFIED.
The fully clothed male body discovered floating in Boston Harbor last Friday morning has been identified as Caesar Anthony Cipriano of Dorchester. How Cipriano, 26, ended up in the water is not known. At this time, police have no evidence of foul play, but are investigating. Cipriano, an employee of the Massachusetts Trial Court, was identified by his father, Francesco Cipriano, also of Dorchester.

45

Zelia Valdes accepted Jack Ralston's extended arm as they joined others walking out of the crowded stone church. Under late-morning sunlight, they acknowledged acquaintances with nods and small smiles. A number of members of the press were camped on the sidewalk at the end of the concrete walkway, drawn to the memorial service for Judge William Bettinger by the list of prominent mourners. The governor, three United States Senators and two justices of the United States Supreme Court were among those in attendance. Seeking to sidestep the crowd, Zelia and Jack walked to an empty memorial garden tucked alongside the church.

Zelia sat on a granite bench while Jack remained standing. As he shook a pair of cigarettes from a pack, Zelia reminded him of the times they would step onto the fire escape at the Public Defender's Office to sneak a smoke and share stories that kept criminal defense attorneys laughing, and sane. She reached her hand out for the Marlboro.

"Quite a turnout for the judge," Jack said, extending a plastic lighter to Zelia.

Zelia lit up and said, "Yes, it was. A lot of important people. Ironic in a way. William did a lot in his life for the little guy. He really loved those in need."

Jack was pleased with Zelia's observation. It provided a segue for a subject he intended to broach. He lit his cigarette, and then said, "William also loved you."

Zelia was taken aback by Jack's naked statement.

"Why do you say that, Jack?"

"Because it's true, and, if you don't know, I thought you should. Although the judge didn't expect to die when he was taken to the hospital last week, he was afraid he may be incapacitated for a good while. As he was being put in the ambulance at his home, he had his cook call and ask me to meet him at Mass General that evening, which I did. When I saw him at the hospital we had quite a conversation. He asked me to do certain things he could not do himself. He also told me things, including his feelings for you."

"Really?"

"Yes, Zelia, really." Jack allowed himself a nervous cough. "The judge was very direct. He prefaced his comments by saying that he was in love with you, and he would do anything to protect you. The reason he told me that was to give me the opportunity to back away from agreeing to help him accomplish certain things. If I thought he was simply blinded by his love for you, he'd understand my making decisions with an objective eye."

There were a few moments of silence, then Zelia asked, "What do you know, Jack?"

"The judge took me into his full confidence. He told me everything you had told him, and how you had carried the burden of keeping this Gardner Museum information to yourself, by yourself, for years."

"He told you everything about it?"

"As far as I know, he did. He told me about the huge dilemma you faced when Eddie Smelton dropped the bombshell on you about his robbing the Gardner Museum. He also told me about your visits to Eddie's North Cambridge home to try and persuade his mother to let him return the paintings. The judge also mentioned you paid for renovations to the Smeltons' house to protect the paintings," Jack's smile returned, "and your short-term storage business. Then he told me about your being followed by the private investigator whose severed head turned up later. Yes, I think he told me everything, Zelia."

Zelia's face reddened. "I, I don't know what to say, Jack. I know I could have leaned on you, reached out to you, but it wouldn't have been fair. I'd have put you in the same box I was locked into. I couldn't do that to you. It could have ruined you, your career, just knowing these things."

"I wish you hadn't spared me, Zelia."

"Initially, Jack, I turned to Judge Bettinger because I found out I was being followed. The judge had always been a rock for me, and I was hoping he could discover, somehow, what was happening, why someone would be interested in me. I didn't intend to involve him in the Gardner situation, but everything just seemed to flow from that first call. I came close to letting you know about the docent last fall. The fellow I told you about after dinner at the Elms, the man I was speaking to in the bar when you arrived, he was ..."

"Eddie Smelton," Jack said, completing Zelia's thought. "I confirmed that as soon as I talked to the judge."

"Confirmed it? What do you mean?"

They both knocked the glowing tips off their barely-smoked cigarettes on the legs of the stone bench. Jack ground the remains into a mulch bed with his heel. Zelia reached up and took Jack's hand. He sat beside her on the bench.

"Let me back up a bit, Zelia. I'm sure the judge called on me to help him out because I had asked his advice a few weeks earlier about how to handle a client of the Public Defender's office. I'd told him that she, this client, seemed to have good information that could possibly lead to the discovery of someone who was involved in the Gardner robbery. He asked me to sit on my information for a while, which I did. I wondered why he wanted to delay anything. I found out when I saw him at Mass General.

"His immediate concern was that if my client's tip resulted in a new investigation, your involvement with Eddie and the paintings might be discovered. But, even before the judge ever mentioned Eddie to me, I had been told by the client that it was very likely that a Gardner docent named Eddie was involved in the robbery. It occurred to me that it was probably the same Eddie you told me about last fall."

"Two and two is still four," Zelia said.

"Yes, but I didn't tell you about my client's tip because I had no idea of the depth of your involvement with Eddie and the paintings until the judge told me."

"That must have been an eye opener."

Jack smiled. "Yes. You could say that. The judge told me because he was afraid that your actions would never be understood by the public, and how that could impact you. Because he couldn't do anything from his hospital bed, he asked me to intervene with Eddie. He thought something had to be done, and in a hurry."

"Intervene? To do what?"

"Primarily, to convince Eddie that, if the paintings were discovered at his home, or he was involved in an investigation, there was no reason to tell anyone that you knew about anything, or were involved in any way. The judge was also hoping that if Eddie was told about new evidence that could point at him, it might put enough pressure on him to consider returning everything to the museum. If he decided to return the paintings, deals with the prosecutors might be possible."

"Was your client's information behind the FBI raid at Eddie's home?"

"No. I'm sure it wasn't. I don't know what triggered the raid. My guess is that it had something to do with the murdered private investigator who was following you. I think it could be that somehow this Basil character discovered the paintings were at Eddie's house, told somebody about his discovery, and got decapitated for his trouble. That would have given someone else a clear shot at a huge reward."

Zelia massaged her forehead. "Oh, Jack, I can't help feeling that somehow I've been responsible for so many terrible things that have happened. I could have stopped everything so long ago." Tears welled in her eyes.

"Don't do that to yourself, Zelia." Jack stood and led Zelia to her feet. He wrapped his arms around her and she melted into him. Their minute of silence was invaded only by a few chirping birds. Jack pushed a strand of Zelia's hair aside and looked down into her eyes. "You were obligated to act in a certain way as Eddie's attorney, and that's what you did. When you faced dilemmas, you followed the dictates of your conscience. That's the most anyone can do. There's no black and white in a lot of situations, but you absolutely handled this whole, crazy thing correctly."

Even though alone in the church garden, Jack spoke quietly as he and Zelia walked a narrow path among the flowering bushes.

"Here's the picture, Zelia. I met with Eddie just before I ran into you in the Mass General lobby last week. He told me he had moved the paintings from his house. I don't know where he put them, and I don't want to know. Eddie's mother has been admitted to a nursing home and is non-communicative. Eddie thinks she'll die soon. He assured me that the last thing he would ever do is tell anyone about your visits to his home, or your storage of the paintings. I believe that you're safe regarding your knowledge of where the paintings have been kept all these years, and your other involvement with them."

"The newspapers said the FBI found Eddie's house empty," Zelia said. "The Bureau won't stop looking for Eddie, for the paintings."

"The FBI may not have to find the paintings, Zelia. As Judge Bettinger was hoping, Eddie intends to have everything he took returned to the museum. He told me he is working on a plan to do it. I'm meeting him on Monday to hear his idea. Eddie has impressed me in many ways. I won't be surprised if whatever he decides makes a lot of sense." Jack took Zelia's arm to lead her from the garden area. "What do you say I get us back to the city? Then, lunch at Lucia. I'm not expected back in the office today."

"First, Jack, can I ask a huge favor?"

It took forty-five minutes for Jack's Chevy Bel Air to take him, Zelia and Thurgood from Wellesley to the North Shore coastal town of Marblehead. It was here, on a promontory at the edge of the Atlantic, that Zelia had scattered the mingled ashes of her husband and son. A skeptic of the afterlife, Zelia, nonetheless, talked to her two Davids. Her visits to the area were at least twice a year, and also when prompted by significant events in her life. Her husband and son held the status of confidants. Standing alone near the edge of the bluff, she stared out at the cold blue water.

Jack stood back a respectful distance, Thurgood on his haunches at his side. He watched the slender figure of the woman he loved. A friendly mid-day wind was having its way with Zelia's hair. After a few minutes, she turned and gestured for Jack to join her. She threaded her arm through his, smiled and turned him toward the ocean.

"Say hello to my Davids, Jack. They agree it's time we had some more company. I've told them all about you. I know they'll like you."

Lunch at Lucia would wait for another day. Jack was pleased it was one of those days that his apartment was habitable. Thurgood lapped up the remains of the Chinese take-away meal, abandoned his attempts at joining post lunch bedroom antics, and curled up in a corner.

46

The day following Judge Bettinger's service, Zelia stood by the living room window, next to her writing desk. She stroked her cat that had hopped onto the desk, seeking a place in the sun. Zelia was staring across Pinckney Street at cobble-stoned Louisburg Square, its small grassy park contained by its wrought iron fencing, but her mind was elsewhere. The staggering effects of the deaths of William Bettinger and Tony Cipriano had waned somewhat, helped by Jack's kind and thoughtful words, but she was still shaken and saddened. She found it easier to accept William's death because he had lived a full life before an innocent death. He was given the opportunity to contribute, and those his life had touched were better off.

But Tony was young, his life ready to blossom. Others would have gained from his continuing to live. They were denied. Tears flowed at Tony's funeral Mass from his friends and former co-workers at the meat packing plant and the courthouse. But it was seeing Tony's dazed, elderly parents, clearly in shock, that had staggered Zelia. It was a memory she knew she would harbor forever. Why would a God permit children to die before their parents left this earth? How often she had asked that question.

She knew that Tony's death, even though an apparent suicide, was at the hands of others. She was certain that Cosmos Theopoulis's radio interview was the last straw for Tony. Zelia had no words to adequately describe Attorneys Metcalf and Poole, whom she knew had packed the camel's back with their venomous deceit in the first place. Whatever sanctions the legal system and community may impose on these men, lawyers who had disgraced themselves in a profession that provided so much opportunity to contribute, would never be sufficient.

Zelia was comfortable that she had done the right thing in upholding the sanctity of the attorney-client privilege over the years. Her further involvement with the stolen art, and how it could be perceived if made public, was another matter. God only knows who the private investigator may have told that he followed her to Eddie's home - the primary suspect's home, the site of the abandoned museum room. And it was likely just a matter of time before the renovation contractor connected the dots, if it hadn't already done so. In the wrong hands, the knowledge of her association with these things would be embarrassing at best, used to attempt extortion at worst. It would be a disaster waiting to happen.

Criminal or not, regardless of the circumstances, to herself she could not justify her actions, particularly one of them. She felt she had reaped an enormous, personal benefit from the Gardner theft for the past five years - her private viewings of Vermeer's masterpiece, *The Concert*. Zelia Valdes now judged her own behavior. She shooed Blanco from the desktop, sat and reached for her writing paper and pen.

Dear Governor, It has been my great honor to serve as a judge of the Massachusetts Superior Court...

The heated rocks fizzled and a plume of steam surged toward the ceiling. Cosmos Theopoulis tossed the ladle back into the wooden water bucket and climbed to the top bench in the sauna, feet dangling in the air. He looked toward the lower bench across the room. Roger Metcalf was wiping his brow with a towel. The lawyer was wondering why the invite to sweat with Cosmos.

"Never hot enough," said Cosmos.

"It sure as hell is hot enough for me," Roger said as he looked at the green-stained soles of Cosmo's feet. "Still running, I see."

"On that turf course every day. Gotta keep fit. Keeps me young. Vision's twenty ten. Never popped a Viagra in my life. By the way, what's going on with Poole? Vacationing down in Ptown with his boy-toy?"

"He's taken a leave of absence from his firm. I'm still using their resources and people on our appeal, but Frederick's no longer personally involved with the case." Roger hesitated a moment, then continued. "Actually, he's in rehab. He's finally trying to treat his problem."

"Heh. Hate to tell you, but there ain't a cure for being queer."

Roger leaned back against the sauna wall and closed his eyes. "He has a substance abuse problem, booze. My guess is he'll retire. His health isn't great."

"Good riddance. By the way, you guys in any trouble over setting up the law clerk? I know the feds were looking into it."

"Glad to say that's history. The US Attorney's investigation is over. No charges, no indictments. The Justice Department concluded we may have been overzealous, but that's all. As far as I'm concerned, you can't be overzealous when you're representing a client."

"Doesn't hurt to have the victim take a header off the Tobin," Cosmos said.

"We were able to call in a few favors," Roger added. A lot of good people spoke up for us. Connections never hurt."

"You've been doing a decent job since that shit-ass trial ended," Cosmos said. "The info from that law clerk was priceless. Then he killed himself, and that just proved he fucked up, and he couldn't handle it. Not your fault. He got involved where he shouldn't have. It's that simple." Cosmos took a towel off the bench and draped it over his head, leaving his face clear. Roger thought of Mother Theresa. Cosmos continued, "I know a lot of lawyers, and they keep telling me what you keep telling me - the chances on appeal look pretty good, that the judge really fucked up."

"I expect the case will be scheduled in the Appeals Court early next year," Roger said. "We should have a decision by next summer. As you know, between now and then, the lower court judgment is stayed. Nothing changes here at Finish Line."

"I know you were looking to become a judge. Anything available?"

Roger's attitude suddenly shifted from guilt about the trial verdict Cosmos had resurrected, to optimism. "Well, actually, I was hoping something would open up in the superior court, but right now the best bet is probably the Boston Municipal Court. Judge Meagher is retiring at the end of the month. If I could get appointed to the BMC, I'm sure I could get bumped up to the superior court in a year or two."

"Done. I'll tell the governor when he gets back from Tahiti, or wherever he's disappeared to."

"Done? Just like that?"

"C'mon, Metcalf. That horse's ass would still be a state rep if I hadn't bumped into him at the track's clubhouse a few years back. Couldn't pick a winner, either. Don't sweat it. You'll be all set."

"I don't know what to say."

"Don't say squat. When it happens, just remember how you got to be a judge. Pour some more water on the stones."

While Roger and Cosmos were sweating in the sauna, Deputy Sheriff Alan Silver stood in the reception area of Keene & Metcalf's law office. He held a three page *subpoena duces takem* issued by the Massachusetts Board of Bar Overseers in his hand. The receptionist placed her phone on its cradle and looked up from her desk.

"Mr. Metcalf's secretary says he's out until late this afternoon, sir."

"Be sure he gets these papers, please."

47

Two United States Marshals, one tall, one short, both featuring solid builds and wearing blue suits and red ties, stood outside the closed door of a secure conference room tucked into the interior of the Moakley US Courthouse in South Boson. It was early afternoon on a Monday in late September. Inside the windowless room, Jack Ralston stood by the door. Four other men, three in suits and ties, one in casual attire, sat at an oblong conference table that held only a single telephone. The men at the table had accepted invitations to the meeting after each had received a hand-delivered copy of a letter. The letter's content had been quick to get their attention.

Re: The Gardner Museum Robbery
To Whom This May Concern,
    Because I am hospitalized and don't know when I will be discharged, I have requested that Jack Ralston of the Public Defender's Office act in my stead, as well as in his own right, to take steps that we anticipate will result in the quick return of all of the artwork stolen from the Gardner Museum in 1990. If we are to be successful, a good amount of cooperation and discretion will be required from third parties, such as you. The details will be explained by Jack.
    You will have a number of questions regarding how we acquired access to the artwork; however, because of our attorney-client relationships with the person or persons involved, those questions will have to remain unanswered. We can say that we are both convinced

that there was never any intention to profit monetarily from the theft. Now, our goal is simply to get the art back in its rightful place so it can be appreciated by the public.

I ask that you consider any request Jack may make of you and, if at all possible, that you comply. Finally, and pardon the melodrama, please destroy this letter as soon as you have read it. If it falls into the wrong hands, it could botch things beyond repair - it's time for the paintings to go home! Thank you so much for your cooperation,

William Bettinger, US Court of Appeals, Retired

All those invited had accepted when Jack followed up with a phone call. He asked the participants to come to the meeting alone, without a hint to anyone that the top brass of law enforcement in Massachusetts was gathering.

Federal, state and Suffolk County chief prosecutors, along with the special agent in charge of the Boston FBI office sat, fidgeting, at the table. Boston's habitually late police commissioner had yet to arrive. Jack glanced at a wall clock, assured the men in the room that the commissioner would show up any minute, and sat at the empty end of the table. He thought back to a pair of meetings at Harvard the previous week.

Four days earlier, Jack had succeeded in satisfying a requirement from Eddie as part of an overall plan that would result in the return of the Gardner artwork. A few weeks ago Eddie had told him of his proposal. Jack wasn't sure it had legs, but promised he would do what he could to morph the docent's wishful thinking into reality.

On the past Thursday, Jack had met with four members of the Harvard College Board of Trustees for a private lunch at the Harvard Faculty Club. The Board members comprised its standing committee on institutional charities. The meeting had been arranged with the cooperation of the Director of the Harvard Art Museums, who made it clear to the members that the university's president was in full support of what would be proposed.

Jack's opening gambit was to pass around copies of Judge Bettinger's letter. Once the judge's thoughts had been digested, Jack collected the copies and made his pitch. A few polite questions followed, which Jack mostly avoided answering. By the time dessert had been served, the committee had assured Jack that, upon his request, one million dollars would be deposited in a local bank account, and a trust instrument would be prepared pursuant to his instructions. The handshake agreement required no further information from Jack regarding the prospective use of the funds. Smiling Board members, delighted with their participation in the clandestine search and recovery mission, saluted Jack and then dug into their servings of cheesecake.

Succeeding with Eddie's demand was easier than Jack had anticipated, by far. It occurred to him that the committee's eagerness to cooperate could have had a financial basis - was it Harvard that had put up the five million dollar reward for the return of the stolen art? Was the committee in the process of saving its college four million dollars?

His business with the charity committee happily concluded, Jack left the Faculty Club about a half an hour before his second meeting of the afternoon, scheduled for three o'clock with the dean of the Harvard Law School, Owen Williams. The dean had agreed to meet with Jack at the request of a US Appeals Court judge who had been a close friend of William Bettinger. Dean Williams also knew Jack as one of his former students at Yale Law, and as chief counsel for the Massachusetts Public Defender's Office, a cooperative link in the law school's intern program. At the end of a phone conversation with Jack earlier in the week, Williams had promised to do what he could to help. As they had discussed, the cooperation of a third party was essential. Crossing the Harvard Yard, Jack hoped the dean had secured that cooperation.

Eight years previously, the Harvard Law School had offered its deanship to Williams, a popular Yale Law School professor, who readily accepted the prestigious post. Many Yale Law alumni residing or working in the Boston area, including Jack, were invited to a reception introducing Dean Williams to the Boston legal community. As he stood in a lengthy queue waiting to greet and congratulate his former Conflict of Laws professor, Jack enjoyed an impromptu conversation with Jonathon Hughes, a fellow Yale Law graduate who had preceded him by a few years. Since that day, Jack had noticed Hughes' name mentioned in the news media on a politically connected basis. Now, almost a decade later, Jack doubted Hughes remembered him, but he was sure Hughes remembered Dean Williams.

With time to burn before meeting with the dean, Jack strolled through the Yard at a leisurely pace, appreciating his surroundings. It was a sun-filled, early fall afternoon. Students, some newly arrived, some returning to campus, crowded the footpaths. Jack wondered how many of the kids understood how fortunate they were, as he had been, to be at a top-shelf college. Sure, for many there had been plenty of hard work and serious problems overcome to get this far. But he hoped they wouldn't fall into the trap of forgetting the insurmountable obstacles they didn't have to face. For so many of equal potential, even a high school diploma was pie in the sky.

Jack's spirits were high. Harvard was in - at least its money was - and that was what he needed. What was left to satisfy the wishes of both Judge Bettinger and Eddie Smelton was cooperation from law enforcement, from all the major players. Jack noticed a few students seeking good luck by rubbing the left foot on the nearby statue of John Harvard. Jack didn't believe in luck, but he did believe in opportunity. He thought opportunity was knocking, and hoped Dean Williams was going to tell him he would agree, if necessary, to open the door for it. If so, Plan B would be available to Jack in the upcoming week. He had learned early in his career - always have a Plan B.

Boston's top cop was twenty minutes late for the meeting at the Moakley courthouse. The police commissioner was greeted at the door by Jack. As she stepped to the conference table, her "Sorry, gentlemen." was met without reaction by the assembled men, each of whom had experienced her tardiness more than once.

Jack, standing at the head of the table, thanked the participants for coming. He then prefaced his remarks by explaining that the trustees of the Gardner Museum had a singular goal, the return of its property stolen in 1990. The museum was in full support of any decision made in today's meeting that would further that goal, even if it meant the perpetrators of the robbery, or any others that may have been involved with the stolen art, never paid for their crimes. He then began what he expected would have to be the most persuasive argument he would ever deliver.

By late afternoon the invitees had deconstructed Jack's argument and, all but one, agreed to cooperate and try to make his suggestion work. Then, amongst each other, they did their share of cajoling, promising, chest-thumping and horse trading, as a full group and in smaller units spun off to a conference room across the hall. They had bargained about everything that came to mind - where they would be listed in a press release, where they would stand at a press conference, how long they would speak, and what they could and could not say. Even though some, perhaps most, of the participants probably agreed with the Suffolk County District Attorney - "C'mon, this just isn't ever going to happen." - all but a single holdout had secured what they considered to be the best deal for their organization. Maybe, they figured, the DA was wrong, and this was going to happen.

At four-thirty, the only obstacle to Jack's success was embodied in Thomas H. McBride, Special Agent in Charge of the Boston Office of the FBI. When the door closed behind the departing Massachusetts attorney general, Jack was left alone in the main conference room with McBride. The others left their assurances of cooperation, but only if the Bureau was also on board. They agreed that notice of the Bureau's cooperation was required by eight o'clock the next morning,

From early afternoon McBride had insisted, without providing any evidence to support his claim, that the FBI was on the verge of arrests and recovery of the stolen Gardner properties. His later comments during the day were only slight variations of his first: "Why make a deal with anybody at this point? Why not the whole enchilada - the paintings and the prosecutions? That's what the public expects - they don't want these shitbums to walk - and that's what the Boston office of the Federal Bureau of Investigation intends to deliver. In case you guys forgot, this wasn't a stick-up at the local Seven-Eleven."

Jack wasn't surprised that McBride was the fly in the ointment. When he was planning the arguments he would make to the prosecutors, he found himself spending an inordinate amount of time trying to figure out how he could get the FBI's local boss on board. He had known all of the conference invitees for a number of years, some more than others. He'd felt he had a very good shot at convincing all, but, perhaps, McBride. But he had to deal with him. No FBI agreement, no deal.

Jack and the FBI agent first crossed paths four years earlier when McBride testified at a hearing to remove a criminal matter from state to federal jurisdiction. Since then, they had seen each other at an occasional conference or seminar. Jack was unimpressed. Unlike so many men and women who were able to keep a civilized lid on dealing with crime on a daily basis, McBride was often arrogant, and certain he was always right in his opinionated comments. Whenever the FBI agent came up in Jack's conversations with others in Boston's close-knit legal world, the assessments were consistent - ambitious asshole. Jack knew it was a going to be difficult at best to tear this dog from the Gardner Museum bone.

Even with his misgivings about McBride's agreeing to anything, Jack knew why the federal agent was willing to attend the meeting. If, somehow, Jack was able to pull a rabbit out of the hat, McBride would want to be on stage as part of the act, not in the audience. Also, the agent knew the only way to interfere with whatever was going to be proposed was to do so in person. As anticipated by Jack, after all the arguments made throughout the afternoon, McBride would only agree that the coffee sucked.

Now, after fifteen minutes of one-on-one discussion with Jack, McBride realized he and the Bureau would get no special praise or be singled out from the other agencies if the stolen art ended up back at the Gardner. Out of deference to the other prosecutors involved, Jack was not budging on a promise of equal treatment. As McBride gathered up a few sheets of paper, he muttered "Thanks for nothing." Jack asked him for just a few more minutes of his valuable time, promising it would be worth it.

Without giving the FBI agent a chance to say no, Jack quickly stood from the table and left the room. On his way across the hall to the alternate conference room, he gave a dollar bill to a marshal and asked if one of them could hastily find a vending machine and bring a candy bar to the FBI agent he had left in the main room. Jack walked into the room across the hall, leaving its door ajar to keep an eye out in case McBride decided to bolt.

Jack rarely sought favors, and when he did it was out of necessity, a result of absolutely no viable options, and for only the worthiest reasons. Now, alone in the room, he pictured his fellow Yale Law graduate, Jonathon Hughes, he'd met while waiting in line at the reception in Cambridge eight years ago. Using his cell phone, Jack called a direct number that rang in the office of Dean Owen Williams at the Harvard

Law School. His call was answered immediately. Jack responded with his urgent message.

"Sir, as we anticipated, your assistance is necessary. I can't get Agent McBride to bend at all. He seems to relish being the only holdout. Could you please have the call made to the number I gave you this morning? And please, sir, as soon as possible."

"No problem, Jack. Everything's in place. It will be just a minute or two."

Jack dawdled half a minute or so, then walked across the hall, past the tall marshal guarding the door, and back into the main conference room. He closed the door and sat across from the sullen McBride who drummed his fingers on the table as he gave Jack a cold stare. Jack explained that there would be just a very slight wait for a phone call that he assured McBride was critical. The FBI agent shook his head, stood and said he'd already wasted the fucking afternoon. Jack also stood, thinking of how to delay McBride, considering physically blocking his path to the door, when it suddenly opened. As the shorter of the two marshals walked in and held a Snickers candy bar out to the FBI agent, the phone on the conference table rang. Jack answered it, and then looked at McBride.

"It's for you, Agent McBride. It's the Bureau's director, Jonathon Hughes."

48

Standing on the south side of the mammoth red brick City Hall Plaza, Jack Ralston held an unlit Marlboro in one hand, a lighter in the other. His tie was loose and his suit coat draped over his arm as he enjoyed the early fall weather. He was looking across the broad concourse at the concrete edifice that served as the city's administrative center. Boston City Hall seemed to be elbowing its neighboring buildings out of the way, making a bully's claim to what used to be Scollay Square - playground of sailors on leave and local college students - now, since the sixties, Government Center. Jack's thought, shared by many, was that the building said as much about the city as Back Bay brownstones did not. He was convinced that if one more truckload of cement had been poured, the earth would have split. But architectural critique was for another day. Today belonged to Eddie S. Smelton.

Jack was anxious to confirm to Eddie that the plan, including Eddie's requirement that Julie Santos benefit, was positioned to become a reality. He was surprised Eddie chose the plaza to meet, thinking the man whose face adorned post office walls would have preferred invisibility. Since the FBI's Labor Day raid on Eddie's North Cambridge home a little over a month ago, rumors, along with lead stories in local papers and on TV newscasts, suggested a major break in the case of the Gardner Museum heist was at hand. Within hours of the FBI discovering that the small house on Rindge Avenue was vacant and empty of furnishings, the Bureau had placed Eddie in the top three on its "most wanted" list. His picture, along with pictures of his now abandoned North Cambridge home, including its fire-proofed "museum annex," were featured in newspapers and magazines around the country. Eddie's failure to return to his post at the Gardner Museum seemed to clinch his involvement.

The city buzzed with anticipation as the search went on for the now notorious, and missing, docent, and the stolen masterpieces. National TV tabloid shows had been quick to pick up the story. They promoted the image of a cunning cat burglar on the lam. But, in short order, the tables turned. Eddie's image as a cat burglar had been emphatically debunked by an enterprising city beat journalist from the *Boston Herald. GARDNER PERP?* was the headline above a photograph of an overweight, bespectacled Eddie culled from a museum story the reporter dug out of her newspaper's morgue. The next day, an anonymous source provided both Boston daily newspapers with copies of years of Mrs. Smelton's prescription bills, along with copies of Eddie's canceled checks in payment.

Interviews with former neighbors and museum colleagues helped to morph Eddie from a suspected burglar akin to a resurrected David Niven, the smooth, urbane thief of *Pink Panther* fame, into a humble, hard-working and devoted son who, without complaint, had accepted his lot in life as personal caregiver for his invalid mother. Shortly after Eddie's image had been recast, Pinecrest Manor Nursing Home reported to the city of Cambridge records office that Constance Smelton had died of heart failure.

Then, with no discernible source, a rumor began ricocheting around Boston like a pinball launched onto a machine's playfield - *the Gardner masterpieces were safe, in friendly hands, and on their way back to the museum.* Just as flippers, bumper caps and springs keep the shiny chrome ball in motion, radio talk shows, newscasts and citywide banter kept the Gardner rumor rolling. The excitement was palpable. The public's attitude towards the presumed perpetrator of the Gardner heist had undergone a massive shift. "Eddie-mania" took hold and spread throughout the city.

From the hair salons on chic Newbury Street, to the furthest bleacher seats at Fenway Park, the celebration of Eddie's redemption was in full swing, shared, just briefly, with Pedro's game five win over Oakland. The wind had been taken from the manhunt's sails, replaced by a growing euphoria for Eddie Smelton, who was described on last night's edition of **60 Minutes** as "this suspected art thief, and most decent docent."

Eddie was now walking toward Jack, the morning sunlight reflecting off his eyeglasses. "Hi, Mr. Ralston," was accompanied by a half arm wave and smile. Jack dropped his unlit cigarette into a red bucket provided to keep the plaza's brick floor clean, walked to meet Eddie and shook his hand.

"I feel like I'm in the company of royalty, Eddie," Jack said as the two men started to walk across the plaza in the direction of the JFK Federal Building. "It's amazing what some well placed PR can accomplish. You could be elected mayor, if you don't get arrested first."

"I believe in hiding in plain sight. You said on the phone that everything is all set. That's great, Mr. Ralston."

"It is. All the pieces are finally in place. There was some resistance, but we were able to overcome it. The District Attorney was hesitant to get involved because the FBI was telling him that they were about to crack the case. When they couldn't give him any evidence they were on the verge of finding the paintings, or you, the other agencies involved were able to persuade the DA to cooperate. I've known and dealt with him for years. He will do what he says. He's agreed to an outright dismissal of the recent drug charges against Julie. She's safe. She has also been given immunity for any involvement with the museum theft, even though I don't think she had any liability there."

"So, Julie's in the clear. That's great. And the trust fund?" Eddie asked.

"Harvard has provided one million dollars. The money is deposited in a private account opened at the Cambridge Trust Company for Brandon Santos and Julie Santos. The bank will act as trustee. Under the terms of the trust, the money is to be used for the benefit and welfare of Brandon and Julie. Of course, Eddie, that will include educational expenses for Brandon, college tuition in particular. Any funds remaining after Brandon is finished with his schooling are to be divided evenly between him and his mother. The trust is filed with the Suffolk Probate Court. It is impounded to keep it from public scrutiny."

"When will you tell Julie?"

"I've already met with her and told her. It was important that she approved of this deal before I finalized anything."

"Did you think she might say no?"

"I wasn't sure what she'd say. I told you she decided a long time ago not to look for any reward for information about the break-in. But when I explained that you were not sure about returning the paintings if she wouldn't go along with the trust fund, she said okay."

Eddie turned to Jack and smiled. "That was a lie. I would have given the paintings back anyhow. But I did want Julie to get a reward. She deserves it. She kept quiet about me all these years and then, when she had to do something to be sure her son stayed with her, she kind of cracked the case."

"Julie did ask why Harvard had to come up with the money, so I told her you thought Harvard had mistreated your mother. She said she understood why you wanted Harvard to pay."

"I think she has a lot of principle," Eddie said.

"I agree. She intends to pay her family's living expenses without using the trust fund, but knowing it's there for Brandon if something happens to her sealed the deal. Julie expects great things from her son. She understands how expensive college tuition is, and that it gets more expensive each year. She was in tears, Eddie. She was very happy. She wanted me to tell you how grateful she is. For herself, but mostly for her son."

"Family always comes first, Mr. Ralston."

"By the way, I got to meet Brandon. He's like most five or six-year olds. Rambunctious. Loves dogs. You'd like him, Eddie. He seems like a real nice kid."

Eddie nodded his head, saying, "I'm not surprised." He paused a moment, then said, "I wonder what Harvard will say happened to its million dollars."

"My guess is they'll probably just mingle the expenditure with some other art project. It's kind of pocket change over there. The Harvard trustees are anxious to see the paintings go back to the Gardner. Along with a lot of money, Harvard has a lot of influence. They really helped us out, Eddie, in more ways than one." Jack decided to keep his theory that Harvard had probably saved four million dollars to himself.

A young mother pushing her twins in a stroller seemed to examine Eddie as she approached him and Jack. She drew smiles from both as she raised a thumb.

"I wouldn't want to see the museum have to pay anything. They won't have to, right?" asked Eddie.

"That's right. The five million dollars offered as a reward by the Gardner won't be paid to anybody. That reward was to be paid only if a tip led to an arrest, or discovery of the paintings. The tip that led to the raid on your house did neither. By the way, I understand the information given to the FBI came from one of the real bad guys in the city. It did not come from an ordinary citizen."

"I was thinking it might have been Tommy, the paperboy. That maybe the door to the room with the paintings was left open one day."

"Nope, it sure wasn't the paperboy."

The two men were quiet for a few moments as they continued walking. Then, Eddie asked, "You're sure no one will try and find out things from you about where you got the paintings, where they were kept all this time, and other stuff, like who else might have known about them?"

"Yes, I am sure. The state attorney general, the DA's office, US. Attorney and the Boston police have all agreed to leave me alone and ask no questions. They all know I'm not able to tell them anything that could possibly lead back to my client. I couldn't do that even if I wanted to because everything you have told me is confidential. I'm your lawyer.

"But, Eddie, as we talked about, the authorities I dealt with aren't willing to give you personal immunity because of the precedent it would set and because this robbery was news around the world. But they all agree that, because of the time that's passed, it's really unlikely they will ever pursue an arrest in this case. Also, with no direct evidence of who took the paintings and where the paintings were kept over the years, I don't think they'd ever be able to patch this together for an indictment. Even if they could, they wouldn't be confident a jury would ever convict you. They know all that. They'll all take credit for applying pressure that helped get the paintings returned and leave it at that." Jack paused a moment, then added, "Maybe."

"Maybe?"

"Yes, maybe. I don't think this will happen, Eddie, but I know at least one, maybe two, of the agencies involved are making a push to claim the case was solved by hanging the robbery around the necks of a couple of local, and very dead, mobsters. They'd suggest the robbers tried, but were not able to sell the paintings, then died. If they decide to try this, they also plan is to say that an anonymous tipster told them that the paintings were stored in an old coal bin in a church cellar for all these years."

"Why would they do that, Mr. Ralston?"

"Because they know it's just about impossible they'll ever prosecute anyone for this crime. Once the stolen art is back at the Gardner, legal authorities really want to close this case. It's not one they're proud of."

"Can they do that, Mr. Ralston, blame dead people who didn't do it?"

"They can try. But I can't believe they can keep a scheme like that under wraps. Anyhow, it's out of my hands the second they take possession of the paintings. I've agreed to stay out of the picture, and say absolutely nothing about the robbery, or this agreement. As far as the rest of the world is concerned, I had nothing to do with this. They don't know who I am, and that's the way I want it.

"We'll know what they decide to do pretty soon, Eddie. A press conference from the museum's atrium is scheduled for this Friday, at noontime. One thing I do know is that the police and the FBI will say they aren't looking for you anymore, that you're no longer considered a suspect. You'll be able to move around without fear of arrest. No more hiding."

"I usually don't watch TV, but I'll be sure to see that."

Eddie stopped walking and turned to Jack, who stopped beside him. "You're not in any kind of trouble for doing all this, are you? Is it a crime to help to get money for this trust for Julie? Like aiding and abetting, or something like that?"

"No, and to be sure I was doing the right thing, I ran the situation past the agency that's in charge of lawyers in Massachusetts. I didn't tell them who, besides me, is involved. They gave me written assurance that my involvement in the return of the paintings, including the trust fund, doesn't violate any ethical standard. They actually encouraged me to do what I could to see that the deal got done."

The men resumed walking, turning back in the direction of the Government Center **T** entrance. They traded smiles with a uniformed police officer walking in the opposite direction.

"You said it was best to keep Judge Valdes out of the whole thing. Not to try and make any deals to protect her. Is that what happened?"

"Yes, and that's exactly what she wanted, no favors, no preferential treatment. As far as I know, there are only three people who are aware that she ever had anything to do with the missing paintings," Jack said as he turned to Eddie, "me, you and her."

"I'm glad it turned out okay for her. She was always real nice to my mom."

With a smile and a wave, Jack acknowledged an assistant district attorney crossing the plaza. He then turned back to Eddie. "The Gardner Museum heist, or," Jack smiled, "maybe it should be called the Gardner Museum lending program, is about to be history."

"I don't know how to thank you for all you've done, Mr. Ralston. Can you get paid by Harvard for all your work?"

"Thanks, Eddie, but no fee. That's out of the question. Being involved in getting the paintings back on the walls at the Gardner makes me feel like I'm doing something valuable for my adopted city. That, and being able to help out some awfully good people, is plenty of pay for me. By the way, how are *you* fixed for money? Can you get along okay?"

"No problem there. I have a lot of money left over from the home equity loan I took out on the house when my mom went into the nursing home. I don't have to pay it back because the house was worth more than I borrowed. The bank can sell the house and get all its money back."

"I have copies of the trust documents for you. I'll send or deliver them whenever you say to wherever you say."

"No thanks. I don't want any copies of anything," Eddie said as the two men approached the **T** station entrance on the edge of the plaza.

"Eddie, I won't ask you what you're going to do, or where you're going to do it. I just hope you have a great rest of your life."

"I've always wanted to see Europe's museums in person, not just in books. Maybe I'll finally get there." A smile lit Eddie's face. "Venice, Prague."

Now just steps from the **T** subway entrance, Jack and Eddie stopped walking. Eddie pulled a key from his pants pocket and handed it to Jack. "Unit eighteen, the Storage Bunker, near Sullivan Square in Charlestown. As of an hour ago, all thirteen items taken from the museum were there. They're all in top condition. I've been living in the storage unit with them for about a month." Eddie smiled. "The locker is rented under the name of J. F. Millet."

Jack slipped the key into a pocket and reached out and grasped Eddie's shoulder. "Eddie, if you ever need anything, anything at all, you sure as hell better call me first."

Jack tightened his grip on Eddie's shoulder as they shook hands. Eddie turned and walked away. Jack watched him disappear down the steps leading to Boston's ancient subway system.

49

By mid-October, the stolen masterpieces were back on the walls of the Gardner Museum, delighting the throngs that lined up each day to welcome them home, many of whom were inside a museum for the first time. The "Curse of the Bambino" was still hexing away - the Sox had lost to the Yankees in seven and could forget about the World Series, again. The die-hards were adding the well-worn *Wait 'till next year!* to their salutations, hoping the magic, absent from Fenway since 1918, would return in 2004. *Dream on* was often the response.

At the county courthouse on Route 6A in Barnstable, a gilded codfish suspended from the high ceiling watched over the quiet main courtroom, splashed with late afternoon sunlight. An assistant district attorney and a defense attorney, both reading police reports, sat at counsel tables fronting the judge's elevated bench. A pair of defendants, leg chains linking them together, sat in the dock off to the side, a county jail officer on the bench behind them. An elderly court officer catnapped in his chair next to the empty jury box, and a bored assistant clerk shuffled papers at her desk. All were waiting for the Barnstable Superior Court judge to take the bench and rule on the pair of late bail reviews sent over from the Cape's main district court.

Roused from his half-sleep by a sixth sense, the court officer broke the quiet in the courtroom by intoning the familiar "All rise!" just a moment before the judge strode in from chambers. The clerk called the first case.

"Commonwealth versus Jensen."

Standing straight and tall, the newly-minted assistant district attorney declared in a firm voice, "Joseph I. Mulligan for the Commonwealth."

The defense attorney scratched through the sleeve of her tan suit coat at a nicotine patch and then identified herself. "Attorney Zelia Valdes from the Mass Public Defender's Office, representing Michael Jensen, Your Honor."

Once the bail reviews were concluded (one reduced, the other maintained), Zelia left the old granite courthouse by the rear door and walked to a convertible, top-down, parked at curbside. Jack Ralston reached across the seat and popped the passenger door open. The trip down Cape to Provincetown would take about an hour. If they meandered for another hour or so, a choice made easy by the quaint Cape villages on the route, they'd arrive at the Mews just in time for their seven o'clock dinner reservation.

"By the way, Boss, what did you do with Thurgood for the weekend? Put him in a kennel?" Zelia asked, pulling the passenger door closed.

"No, no. He wouldn't go for that. His new best friend is dog-sitting."

Zelia smiled. "His name is Brandon, maybe?"

Jack pulled the Bel Air onto The Old King's Highway. "It is. And it won't be easy breaking them up."

Zelia rested her head on the seat back and closed her eyes. She wondered if the voice in her head would ever leave for good. *'Oranges and Lemons, ♫ say the bells of ♫ St Clement's.'*

Earlier in the day, Frank Cipriano sat on a hard plastic bench in a Blue Line train, hands folded, head bowed. It was Friday, and he was on his way to East Boston to visit his fellow Korean War veteran and buddy, Vito. When he'd left his Dorchester home, his wife, Anna, was sitting at the kitchen table, rosary beads in hand, tears welling in her aging eyes. He thought of her, and of her tears, constant since Tony's death, and he thought of Tony. Was he really gone? Would this nightmare ever end? Thank God for Vito. Frank needed his good friend, his confidant, now, more than ever.

Screeching and squealing, the train lurched to a halt at Beachmont station. Frank got off and walked down the elevated station's staircase to the **T** exit, and then the short distance to Vito's apartment. It was on the second floor of a triple-decker adjacent to the racetrack.

Cosmos Theopoulis was on his daily run over the Patriot Downs turf course. It was between the seventh and eighth races on the Friday card. Wearing his usual black running shorts, gray T-shirt and, as always, barefoot, he reached the backstretch of the racetrack. As he often did, Cosmos mulled over various things as he jogged. Most days his thoughts involved his legal problems. Often he was upset. Today he was upbeat.

Everyone tells me there's a good chance the Appeals Court will send the case back for a new trial, and Zelia Valdes won't be around this time. Quit the bench. Thank God. By the time he reached the red and white half-mile pole, Cosmos was thinking about what the governor told him at lunch today - the nomination of Roger Metcalf to the Boston Municipal Court bench was on hold, waiting for a Board of Bar Overseers decision on its disciplinary investigation. *No point in nominating someone if he's likely to be disbarred, the governor figured. For once the numbskull got something right. Metcalf? What do I give a shit? The son of a bitch cost me a fortune, and I'm still not out of the damned woods.*

Cosmos, arms pumping, raised his head and looked into the distance. Just beyond the turn at the top of the backstretch he saw the trackside neighborhood of three-decker homes. He was able to make out two guys on a second floor, rear porch. One of them appeared to be sitting, and was mostly obscured by a waist-high railing and balusters. The other, standing, seemed to be watching him through binoculars. Cosmos gave him a wave.

Binoculars glued to his eyes, Vito waved back, and then spoke to Frank. "Ten to fifteen; right to left; half value; target clear; four hundred meters. Send it."

About the Author

Over the years of his general law practice, Tom Kenny has heard numerous unusual (some may choose a different adjective) stories from persons of all stripes. Some from the witness chair, some from across his desk. Years ago, he decided to create his own tales of human interactions, and his efforts have resulted in three novels. (Clients need not worry, these are fables.) Last year *The Morning Line* was published, and *The Docent* now follows. Tom lives and practices law on Cape Cod.

To contact the author, please email him at:
tomkennybooks@gmail.com